To R[illegible]
our oldest and dearest
friends. Enjoy!!
[illegible]

Cop On The Run

by

Arnold M. Pine

1663 Liberty Drive, Suite 200
Bloomington, Indiana 47403
(800) 839-8640
www.authorhouse.com

This book is a work of fiction. Places, events, and situations in this story are purely fictional and any resemblance to actual persons, living or dead, is coincidental.

First published by AuthorHouse 08/17/04

ISBN: 1-4184-6764-2 (e)
ISBN: 1-4184-2368-8 (sc)

Printed in the United States of America
Bloomington, Indiana

This book is printed on acid-free paper.

Acknowledgments

First, and foremost, to my wife, Charlotte, for working so hard on this project, whose love and encouragement are chiefly responsible for its completion. And to my daughter, Andrea Pine-Grimaldi, a professional Occupational Therapist, whose advice and technical assistance led me through the care and treatments for paraplegics.

Chapter One

"What a come down," Peter Santini thought, as he drove his newly purchased 1981 Buick Century along the pitch black New York Thruway. "This feels like a piece of shit."

The car really wasn't that bad. The body was clean, the white paint obviously cared for. With only 68000 miles on the odometer, the car had plenty left, and for only eighteen hundred dollars, it was a good deal. What was important, he could drive it anywhere in the United States and not be conspicuous. He registered the car under the name of Robert Fellini. The real Robert Fellini had died on Flatbush Avenue about a year ago, a mugging victim.

Peter had found the victim's wallet on the sidewalk, money missing, but his driver's license, social security card and credit cards intact. Peter had slipped the wallet into his own pocket, sure he could find a use for it. The first thing he did was notify the Motor Vehicle Bureau of Fellini's change of address to a post office box that he had rented. Then he got a photographer who owed him a favor to put his picture on the driver's license. This morning he bought the Buick, registered it and got insurance under the assumed name.

He was on the run. Who could believe it? Peter was decorated nine times in his twenty three years of service, and a member of the Honor Legion, as befitted a member of a police family. The Santini's were members of the New York City Police Department for three generations. His grandfather, Frank, put in thirty years and in 1950 was killed in action in Times Square, earning him the Medal Of Honor. His father, Frank Jr., retired as a sergeant in 1981 after thirty five years of service, earning fifteen citations. Peter was the oldest of Frank's four children on the force, and was assigned to the 78th Precinct in Brooklyn. His twin sister, Betty, was a detective in the 23rd. Squad. Then came Michael in the 62nd, and Jimmy, a mounted cop at the 102nd in Queens. All were proud to be cops and family gatherings sounded like the back room of a station house. All were straight, honest and clean, until Peter fell from grace and became dirty.

He prepared well for this eventuality. Peter had a new identity, complete with papers and plenty of cash. He patted the strong box on the seat next to him. It contained over sixty thousand dollars He smiled when he thought of the three safe deposit boxes he owned, filled with more than three times that amount. He left in haste, but was determined not to get caught. The last thing he wanted was to be sent to prison, to live with hundreds of men he sent there. What a welcome that would be. He gripped the steering wheel tighter and glanced at the speedometer. Sixty miles per hour. No more than that. He had to learn to practice patience, to be the man that nobody noticed. Where should he go? Nebraska? Montana? Boise, Idaho? Does anybody really live in Boise, Idaho? Well, he'd have to find out.

"Onward to Boise, Idaho," he thought. "I feel like a fucking pioneer. `Go west' the guy said. The pioneers went with their families, God knows when I'll see mine again."

He thought of his two pretty little daughters, Tessi, 8 years old and Marci, 6, and a lump grew in his throat. Both had blonde hair and blue eyes, replicas of their Irish mother, Alice. Peter had mixed feelings when he thought of Alice. Once he had loved her with all his heart, but after the birth of their second child, Alice decided she didn't want anymore children. She closed her legs to him, quoting her parish priest, who told her that sex was for pro-creation only. Easy for him to say. He didn't have to sleep with a beautiful woman who screamed "sin" every time he laid a hand on her. That was the start of it all. That's what drove him to the streets. That's why he was running now.

"You bitch, it's all your fault," Peter shouted, as he clutched the wheel tighter. "I lost my fucking pension, my job, my honor and my family because of you. Damn you, Alice, Damn you."

Tears blurred his vision as he struggled to see the road in the black night. He turned on the radio and all he received was static, as he twisted the knob from end to end.

"I can't believe I bought a car without a fucking radio," he thought, pounding on the dash board. "I hope its got a spare and a jack."

His anger eased a bit when the headlights illuminated a sign that read "Service Area,

Five Miles Ahead." Peter felt a pang of hunger and when he glanced at his gas gauge, he saw that the car needed fuel also. Five minutes later, he pulled into the service plaza and was surprised to see so many cars.

"This is where they all hang out," he thought.

Peter decided to eat before gassing up, and pulled into a parking spot near the restaurant. Inside, he used the facility, washed up, and entered the diningroom. At three in the morning only the cafeteria was open, but he was able to get a hot meal. Peter sat at the last empty table. Midway through his meal, he saw a large man standing before him, holding a tray of food. The man was a state trooper. Peter's heart sank.

"Mind if I join you?" the trooper said, "All the tables are taken and you're alone."

"Not at all," Peter stammered, "Be my guest. I'd rather meet you in here than on the road."

"That's a good one," the trooper said, laughing. "I never heard it before, and I eat here every night."

The trooper set his tray down and sat, putting his hat and gloves on an empty chair. Peter tried hard to act "cool." He was never a fugitive before, only the pursuer, and he had to think about every word or motion. He wanted to get up and leave, but he was sure that would arouse suspicion. He forced himself to stay and make small talk. The trooper turned out to be a country hick, not as sharp an officer as Peter was accustomed to. A New York City police officer probably had more activity in one week than these troopers did in twenty years. When he finished his meal, Peter said his goodbye and left. The trooper seemed disappointed at Peter's departure. He had half an hour left on his meal period and no one to talk to.

When the attendant finished pumping the gas, Peter pulled out his wallet and paid in cash. He was shocked when he realized he pulled out the wallet with his true identity. Suppose a trooper stopped him and he pulled out this wallet, he'd be a dead duck.

"Damn you, start thinking like a felon, or you won't last a day," Peter thought.

He pulled his car over to the air pump and got out to check his tires. He took the money out of his own wallet and transferred it to the Fellini wallet. Then he took the Santini wallet, wrapped it in a napkin, and hid it in the springs under his seat. From now on he was Robert Fellini. It was a sad occasion. For forty-four years he was fond of Peter Santini. He couldn't dispose of the other wallet. Someday, he might need his old identification. When he pulled back onto the highway, Robert Fellini was driving the car and Peter Santini was hiding under the seat. From now on, they would have to be inseparable. Each would have to depend on the other, look out and protect the other, until death. It was going to be a strange but necessary marriage.

Robert would need a biography, a story to justify his roaming the country alone. He could be a widower. No. Then he would have to explain why his children weren't with him. He couldn't write off his daughters. That would break his heart. He could be divorced and his daughters, logically, would be with their mother.

"Yes, that's it," he said, "My wife ran away with another man, a prosperous man, taking the children with her," he thought. "I divorced her, sold my unsuccessful contracting business, and hit the road. Now, I'm free to go any place I damn please."

Dawn was breaking on the New York Thruway and Robert yawned. He hadn't slept for thirty-six hours and had been driving for over ten. He was passing the suburbs of Buffalo, and the Thruway was soon coming to an end. Robert read signs that lodging was available at the next exit, and he decided to get off. A small motel struck his fancy, and he checked in. He showered and went directly to bed, putting his money box under his pillow. Robert slept dreamlessly for ten hours.

Chapter Two

The sound of a vacuum cleaner in the hall woke Robert. He opened his eyes and looked around the strange room, totally confused. He sat up, looked at his watch. It was just past three in the afternoon. He fell back on his pillow. What was his rush? He had nowhere to go, nothing to do.

The vacuuming stopped and now the darkened room could have been the inside of a tomb. Robert always loved to be awakened by his two daughters bouncing on his bed, and when he would open his eyes, they'd smothered him with their kisses. Then followed a period of nagging and pleading for a story. He always played hard to get, but eventually gave in. It was the highlight of his day to lie there with an arm around each of his beautiful daughters, and tell them outrageous stories where one was always the hero, saving the other from a terrible fate. They would howl with glee at the end, and the victim would always remind him that in the next story, she would be the hero.

At the end of the story, dutiful Alice would have a hot breakfast ready for him. He never gave it much thought, but now he realized he loved that life. It was as close to heaven as a man could get. Peter Santini, alias Robert Fellini, felt all choked up and tears filled his eyes.

"Stop thinking about it, you stupid bastard," Robert said to himself, "You have to figure out what you're going to do. How to save your ass."

Robert got up and went into the bathroom. He spent his usual hour there and when he came out, was ready to meet his new challenges. Robert turned on the TV and pushed the buttons until he found a news program.. There on a split-screen picture was a photograph of Peter Santini in his police uniform, and a live picture of Captain Whalen, his C.O., being interviewed by a reporter.

"Do you think he's dangerous?" asked the reporter.

"A cornered rat is always dangerous," answered Whalen, "And we all know `a cop gone bad' is a rat."

"Does Police Officer Moran have a chance to recover?"

"He has youth on his side and the prayers of his family and twenty five thousand police officers," Captain Whalen answered with a catch in his voice.

"Is it true that the Santini family were the first of the departmental volunteers to give blood?" the reporter asked asked.

"Yes, it's true. Retired Sergeant Santini, his two sons and a daughter, all cops, gave blood for Moran, and all promised to bring Peter back to stand trial. They are making a video now to convince Peter to give himself up."

"I'm sure the prayers of the entire nation are with Police Officer Moran for a complete and speedy recovery. He is, indeed, a remarkable young man," the reporter concluded, as he signed off.

A full screen shot of Peter Santini's handsome face followed, with a graphic of a toll-free phone number to be used by anyone with information about the fugitive.

Robert was shocked. His face and his story were known nationwide. Hiding his old wallet under the car seat wasn't going to make it . The picture of Peter shown on the TV was taken when he was in his late twenties, and displayed a full head of hair. Now at forty-four, his face showed maturity but he still had that shock of black, curly hair. His appearance had to be changed, but not too much to make the picture on Robert's driver's license useless.

He opened his valise and found the small sewing kit he always carried. He took the scissors and went into the bathroom. Carefully, he cut off all his black curly locks, leaving only closely trimmed hair around his ears and the back of his head. Then he lathered his head and shaved all the areas he cut with the scissors. His hand holding the razor, hovered above his mustache, ready to cut it off. Then he lowered the razor, and decided to keep the mustache. He could disguise himself with the bald head, and a pair of horn-rimmed glasses, but he could look a lot like his picture by removing the glasses and wearing a baseball cap. The man that checked out of the motel looked at least fifteen years older than the man that checked in.

After leaving the motel, Robert walked across the highway into the mall. He located a pharmacy and entered. He found a display of reading glasses. He tried on at least twenty pairs of horned-rimmed glasses until he found a pair with a very slight magnification. He could live with them. He paid for the glasses and wore them out of the store. No one paid him any mind and he entered a diner with confidence that he wouldn't be recognized.

After eating, Robert walked back to his car to do some heavy duty thinking. He never dreamed that his fight with his partner, which resulted in an accidental shooting, would gain nationwide notoriety. Now he couldn't go to small town in middle America, for as a man of obvious Italian descent, he would always stand out. He had to make a life for himself among Italians, where he wouldn't be noticed. He could understand, but couldn't speak the language. As a fourth generation American, he wouldn't be expected to.

Robert drove into downtown Buffalo and was gratified to see that a large number of businesses were under Italian names. He drove slowly through the city and the worse the neighborhood became, the fewer Italian names he saw. Robert stopped the car outside a store that sold newspapers and bought a paper. The story of the fight between Peter Santini and Pat Moran was in bold headlines on page three. The pictures of both police officers were shown in the third column of the story. A nation wide hunt for Peter Santini was in progress. Robert was glad that he stayed in New York State, where the license plate on his car would draw no attention.

The police were covering all air and bus terminals. The paper reported that Santini fled in a great hurry and left his car in his garage. This brought a smile to Robert's face. He had planned for a possible escape for several months, and was well prepared.

He turned the pages to the classified section and looked for a furnished room. There were three rooms available in downtown Buffalo and one in a suburb called Eggertsville. Robert spent three hours finding the three available rooms in the city. He turned each one down. There was no way he could live in the filth he found. The room in the suburbs listed a phone number, and Robert called it to see if the room was still available. A pleasant sounding voice informed him that it was and gave him directions to find it.

It was just getting dark as Robert pulled up to a large, well-kept house on a quiet, tree-lined street in Eggertsville. It was a middle class neighborhood, and the cars parked in front of the houses were several years old. He rang the bell and was greeted by a plump, dark-haired woman of about fifty.

"Are you the man that called about an hour ago?" she asked.

"Yes," Robert answered, "My name's Robert Fellini."

"Come in, Mr. Fellini. The room's on the third floor. By the way, I'm Mary Russo," she answered in a soft voice, as she extended her hand to him. "Come in, please."

Robert followed her up a wide, highly polished staircase, and noticed the house was beautifully furnished and neatly kept.

"There's only two bedrooms on this level and one bathroom," Mary said, in a voice hardly above a whisper. "An elderly gentleman who writes, occupies this one," she said, pointing at a closed door.

The sound of a loud typewriter could be heard from inside the room. The next door she opened revealed a large bathroom with an old-fashioned footed bathtub.

"There's a shower in that tub," she said, answering his question before he could ask it. "The last door is the available bedroom."

She opened the door to a very large bedroom. There were three windows, cross ventilation, a large, mahogany, four-poster bed, an old triple-dresser, a desk with a lamp and a chair. The walls were covered in a bright, flowered wallpaper, and there was a large hooked rug on the floor. It looked like a nice, clean, comfortable room.

"The room is a hundred dollars a week, paid in advance. You get fresh towels everyday and fresh linen once a week. What do you do for a living, Mr. Fellini?"

"Nothing at the moment. I just came through a messy divorce, and I sold my contracting business. My wife got custody of my children and I felt like I was going to explode. I left town to keep out of trouble. I'll be looking for a job tomorrow, but I have enough money to carry me for a while, so you needn't worry," Robert said, sadly.

Mary Russo looked Robert up and down, and noticed that his clothes were expensive looking, well-kept and clean, and that his shoes were polished. She smiled approvingly.

"There's absolutely no cooking allowed in this room. But, you can keep cookies and fruit and things like that. I should've told you on the phone and saved you a trip. I don't allow smoking anywhere in this house. Is that clear?" Mary asked, sternly.

"That's fine with me. I don't smoke."

"Fine. You can bring your bags in after you pay me. Will it be check or cash?"

"Cash," Robert said, with a slight smile. "By the way, can I bring in a TV?"

"No, but you can rent one of mine. Five dollars a week, in advance. You don't need an antenna, just plug the set into that wall jack. I have a master antenna on the house," Mary replied, proudly.

"How many tenants do you have?" Robert asked, trying to figure out her monthly income.

"Three spinster ladies on the second floor, but they eat in. I don't cook for gentlemen lodgers," she added, coldly. "Remember, no hanky panky with the ladies. This is a Christian house."

"Don't worry about me, I'm not interested in women. Especially after the beating I took in court."

"Ha, that's a good one," Mary said, laughing loudly. "I'll store your bags in the basement after you unpack, okay?"

"That's fine. I appreciate it," Robert replied.

"I like to make my guests feel welcome," Mary said as she eyed Robert up and down, giving him an uneasy feeling in his crotch.

By ten-thirty that evening, Robert was settled in his new home. His bags were unpacked and stored in the basement, and he had eaten a good meal at the Scotch and Sirloin. During his absence, Mary had brought up his TV and connected it. Robert stripped down to his shorts and opened all three windows. A warm breeze made the lace curtains do a strange sensuous dance. It was a humid night for the end of May and made Robert think that air conditioning might be a real need in the near future.

"She probably rents those, too," he muttered under his breath.

He turned on the TV and tuned the volume very low. Robert switched from channel to channel and found the three major networks and two local stations. It was a far cry from the thirty channels he received on cable back in Bellmore. He tuned in NBC to catch the second half of LA Law. Robert doused the lights and stretched out on top of the covers.

"Damn. I have to get out of bed to shut the goddam TV," Robert mumbled under his breath. "What a pain in the ass."

The episode on **LA Law** was a repeat and Robert had seen it months ago. He was too lazy to get out of bed to change the channel, so he closed his eyes to rest them. Before he knew it he was fast asleep.

A sudden noise startled him, and he opened his eyes in a pitch black room. He immediately sensed a presence in the room. He could hear somebody breathing. He reached under his pillow and felt for his money box. It was still there.

"I have to rent a safe deposit box in the morning," he thought.

A car passed through the street below and its headlights momentarily illuminated the room. Robert saw a figure pressed against the wall next to the dresser. He quietly crept out of bed and lunged for the intruder. He grabbed the person around the throat and cocked his right fist to deliver a blow.

A muffled scream escaped from the person's throat and it sounded female. So Robert held up from delivering his punch. He transferred his right hand to the person's throat and groped for the light switch in the dark with his left. He found the switch and turned it on, revealing Mary Russo with a look of terror frozen on her face.

Robert released his grip on her throat and Mary slumped to the floor. He gently helped her to her feet and led her to the bed, and held her as she weakly sat down.

"What the hell are you doing in my room crawling around in the dark?" Robert growled, as his heart pounded. "Were you trying to rape me?"

"Oh God, no," Mary whispered, still too terrified to speak, both her hands trembling.

Robert sat down on the bed and took Mary's hand in his. "Just calm down and take a deep breath," Robert said, gently. "Then take your time and tell me what's going on."

Mary, realizing that she was sitting on a man's bed who was clad in only a pair of jockey shorts, while she wore only a shorty nightgown, jumped up and fled from the room.

Robert laughed, got up and shut the door. He put out the light and returned to his bed. He glanced at his alarm clock. It was one-thirty.

"Jesus," he thought, "What an experience. I'll never get back to sleep, tonight."

A few minutes later, Robert heard a gentle tapping on his door. He jumped out of bed and put on the light. He opened the door and there stood Mary Russo, dressed in a long, bulky bathrobe. She had an embarrassed look on her face.

"May I come in for a minute?" she whispered, "I owe you an explanation."

"Sure," Robert answered, taking a few backward steps.

Mary entered and shut the door behind her. "Sit down, you make me nervous," she ordered.

Robert sat on the bed as Mary paced back and forth.

"I don't know how to say it without sounding stupid," she said, speaking very softly. "My room is directly below this one. About a quarter after one, I awoke hearing voices and music. I realized it must be your TV and that you must have fell asleep. I tried to cover my ears but the sounds bothered me. I came upstairs and tapped on your door, but you didn't answer. I decided to sneak in and shut the TV and sneak out again. I tripped over your goddam shoes and woke you. You almost crushed my windpipe. I never felt such strong arms," Mary whispered, as she looked over his almost naked body.

"Yeah, you know about the Italian love-affair with cement. It's hard work and builds a lot of muscles," Robert answered, with an apologetic tone in his voice.

"Could you go for a cup of coffee?" Mary asked, suddenly. "I know I could. You scared the shit out of me and I'll never be able to go right back to sleep."

"Sounds good. I'll just put on my pants."

"Don't bother. I was married for twenty years and my husband always walked around the house in his drawers. I rather liked it," Mary said, smiling sweetly.

"Well, a guy can't disguise his feelings when he's only wearing jockey shorts. A woman doesn't have that problem," Robert laughed, as he pulled on his pants.

"I think I'm going to like you, Mr. Fellini. Follow me to the kitchen."

Chapter Three

Sitting around the kitchen table, drinking coffee at two o'clock in the morning with Mary Russo, brought back fond memories to Robert. He missed the warmth of the Italian household he grew up in, where sitting around the kitchen table, just bullshitting, was a frequent event.

After he married, his cold Irish wife, Alice, was always in bed by ten, and he spent his nights alone in his den, watching TV. Her "beauty sleep" always meant more to her than companionship. She didn't seem to care when he took to the streets on the nights he wasn't working.

Mary chatted easily, smiled often, and Robert liked her round, not quite pretty face. Compared to Alice, she was almost a dog. But he could never remember Alice sitting at a table, just talking and being relaxed. The only times Alice was ever relaxed were the times she got together with her Irish brothers. They drank beer till they couldn't stand. Sober, she was always serious. This was reflected in her tidy house, her tidy clothes and her tidy children.

Tess and Marci never had the fun of messing up the house like Italian children or running around the house whooping and hollering with their friends. Friends or pets or games were never allowed in the house.

"My husband died five years ago, and I've been renting rooms ever since. Just to get by. He didn't believe in insurance," Mary said with a sigh.

"How'd your husband die? He must have been fairly young," Robert said.

"He was young. Just forty-five same as me. He got whacked," Mary said, with tears filling her eyes.

"Whacked?"

"You know, killed, murdered, rubbed out? Those sons of bitches killed my Mario."

"Why?" Robert asked, feeling a kinship with this woman, who'd had her share of trouble. "Who?"

"I never told anybody this," Mary said, in a conspiratory manner. "Mario was a bookie for the mob. They said he was skimming and they shot him."

"Was he?" Robert asked.

Mary was silent for several moments, then answered in a whisper, "Yes. He did it for us. We sent two girls through college. Nobody else in the mob did that. We were saving for a vacation. We never had one. After they killed him, they came into this house and tore it apart, looking for cash. They found some of our hiding places, but not all. I had enough left to fix up the house and make small weddings for my daughters. I get along."

"Don't you have family? Brothers or sisters?"

"I have two brothers, but they're both in the mob. They're forbidden to help me. I don't care, I have a good life here."

"I give you credit, you're a brave girl," Robert said, patting her hand.

"Ha, some girl. I'm fifty years old. I'm older than you. Just a fat old bag."

"I wouldn't call you fat. Plump, maybe. You looked pretty good in that short nighty," Robert said, smiling.

"Don't say things like that," Mary snapped, blushing, "I was very happy with my husband for twenty years. It's hard to be alone after so many years. I'm vulnerable. Don't tease me or hand me a line."

"I apologize. I feel so comfortable with you. Talking familiar seems natural. I meant no disrespect. It feels good to be in an Italian house again. I'm running away from a cold woman and a cold house. If it wasn't for my kids, I would've run long ago."

"I think we better call it a night," Mary said, standing. "I never told anybody the things I told you, and we only met a few hours ago. I don't know why. Maybe, because you scared the shit out of me and then you were kind. You threw me off. Things'll look different in the morning. Goodnight, Mr. Fellini. Put the lights out when you're done with your coffee."

Robert watched the sad woman leave, and sighed. Things looked a little brighter than yesterday, but he was still in deep shit.

Robert slept for three hours and awoke at six-thirty. He donned his bathrobe, grabbed his toilet kit and a towel and headed for the bathroom. The door was locked and a grumpy voice called out.

"I'll be out in thirty seconds, hold your water."

"That's about as long as I'll be able to hold it," Robert answered.

Robert heard the doorlatch squeal as it was unlocked and the door opened, revealing a tall, gaunt man, about seventy. He had a weathered face and a full head of white, wavy hair.

"Kurt Bauer," the distinguished-looking man said, as he extended his hand.

Robert shook the hand and was surprised at the firm grip the old coot had. "I'm Robert Fellini. Glad to meet you," Robert offered, without smiling.

"Tap on my door when you're ready to eat, and I'll show you where the good, cheap restaurants are," Bauer said. "Got a car?"

Robert nodded.

"Good, I don't," Bauer answered tersely. "I'll be waiting for you."

By seven o'clock Robert was dressed and ready to go out. He put his money box into a paper shopping bag, and tucked it under his arm. Upon leaving, he slammed the door and checked to see if it was locked. He stopped in front of Bauer's door and knocked.

The sight of the old man, as he stepped through the door, brought a huge smile to Robert's face, and he struggled to suppress a giggle. The old coot was actually wearing a beret and a long scarf that was thrown jauntily over one shoulder, like a Hollywood version of what a writer should look like.

"Let's go, young fella," Bauer grumbled, "And wipe that shit-eatin' grin off your face."

Chapter Four

"What're we going to do now, Sarge?" asked Michael with a whine in his voice.

"Don't call me Sarge in my own house, you little shit. If I ever called my father anything but Papa he'd blacken my eye," Frank roared, as he paced back and forth at the head of the diningroom table.

"Okay, Pop, I didn't mean anything. Take it easy. With your blood pressure, you're gonna blow a gasket," Michael mumbled.

Frank pulled out his chair and wearily sat down. He stared at the faces of his handsome children and his own face sagged, revealing the terrible burden he was carrying.

Betty, like her twin Peter, was forty-four years old. She was unmarried, and was sworn in twenty-three years ago in the same class with Peter. How proud Frank was that day. Four years later, Michael the whiner was sworn in at the age of twenty-three, and was now thirty-nine years old and had three children, all boys. Then came Jimmy. At the age of twenty-one he was almost too pretty to be a boy. He struggled with the dilemma whether to follow his heart and become a priest or follow the family's tradition and be a cop. He buckled under his siblings' pressure and was sworn in twelve years ago. Now, at the age of thirty-three, his only love was his horse, Frieda.

Frank began to speak. "For seventy-two years the Santini name brought honor to the Job and to this family. My father was buried with the Medal Of Honor and ten other citations. I retired with fifteen citations, Betty has twenty, Mike has five and Jimmy has three. Even that scumbag Peter has nine, including three Commendations. That's sixty-three citations for this family. A great honor?" questioned Frank, as he scanned the faces of his children. "Bullshit," he roared, as he pounded the table with his gigantic fist. "All forgotten, brought down to the sewers by your brother. May the Saints curse his name for eternity."

Frank pounded the table over and over again with both fists as tears streamed down his weathered face. No one at the table dared speak, fearing to show the terrible emotion they all felt. After a lengthy pause, Frank started to speak again.

"Your brother must be found and brought back to stand trial. The only way a Santini will be able to hold up his head again is if a Santini brings him in. Understand me?" Frank shouted. "Somebody at this table better hunt down that son of a bitch and drag him into court. I've been out of the Job for eleven years and lost most of my contacts. I think I'd kill him if it was me that found him. Somebody at this table needs to take a leave of absence and hunt him full-time. Coordinate the efforts of the rest of us. We'll never know peace until Peter's brought to justice by a Santini. Do I make myself clear?"

"How're we going to choose?" Jimmy asked meekly, "Draw straws?"

"No," Betty whispered, sighing perceptibly. "It has to be me. I don't have family to come home to. Besides, I know how he thinks. Until we got on the Job, not a day went by I wasn't getting him out of one jam or another. If it wasn't for me, Peter would have gone up the river by the time he was sixteen. Maybe I should've let him," she sobbed. "Then we wouldn't be sitting here now."

Michael said, "She may have to follow Pete across the country. It's not safe."

"You stupid ass," Betty exploded, "I've put in twenty-three years on the streets. What could be worse? Besides, I'm the only one at this table with investigative experience. I didn't make first grade because of my looks. I earned it."

"Then it's settled," Frank said sadly. "Betty's the one. Honey, would you do me a favor?" Frank asked as tears filled his eyes.

"What?" Betty asked, as a lump rose in her throat.

"Would you go to mass with me tomorrow morning?"

"Sure, Pop, sure."

Sitting in the diner, Robert tried to concentrate on Kurt Bauer's dissertation about his latest novel. The writer had a slow, clipped delivery with a droll sense of humor. A typical New England Yankee. Robert became anxious to get the old man back to the house so he could get on with his chores. He felt uneasy about leaving the strong box in the car under the driver's seat, filled with sixty thousand in cash and two loaded pistols. The small bank he noticed in the mall as they drove up to the diner would do nicely. After dropping Bauer off at the house, Robert returned to the bank and opened a checking account and rented a large safe deposit box. He left most of his cash, his old wallet containing his true identification, and his service revolver in the box. He tucked the holster containing his off-duty Beretta under his belt in the small of his back and covered it with his jacket. Robert left the bank with a sigh of relief, feeling pleased that his escape had come off without a hitch. The stubble on his scalp itched slightly and he realized he would have to shave his head daily along with his face to protect his disguise.

Having picked up a newspaper in the stationary store, Robert returned to his car to scan the want ads. He was looking for a job that paid daily and preferably off the books, so his pursuers couldn't get a fix on him. On page three of the Want Ad section, a one-inch square in bold print jumped out at him.

Laborers Wanted	**Day Workers or Permanent.**
Ace Demolition Co	**Report to Job Site.**

Barnum Street and Marcy Ave.

Robert found the location on his street map of downtown Buffalo and estimated it to be about a twenty minute drive. Rush hour being over, Robert made the trip in eighteen minutes. The demolition site was a six-story brick building surrounded by a structure of beams covered with a layer of old doors. A cloud of dust hovered over the entire area.

Robert counted six men moving on shaky scaffolding, each carrying a hefty crowbar. All wore safety helmets. There was a filthy-looking trailer parked at the curb with the door open. Robert observed a burley, unkempt man sitting on a wooden chair that was leaning back against the wall. His feet were on top of a cluttered wooden table and he appeared to be reading a Playboy magazine. His yellow hard hat was pushed back on his head, revealing a deeply wrinkled brow and bushy black eye-brows.

As Robert approached him, he noticed a bush of black hair sticking out from his open-collared, filthy shirt. It resembled a pad of steel wool. The man was chewing on a black cigar. Robert knocked on the door and the "gorilla" turned and looked him over, slowly.

"What can I do for you, dude?" the man growled.

"I'm here in response to your ad," Robert answered, suddenly realizing that he was grossly over-dressed for his surroundings.

"We ain't hirin' no accountants today," the man said as he dropped his heavy booted feet to the floor.

"I'm applying for the laborer's job," Robert said slowly and deliberately, as his temper started rising.

"Huh," the man said, as he belched, sending a heavy odor of garlic in Robert's direction. "You look like a Paison and Paisons don' take jobs like dis anymore. We hire mostly winos, ya know. You on da lamb?"

Robert's eyes narrowed to mere slits and he struggled to control his voice as he answered.

"That's none of your fucking business. I'm strong and I show up everyday, cold sober, ready for work. You need references for this fucking job?"

"Sorry, Pal, I didn't mean to pry. We work from seven to four-thirty. Fifteen minutes for lunch. No booze on the job. Pay is fifty bucks a day, cash.

"That's less than six dollars an hour," Robert replied, shocked.

"It's a helluva lot more when ya figure we don' take out any tax. Take it or leave it," the ape bellowed.

After a short pause, Robert answered softly, "I'll take it."

"Okay. You better find some work clothes, steel-tipped boots and a good hardhat. Then show up tomorra mornin' at seven. Capishe?"

Robert nodded and left. He got into his car and sat there. He felt no elation at landing the first job he applied for. Compared to the money he made as a twenty-three year veteran of the New York City Police Department and the hundreds of dollars he made each day pimping for the Miranda twins, fifty bucks was chicken-feed. But there would not be any Social Security or tax records filed for Robert Fellini, or Peter Santini. That, at least, was a plus.

Shopping for work clothes and dinner at the Scotch and Sirloin took up the rest of Robert's day. Then it took him almost an hour to find his way back to Mary Russo's boarding house. He let himself into the house using his new key. On the way to the stairs, he passed the dining-room where the three spinsters and Mary called friendly greetings to him.

He responded with a nod of his head and a wave of his hand. Robert climbed the two flights of stairs to his room. Once inside, he busied himself with putting his new clothes neatly away in his dresser. When finished, he turned on his TV and tuned in the local station. He removed his shoes and stretched out on the bed to watch the news.

Loneliness was a new and strange sensation to Robert, for he missed his daughters terribly. Even Alice would be nice to have around at the moment. He couldn't attempt a call home. He was positive the phone would be tapped. He made it through the financial report and the world wide report, but his eyes were closing when he heard the reporter announce that the New York City policeman wounded in a fight with his partner had just died. Robert jumped off the bed and kneeled in front of the TV. The official picture of Stephen Moran flashed on the screen and the numbers 1967-1992 appeared under the picture. Then a picture of Peter Santini, in uniform, appeared with the caption, "Killer" underneath. The reporter was shown interviewing Captain Whalen, and later stopping several police officers as they went in and out of the station house. All described the grief they felt and all paid homage to Moran's family. When questioned about how they felt about their brother officer, Peter Santini, the alleged killer, they all answered "No Comment."

Robert turned off the TV and sat down on his bed. Suddenly, he was nauseous. He struggled to keep his dinner down, but it was too late. It was going to be a race to see if he could make the toilet bowl before his dinner left him. He won. But he lay on the bathroom floor with his head near the toilet bowl for many long minutes before he had the strength to get up and clean himself. When he returned to his room, he undressed and collapsed onto his bed, moaning like a wounded dog.

"Say it, you dirty bastard, say it. Murderer...Killer...Cop-killer. Fucking coward. Say the rest of it. Pimp. Drug Pusher.

Dirty, dirty cop."

Robert rolled onto his stomach and buried his face in the pillow. He allowed the sobs to come. He held the pillow tightly to his face with his left hand as he pounded the mattress with his right hand. Never since his flight began did he ever think of himself as a possible killer. He lived with the fact that he was a dirty cop for a long time. Even prided himself that he was so clever to become a rich man without having to share with anyone. Prided himself that he had an escape plan if his deal blew up. Prided himself that the escape plan worked so well.

"Moran wasn't supposed to die!" Robert thought. "Fucking Moran... you screwed everything up! Now I don't even have the option to go back. My father would kill me with his bare hands. Everybody on the Job ashamed they ever knew me. Alice telling Tess and Marci that she knew it all the time... that I was a fucking bum."

Chapter Five

A slight smile appeared on Detective Santini's face as she shut down the computer. She stretched like a cat to get the kinks out of her limbs, sore after five hours on the machine. Betty felt tired.

After she accepted the assignment from her father to hunt down her twin brother and bring him back to stand trial, Betty thought of nothing else. She knew she was a fine detective, well schooled in all the latest techniques, and confident when she followed her instincts while tracking her prey. After sixteen years as a detective, Betty had a large network of "snitches" on the streets of Manhattan.

But Peter had worked in Brooklyn his entire career and her "snitches" would be of no value to her. She would have to put herself in her brother's mind, think like him, feel like him and react like him.

The previous night she spent most of the time tossing and turning, her mind concentrating on her brother's lifestyle the past year. Every few months he would call her to meet him for dinner. His need for these meetings was greater than hers. They were very close before his marriage, ten years ago, but since then Betty stayed away, unable to take that cold fish, Alice.

When they were alone together, Peter immediately reverted to the ways of his childhood. He told her everything, trusted her implicitly. She was his pal, his mentor, his confidant, but he would rarely follow her advice, her example or her ethics. Peter had an evil streak in him. He was wild and before they got on the Job, always came to her whenever he got into a jam. Betty fix this. Betty fix that. I know you'll help me Betty. And Betty did. Betty had been a fool. Now she was his hunter.

She knew Peter wasn't overly bright, but she knew he was cunning and had no conscience. He would use people to gain his own ends without batting an eye, and would become enraged if he was refused a favor. But he was handsome and beguiling. Most people loved him, and very few people ever turned him down. Peter told her that his wife cut him off completely, and that he turned to the streets and the bars for his sex. That's where he met the Miranda twins and became involved with them. She knew that he set them up in an apartment in his sector, so that he could steer johns to them and supervise the operation while he was working. He bought cocaine from the pushers in his sector and the girls dispensed it as part of their fun and games. It was a highly profitable venture for Peter, and his old partner, Jack Wilson, didn't make any waves. Jack was always studying for sergeant. When Peter threw him a few bucks now and then, Jack was happy. Peter took care of Captain Whalen, too, and never had to worry about supervision. Although Peter was an entrepreneur of a whore house, he took care of business in his sector. Always among the leaders in his precinct for felony arrests, he had a very high conviction record. He wouldn't accept graft even though he paid it. He was a role model for some of the younger cops, but socially, he was a loner. He never drank or partied with the men he worked with and nobody, with the exception of his partner, knew his business.

After Jack Wilson made sergeant, Stephen Moran became Peter's new partner. Observing quietly for a few months, Moran questioned Peter's frequent visits to the apartment on Fifth Avenue. When Peter finally told him what was going on, Moran rebelled and refused to cooperate. They became enemies. The fight was inevitable.

Betty felt that Peter would avoid public transportation in his flight for freedom. She would not waste her time tracking Peter through bus, rail or air terminals. Peter would flee in a car and since he left his beloved Acura Legend in the garage in Bellmore, Betty felt Peter had new wheels and she would have to find them. The first thing she did was plead with her commanding officer to allow her to take her five week vacation, even though she was scheduled for one later in the year. After forty-five minutes of bargaining, and telling him the reasons she needed the vacation, he finally gave in. He even consented to let her use whatever means were necessary to catch her brother. He even wished her luck.

Tying into the motor vehicle records, Betty got a read out of all the vehicles registered the day her brother disappeared. There were thousands. Betty decided to concentrate on the Brooklyn list, feeling that Peter was most comfortable there. The Brooklyn list showed 347 for that day. Knowing Peter's conniving mind, she felt that he must have been prepared for a possible flight, and probably had somebody else's papers. Not very hard for an experienced street cop to obtain.

Perusing the list, an Italian name with a post office box for an address jumped out at her. She checked the name on the computer to see if there was any police activity connected with the name, and there was. A Robert Fellini was D.O.A. on a street in Brooklyn fourteen months ago. The police officer that handled the Aided Case was Peter Santini. No wallet was found on the body. Bingo!

Robert reported to the demolition site fifteen minutes early. His new work clothes, new boots and shiny yellow hard hat set him apart from his bedraggled co-workers. He was clean shaven and alert compared to the winos with their red eyes and boozy breaths.

"Ya still look like an accountant to me," growled the disheveled boss as he handed Robert a crowbar. "What do we call you anyway?"

"Call me Bob, and don't worry. You'll get your money's worth out of me."

"We'll see," the boss replied, as he lit up an El Ropo. "By the way, ya can call me Sal. Now get your ass up the scaffold, and do what the other guys are doin'."

After watching the other men strip the walls of the apartment with their crowbars, Robert picked up the technique in a few minutes and soon was surpassing the best of them. Sal climbed up the scaffolding and handed Robert a pipe cutter.

"Ever use one of dese?" he asked.

"No," answered Robert, "But it doesn't look like you have to be a rocket scientist to learn. Show me."

"I want ya to cut out all the copper pipes and throw 'em on that pile down there. Capische? Now watch me, it's real easy."

Robert watched Sal skillfully cut the copper pipe in about thirty seconds, and reached for the cutter. Sal smiled as Robert made a clean cut with the tool.

"You're a quick learner. You'll do okay. You do all the cuttin'. It's easier than rippin' the walls out," Sal said as he climbed down the scaffold and entered the trailer.

At noon Sal blew a whistle and the men stopped working. They drew paper bags from inside their shirts and sat on the scaffolding to drink their lunch. Robert forgot to bring anything to eat, so he kept on working.

"It's lunch time, asshole," Sal yelled up at Robert. "I didn't bring anything so I might as well keep working," Robert answered. "Well ya ain't gonna get paid fer it." "I didn't expect to," Robert answered.

By the end of the day, Robert didn't look like a rookie any longer. His work clothes were filthy and he had a slash on the left shoulder of his shirt. His boots were dirty and scuffed. There was a big callous on the palm of his right hand and a laceration across the knuckles of his left hand. He lined up with the rest of the men outside the trailer to get paid.

When Sal handed him two twenties and a ten, he said, "Ya did good, kid. Surprised me. Showin' up tomorrow?"

"You think I spent all that money on my work clothes for one day? Yeah, I'll be back."

"That's good, kid. See ya tomorrow," Sal said, as he playfully punched Robert on his right shoulder.

Robert's eyes narrowed as his temper flared, but he forced himself to smile and said, "See ya."

Robert walked the long block to his parked car and threw his hard hat into the trunk. He opened the door and was about to slide in when he noticed how filthy his clothes were. He shut the door and looked around. Across the street was a newsstand. He bought a newspaper and a chocolate bar. He spread some newspaper pages across the seat, and promised himself he'd buy a plastic drop cloth to spread over the seat as soon as he found a paint store. When he ate the candy bar, his stomach pleaded for more.

Robert saw Mary on her hands and knees working in her front flower garden, as he parked his car in front of the house. He felt dead tired as he approached her.

"Hi," he called, waving his hand.

"Hi, yourself," Mary answered with a smile, then called out as she watched Robert start up the front steps, "Wait a minute, Mr. Fellini. You're not walking across my clean carpets in those filthy clothes. Use the cellar entrance. C'mon follow me."

Robert followed Mary around the house to the backyard, and observed Mary's fully packed jeans wiggle back and forth. He wondered if those big buns would be hard or soft to the touch. Mary went down through the open cellar doors into the dark basement and Robert followed. She skillfully maneuvered between large cardboard cartons, old dusty luggage and various pieces of broken furniture, pulling on light chains as she went. Finally, she reached a closed door, opened it and put on the light, revealing a room with a washer, dryer, and shelves filled with boxes of laundry products. Mary entered and stood aside as Robert followed, then closed the door.

"Take off your clothes," she ordered, and I'll wash them for you."

Robert, surprised, stammered, "You don't have to do that."

"I know I don't have to," she said softly, "But I don't mind. It's been a long time since I washed a man's dirty clothes. C'mon, take 'em off."

Robert, long conditioned to taking orders from a burly Italian woman, reacted automatically, sat down on a chair, removed his filthy boots, then his shirt and pants.

Mary grabbed the clothing and threw them into the washing machine. "Might as well give me your socks, too," she said sternly, holding out her hand.

Robert timidly removed his socks and handed the damp, smelly things to Mary.

She nonchalantly took them and put them into the machine, then pushed some buttons, closed the door, and leaned her pelvis against the machine as it commenced to make the noises of its task. "I must be fucking crazy," she muttered under her breath.

Robert sat there, observing this disheveled woman, her own jeans stained with the dirt she had been digging in. One of her shirt tails was hanging out, her hair tied tightly with a ribbon and hung down the back of her shirt, revealing beads of sweat on her neck.

"Earthy," Robert thought as he watched her buns jiggling with the vibrating machine. "A regular Anna Magnani."

Robert stood up, sweating in the dank room. Dressed only in his jockey shorts and a T-shirt, Robert moved next to Mary and closed his arms about her waist. He pressed tightly against her and could actually feel the vibration of the machine through her. For several seconds they stood like that, and

Robert became rock hard as he pushed against her ample buttocks.

Suddenly Mary stiffened. She whirled around and pushed Robert away. With both fists tightly clenched, she approached him. "You filthy pig," she growled. "Don't you ever put your paws on me again unless I ask you to. Or I'll rip your balls off. Understand?"

Robert retreated until his back touched the wall. "I didn't mean anything, Mary, it just seemed like the natural thing to do. I really apologize. I won't do it again, honest," he whispered.

"Get your ass up to your room. I'll bring your clothes up when they're finished."

"You want me to walk through the house in my underwear?" Robert said in surprise.

"The old ladies aren't home yet. So don't worry, nobody'll jump you," Mary said sarcastically, as she glanced at the bulge in his jockey shorts.

After his shower, Robert wrapped himself in a big bath towel and stepped into the hall. He saw Kurt Bauer standing in his open doorway.

"Want some company for dinner?" said Kurt.

"Sure, I don't mind," Robert answered, "Give me ten minutes to get dressed."

Ten minutes later, Kurt, overdressed for a warm summer's evening, had on a shirt and tie, plaid sports jacket, and his goddam beret tilted jauntily over his right eye.

Robert wore a short-sleeved shirt, tan, with an alligator on his breast pocket. He wore tight, tan slacks with a matching belt and ox-blood loafers.

As the two walked down the steps, the old, stooped author made Robert look like a virile, handsome stud in comparison. When they passed the dining room, the three old ladies and Mary were seated at the table busily eating their dinner.

"Good evening, ladies," Kurt called, waving a greeting with his right hand.

Robert said nothing, but waved his right hand.

The three old ladies, all smiling, giggled an answer. Mary, blushed scarlet, just stared into her soup.

Chapter Six

Betty Santini sent out an APB on Peter Santini, wanted for the murder of a brother police officer. He was possibly using the alias of Robert Fellini, and possibly driving a 1981 white Buick Century. She gave the identification and license numbers. The latest available picture of Peter Santini was sent over the wires, and the 23rd Squad and its phone number were given as recipient for any possible information.

Betty spent hours contacting her friends in the media, calling in some markers, trying anything to keep the story alive in the papers and on TV. She spent days following false leads that came over the phone, and hours arguing with the two detectives in the 78th Squad in Brooklyn that were investigating the original U.F.61 complaint of Peter's crime.

A message was received at the 23rd Squad from a State Trooper Quinn, who patrolled the New York Thruway. He left a phone number. Betty called the number and spoke to him.

"I saw that picture of the fugitive cop that you sent out," Trooper Quinn said, "And it looked like a guy I sat with at a table in one of the rest stop restaurants. I remembered him because he had a good sense of humor."

"Do you remember what day and what time you saw this man?" Betty asked anxiously, thinking that her brother did have a good sense of humor, in a wise-guyish sort of way.

"Well, I remember it was on my first tour back from my vacation, so it had to be May Twenty-seventh and it had to be at three in the morning, because that's when I always eat on my late tour."

"The timing's perfect, trooper, and it gives me a fix on him. Thank you."

"That's okay. I hope you catch that fucking cop-killer and put a slug in his brain."

Betty hung up and a shiver ran up and down her spine. That son of a bitch trooper was talking about killing her twin brother. Betty felt a lump in her throat, so big she felt she was going to choke. Could it come to that? Could she kill her brother? She always knew there was that possibility whenever she hunted a killer, or any felon for that matter. But her brother? She couldn't answer that right now and said a little prayer that God keep her from ever being in that position. The squad room suddenly became oppressive to Betty. She felt she needed fresh air to think.

Driving over thc Brooklyn Bridge toward the brownstone house Betty owned on Henry Street in the heart of Brooklyn Heights, she reviewed the progress she was making. She had the alias her brother was using, the car he was driving, and the direction he was going.

"Oh brother of mine, where are you hiding?" Betty mumbled out loud as she came off the bridge and made a right turn onto Tillary Street. As she waited for the light to change at Fulton Street, an idea jumped into her head. She could put Peter's picture on her computer screen and alter it with different disguises and print up all the possibilities. She couldn't wait to get started.

After dinner, Robert stripped down to his jockey shorts, turned on the TV, turned off the lights and stretched out on his bed. A warm breeze gently moved the curtains back and forth, but did little to cool off the room. Robert thought about asking Mary to rent him an air conditioner. He couldn't sleep well in a hot, humid room. He dozed off now and then, never watching an entire program all the way through.

He woke in a hot sweat, and sat up, feeling a dull ache in his loins. His jockey shorts bulged as his penis fought to escape its confines. He laid back on his pillow and exhaled noisily.

"I was actually dreaming about my landlady," Robert whispered under his breath. "Shit, I'll never sleep now. Maybe I can scrounge up a cup of coffee."

Robert got out of bed, put on his bathrobe and slippers and slipped quietly from his room. He tip-toed silently down the staircase, past the darkened diningroom and into the bright kitchen. To his surprise, he saw Mary sitting at the table, her hands wrapped around a coffee mug. Her dark complexion deepened a bit when she saw Robert standing there.

"I don't remember inviting you into my kitchen," Mary growled.

"I couldn't sleep very well. I thought a cup of coffee might help," Robert answered sheepishly.

"I'm glad you couldn't sleep, you son of a bitch. Because of what you did yesterday, I couldn't sleep. You acted like a fucking pig. I've been trying to decide whether or not to kick your ass out of this house, but I hate to give back money."

"Don't kick me out, Mary. I apologized and I meant it. It won't happen again."

Mary's angry face softened a bit, and she asked, "What made you feel you had the right?"

Robert hesitated, searching for a good answer. "The only excuse I can give is that it felt natural. Sitting there in my underwear, watching you doing my laundry, made me feel... safe. Yeah, safe. That's the feeling that came over me. And I wanted to hold you close. It was a natural reaction, but you were right for shooting me down. I was out of line."

"That's bullshit. I felt your thing pushing into my ass."

"I won't apologize for my thing, as you call it, getting hard when I held you close. You felt warm and soft. And damn it, I find you very sexy. I apologize for taking the liberty to hold you in the first place. To surprise you like that."

"I wasn't surprised," Mary whispered, "All you Guinea studs think with the wrong head. I was brought up with two brothers."

"What's that supposed to mean?

"They were always putting their hands on me, coppin' a quick feel whenever they could," Mary said with a sneer.

"You can't make a general statement like that," Robert answered, suddenly defensive. "I grew up with a twin sister, and I never thought of touching her like that. Never."

"Aw, drop it," Mary said, rising and walking to the stove. "You still want that cup of coffee?"

"Yes."

"Then sit down."

Mary brought the steaming cup, set it down in front of Robert and sat down, wrapping her robe tightly around her. They sat there quietly, staring at one another for several minutes. Finally Mary broke the awkward silence,

"Listen to me. I'm going to put a hamper next to the washing machine. Every day after work, put your dirty clothes in it. I'll wash'em once a week. Oh, yeah, on your way out in the morning, hang your bathrobe in the laundry room so you can walk through my house in a civilized manner in the afternoon. I don't want you to scare the old ladies, showin' off your big cock."

"Oh, so you noticed?" Robert answered, smiling.

Mary got up and left, calling over her shoulder, "Make sure you put out the lights when you're done."

Three days passed, and Robert was turning out twice the work as any of the winos. He learned to stop at a Deli on his way to work to pick up his breakfast and lunch. After work, he dropped his filthy clothes in the hamper, showered, and went to dinner alone. He avoided the late night trip to the kitchen. Instead, he spent hours scouring the papers and TV news for any follow up on his case. Nothing. Robert had no contact with anyone in the house.

On his fifth day at work, as Robert approached the trailer-office to get his daily assignment, six winos were sitting on the curb in front of an empty, parked police car. Robert heard loud voices coming from the trailer. He looked inside and saw Sal sitting at his table and a large uniformed sergeant waving his arms.

"Look at this place," the sergeant bellowed. "The pedestrian bridge has gaps in it, the scaffolding is unsafe, and the sidewalk's filthy. I'm closing this job down."

"I got a permit," Sal pleaded.

"You ain't got all the permits," the sergeant yelled, arms waving again, "The captain's unhappy, the sergeants are unhappy and the sector cars are unhappy. So this job is history."

"Sounds like a fuckin' shakedown to me," Sal said belligerently, getting to his feet.

"Bullshit," the sergeant yelled, the veins in his neck bulging as he stood nose to nose with Sal. "Everything I said is strictly legal. It's all on the books."

Robert entered the trailer and tapped Sal on the shoulder. "Why don't you let me handle this, you're getting too excited. Remember your bad heart?" Robert said as he winked at Sal.

Sal threw his hands in the air and stomped heavily out of the trailer.

Ten minutes later, Robert and the sergeant emerged from the trailer, both smiling. They shook hands and the sergeant got into his car and left. Sal looked so surprised he almost swallowed his El Ropo.

"What the fuck did ya say to him?" Sal asked as he grabbed Robert by the elbow and led him back into the trailer.

"Aw, it's just a game they play," Robert explained, smiling. "What do you know about this game? You're on'y a laborer."

"Back in New York I was a contractor. They played the game there, too. I set up a pad with the station house. A sergeant will be around every week to pick up. By the way, you owe me fifty bucks."

Sal sat down heavily in his chair, scratched the hair on his chest and muttered, "The bastard wouldn't talk money with me. How'd ya do it?"

"Well, I noticed you weren't the greatest diplomat in the world. Just took a little finesse, that's all."

"Okay, okay, I'm just a fuckin' bum, but I'm the boss. Get those fuckin' winos up on the scaffold. We got a buildin' to rip down," Sal said as he slapped Robert on the back. "By the way, Bob, thanks. I appreciate what ya done. See me after work, I wanna discuss someting with ya."

After work, Robert was invited into the trailer and Sal was gracious as he offered Robert a seat. He even went as far as offering him an El Ropo, which Robert declined.

"I'll get right to the point, Bob," Sal said, as he leaned his chair back against the wall. "I'm lookin' fer a partner, a guy with a little education, a guy with a little class. I know I'm just a slob, but I got a little dough, and I can get these little jobs. But if I had a guy like you, a guy that looks like a fuckin' accountant, we could go fer the really big jobs. Where the real dough is. Interested? Ya got any money to invest? Talk to me."

"You took me by surprise. I'll have to think about it. I'll let you know," Robert said as he stood up.

"What's the matter with you? Ya ain't got the money? That ain't no sin. We can work somethin' out."

"It's not the money, Sal. I just don't know if I want the responsibility right now. I'll let you know."

"Geez, I'd love to have ya. Ya handled the situation this mornin' just lika pro. Think about it, serious like."

"Sure, Sal, sure. I'll give it serious thought."

They shook hands and Robert left the trailer.

Chapter Seven

Driving home, Robert gave serious thought to Sal's proposition and felt flattered that Sal recognized his ability. He knew that he had to maintain a low profile, but his ambition was still a strong force to be reckoned with. Nobody would look for him in a legitimate business venture.

"Don't rush into anything, schmuck," Robert thought. "Play it cool, think it out."

Robert felt alive, no sign of fatigue, even after a full day of strenuous physical labor. For the first time in a week he felt really hungry.

"A good Italian meal would hit the spot, and to get Mary into bed would be a great desert," Robert thought with a smile.

He remembered how warm and soft she felt the other night when He held her close. He got hard then feeling her, and he got hard now thinking about it.

"Should I ask her out to dinner tonight?" he wondered. "Nah, too soon. She's still pissed off at me. I'll shower, get dressed in a jacket, and drive back to Buffalo, to Maria's Restorante. Looks like a swanky restaurant and I'm dying for good pasta. Maybe veal parmesan."

Mary was kneeling in her flower garden as Robert pulled up onto the driveway.

"Hi, Mary," Robert called.

Mary answered with a wave of her gloved hand, but Robert was almost certain he detected a slight smile in the corner of her mouth, and her facial color deepened a bit.

"She's hot for me, too," Robert thought as he got out of the car. He ducked his head as he went through the cellar doors, wound his way through the dark cellar to the laundry room, and quickly undressed. He dropped his dirty work clothes into the almost full hamper, and donned his bathrobe.

Mary entered the room. "I'll make a wash after supper, but I won't bring it up to your room till the old ladies are asleep," Mary said, avoiding his eyes. "I don't want anyone to know I'm doing your laundry."

She turned her back to him and immediately left the room.

"What a queer duck," Robert whispered under his breath.

After showering, Robert dressed in his tan slacks, tan sport shirt, brown loafers, and his best brown sport jacket. Inspecting himself in the mirror, he nodded his approval, put out the lights and closed the door behind him. He walked to the staircase and stopped.

"I feel undressed without my piece," he thought. "For twenty-three years I never went out without a gun, and that restaurant is in a tough part of town," he reasoned.

He went back to his room, removed his off-duty revolver from its hiding place inside his work boot. The snub-nosed .38 was encased in an inside-the-belt holster. Robert tucked it inside his pants, ran his belt through the loop, then buttoned his jacket. Now, he felt dressed.

He arrived at Maria's Restorante at about eight-thirty. The small parking lot was full and Robert had to park a block and a half away, in front of a darkened factory building. He was seated right away, even though there were several parties waiting. A table for one was easy to get.

The atmosphere was cozy, the room fairly dark, the tables lighted by candles stuck in old wine bottles, covered with red checkered table cloths and matching napkins. Music was supplied by two roving musicians, both old, bald and fat. One played an accordion and the other a violin. They were good and people stuffed dollar bills in their pockets.

Service was slow but the delicious food made the wait worth while. It was nearly eleven when Robert left the restaurant. He felt stuffed but very satisfied. He would certainly return, he thought.

Robert walked the block and a half to his car. As he was about to put his key in the lock, he heard screaming. It seemed to be coming from an alley around the side of the darkened factory. He walked to the head of the alley and looked down the narrow street. What he saw startled him.

His first impulse was to run back to his car and get the hell out of there. But as a veteran police officer, he couldn't do that. He looked into the dark alley and saw a police car about a hundred feet away. It was illuminated by another car parked behind it with its headlights on. Draped over the right front fender of the police car was a police officer, hatless, with long blonde hair covering the face. By the sound of the screams, Robert knew it was a woman. Her pants were in a heap around her ankles. A huge black man was fucking her from behind, encouraged by two other black men, one of whom was holding a dark pistol.

Robert pulled out his own gun and, crouching against the wall of the factory, crept closer. He could hear the two onlookers urging the rapist to hurry so they could take their turns.

"I always wanted to fuck a cop," the rapist grunted, as he plowed into the diminutive officer. "Her bein' white makes it perfect."

The girl's screams made Robert choke on his anger. His hand tightened on his gun and he wanted with all his heart to shoot the three mother-fuckers. But he was a cop on the run, himself a cop- killer. Every police officer in the country was looking for him. How could he get involved? Robert turned and started out of the alley. He felt bad about the girl, but his own ass was at risk.

After three steps, Robert stopped. His sister Betty's face jumped out at him. He remembered that long ago she too, was raped by three men. His chest filled with such pressure, that he had trouble breathing. There was no way he could abandon this girl. He had to go back to the alley. Could there be any reason for a cop to abandon a fellow cop? Or any man, for that matter, to turn his back on any woman? Robert's rage exploded.

"Drop that fucking gun or you're dead meat," Robert roared.

He fired a shot into the rear window of the car in front of him. The shattering glass amplified the anger in his voice as he yelled, the sound coming from the pit of his stomach. "I'll blow your fucking head off, if you don't drop that gun. Now." Robert fired another shot, this time in the air. The noise sounded like a cannon, reverberating off the walls of the narrow alley.

The youth dropped the gun like it scalded him. He shrieked, "Don't kill me, man, don't kill me, please."

All three of you, turn toward me and put your hands on your head. Now," Robert ordered.

The two youths who were watching turned immediately, hands shooting to their heads. The rapist, his humping stopped, just stood there, his arms still wrapped around the sobbing girl.

Robert fired another shot, this time at the rapist's shoes, missing, but close enough to kick dirt onto his feet.

He pulled out of the girl and turned to face Robert, his penis dangling like a tree-trunk in a storm. Slowly, defiantly, he put his hands to his head.

"Lay down on the ground, and put your fucking faces in the dirt," Robert ordered.

The two onlookers complied immediately, the rapist in slow motion. The policewoman slumped to the ground, sobbing pitifully.

Robert retrieved her automatic from the ground, and put his own gun back in its holster. Covering the three men, Robert slowly inched his way to the girl's side, bending down and helping her to her feet.

"Stop crying, and pull your pants up," Robert said gently, "You still have a job to do."

The girl's sobbing slowed to a whimper. As if in a trance, she slowly pulled up her pants, buckling her gunbelt.

"Give me your handcuffs," Robert ordered.

The girl handed them to Robert. He roughly pulled the rapist's hands behind his back and cuffed him tightly. Tight enough to be painful. Robert then pulled the belts off the other men and tied their hands behind their backs.

"Turn over on your backs and look at me, you sons of bitches," Robert ordered.

The men complied, grumbling protests, offering weak threats.

"All my life I saw rapists caught, go to court and walk. Those that did time, did very little. Their victims suffered their entire lives. Tonight, justice will be served quickly."

Robert bent over the rapist and fired two shots into his genitals. His screams were louder than the girl's.

"You'll never rape again, you fucker," Robert hissed. He repeated the shooting with the other two men, their screams joining the rapist's. "You're all going to be sopranos, now," Robert said, as he wiped the gun with his handkerchief.

Robert put the gun into the policewoman's holster. She was silent now, but her face wore a pained expression.

"Pull yourself together, Officer. You're going to be answering questions for hours," Robert said quietly. "I'll call for backup and for ambulances. Please don't remember me too well. That's how you can return the favor."

Robert opened the door of the radio car and picked up the handset. He identified himself as a civilian aiding a police officer and requested back-up and ambulances. He reported three perpetrators shot.

Robert ran out of the alley, got into his car and sped away with no lights. Six blocks away he slowed down, put on his lights, and exhaled several times.

"Damn it," he yelled, as he slapped the dashboard. "Why do these things always happen to me."

By driving slowly, Robert thought he could slow his pounding heartbeat. In his twenty-three year police career, while trying to apprehend felons, he had occasion to shoot men before, many times. But never deliberately and maliciously as he had done tonight. Slowly his breathing returned to normal and it wasn't long before he pulled up on Mary's driveway.

Suddenly he felt dead tired. He couldn't wait to get in his bed. Robert quietly climbed the stairs to his room. He didn't put the lights on as he stripped to his shorts. With a groan he stretched out on his bed. For the first time in ten years, Robert yearned for a cigarette. For an hour he lay there with his eyes wide open, reliving the night's events over and over. Then he thought he heard a tapping.

He listened... nothing. After several minutes he heard it again, louder. Robert got off the bed noiselessly and slowly opened his door. By the lights in the hallway, Robert made out the form of Mary, holding something bulky in her arms. She was dressed in a shorty nightgown like she wore the first night he stayed in this house.

"I've got your laundry, Mr. Fellini. Can I come in?" she whispered.

"Sure," Robert whispered in return, as he stepped aside to let Mary into the room.

"I waited till everyone was asleep," she stammered, "I don't want anybody getting funny ideas. Where should I put this stuff?"

"On the dresser. I'll put it away in the morning."

Robert lit the lamp on his night table then paced back and forth, nervously, unaware that he was dressed only in his jockey shorts. "Sit down. Say, would you join me in a drink? I need one bad."

Mary sat on the bed and watched Robert pacing. "I'll have a sip," she answered. "What's with you? You look all upset. Something happen tonight?"

Robert paled. "What makes you think something happened tonight?" he retorted, panic rising in his voice.

"I may be a dumb broad, but I'm not a moron, you know. I've seen that look before."

"What look?" Robert asked, defensively.

"Like you got caught with your hand in the cookie jar. If you want to talk, I'm a good listener."

Robert searched in a dresser drawer until he found his bottle of Jack Daniels. There was only one glass on the dresser and he filled it almost to the top with the bourbon. He handed it to Mary and said, "We'll share."

"I can't drink that shit without ice. Want me to go down and get some?" she asked.

He shook his head negatively, and took the glass from her hand. Wearily, he sat down on the bed next to Mary, their bare legs touching. Robert took a long swallow of the bourbon and handed the glass back to Mary.

"Drink. Make believe there's ice in it," Robert said without the hint of a smile on his face.

Mary obediently raised the glass to her lips and took a small sip. She immediately exhaled, exclaiming, "Jesus, how can you drink that shit? My throat's on fire."

"Shush. You'll get used to it. It's good. It'll warm your blood."

"My blood's hot enough already. Here, you finish it. You look like you need it."

Robert took the glass and drained the contents with one swallow. He got up and refilled the glass and handed it to Mary.

"Drink," he ordered, as he sat down carefully next to her. "The more you drink the better it tastes."

Mary took a small sip and held the glass. "What's wrong, Mr. Fellini? You look like you're going to explode."

"I can't tell you my secrets if you're still calling me Mr. Fellini. The name's Robert, or Bob, if you prefer."

"All right, Bob," Mary whispered, color rising in her cheeks. "You can call me Mary." She took another sip and turned toward Robert, her breast brushing his arm.

Robert looked down and saw her deep cleavage. Now it was his turn to blush. "One of those beauties was bigger than both of my wife's," he thought.

He jumped to his feet and started pacing again. He stopped and took the glass from Mary's hand and took a long swallow. Then he handed her the glass and resumed pacing. Suddenly he stopped and kneeled in front of her. "Mary, I did a stupid thing, tonight. I shot three black guys. Shot their balls off, God forgive me."

Mary's eyes widened and she took a deep breath, but said nothing. With her free hand she grasped Robert's hand and squeezed.

"I was getting into my car at the restaurant, and I heard a scream. A woman's scream. It came from an alley and I made the mistake of looking. I saw a woman, a lady cop, leaning over the fender of her police car. This big guy was fucking her from behind. Two other bastards were standing there, urging him to finish so they could take their turns. One was holding a gun. The cop's gun. I don't know what happened to me, I blew my top. I took out my gun and fired off two shots. I scared the shit out of them. Then I ordered them to lie down. I handcuffed the rapist and tied the other two with their belts. The cop was screaming like a little girl and I thought `Suppose this was my sister, what would I do?' I knew what I'd do. I picked up the cop's gun, rolled those bastards over so they could see my face and shot their balls off. I'm a fucking dope, Mary, just a fucking dope," Robert sobbed, lowering his head.

Mary put the glass of bourbon on the floor, reached out and hugged Robert's head to her breast. Robert could hardly breathe, but strangely, he felt safe there.

"Are you a Sicilian by any chance?" Mary asked in a whisper.

Robert nodded, unable to speak.

"So am I," she answered. You did what any Sicilian would do for his sister. But, come to think of it, I don't know any Sicilian that would do that for a cop."

Robert tried to pull away from Mary, but she hugged him all the tighter. His lips were now over her nipple, separated by the flimsy cloth of her nightgown.

"Jesus," Mary whispered, as she rocked Robert's head back and forth, "That drink's gone to my head. I feel a little giddy."

Robert could feel Mary's nipple growing under his lips. He pushed her away and she fell back on the bed and stayed there. Her short nightgown pulled up on her stomach, revealing her panties, and two long, plump but shapely legs.

Robert sat down on the bed and leaned over Mary. Her dark eyes stared into his and her mouth opened, mouthing words soundlessly that he didn't understand. She raised her arms, holding them out to him. Those two huge, wonderful breasts were heaving. Robert bent lower and kissed Mary lightly on the lips, then straightened up tentatively.

"What's the matter?" she whispered.

"The last time I got close, you got pissed off and threatened to rip my balls off."

"I also said unless I wanted you to, and now I do."

She held out her arms to him again and Robert came into them. Their lips met, opened, and their tongues became very busy. Mary lifted Robert on top of her so easily that Robert was alarmed at her strength. He felt like he was being sucked into a vortex of flesh. In his previous experience with women, his wife and the twins, who were small and delicately framed, Robert felt omnipotent, in charge. But now with Mary, her size, strength, and aggressiveness made the issue of who was in charge gravely in doubt.

Somehow, her panties and his jockey shorts mysteriously disappeared and he felt himself entering a wet, hot world, so inviting that he thought it must surely be heaven. But then the ride began, and Robert held on for dear life. He was the star cowboy at a championship rodeo, riding an inspired wild animal. He heard the crowd's frenzied cheering, then realized it was coming from him. "Hold on, hold on just a little longer. Hold on if you want to win," he yelled.

The tempo unbelievably increased, and two powerful arms crushed his face into the twin peaks of the softest flesh he ever felt.

Then, from some distant place he heard a moan, and the pace slackened, like a train coming into a station, and stopped. His coming felt like an explosion that tore the top of his head off, and he was dying. Now he was truly suffocating. At last, the arms relaxed and he could breathe.

"Holy shit," Mary exclaimed, giggling, "I must've stored that one up for five years. Get off me, you're all wet," she said, as she rolled Robert off. "God, it's hot in here. I'll have to rent you an air conditioner.

What's the matter with you? Can't you talk?"

"I will, I will," Robert said, panting. "As soon as I get my breath back."

They laid quietly, side by side for several minutes, holding hands. Finally, Mary broke the silence.

"Would you look at this bed. It looks like they drove a herd of cattle through here. What's the matter with you? You're so damn quiet. Are you sorry it happened?"

"No, Mary, no. I'm glad it happened. I dreamed about it the last couple of nights. I just wasn't ready for it. I never dreamed it could be like this."

"Ever have an Italian girl before?"

"Never did. Everything I did before seems like nothing. Tonight, I felt like a virgin."

"Yeah, they ought to make it a law," Mary said, yawning. "Every man should have an Italian girl before he dies."

Mary turned over on her side, and in moments was asleep. Robert got out of bed, found his jockey shorts and put them on. He found the glass and filled it with bourbon. Then he pulled his chair over to the bed and positioned it so that when he sat down, he could put his feet on the bed. He sat and drank for a long time, looking at Mary's form on the bed and reviewing his long and eventful day.

"Jesus," he muttered out loud, "I'm sure glad tomorrow's Saturday."

Chapter Eight

After completing six different composites of how her brother could alter his appearance, Betty showered and went to bed. She turned on her TV just in time for the eleven o'clock news.

The lead story depicted the cruel and vicious rape of a policewoman in a dark Buffalo alley, and the physical beating she took at the hands of three black youths who overpowered her and disarmed her of her weapon. She was found by her fellow officers in the alley, torn and bruised and emotionally hysterical. They were called to the scene by an unknown hero. Her assailants, all shot in their genitals, were also found in the alley, lying in pools of blood. All four were removed to Buffalo's Mercy Hospital, where detectives were trying to sort out the facts. It was the policewoman's opinion, the hero had to be a retired or off-duty police officer or a military man. She did not get a good look at his face. The investigation was continuing.

Betty watched the rest of the news, then turned off the TV and her lamp and tried to fall asleep. The bizarre case of the raped policewoman wouldn't leave her mind. Betty remembered she was in a similar situation the night of her high school prom and broke into a sweat. Her heart went out to the battered cop.

"Thank God, we didn't ride solo in New York City," she thought. "All my partners over the years were good, loyal guys. We took good care of each other's asses. If

I had to ride solo in uniform, I'd quit the Job, it would've been suicide."

Betty's mind wandered to the man who most assuredly saved the policewoman from certain death. She wouldn't have been left alive to identify her attackers. What kind of man would risk his own life by entering a dark alley, where he was outnumbered by armed men, overpower them and then dole out his own kind of justice? Her brother would. Betty remembered how he had beaten her attackers with a baseball bat when he had learned of her rape. The man stayed long enough to summon aid for all the injured people, then disappeared. Just like the Lone Ranger. Her description didn't exclude her brother, especially if he was now wearing a disguise. He was heading in the direction of Buffalo. The state trooper put him on the Thruway. Why would a hero run away? Why not stay and get all the media attention his brave act deserved? Most cops loved all that attention. But if he, himself, was being sought by the authorities, he'd have to run. Then why get involved in the first place?

Her mind was made up. She would fly to Buffalo in the morning and interview the policewoman. Maybe she could identify one of the composites. That much settled, Betty rolled over and went to sleep.

By noon of the following day, Betty stood in the hallway of Buffalo's Mercy Hospital, pleading with the doctor to allow her to interview the policewoman. The doctor refused, saying the woman was under too much pressure and was heavily sedated.

Betty hung around in the hospital Room until four o'clock. When the new shift of nurses took over, she cornered the RN that was taking care of the policewoman. Showing her shield, Betty took her aside and pleaded, "Please, all I want her to do is look at some pictures. The guy that saved her might be my brother. He's missing and the family wants him back. Just tell her I'm a policewoman, too. She may want to help me. Just ask her, please."

"The doctor left specific orders not to disturb her, but when she wakes up, I'll ask her. It'll be her choice."

"Thank you, Nurse, That's all I can ask for. I'll be in the Hospitality Room.

A few hours later the nurse shook Betty, who had fallen asleep, curled up in a chair. "She agreed to see you, but make it fast. Five minutes, tops. Its my ass if we get caught," the nurse said, furtively.

"Thanks, I really appreciate this. By the way, what's her name?"

"Paula. Paula Stone." Betty was shocked when she walked over to the bed. The girl looked small, her face very pale between the purplish bruises. The IV stand looked like a Christmas tree, it had so many bottles hanging on it.

"Hello Paula, I'm Betty Santini. Thanks for seeing me. I came an awful long way."

"Are you really a policewoman?" she asked weakly.

Betty pulled out her shield case and showed it to Paula.

"Oh, a first grade detective. You must be quite a cop. And in New York City. I'm impressed."

"Stop the shit, Paula. It takes a lot of guts to ride solo in uniform. More guts than I've got, believe me," Betty said, as she sat down in the chair next to the bed. She took Paula's hand in hers.

"Thank you. It's nice of you to say it, but I really don't feel very brave right now. How can I help you?"

"I'm looking for my twin brother. He's also a cop, and I have a hunch he might have been the guy that helped you last night."

"Is he a New York cop, too?"

"Yes he is."

"Then what's he doing in Buffalo?"

"He got into a jam and he ran. I'm going to bring him back."

"I don't think I can help you. It was very dark, and I wasn't in a position to get a good look at the guy. I was draped over the front fender of my car," she said, bursting into tears.

Betty squeezed the girl's hand and waited till her sobbing stopped.

"I'm sorry. But everytime I think about it, I cry. It felt like he was tearing me apart. It was just horrible."

Tears came to Betty's eyes as she attempted to sooth the battered girl. "I know how you felt. I've been there."

"Show me the pictures. The nurse will be in here any second to throw you out. They don't let anybody stay."

Betty took out the six pictures and showed them to Paula one at a time. She shook her head without hesitation on the first three pictures, then hesitated on the fourth. Her cheeks showed a little color but she shook her head no. She barely looked at the last two pictures.

"I'm sorry. I can't help you. Please go."

Betty leaned over and kissed Paula on the top of her head. "Get well fast, kid. Every cop in the country's pulling for you, and I'm glad those bastards got what they deserved."

Betty left the room and waved a thanks at the nurse. She left the hospital, found her rented car in the parking lot, and got in. She sat there for several minutes trying to decide what her next move would be.

"She lied", Betty thought, "It was the fourth picture. I'm almost sure of it. I'll stick around Buffalo a while. Introduce myself at the local station house and maybe I'll get some help. I'll leave copies of the pictures, the registration number of the Buick, and who knows, I might get lucky.

Robert opened his eyes and a rush of feelings hit him, all at the same time. His back ached from spending most of the night sleeping on a chair with his feet up on the bed. He felt the excitement of warm lips on his and a tongue playing tag with his own. The feeling of a hand pressing down on his penis made waking up worth while. He was never awakened like this in all the years of his married life. His wife, Alice, never initiated a single show of affection.

"Good morning, lover," Mary said with a sly smile as she patted his bulging shorts. "I see you're ready for an encore."

"You've got that right, honey," Robert said playfully as he reached for her.

Mary skillfully dodged Robert's attempt to grab her and walked to the door, putting her finger to her lips. "Shush, I have to get back to my room before anyone in the house gets up and sees me. I run a Christian house, remember?"

"It's Saturday morning, for crying out loud. Everybody sleeps late. We've got time for a quicky," Robert said, smiling.

"You don't know how tempting that sounds," Mary whispered. "But better safe than sorry."

"Want to go to breakfast with me?"

"No, but why don't you ask me out for dinner? It's been a lifetime since I had a date."

"You're on," Robert answered, smiling. "Six o'clock okay?"

"No, I still have to make dinner for the old ladies. Eight o'clock would be better."

Mary blew him a kiss and slipped noiselessly out of the room. Robert felt warm all over. Maybe his luck was changing. He felt fate smiled on him by giving him such a safe, snug harbor amidst the storm of life-shattering events of the past few weeks. To be up-rooted from his family, the Job, and his business was traumatic. He missed his daughters so much.

"God, I've got to call them after breakfast," he thought.

Last night brought another human being into his life. A warm, live woman, bursting with passion, who seemed eager to welcome him into her life. Knowing the nature of Sicilian women, he hoped this one also would be faithful and be at his side through anything. Yes, just like Betty did, when they were kids.

He sighed, partly for the memory of Betty, and partly for the anticipation of his future relationship with Mary. Robert put on his bathrobe, grabbed a towel and his toilet case and headed for the bathroom. Seven o'clock on a Saturday morning and he was up and about, when he could sleep late or just lounge around. He felt good.

Kurt Bauer was coming out of his room as Robert left the bathroom. "You're up early for a Saturday," Kurt drawled, "Want company for breakfast?"

"Sure, sounds great."

"Fine, give me twenty minutes."

When Kurt lit up his pipe after they had both finished a hearty breakfast, Robert excused himself and went to the phone booth. He had a pocket full of change and was anxious to speak with his daughters. He dialed and Alice answered the phone.

With a voice dripping with hate, she said, "You have a lot of nerve calling this house, you lousy pimp. You slept in my bed, ate the food I cooked for you and all the time you were running a whorehouse. You bastard, you touched my daughters with your filthy hands. You're no longer welcome in this house, so don't even phone."

"Don't you dare hang up on me, Alice. Remember, it's my house too. I pay all the bills. Now put Tess and Marci on the phone."

"Drop dead, you son-of-Satan," Alice shouted as she slammed down the phone.

Robert looked at the dead phone as if it was responsible for the betrayal he just experienced. He returned it to its holder with such vehemence that it was a miracle it didn't shatter. Robert returned to the table, his face ashen from the rage he felt.

"Bad news?" Kurt asked.

Robert's furious expression stopped further conversation. "Let's go," he said.

Not a word was spoken on the ride back to the house. Silently, they entered the house and climbed the stairs together. As

Kurt opened his door, he turned to Robert and asked, "Dinner?"

"No," Robert answered quickly, "I have a previous appointment."

"That's okay," Kurt said, stepping into his room.

"Kurt," Robert called.

What?" Kurt answered, poking his head out the door.

"I'm sorry,"

"Shit happens," Kurt said, closing his door.

Robert felt uneasy as he descended the stairs at eight o'clock to meet Mary. This morning he felt as high as a helium balloon after the wonderful night with her. The phone call to Alice deflated him. He had spent the rest of the day indulging in self-pity and negative thoughts. He almost canceled the date. A smiling Mary was waiting for him at the bottom of the stairs, and his first sight of her stopped him dead in his tracks.

"Mary, you look beautiful," Robert blurted out.

Color deepened Mary's rouged cheeks. "Look at me. Fifty years old, and I blush at a compliment."

"You do look beautiful, and younger somehow."

"Well, I spent good money at the beauty parlor. I haven't been there for years. But today, I went for the whole shebang. Hair, facial, nails, even my toes. Then the cosmetician did the rest. You like?"

"I don't like, I love."

Robert descended the remaining stairs and embraced Mary, attempting to kiss her. She pushed him away.

"Don't, you'll ruin the paint job."

"Your dress is gorgeous," Robert exclaimed, as he looked Mary over from head to toe. "It makes you look thinner."

"I like the dress too," Mary said, "But the thinner comes from a new girdle. It's so tight, I don't know if I'll be able to eat."

"You did all this for me?" Robert asked, amazed.

"Don't flatter yourself. A little for you but mostly for me. I was really a nice looking broad once, but I've been shlumping around for a long time. Nobody to look nice for. Last night made me feel alive. I did it for us."

Robert's spirit soared. This woman pumped him up everytime he saw her. "She's no young chicken," he thought, "but she puts lead in my pencil."

Monday morning Robert worked with enthusiasm, feeling an inner peace that was missing for years. The past weekend seemed to have changed his outlook on life, and his new relationship with Mary was the most rewarding he had ever experienced. Deep passions were unleashed during their sexual encounters on Friday and Saturday nights, and the three times on Sunday. He felt a new confidence he never felt before. Dining out with Mary was so natural, so enjoyable, it emphasized how tension filled his life with Alice had been. The down side was that all this new intimacy was bringing on a new feeling of guilt. Should he reveal his past to Mary? Would he lose her if he did?

Robert was shocked out of his reverie, when he looked out of the fourth floor window where he was working and saw a uniformed police officer examining his Buick a half a block away. The officer looked in the windows then wrote in his memo book. He reached inside the patrol car and brought out the radio handset. He transmitted a message while reading from his memo book. Robert's world came crashing down. His car being under police scrutiny meant there was an alarm out on it. Somehow, his escape plan was known, and his new identity transmitted to all police departments.

The officer got into his patrol car and settled down to wait for the car's owner. Robert felt panic overcoming him. He had to stay calm. He would force himself. He remembered his off-duty revolver was still under the driver's seat. His fingerprints were all over the car. He had to get the car back for a little while. But how? A diversion. Yes, that's it, he needed to create a diversion to get the cop away from his car.

Robert compiled a mound of trash, anything that would burn rapidly. Then he walked down to the third floor where the rest of the laborers were working and mooched a cigarette from one of them. The wino also gave him a book of matches and told him to keep it. Robert went back to the fourth floor and worked a while. When he thought the time was right, he started the fire. When the fire gained some headway and spread to the walls, Robert shouted the alarm.

The winos on the third floor took up the call, alerting Sal in the trailer. Seeing the smoke pouring from the fourth floor, Sal ran for help. He spotted the parked police car a half a block away and ran towards it, alerting the policeman.

The officer immediately radioed for fire assistance, then drove to the smokey demolition site. He tried to free the area of vehicles to facilitate the arrival of the fire department.

In the confusion, Robert slipped away, got into his car and drove home. He washed then changed his clothes, got back into his car and drove to the mall, to his bank. He closed his accounts and emptied his safe deposit box. Then he went back to Mary's driveway. He found some kerosene in her garage which he used to wash the car thoroughly, inside and out, including the trunk. Then he removed the plates and threw them down the sewer.

Robert drove back to Buffalo, to a busy neighborhood, and parked the car. He walked for a few blocks till he hailed a cab and was driven back to Eggertsville, getting out at the mall. There would be no taxi records to Mary's house.

The five block walk back from the mall seemed like the longest walk he had ever taken, for it was then he decided to reveal his past to Mary.

Chapter Nine

Betty's phone at the Howard Johnson Motor Inn rang. She rushed to pick up the phone, knowing the only people who knew where she was were the detectives at Buffalo's Downtown Precinct.

"Detective Santini?" asked the deep voice of Detective Mullin.

"Yes, this is she," was the excited answer.

"Detective Mullin here, but don't get your balls, I mean hopes in an uproar," he said with a chuckle, "We have something to report to you."

"What, what," she pressed.

"Your hunch may be right. That '81 white Buick you think your brother was driving was seen in downtown Buffalo. But now it's gone."

"Wasn't the car watched?" she screamed.

"The officer that spotted the car was keeping it under surveillance, but a fire broke out half a block away. It took priority. When he returned, the car was gone. But at least we know for sure your brother's in the Buffalo area. We'll double our efforts, since we know what we're working on is more than just a hunch."

"Thanks, Mullin, I appreciate your notifying me so quickly. I know you had to go out of your way."

"Hey, that's okay," he answered quickly. "I'd sure hate to be in your shoes, hunting down your own twin brother. By the way, bring in those composites of your brother, we'll send out copies all over the city."

"That's swell, Mullin. If I can ever do anything for you, just ask."

"You can."

"Anything," she repeated.

"How about dinner tonight? I'm alone and you sound like you could use some company, too."

After a pause Betty answered, "Okay, but I don't have anything fancy to wear."

Detective Mullin lit up a cigar. The food, sirloin steak, french fries, and corn-on-the-cob was extremely good fare for an Irish pub.

Betty felt relaxed for the first time since her brother disappeared, as she sipped from a large stein of beer. Beer certainly wasn't her favorite drink with dinner. Red wine was what she grew up on and still preferred. But being out with an Irish Dick in an Irish pub, beer seemed like a good idea. Betty was still on her first beer while Mullin was finishing his third.

"I hope the cigar smoke doesn't bother you," he stammered.

"Not at all," Betty answered, "Dinner at my father's house resembled an opium den. Everyone smoked, even my mother."

"But cigars?"

"My father, and even my grandfather when he was alive. It brings back fond memories," Betty said smiling.

"That's swell. These days I get dirty looks whenever I light up. You're a welcome change."

"Are you married, Detective Mullin?"

"Please, call me Frank. No, I'm an old bachelor. Never married."

"You're not so old," Betty said with just a hint of a smile. How come you never married, Frank?"

Frank chomped on his cigar, twirling it around with his fingers as he searched for an answer. "I don't know, really. The Job took up most of my time, and I never cared for any of those Irish women my family and my parish priest tried to fix me up with. I'm not a fag. I've had a lot of women, but no relationships. At forty-eight, there's no hope for me. How about you? You married?"

"No," Betty answered, running her finger around the rim of her beer stein, making it sing. "I guess my answer would be the same as yours. Except I'd substitute Italian men for your Irish women. The parade has passed me by too. I'm forty-three."

"That's not so old. You're still young enough to have kids."

"I never pictured myself a mother. The Job was my only interest. I'm sick and tired of the same old questions. `When are you going to get married? Are you a lesbian?' I just never met the right guy."

"Are you?" Frank asked softly.

"What?"

"A lesbian?"

"If you weren't so goddamned big, I'd deck you. But no, I'm not a lesbian."

"Well, you're awfully pretty not to have married. I can't believe there's so many dumb cops in New York. I figure one of them should have nailed you. At least you would have had the Job in common."

Betty blushed. "Thanks Frank. It's been a long time since I got that kind of a compliment."

"C'mon, Betty, let's get out of here. It's early yet. Did you ever see Niagara Falls?"

"No."

"You'll love it. It's one of the most beautiful sights in the world."

"But it's dark," argued Betty.

"You'll see. You'll see."

"Betty, I didn't want to mix business with pleasure, but we found the Buick," Frank said with a frown as he drove.

"Why didn't you tell me that earlier? Take me to it, now."

"There's nothing to see. Your brother's a smart cookie. The car was absolutely clean.

In fact, it was washed with kerosene, inside and out. It's just a car, take my word for it. The only thing the car told us is that he's on to us. He knows we know he's here."

Betty leaned her head back on the car seat and closed her eyes. Turning to Frank, she spoke slowly and softly. "I have to figure out his next move. He's my twin. I could always do that. He knows that too. My only advantage is that he doesn't know I'm in Buffalo.

Robert found Mary watering her vegetable garden on the side of the garage. He shut the hose cock on the house, cutting off her supply of water. She examined the nozzle of her hose as if she expected an explanation for its failure to produce, then looked around and saw Robert standing there. Mary's face blushed at the sight of him.

"Hi, honey. I didn't hear you drive up," she said, dropping the hose and removing her gloves. "What're you doing home so early?

And all cleaned up, too? Didn't you go to work today?"

Robert was dead serious as he approached Mary and took her hand. "We have to talk, Mary, right away."

Mary clutched her heart. A look of fear appeared on her face. She crossed herself and said a silent prayer. "Come in the kitchen, I'll make coffee," she said somberly.

Robert followed Mary up the back porch, into the kitchen. He took a seat at the table facing the stove, and watched her fiddle with the coffee pot.

"Let's have it," Mary said softly, "It won't get any easier by delaying it." After putting the pot on the stove, Mary continued to stare at the pot. The muscles in her back tensed, as if she was expecting a lashing.

"Sit down, Mary, and look at me. I can't speak to your back," Robert ordered gently.

Mary sat down, putting both hands on the table, her left hand squeezing her right.

Robert cleared his throat, and in a barely audible voice, said, "I don't know where to begin."

"How about at the beginning?"

"The beginning was several years ago," Robert said softly, making eye contact with Mary, his eyes begging her to be patient. "Ten years ago, I married a beautiful Irish girl named Alice. During our engagement, whenever we had sex, she would end it with a crying jag, accusing me of leading her straight to hell. The next day she'd go to confession. I should have seen the handwriting on the wall, but she was so beautiful and I loved her. I convinced myself things would get better after we married. They didn't. After two children, she wouldn't let me touch her. Her parish priest told her sex was for procreation only. Everything else was a sin. His advice was law to her, and she locked her legs. You don't know what I went through, lying next to such a beautiful woman and staring at the back of her woolen night gown. She could have been wearing a chastity belt and thrown the key away. I never told you, Mary, but I was a police officer." Robert looked at Mary's face and saw she was astonished.

"I knew there was something about you," Mary blurted. "I could feel it. But never in my entire life could I imagine myself kissing a cop. My dead husband must be turning over in his grave. Go on," she sighed.

"I'm not very proud of what happened next. For almost five years, I lived a celibate life. It was torture. Then I began to hang around the bars after my shifts. I was drinking heavily, and little by little I began to weaken. I was flattered by the flirting women that hung around the bars. They started to look better and better. One night, a pretty Puerto Rican girl did a number on me. I was drunk enough to blame it on the booze. She took me to a room and we started to fool around. I thought the booze blew my mind, because I saw two of her. She had an identical twin, and they were in business together. For a sex-starved, healthy male to find himself in bed with two young, gorgeous girls -- who knew so many games that I never knew existed-- surpassed my wildest fantasy. I had them every night for several weeks, but it cost me plenty. I wanted them all to myself, but they laughed at me. They said I couldn't afford them, that they could make a fortune on the streets. I couldn't give them up, so we worked something out."

"Instead of their hustling the streets, I set them up in an apartment in my police sector. I steered customers to them. They worked for me. We were successful beyond my wildest dream. All the storekeepers begged for reservations during the days. The bartenders sent customers at night. The girls and I were getting rich. The girls even sold drugs to the customers that I supplied." Mary wore a solemn expression as she listened. "You sound more like a hood than a cop," she whispered.

Robert ignored her remark and continued his narrative. "It took a lot of my time while I was patrolling. I worked a very active precinct. I was an active cop. I led the precinct in arrests every year to keep the supervisors off my back. But all my spare time was supervising my whorehouse. My partner didn't mind, he was busy studying for sergeant. The weekly envelope I gave him, made things even easier."

"But then my partner, Jack Wilson, made sergeant and was transferred. My new partner, Steve Moran, was a ball breaker. He objected to my business. When I offered him money, the kid threw it in my face. Things went from bad to worse and he threatened to lock me up. One day we fought, and he pulled his gun on me. It accidentally went off and Moran got shot.

Mary gasped, "Oh, no. What a shitty break."

She covered her face with her hands and wept silently.

Robert continued speaking as if in a daze. "I ran. I was prepared to run for a long time. I had a new identity with all the necessary papers. Then Moran died and my picture was all over the papers and TV. I had to change my appearance and I did. From Brooklyn, I wound up in Eggertsville, living in a boarding house and falling in love with my landlady."

Robert took a deep breath and continued. "Anyway, I saw a Buffalo cop going over my car today. They had me made. I covered my tracks, so I'm sure nobody could have followed me. So, here I am, Mary. Where do we go from here?"

Mary's eyes filled with tears, her fists tightly clenched on the table. "What do you mean *We*?" she hissed. "You think I"m a fool? I know you're just using me. I won't go anywhere with you and have you dump me when it's convenient. Get out of my life."

Mary's sobs seemed to come from deep within her chest. Robert got up from the table and walked behind her. He put his arms around her, hugging her tightly. "Then it's settled. Since you won't come with me, I'll stay here with you. I won't run."

"Why is it I can't believe you?" Mary sobbed.

Robert walked back to his seat and picked up the paper bag from the floor. He removed the large steel box and handed it to Mary. He said, "You keep this. Without it I can't go anywhere. I'm trusting you with my life."

Mary took the box and put it on the table. Her crying stopped. With tears still creeping down her cheeks, she looked Robert in the eye and whispered, "What do you want me to do with this?"

"Open it," he ordered.

Obediently, Mary opened both latches and raised the lid. A large and a small pistol lay half hidden in their holsters, cushioned by neatly stacked bundles of money. Her eyes bulged from surprise.

Robert removed the small pistol and tucked it in his belt. He shut the box, put his hand under Mary's chin and turned her face towards him. "Hide this. Don't tell me where you put it. It's your insurance policy that I won't leave you, and it's yours if anything happens to me."

Mary looked in Robert's eyes for a long time. "I must be nuts," she said with a sad smile, "to go through this a second time."

Robert got up from the table and started pacing. His mind raced as he tried to formulate new plans. "First, I'll have to change my appearance," he muttered, mostly to himself. "I'll let my hair grow in, and grow a Van Dyke. I'll keep the glasses."

"You mean you're not bald?" she asked, surprised.

"No, I have thick, black hair," he said, wistfully.

"I can't wait to see it," she said fondly.

"I need a new name, new social security card, driver's license, and a new car. Can you help?"

"My brother has the connections to get you the papers. The family told him not to have anything to do with me, but I think he'll help me. He was the only one of my brothers who looked after me."

Robert paced in silence for several minutes.

"Could I make a suggestion?" Mary asked timidly.

"Sure," Robert answered, surprised. "Jump right in."

"If you used the name `Russo', I could say you were my cousin. You could get mail here or use my car without raising suspicions. But keep the name `Robert'. Everybody here's used to calling you that," Mary said, her voice getting louder as her plan became clearer.

"You've got something there," Robert said quickly. "I tell you what, take some of that money and buy a new car. Make it a four-wheel drive car. Yeah, there might come a day when we have to make a run for it, and a four-wheel drive truck might come in handy. You buy it, register it, get insurance. If I use your address on my driver's license, I could always say I was your husband. If I was stopped by a cop, everything would jibe. Great. Mary, you're a doll. A doll with brains. You'll make a swell partner."

Mary smiled warmly as she wiped away happy tears. "You start on your appearance and I'll take care of the car tomorrow," she said with a wispy smile.

Robert stopped pacing, stood behind Mary and put his arms around her, kissing the back of her neck. "Thanks for being my partner," he whispered, shyly.

Chapter Ten

For five days, Betty and Detective Frank Mullin toured the city, showing the composite pictures of Peter Santini alias Robert Fellini to hundreds of countermen, headwaiters, waitresses, gasoline attendants, barbers, anyone who might have waited on him, all with negative results.

Frank admired betty's energy, she never seemed to tire. He longed for the day to be over, so that he could escort her to one of his favorite restaurants, relax and enjoy the company of this extraordinary woman. Never, in all the days of his long bachelorhood did he meet a woman with whom he felt so comfortable. Even without Job-talk, he found they had much in common, and several times they talked well into the night. The few occasions when he held her hand or touched her accidentally, it thrilled him. He felt like a teenager. With his hormones more active than they've been in decades, he longed to bed this woman, but he didn't have an inkling of how she felt about him.

Later at night Frank and Betty were dining in one of Buffalo's most popular seafood restaurants, overlooking Lake Erie. They sat in a secluded corner of the outdoor patio, so deeply engrossed in conversation that neither noticed that the bright, full moon had disappeared under a deep blanket of ominous clouds. While they were quietly enjoying a cup of coffee, they were surprised by a sudden deluge of a summer downpour. They got up and ran for cover into the diningroom, but too late, they were both thoroughly soaked. After paying the bill, they waited patiently under the front canopy of the restaurant until Frank's car was delivered by one of the drivers of the valet service.

Frank shivered as he drove. He glanced at Betty, who was clutching her pocketbook to her chest, her hair wind-blown. She was curled up on the seat, trying to get warm.

"Care for a drink for medicinal purposes?" Frank asked with a smile.

"Hurry. I'm freezing," Betty stammered.

"Okay, Charley O's is just down the road. We'll be there in a minute."

True to his word, Frank turned off the avenue into a parking lot that was lit by a sign in red neon letters that spelled "Charlie O's." Frank parked as close to the back door as he could get. They sat and watched the rain pelting down.

"Are you ready to make a run for it?" he asked.

"Ready as I'll ever be," Betty answered with a whine in her voice.

"Can you run in those high heels?"

"Watch me."

They opened the car doors at the same time and sprinted for the back door of the bar. Betty ran, holding her large pocketbook over her head to protect her hair, her heels clicking and clacking on the wet pavement. Frank laughed as he ran behind her.

"What a sight you were," he giggled as he opened the door. "I never saw anything more female. And you're supposed to be a tough cop from New York City."

"Fuck you, Frank," she said, as she brushed the water from her dress.

"Follow me. We have to go through the kitchen."

Betty followed Frank through a maze of sinks, ovens and work tables until he reached the swinging door to the bar. He noiselessly opened the door, and spread before them was a scene that shocked the two veteran police officers. They saw one big man in front of the bar, holding a gun on two bartenders and two waitresses. A second man, behind the bar, holding a gun in his left hand, was looting the till with his right. There were four or five patrons lined up against the rear wall.

The police officers instinctively reacted, both springing into action. Frank pulled his gun from his shoulder holster as Betty took her small revolver from her pocketbook.

Frank advanced quickly and silently behind the man who was rifling the till. He attacked him, disarming the man, and getting him in a choke hold. The gunman covering the bartenders, whirled around and fired at Frank, knocking him down.

Betty fired one shot, hitting the gunman in the throat. She then pounced on the other unarmed man, beating him in the face with her big pocketbook. He advanced on her and she fired a shot at him, intentionally just missing his face.

The man's eyes bulged in terror. Betty ordered him to his knees with his hands behind his head.

Frank got to his feet shakily, rubbing the side of his head. He removed his handcuffs from his belt and cuffed the unhurt gunman.

Betty exhaled a huge sigh, and ran to Frank's side, examining the left side of his head that was covered with blood.

"Oh God, Frank, you're hit," she yelled with a sob in her voice.

"Take it easy, kid," Frank answered, "I'm okay. The bullet just grazed me. It's only a scratch. You okay?"

"Yeah. Just a little weak in the knees."

"That's only natural. Honey, you did great. You just dispelled any doubts I ever had about lady cops. I don't know anybody that could have done better."

"Is that other guy still alive?"

"I'll check," Frank said, as he picked up a wet towel from the bar and wiped the bloody side of his head. He walked out from behind the bar and bent over the fallen gunman. After a quick examination, Frank called out, "He's still breathing." Then he went to the phone and called for an ambulance and backup.

"You start taking statements from the customers, I'll work on the help," Frank told Betty.

Within a few minutes, screaming sirens could be heard, and flashing red lights flooded all the windows. Moments later the room was filled with excited policemen. The paramedics arrived and tended to the wounded gunman. The confusion increased greatly when the media arrived, reporters, photographers, and TV cameramen crowded every available space.

Frank pulled Betty aside and handed her his car keys. "Take my car and get back to your hotel before you blow your cover. I'll make sure you get full credit for this collar, but I don't want your name or picture spread around. After I clear everything up, I'll drop over. Wait up for me."

"Get your head tended to first. Your scratch might get infected, "Betty answered, as she patted Frank on the cheek.

Frank self-consciously leaned over and kissed Betty on the forehead. Then he smiled and whispered in her ear, "Beat it, Tiger."

Betty got lost trying to find her way back to the airport area where her Howard Johnson motel was located. She had to stop at an all-night gas station to get directions, But between the gas attendant's broken English and Betty's complete ignorance of the city, she got lost again and had to stop for directions a second time.

One hour and ten minutes after she left Charlie O's, Betty finally pulled up to her motel. Dead tired, she dragged herself up to her room and hastily undressed. She took a long, hot shower, and reflected on the evening's events. She shivered, even though the shower was filled with steam. She prayed that the man she shot would survive. Although she was involved in many shootouts in her long police career, Betty never killed anyone. She knew many officers that did, and they all suffered psychological damage. She didn't even have the luxury of family support. Her only living relative within five hundred miles was her twin brother, who she dearly loved. But she was stalking him. Her relationship with Frank was getting warmer, but she certainly didn't know how she was going to handle that.

"How did I suddenly get so fucked up?" Betty said out loud, as she rubbed her body vigorously with a thick, soft towel.

Robert walked into the kitchen with a newspaper under his arm and took a seat at the kitchen table facing Mary, who was busy at the stove.

"I love that car," Robert said, referring to the brand new Ford Explorer that Mary brought home that morning. "I love the way it handles. It must have every option that Ford offers."

"Yeah, it's easy to shop when the money isn't yours. You said buy loaded, I bought loaded. You'll have to teach me what all that four-wheel drive crap is all about."

"Someday, I'll take you on a picnic in the country and we'll drive off-road. Then you'll see how much fun it is," Robert mumbled as he spread the newspaper on the kitchen table.

The headline story about a police shootout in a city bar took up the whole front page, with a color picture showing the paramedics treating a wounded gunman. Robert, the ex-policeman, was always fond of reading about the exploits of other policemen, since he was often the main attraction of many good stories. Now, he was the heavy and the subject of a nationwide search. Robert read the story out loud to Mary. It described the exploits of an undercover female detective and her role in capturing armed gunmen that were holding up a bar and grill. She shot one and forced a second to surrender. Her partner was shot, but not badly wounded. After the arrival of other police officers, the female officer went into hiding to protect her identity.

Robert whistled after reading the story.

"Some story. Reminds me of my sister Betty," Robert muttered under his breath.

"Your sister a cop, too?" Mary asked, as she turned to face him.

"Yeah, I come from a whole family of cops. My grandfather was a hero-cop, killed on the Job. My father retired as a sergeant. He was also a hero. My twin sister, Betty, is a first grade detective, and I have two brothers on the Job."

"Wow," laughed Mary, "I come from a long line of hoods, dating all the way back to Sicily. We make quite a pair."

Mary poured two cups of coffee and sat at the table facing Robert. Her face turned very serious. "Do you have any plans, Bob?"

"I'm starting to put some thoughts together," Robert said slowly. "As soon as your brother gets me those papers and my new driver's license, we're going to take a trip."

"Where? What kind of trip?" Mary asked.

"Brooklyn for a few days. I've got a few safe deposit boxes I want to clean out.

And I want to check around to see just how hot I really am. Then we'll shoot out to Long Island, to Bellmore. Maybe, I'll get a chance to see my little girls. I miss them more than I could tell you."

"Won't that be dangerous?"

"We'll see. I certainly won't take any chances. My hair and beard are growing. When we get back home, I may buy into a business. I've been giving it some thought."

"What kind of business?"

"Demolition. My boss offered me a deal. A partnership. I'm thinking about it. It's something I could handle. I think I'd be safe. The people he hires aren't exactly the type to ask questions or have anything to do with the police. I could handle the contracts and the business deals, while Sal handles the actual work. I'd be sort of an executive. I have to do something. I'm going crazy."

"Please don't rush into anything. Think things out carefully," she said quietly, her eyes pleading with him.

"Don't worry, I will. Hey, let's go upstairs for a matinee, before the old girls get home."

"Before dinner? Are you nuts?" Mary asked, getting up eagerly.

Chapter Eleven

The sun shining through the window into her eyes woke Betty. She was dressed in her nightgown, covered with a bathrobe. Expecting Frank, she hadn't made the bed. She had fell asleep on top of the covers while watching an old movie on TV.

When she opened her eyes she saw a picture of Charlie O's. The camera was panning the parking lot, the front of the building and finally inside. The camera zoomed in on the wounded man lying on a stretcher, showing two paramedics hooking up an IV. The anchorwoman was extolling the virtues of a clandestine hero cop, who disappeared to safeguard her identity. She was proudly emphasizing the fact that a female detective had to rescue her male counterpart.

Betty laughed. A knock on the door brought her to her feet and she switched off the TV. She opened the door and admitted a tired looking Frank. His clothes were wrinkled from last night's rain and he wore a white bandage on his left temple.

"I'm sorry to be so late," he said as he gave her a hug, "The paperwork took forever. Then the bastards from Internal Affairs weren't satisfied with my story about you. They grilled me for hours. They had trouble locating the right people in New York in the middle of the night to verify my story."

"How'd it wind up?" Betty asked, smiling.

"I'm not entirely sure. Your boss at the twenty-third squad praised you to the sky, and threatened an invasion of thirty thousand cops from the city if they tried to sully your reputation. It did my heart good to see the disappointed looks on the faces of those bastards. They enjoy zinging any cop, but especially good cops. Jealousy, I suppose. They want to interview you this afternoon. Fuck 'em. You don't have to go. You deserve the Medal Of Honor, and I'm going to see you get it."

"I'll go. What happened last night could have happened to anybody."

"Yeah? But not everybody would have handled themselves as good as you did. Man or woman. I never thought I'd ever say it, but my hat's off to your department."

"Stop the shit, Frank. We just did our job. We were lucky. If one of those customers was hit by a stray bullet, the media would have crucified us. There's a very fine line between hero and bum. It happens all the time."

"Bullshit. There was no luck involved in your shooting, and under fire no less. It took skill and guts, and you showed both. I'm proud of you."

Betty blushed. "Do you want me to order breakfast from room service.?"

"Not for me. I'm bushed. I'd like to take a shower and grab a few Zs. Mind?"

"No, no," Betty said quickly, feeling strangely relieved. "I came here to find my brother and I've got a lot of things to do. How long do you want to sleep? I assume you were ordered to bring me to the IA."

"Wake me between noon and one. We have to be downtown by three. We'll grab a bite before we go."

Betty watched Frank enter the bathroom, stripping off his clothes as he went. She couldn't help thinking that this was a real man. A good man, a man she could respect and even grow to love. But could she let him make love to her? A feeling of panic overtook her as she thought about it. To have a man touch her was like a claustrophobic getting locked in a dark closet. Did she hate it or was she just afraid? She had the answer to that one. She could remember vividly when she had loved it.

She drove slowly through the congested streets of Buffalo to a section highlighted on her map that Frank and she had not covered yet. A pile of the composites of Peter's face lay on the seat beside her. After reaching the neighborhood, Betty went from store to store, questioning the proprietors and leaving the composites everywhere. Sooner or later, someone would recognize Peter. She knew he was here in Buffalo. At eleven-thirty, Betty headed back to her car from the half hour trip back to her motel.

Betty opened the door of her room and was greeted by sounds of snoring. So loud, a vision of a wounded walrus jumped into her mind. She walked over to the bed and stared down at the man, who seemed to be working hard at his sleeping. He was a rugged looking man, so huge he seemed to fill the double bed all by himself. He was lying flat on his back with his arms extended, like Christ on the cross.

She gently shook his shoulder causing him to jump. His quick action startled her, and she stepped back a step or two.

"What time is it?" he said, rubbing the sleep out of his eyes.

"Twelve fifteen," Betty answered.

Frank pulled the cover from his body and jumped out of bed. He was only wearing his shorts, revealing a thick, muscular body, every inch covered with black hair. When he stretched, he looked massive. Betty envisioned him crushing her with those huge, hairy arms. He made her feel tiny, inconsequential. When he took a step towards her, she stopped him with a command.

"Get dressed, Frank. We don't have much time if we want to get something to eat."

Her authoritative tone stopped him in his tracks, and he stared at her. Without a word, he turned and headed for the bathroom where he had left all his clothes.

A few hours later, Betty and Frank sat in the stark office of the Internal Affairs interrogators. Betty was questioned at length as to why she was in Buffalo investigating her brother's case, even though she acknowledged that she was not the official officer assigned to the case.

"I'm on vacation. I"m here at my own expense on my own time. The Code of Criminal Procedure of The State Of New York states that I'm a peace officer everywhere in the state of New York. That's why I took official action last night when a felony was committed in my presence. It was my duty. My request to remain anonymous is consistent with my pursuit of a police officer charged with murder. I believe he's in the Buffalo area. I'm here with the blessing of my commanding officer, who I'm sure you've already spoken to. The two morons from Brooklyn assigned to this case are still in Brooklyn. Detective Mullin from Buffalo Homicide was assigned to this case and is assisting me. Does that answer your question? Frank and Betty were both First Grade Detectives, and outranked the interrogators.

"I'm sorry, Santini," the younger of the interrogators said, "But I can't keep your pedigree out of the official reports. You shot a man, for chrissakes. I gotta do my job. I can't worry about New York City."

"Jumpin' Jesus," Frank shouted, as he jumped out of his chair and approached the interrogators' desk. He pounded his huge fists on it. "This officer saved my life last night. Doesn't that count for anything? She deserves cooperation from this department by just asking for it. She didn't have to earn it, but she did. If anything leaks from this office to jeopardize her investigation, I'll personally come back here and break your arms and legs. That goes for both of you. Comprende?"

The two young sergeants looked shocked. Both started to speak, but Frank's huge fist pounded the desk again, causing everything on it to jump in the air, and both sergeants decided it was wiser to say nothing.

"Let's go, Santini," Frank growled as he pulled Betty from her chair. "I'm going to buy you that drink I promised you last night."

It took Robert almost seven hours, to make the trip from Buffalo to New York City.

"Driving the speed limit is against my religion," Robert said sourly as he maneuvered the Explorer through mid-town traffic.

Mary looked bewildered as she gazed up at the skyscrapers. This was her first visit to the big city, and seeing the panorama in person was almost frightening. She wasn't prepared for the traffic gridlock. In comparison, Buffalo was a hick town. She flinched each time a taxicab passed them. Mary screamed when a taxi, approaching from the oncoming lane, swerved at the last second to avoid a head-on collision.

"Don't ever ask me to drive in these fucking streets," Mary gasped, holding a hand to her chest. "Who drives those cabs? Lunatics? When are we going to be there?

Robert laughed. "You sound like my kids. `When are we going to be there? When are we going to be there?'" he mimicked. "That's the Marriot up ahead. I hope they have our reservations."

Mary looked in awe, as she watched big-league professionals at work. In minutes, the bellhop took their luggage, the garage attendant took their car, and the desk clerk gave them their key. She watched Robert sign the admission card "Mr. and Mrs. Robert Russo."

"Forgive me, Mario, but you've been dead a long time," Mary whispered, as she crossed herself.

They followed the bellhop toward the elevators. Mary nudged Robert in the ribs, as she looked around the lobby. "This place is magnificent, just like in the movies. There's more people in this lobby than in all of Eggertsville. Is it safe?" she whispered.

"Don't you know? The best place to get lost is in a crowd. Nobody notices anybody, they just go about their business."

The bellhop opened the door of their room on the thirty-second floor, put their valise on the bed, opened the drapes and adjusted the air conditioner. He smiled when he saw the large bill Robert put in his hand.

"My name is Henry. If you want anything, call the service desk and ask for me. I'll take good care of you," he said as he gave Robert a big wink and closed the door behind him.

"Why'd he wink?" Mary asked.

"Just acting cool. I guess he figures us for hicks.

"Well, he certainly figured me right," Mary giggled.

"Come over to the window and look at this magnificent sight. Like no other in the entire world," Robert said proudly.

Mary walked to the window and looked down. It was dusk, and lights were coming on all over the city, shining like millions of diamonds. She gasped, and grabbed Robert around the waist.

"Jesus Christ," she yelled, "I just lost my stomach. Hold me, I feel dizzy. I was always terrified of heights."

Robert laughed. "Maybe tomorrow I'll take you up to the top of the Empire State Building or the World Trade Center. Then you'll know what high really looks like."

"Fuck that, this is high enough for me. Look, the cars look like ants down there. Close the drapes, please. I'm starting to feel sick."

Robert closed the drapes and picked up the phone. He dialed the service desk and asked for Henry.

"Henry, there's a double sawbuck in it for you if you can get two good seats for `*Les Miserables*' for tonight.

"I know there's not much time. If there was I wouldn't need you," Robert said, falling into a New York accent. "And bring up a bottle of good French champagne, to get us in the mood."

He waited for Henry's response, which took a moment. "What? If you can't get the tickets, who needs the French champagne?" Robert shouted, slamming down the phone.

"Why were you so rude?" Mary asked, it's not like you."

"When in Rome," Robert mumbled.

"What does that mean?" Mary asked, with an annoyed look on her face.

"It means," Robert answered slowly and patiently, "That when yer in New York City, ya act like a New Yorker. Capishe?"

Mary answered by throwing her high heeled shoe at him. Robert responded by tackling her onto the thick carpeting, and kissing her deeply. His hands roamed over her body, making her shiver.

"I think I'm going to like New York City," Mary whispered, then pulled Robert's head down for another kiss.

Chapter Twelve

"Last night was the best time I ever had. Thank you. I never saw a stage show in my entire life, and seeing it from the third row was magical. I cried my eyes out," Mary said excitedly. "Did you like it?"

Robert concentrated on getting out of the parking garage and into traffic. That accomplished, he turned right onto Broadway and headed downtown toward the Brooklyn Bridge.

"Well, did you?" Mary asked.

"Did I what?"

"Like the show?"

"It was okay."

"You lying bastard. Tears were pouring from your eyes. I was watching you."

"Yeah," Robert answered, "It was great, but a little too sad for me. I enjoyed the restaurant more. Best food I had in a long time."

"It was like a fairy tale," Mary exclaimed, clapping her hands together. "Dinner at Sardi's. I read about it, saw it in the movies, but I never dreamed I'd ever be there. We were sitting around all those elegant people. I felt like Cinderella. I don't remember what the food tasted like, but I remember it was very expensive. Now I can say I was there. Can we go to some other famous place?"

"No, Mary we can't. Remember, I'm on the run? I took a helluva chance going out in public when the whole police department's looking for me. I did it for you. I wanted to give you a special treat. Now we have to go underground again. We came here for two things. First, we clean out my safe deposit boxes, then we go out to Long Island to see my kids. They'll tell their mother they saw me and she'll spread the alarm. Under no circumstances are my kids to see this car. By the time they get home, we should be well on our way back to Buffalo. Capishe?"

"Capishe," Mary said, disappointed.

"I enjoyed fooling around on the carpet and later in that big bathtub, the best," Robert said, slyly, changing his demeanor to one at ease.

"You're just a degenerate," Mary giggled, "But I must be one too, because I loved it. My husband never did any wild things like that, even when he was young."

"Ha, after my daughter Tess was born, I didn't get laid for over five years, sleeping in the same bed with Alice," Robert said, sullenly.

"She must be a real nut case," Mary said. "Didn't she know what she was missing? You're a great lover."

"Ha," Robert said disgustedly, "She cried after everytime we made love. The next day... right to confession. How good could I be?"

"She's an Irisher, what does she know?" Mary exclaimed, waving her hand to the sky. "Give her a bottle of beer and she thinks she's coming."

"There's the Brooklyn Bridge. Want to buy it?"

"Very funny. It looks really old."

"It is, way over a hundred years."

"I don't care for the neighborhood. All I see are Orientals."

"Dope. This is New York's famous Chinatown," Robert said, as he directed his car onto the bridge.

"Oh, my God," Mary said, grabbing Robert's elbow, "Is this old bridge safe?"

"Are you kidding? Look at those towers. Solid granite. This is the strongest bridge ever built. Relax."

Mary looked like she held her breath all the way across the bridge. She exhaled deeply as Robert exited made his way onto Adams Street and gridlock in Brooklyn.

"So, this is Brooklyn," Mary said, looking around. "Looks just like Manhattan."

"Only around here," Robert said patiently, "this is the downtown area. Courts, big buildings, big business. In a few minutes, it'll be strictly residential."

Fifteen minutes later, Robert pulled up in front of a large bank on Flatbush Avenue. He reached under his seat and pulled out a large paper shopping bag. Turning to Mary, with a very serious expression on his face, he said, "Honey, I should be out in a few minutes. Get into the driver's seat. If I run into trouble, or if there's a hold on the box and it takes me longer than a half hour, take off. Drive around the block for another half hour and if you don't see me, go home."

"Are you crazy?" Mary shouted. I'll never leave Brooklyn without you. You're my life now."

"Okay, okay, say a little prayer for me."

Robert leaned over and kissed Mary's forehead, then opened the car door and disappeared into the bank. The last thing he heard before the car door closed was a deep sob from Mary.

Fifteen minutes later, Mary saw Robert emerging from the revolving doors. He had a broad smile on his face and the paper shopping bag he carried was noticeably bigger and fatter.

After getting behind the wheel, Robert gave Mary a peck on the cheek and said, "Boy, that went great. The clerk looked bored out of her tree. She never looked at my face, not even once. We'll wait here a few minutes to see if there's any unusual activity. Then we'll go to the other bank on Dekalb Avenue. It's only a few blocks away."

"I think I held my breath all the time you were in there. Thank God, everything went smoothly," Mary said.

Robert emerged from the second bank with the same big smile he had the first time.

When he got behind the wheel, he handed Mary the shopping bag. "Here you are. You take charge of it. With the other money I gave you, we have almost two hundred thousand dollars to live on. You know I won't leave you as long as you have the money. Don't tell me where you hide it. Like I said, it's your insurance policy."

"Please, Bobby, don't talk to me like that. I trust you, and I love you. You'll know where the money is. I don't want the money to be the glue that holds us together. I want it to be love and trust. Capische?"

"Capishe," Robert answered, grinning. Now I have another treat for you. A few blocks from here is Junior's Restaurant, one of the best places to eat in all of Brooklyn. I ate there a lot when I was a cop here."

Robert made a U-turn on Dekalb Avenue and headed south. Four blocks later, he pulled up to the curb next to a fire hydrant, outside the restaurant.

"Get out a piece of paper and a pen," Robert ordered. "I don't want you to make a mistake on the order."

"Aren't we going to eat inside?" Mary asked, surprised.

"No, I'm too well known in there. Can't take the chance. Ready?

Robert dictated a huge order of succulent delicacies that put a look of amazement on Mary's face. "And don't forget the napkins. My partners always forgot the napkins."

"Hand me the shopping bag," Mary said with a sly smile."

"What for?" Robert asked seriously.

"To pay for the check, silly."

"Hurry up and get your ass in there, I'm parked at a hydrant," Robert answered, trying to keep a straight face.

"Where are you taking me?" Mary asked as she watched Robert drive through narrow streets among tall, dirty looking warehouses.

"To an old dock where all the daytime cheaters go on their lunch hour. We won't be noticed there."

Robert drove slowly, winding his way through the parked cars, to find a space near the water.

"Oh my God, did you see that?" Mary shouted.

"What, what?" Robert responded quickly.

"In that red car, they were fucking in the back seat. In broad daylight, for chrissakes. They were naked!"

"That's unusual," Robert answered, giggling, "Look in the other cars. They're all fucking with their clothes on. They only have their lunch hour to do it."

"I thought you were kidding. This is disgraceful."

"Give 'em a break. They're all consenting adults," Robert said, as he parked the car alongside the dock.

"Ugh," she said disgustedly, look at all the used condoms laying on the ground. How could you want to eat here?"

"Unpack our lunch," Robert ordered, "Those rubbers aren't going to jump in the windows. You're quite safe."

It was one-thirty when Robert drove up the winding ramp to the Brooklyn-Queens Expressway, on their way to Bellmore, Long Island.

"If we don't run into a traffic jam, we'll be early," Robert said as he entered the fast moving traffic and maneuvered to the left lane.

Robert wore an anxious look. He was worried how his children would greet him after an absence of almost three months. It was early September, and the children had gone back to school.

At two-fifteen Robert pulled off the Wantagh State Parkway at Hempstead Turnpike and made a left turn onto Bellmore Road. Ten blocks later, he pulled into a parking space in front of a pretty split-level house. Mary could see the school grounds two blocks away.

"I want to be waiting at the gate, when they get out at two-thirty," Robert said nervously.

"Won't Alice be there to pick them up?" Mary asked.

"No. They're old enough to walk home by themselves. The house is only four blocks from the gate. We only picked the kids up if it was raining. You stay here. When I leave the kids, I'm going to walk in the opposite direction, then around the block."

"Do you want me to turn the car around and park in the other direction?" Mary asked, timidly.

"Yeah, that's a great idea. We'll be able to get away faster. Keep the engine running and the passenger door unlocked."

Robert leaned over and gave Mary a peck on the cheek, then got out of the car.

"Good luck," she called.

"Thanks," was his worried answer.

Robert crouched at the gate, as he scanned the hundreds of children that crowded the walk on their way to the street. He spotted Marci busily chatting with a girlfriend. His chest tightened as he looked at his pretty blonde daughter. She walked towards him. The child resembled her mother, and would grow up a blonde beauty like Alice. When Marci was five feet away, Robert stood up and called, "Marci, over here."

"Daddy," she screamed, and flew into his arms. Her books were gripped behind his head as she covered his face with kisses.

Robert held Marci around the waist as he hugged her to his chest. Then he felt fists pounding him in the back. He turned around and saw the tear-streaked, beautiful face of his first-born daughter, Tess. She was tall for eight years, blonde and delicate, almost a small clone of her mother.

Robert bent down and drew Tess within the circle of his arms and squeezed the two girls to his heart. All three faces were now full of tears, and Robert was too choked up to speak. The two girls were both chattering away at the same time, and Robert couldn't make any sense of what they were saying. Finally, he calmed them down and was able to get a word in.

"One at a time, sweethearts, so I can hear you."

"Oh, Daddy, did you come home for good?" asked the excited Tess."

"No, Honey. We only have a few minutes, then I have to leave."

"What did you bring me?" asked the younger, Marci.

"Girls, I'm sorry, but I was in such a rush, I couldn't get you anything. But if you tell me what you want, I'll send it to you. I promise."

Tess pouted and turned her head away.

"What's the matter, baby? Why're you turning your head away?" Robert asked.

"Mommy said never talk to you, forever and ever."

"Why, Honey?"

"Because she said you left us flat, and because you're a bum. Are you a bum, Daddy?"

"No, Honey, I'm not a bum."

"Then why did you leave us, Daddy?" Marci chimed in.

"Because I got into trouble and I had to go away," Robert said with a gasp in his voice, "Can you forgive me, girls?"

"I can," Marci said eagerly.

"Me too," Tess answered.

"Take your hands off those children," a familiar, angry voice shouted.

Robert turned around and saw his wife, Alice, running towards him. Her face was contorted with anger, but somehow retained its beauty.

"You son-of-a bitch," she shouted, as she flew at him, raking his face with her nails.

Robert released the girls and tried to defend himself as blood poured down his face.

"Stay away from us, you pimp," Alice shouted, as she tried again to scratch his face.

Robert caught her hands in his, and held them tightly.

"Calm down, Alice, "he pleaded. "Everybody's staring at us."

"Drop dead, you bastard. I hope someone called the cops. Help, help, this murderer is trying to kidnap my children," Alice screamed.

Robert released Alice's hands, kneeled down and kissed his daughters.

"I love you both with all my heart, and don't forget it. No matter what anybody says about me, stick up for me, love me, because I'll love you till I die. Goodbye, girls."

Amid the stares of the crowd, Robert sprinted away, in the opposite direction of his parked vehicle. He circled the block, looking over his shoulder, but saw no one following him. When he finally reached the Explorer, he jumped in behind the wheel of the idling vehicle and took off as fast as he could. In less than a minute he reached the Wantagh Parkway and got on, heading south.

"Aren't you going in the wrong direction?" Mary yelled.

Robert, still puffing from his long run, took a long time before he answered.

"We're heading for the Verrizano Bridge, to Jersey. Then we'll take the Jersey Turnpike to the Pennsylvania Turnpike. We'll take that to Pittsburgh, then go north to Buffalo. The cops know I was in Buffalo and will expect me to return there. So the Thruway would be suicide."

"Get used to this, Mary. This is going to be our life. We're always going to look over our shoulders. From time to time we'll have to run, just like today. If you want out, I understand."

Mary looked at Robert for a long time before she answered. "No, Bobby, I don't want out. I want to be with you for the long haul."

"You've got some temper there, Mullin," Betty said with awe in her voice.

They were seated in a booth in a busy bar, located one block from his headquarters. Being late in the afternoon, the place was filling up with offduty police officers of both genders. For the married, coming from the warzone in the streets, it was a place for a calming drink before they embarked on the trip home. For the singles, it was the place to pair off for a nightly encounter, or to join others in a lonely group, eat and drink and tell lies to the wee hours of the morning.

"Temper? That was no temper. Just the Irish in me showing off a little. Don't mind me, I'm just a pussycat," Frank said with a wry smile on his face.

Betty reached across the table and grabbed Frank's hand and squeezed it. "I had a hunch there was a little pussycat in that great big ugly body of yours," she said softly. "You remind me of my grandfather. He was a great big man who treated me like a rag doll. He told me wonderful stories of the Job, the way it was in the old days. I was eight when he died, but he was the one who made me want to become a cop. He was killed in a shootout in Times Square. By the way, his name was

Frank, too. Maybe that's why I liked you from the beginning."

Frank turned red. He wasn't used to talking to a woman like Betty. He didn't know how to handle it. She made him feel like a kid, insecure. She had it all together, so sure of herself.

"Frank, you're blushing. Didn't a girl ever tell you she liked you before?" Betty teased.

"Not one I didn't pay," he stammered. "You want to eat here? The food's good."

"I'd rather not. There's Jobtalk all over this place. I'd rather go to a quiet restaurant where no one knows you and we could be alone. Okay with you?" she said.

"Sure. We had seafood last night. How about Italian tonight?"

"Sounds great, but tonight I pay. You've been feeding me for a week now. It's only fair I pick up the tab once in a while."

"I couldn't do that. Wasn't brought up that way. Besides, I'm a single guy and I don't have anybody to spend my money on.

When we're not working, I don't think of you as a cop, but as a woman. A lovely woman that scares the hell out of me."

"But, Frank..."

"Don't `But Frank' me. I pay, and don't bring it up again. C'mon, let's go. I know a great Italian restaurant called Maria's. Wait'll you taste that food. You'll think your mother did the cooking."

As Frank was paying the check, his beeper went off. "One of these days I'm going to enjoy throwing this gadget into a dumpster," Frank grumbled, as he led Betty towards the phone booth. "Someday, I'll get my privacy back."

Frank dialed his office, and Betty watched from outside the booth. She saw him nod his head a few times before he hung up the phone. When he turned around, his face wore a serious expression.

"What is it. Tell me," Betty implored.

"My office got a call from your C.O. It seems he got a very excited call from your sister-in-law, Alice. She went to pick up her kids at school and found them in a clinch with your twin brother. She scratched up his face pretty good before he took off and disappeared. She didn't see what he was driving, but she did say he was wearing a Vandyke beard and horn-rimmed glasses."

"Let's sit down. I've got some fast decisions to make."

Frank led Betty back to their table and summoned the waiter. He ordered two coffees.

"I didn't expect Peter to be back on Long Island," Betty said, weakly. "I know he's crazy about those kids, but it would take something very important for him to expose himself like that."

"He left in an awful hurry," Frank said, maybe he went back to clear up some loose ends. Maybe after five weeks, he thought the pressure let up a little and he could safely sneak back. And while he was there, spend a few minutes with his kids. I'm sure he didn't figure on getting caught by his wife. You think he's holed up in the City?"

"Absolutely not," Betty asserted, "He knows how hard New York cops push to catch a cop-killer. He's gone, I'm sure. But where? Back to Buffalo, where he's had five weeks to get situated? But he knows he blew his cover in Buffalo. Maybe he headed the other way -- out east on the Island. No, I've got a feeling, call it a hunch if you want. My beloved twin is coming back to Buffalo. I don't know if he found out I was here. But if he did, I'm sure he showed himself back east just to get me on a plane and out of here. What do you think, Frank?"

Frank rubbed his chin before answering. "You make him sound like a sharp piece of work. I don't know the guy, so I have to go with your instincts. But if you think he's headed back here, let's change that composite of your brother and add a Vandyke. Then we'll fax it to every state trooper barrack on the Thruway. It's only a little over an hour since your sister-in-law spotted him. C'mon, let's go. We'll eat later."

"Frank, I've got a favor to ask you."

"What?"

"My vacation time is up in two days. Do you think your C.O. could call mine and have me temporarily assigned to your command? After all, it is a murder we're working on, and I'm the best qualified person to assist you. What do you say?"

Frank squeezed Betty's hand and looked her in the eye, "I agree. I'll try and swing it, even if I have to call in every marker I hold on my boss. And you know what," Frank added, lowering his eyes, "I don't care how long it takes to catch your brother, I never felt like this for any partner I ever had."

Chapter Thirteen

It was two-thirty in the morning when Robert finally parked the Explorer on the driveway of Mary's home in Eggertsville. Mary was sound asleep and had been for the past two hours. Robert stretched, then shook his hands to get the kinks out of his aching arms. He looked over at Mary and admired her round face, so peaceful in repose. Reminded him a little of his mother. Gently, he shook her shoulder, only to be repaid with a sharp slap across his face.

"Jesus Christ," Robert yelled, rubbing his cheek. "The next time you fall asleep on me in a car, I'm going to handcuff you to the door. You're dangerous lady."

"Oh, I'm sorry, Honey, I didn't mean to hit you," Mary said, sheepishly.

"Do you always wake up swinging?" Robert asked.

"Afraid so. I've done it since I was a child. A natural reaction, I guess."

"What's so damn natural about swinging at the person who wakes you."

"I told you I grew up with four brothers, and if any one of them touched me when I was sleeping, I swung."

"Here," Robert said as he handed Mary the shopping bag filled with money. "Hide this when we get inside. Tomorrow I'll buy a floor safe and install it in the cellar. Only you'll have the combination."

"No, Bobby, that's not the way I want it. We're in this together. We have to trust each other."

"We'll talk about it in the morning," Robert said, yawning. "Open the door, I'll get the valise."

Walking up the stairs behind Mary, Robert playfully patted her behind. "Want to fool around a little before we hit the sack?"

"Shush. You want to wake the old ladies?" Mary scolded with feigned anger. "I thought you were tired."

"I'm tired, but the little guy down here has a mind of his own."

Mary giggled. "That thing never gets tired."

"How about it?"

"Okay. It serves me right, getting mixed up with such a young stud. I'll be up in a little while. After I'm sure everybody in the house is sound asleep. Don't lock your door.

Later, as they lay naked on top of the covers, locked in a tight embrace, a cool breeze from the open windows blew the drapes into a weird ballet as it washed over their sweaty bodies.

"How was it, Honey?" Robert asked, in a proud but exhausted voice.

"Do you always have to ask? It was great, better than great. Do you want me to pin a medal on your cock?" Mary said sarcastically.

"Why're you getting so pissed off?'

"After a good lay, I don't want conversation. I want afterglow."

"What the fuck is that?" Robert asked in a loud voice.

"Shush, you idiot. You want to broadcast to the entire world?

Sometimes I wonder about you," Mary said as she jumped off the bed, grabbing her nightgown. "Come down in the morning after the old ladies leave for work and I'll make you breakfast. Good night."

After finishing his second cup of coffee, Robert pushed his dishes away and watched as Mary cleared the table. "This is no good. I have nothing to do. I'm going to go nuts just hanging around," Robert said, sullenly.

"You can't get a job with that phoney social security card my brother got you. It would only be a matter of time till they caught you."

"I know that. That's why I was giving serious thought of taking that slimeball Sal up on his offer. You know, buying into his business. But after thinking about it, I realized he'd expect me to handle the contracts, legal and illegal. That means exposing myself to the cops. One day, one of them would recognize me and it would be all over. I can't take the chance. You have any ideas?"

"I helped my husband run a small book on the side when he worked for the mob. I still have all the records. We could do that."

"Yeah, look where it got you the last time. A widow at forty-five. No thanks. I don't want the mob after me too. Maybe you and I could run a small mom and pop business, somewhere, in some hick town."

Mary smiled broadly. "That sounds wonderful. We could work side by side. Be together all day as well as all night. It wouldn't even matter if we made money or not. We've got enough to carry us for a long time."

"Bullshit," Robert shouted, his fist hitting the table, "It matters to me. I don't feel like working sixteen hours a day and not making a dime. If we buy a business, it's gotta pay."

"Okay, okay, I was only fooling," Mary said excitedly, "When can we start looking?"

"Just as soon as you can get rid of this house."

"No problem. I'll sign it over to my brother, Vincent. I don't want to bother with real estate agents and all that bullshit. He'll pay me what he can and when he can. He won't cheat me. What do you think?"

"If that's what you want, it's okay with me. Put whatever you want in storage. We're going to leave with whatever we can carry in the Explorer."

Mary looked around the house, sadly. With a tear in her eye she said, "There's nothing here I'd like to keep. The few antiques I have, I'll send to my daughters. The rest I'll leave. Even my clothes are shit. New guy, new things. New life."

Robert was surprised that he felt all choked up. Maybe he wasn't so tough after all, he thought. "Mary, we're going to celebrate. Tonight I'm going to take you to Maria's for dinner. That place has wonderful food. We'll eat till we explode.

"How did you find out about that place?"

"That's the place I ate in the night I shot those rapists."

Mary walked behind Robert and put her arms around him. She kissed the back of his neck and hugged him tighter.

"Thank you for giving me a second chance at life. I've never been happier. Life is so exciting around you, I feel so alive. I never thought I'd ever say this again. Bobby, I love you."

"That's okay, kid. The feeling is mutual."

Mary hit him across the back of his head. "Why can't you say it, you big lug. Say it, say it."

Robert laughed. "I love you, Mary."

Maria's Ristorante was jammed as usual. Robert and Mary waited forty-five minutes to be seated. They requested the non-smoking section, but settled for a table in the smoking section which didn't have as long a wait. Their table was large with four chairs, but the tables were situated very close together, and Robert's back was making contact with a woman's half naked back at the next table.

Midway through the meal, Robert was jostled by a woman trying to squeeze through the space between him and the half naked back. He turned around to complain and looked up into his twin sister's beautiful face.

First, it took on a look of surprise, then shock. Betty shrieked, "Peter," and threw her arms around his neck, then kissed him on both cheeks and finally on the lips.

Robert stood, facing his sister and her companion and said with a controlled voice and a forced smile, "Betty, you and your friend must join us. This is an unbelievable surprise."

Frank moved his right arm, but Robert moved faster, putting his right hand inside his jacket. Frank smiled and resumed his original position.

The waiter seated Betty and Frank at the two vacant chairs and left. The tension at the table was like an electric device, ready to discharge. Faces remained still, but eyeballs were racing back and forth.

Finally, Robert broke the silence, as he reached across the table and extended his hand to Frank, "I'm Betty's brother, Peter. And this is my friend, Florence Romero, who has to leave now, because her babysitter has to be home by ten."

Frank's big paw encircled Robert's hand with such great pressure that Robert stopped breathing in order to prevent his voice from crying out in pain. He strained to keep his facial expression at status quo. When Frank released his hand, Robert felt a surge of gas in his bowels.

"Glad to meet you, Peter. I've been looking forward to it for quite some time. My name is Frank Mullin."

"That's Detective First Grade Mullin, from Buffalo Homicide, Peter," Betty added.

"Thanks, Betty. With his big, Irish mug, I never would have guessed. But I appreciate the warning. Say goodnight, Florence. You better leave now if you want to make it by ten," Robert said as he glared at Mary.

Mary's eyes bulged with anger, but she stood, forced a smile and said, "Goodnight, folks, glad to have met you." and walked from the restaurant like a running back going through a hole in the line.

Robert reached inside his jacket and pulled his revolver from its holster. He put his hand with the gun in full view on the table and covered it with his napkin.

"I'd appreciate it if the two of you would put both hands on the table where I can see them, then we'll have a nice talk," Robert said in almost a whisper.

They complied.

"I don't want any trouble in this crowded room," Frank said icily, his steel blue eyes, drilling themselves into Robert's.

"What the hell are you doing here, Betty?" Robert said, breaking off eye contact with Frank and turning to his sister.

"I came to bring you home."

"How the hell did you know I was in Buffalo?" Robert asked excitedly, with a slight look of strain appearing on his face.

"I'm your twin. Didn't I always know what you were thinking," Betty said, trying to establish control over her brother. "Wasn't I the one who always got you out of trouble?"

"That was a long time ago, Betty. And you're not here to get me out of trouble. But why you?" Robert asked, his eyes challenging his sister's.

"It was Dad's idea," Betty said, with her eyes looking down at the table. "We had a family meeting. Dad said we're a police family with a long tradition and a heroic past. He said you brought shame to the Santini family, and it would take a Santini to erase that shame, by bringing you in. I was elected."

Raising her eyes that were now tearing, and looking into her twin's face, Betty cried out, "For chrissake, Peter, why did you shoot Steve Moran?"

Heads from all the nearby tables turned to hear the answer. A long silence ensued. Finally, Robert spoke in almost a whisper, causing Frank and Betty to lean forward to hear him.

"I never meant to hurt Steve. He was upset with me for giving so much time to my business. I was used to Jack Wilson. He liked it when I was out of the car, so he could study. I expected every partner to go along with me. But Steve wouldn't. He kept threatening to turn me in. I told him to mind his own business. Well, one day, he told me that he was going to lock me up, and he placed me under arrest. I remember telling him to fuck off, and he belted me. His punch felt like a powder puff and I hit him back and knocked him down. He pulled his gun and got to his feet. I told him to put the gun away or I'd shove it up his ass. He threatened to shoot me. I grabbed for the gun and we wrestled over it. The gun went off and Steve was hit. I panicked and ran. You know the rest of the story."

"Why'd you run, Peter? With a good lawyer, you could have pleaded self-defense and beaten the rap. All you had to contend with was the minor charges and the loss of your job. Now you're wanted for murder. Come home with me. I'll fix things, like I always did," Betty pleaded, with tears streaming from her eyes.

"I can't. I made a new life for myself and I'm almost happy. I miss Tess and Marci, but I'm glad to be away from Alice. The last five years with her were pure hell. She was the one who drove me to the bars. I know all about our family history, and I'm too ashamed to go back. I could always talk to you, but I could never face the rest of them. I can't go back, Betty."

"You're going back, fella. Alive or dead, but you're going back. You can take that to the bank," Frank said with a fierce look on his face.

"Okay, that's it," Robert said, pointing the gun at Frank. "Let's all go to the men's room. Now. I'll be right behind you."

Betty and Frank stood, then turned and slowly wound their way through the crowded room. The men's room was the type of facility that allowed only one patron at a time, and it was occupied and locked. They waited outside the room for several minutes until the occupant left. Then Robert pushed his sister and her large companion into the room. He followed and locked the door.

"Face the wall," Robert ordered, "And put your hands on the wall, both of you. Betty, put your pocketbook on the floor."

They complied. Robert lifted Frank's jacket, seeing his holstered gun and a pair of handcuffs. He removed the handcuffs and looked around the tiny room. Being an old building, the room was heated by a two-inch pipe that ran from the floor to the ceiling and beyond. Robert wrapped the handcuffs around the pipe and then cuffed both of Frank's wrists. Then he searched Betty's handbag and found her handcuffs. He repeated the procedure for her. With both his prisoners secured, Robert searched Frank's pockets until he found his keys. He removed the handcuff key and put the other keys back. Again he repeated the procedure for Betty.

"I won't take your guns or your car keys, because I don't want to make unnecessary trouble for either of you. I just need a little time to get away."

"Please don't do this, Peter. Let me take you home," Betty said.

"Sorry," Robert said as he kissed Betty's cheek.

"Fella, you're sure going to regret the next time we meet. And we'll surely meet," Frank warned.

Robert backed out of the tiny room and went back to the table. He dropped a fifty dollar bill on it and left.

Robert stood in the shadows about fifty feet from the entrance to the restaurant and waited. In about three minutes, a young couple came out and walked in his direction, never noticing him. He followed them to their car and waited until the young man unlocked the car. Then Robert jumped him and, at gunpoint, took the keys for the car and ordered them to walk into the dark alley.

Robert sped away, and headed for the airport. He parked the car in the Long Term Parking Lot, wiped it clean of his prints. Then he walked back to the terminal and took a cab to Eggertsville and got off in the mall. While walking the six blocks from the mall to Mary's house, Robert tried to formulate new plans. But he felt so tired and wrung out from his experience in the restaurant, that he couldn't think clearly. It would have to wait till morning, until he rested a bit.

When he unlocked the front door, Mary pounced on him, hugging and kissing him.

"Oh, God, I never thought I'd ever see you again," Mary said, the words gushing from her, "How'd you get away?"

"We never did have desert or coffee," Robert answered, smiling. "So, while you make some I'll tell you the whole story. I won't leave out a thing, I swear."

Robert put his arm around Mary's waist and led her into the kitchen. He sat down at the table, exhausted, and wearily described all the events that Mary missed.

Chapter Fourteen

"I was never so embarrassed in my whole life," Frank grumbled, as he drove aggressively through the almost deserted streets. "I felt like a steer in a slaughterhouse, trussed up on a hook."

"Oh, stop being so dramatic," Betty giggled. "I'm sure worse things happened to you on the Job." "When those uniformed cops came into the bathroom and started laughing, so help me God, I could've strangled them."

"Forget it. At least we didn't lose our guns or shields," Betty sighed.

"Shit, all we lost was our prisoner, our dignity and our self-respect. Not to mention our credibility."

"Please, stop your bitching. It's over. Let's get down to important things."

"Like what?"

"Like dinner. I'm starving. You rave about Maria's, take me there, and then you refuse to eat there. Why?"

"Jesus H. Christ," Frank yelled as he pounded the dashboard with his fist. "Ain't you got no pride?"

"Boy, you really lost your cool. You're using double negatives, and bad ones at that. Are you going to feed me or what?"

"I don't understand you. You're sitting there cool as a cucumber, criticizing my grammar, complaining about being hungry, when just a little while ago your brother slipped through our fingers. You've been looking for him for weeks. Chasing him all over the state. Then he gets the jump on us, makes asses of us, and you sit there smiling as if everything went as planned. Talk to me."

"I'm just happy that he looked so well, had it all together. He looked handsome, didn't he? I had visions of him running like a scared rabbit. Terrified, confused, desperate, a step from being a complete psycho. We'll catch him again, I'm sure of it," Betty said dreamily, as she leaned back in the seat with her arms behind her head.

"You puzzle me, Betty. The way you talk about him, it just doesn't seem natural. You're only his sister."

"You're fucking wrong," Betty shot back, angrily. "I'm more than his sister, I'm his twin."

Not another word was spoken for the next five minutes, as Frank drove more slowly. Then in a quieter, more conciliatory tone, Frank asked, "Do you mind going to my place? I make a great omelet."

"Can I help?" Betty asked, in a softer voice.

"Sure. You can peel the potatoes. I hate that."

"You've got yourself a deal," Betty said, laughing as she playfully punched his shoulder.

By eleven-thirty they were through eating, dawdling at the table, slowly drinking their second cup of coffee.

"Let's get down to business," Frank said seriously, "What do you think he's going to do now?"

"He'll run again, but not right away. He'll plan it very carefully, taking into consideration what he thinks I'll be expecting. Then he'll do the opposite."

"You were right about him coming back to Buffalo after he was spotted on Long Island. I don't know how he made it, with every state trooper on the whole Thruway looking for him."

"He didn't take the Thruway," Betty said assertively.

"How do you know?"

"Must you ask?"

"No," Frank said, shrugging his shoulders.

"Do you think we could identify the woman he was with?"

"Maybe. What name did he call her? Florence something or other?"

"Let me think," Betty said, holding her fist to her forehead. "It sounded like Roman or Romeo."

"Romero, that's it," Frank interrupted. "Florence Romero. I'll call my office and have someone check it out on the computer."

"Don't bother," Betty said softly, "It's a phoney name. I saw a look of surprise on her face when Peter introduced her. I don't think she's too smart."

"It's worth a shot," Frank said as he got up and walked to the phone.

Moments later, Frank returned wearing a little boy's smile on his face. "You were right, as usual. No record. What do you suggest now?"

"How about the motor vehicle picture file? There's a good chance she drives a car."

"Jesus, that would take a lot of work. Maybe we ought to see the Bureau's artist tomorrow morning. We could have him draw up a likeness, then use a few clerks to go through the DMV picture file," Frank said, stretching and yawning.

Betty laughed at him, then said, "I'm getting tired too. Can you call me a cab?"

"What for?" Frank asked, looking hurt.

"I don't expect you to drive me all the way out to the airport at this hour," Betty said tentatively.

"Then stay here tonight, Betty, please," Frank said hoarsely, his face pleading with her. "We're both adults. Long past impetuous mistakes. This isn't a spur-of-the-moment request, I've been thinking about it for a while. I didn't have the guts to ask."

Betty stiffened. She brought her right hand up to her mouth and bit on her fingers. "Why now, Frank?"

"Because of what happened tonight. I think your brother's going to run, and you're going to be right behind him. I'm afraid I might lose you before I can prove how I feel. I think I love you. And I know how much I want you."

Frank reached across the table took Betty's fingers in his big paws and gently cupped them, like he was holding a fragile bird. Then he took a deep breath, his huge chest and neck seemed ready to burst, but words burst from him instead. "Don't you feel anything for me?

Betty pulled free from Frank's grasp and stood up. She began pacing like a lioness in a small cage, only the wringing motions of her hands betraying the battle of emotions going on inside of her.

"You ask a simple question that has a very complex answer. I never met a man like you. I've never been more comfortable with anyone, working or socially. It feels like I've known you forever. I never feel awkward with you or feel the need to make conversation. We're so alike in the way we think. I won't bullshit you, Frank. I don't know if I could sleep with you. I'm forty-four years old, and I've lived by myself all my adult life. I'm very set in my ways. My Catholic upbringing kept me from one night stands and I drove sex from my thoughts. But I'd be a liar if I said I hadn't thought about it since I met you, because I have. It scares the shit out of me. I can't tell if I love you because I don't know what that means. But I can tell you there's nobody I'd rather be with than you. See what you started, you big ape," Betty said, as she burst into tears.

Frank got up from the table and went to her, gently engulfing her in his arms. He raised her face and looked into her eyes, kissing away each tear as it ran down her cheeks. "What now, little girl?" Frank asked timidly.

"Let's call it a night. I'm awfully tired," Betty whispered.

"Okay, okay," Frank sighed. "I'll behave."

"Do you have something for me to wear?"

"Only pajamas. I don't wear them in the summer, but they're laundered."

"That would be fine."

Frank handed Betty a pair of striped blue pajamas, and she went into the bathroom to undress. Frank dimmed the lights, undressed down to his shorts and got into bed. Fifteen minutes later, a very shy Betty emerged from the bathroom wearing only the pajama tops that hung down almost to her knees.

"No way could I handle the bottoms," Betty said apologetically, "They kept falling off. Why didn't you shut the lights?"

"Because I wanted to get a good look at you in my PJ's. You do look awfully cute."

"Well, you got your look," Betty said, blushing, as she put out the lights. Groping her way in the darkness, Betty reached the bed and put a hand on Frank's shoulder. "Mind if I sleep near the wall? I always feel safer there," Betty asked, and without waiting for an answer, climbed over Frank and got under the covers. She tucked her knees under her chin, turned on her side and faced the wall.

Frank shuffled over to Betty, turned on his side, and put his arm over Betty, holding her in place. He moved as close to her as he could get.

Betty tensed, her hands drawn into tight fists. She barely breathed, but her heart felt like it was pounding. Maybe it was Frank's heart that she felt pounding. Fifteen minutes passed, without a word being said.

Then she felt it. Was it her imagination? No, there it is again, against her buttocks, but bigger. She could feel it growing, pressing into her. Betty bit her tongue to keep from screaming.

"They're all the same," she thought, "Even the best of them."

Betty tried to move, to put a little distance between them, but Frank held her like a vise. She was near panic now, perspiration breaking out on her brow. Then it came. She was sure, a slight movement. She could feel his thighs tighten, then release. Then a longer movement, then longer still.

"The son of a bitch was fucking her ass," she realized.

Panic turned to rage. Betty sunk her nails into Frank's arm, causing him to yell and release the grip his arm held her in. She twisted her body around until she was facing him, then kneed him in the groin with all her might.

Frank's groan was followed by moans of agony.

Not able to see his head in the pitch black room, Betty swung both fists in the general direction until she found the range. Once found, she was relentless, pounding both fists into the soft flesh of his face. When the pain in Frank's groin subsided enough for him to catch his breath, a tremendous roar emerged from deep within his chest.

"Jesus H. Christ, Betty. Are you fucking crazy?"

He tried catching her fists with his hands, a tough job in the darkness. He caught one, then a moment later, the other. He pulled her into his arms and hugged her tightly.

"Calm down. Please calm down," Frank pleaded.

Betty responded by sinking her teeth into his hairy chest, just above his right nipple, drawing blood.

Frank yelled in pain, instantly releasing her, and jumped out of bed. He groped along the wall until he found and turned on the light switch. The instant burst of light revealed a grizzly scene. Betty was on all fours in the bed, her face covered with blood, Frank's blood. Frank was leaning against the wall, the bulge in his shorts long gone. Blood was running from his nose, streaming down his neck onto his chest where it was joined by a tributary of blood emanating from his right breast. Betty sat back on her haunches in horror.

"Oh, God. Look at you."

"Yeah, I'm in perfect costume for Halloween." Frank groaned, as he slowly slid to the floor. "I'm afraid to ask what set you off."

"C'mon, you filthy pig. You were fucking my ass," Betty shouted.

"I never had it out of my shorts. I'm not going to apologize because you excited me and it got hard. Nature meant it to be that way. You should be grateful that I'm not queer or too old to get it up. Someday, that little thing will give you a lot of pleasure. I promise you that."

"Don't hold your breath," Betty hissed, as she yanked the cover off the bed, wrapping it around her. She cuddled up on the couch, looked at Frank and ordered, "Put out the lights."

"Aren't you going to wash the blood off your face? You look like a vampire."

"Fuck you, Frank."

Hours later, Betty was still wide awake, huddled on the couch, listening to Frank snore. In her mind she went over the events of a few hours before, trying to figure out why she panicked so. After all, Frank did no more to her than is done almost everytime she rode the subway. Sometimes the culprits sneak in a quick feel as they pound away in the packed subway car. She always got annoyed, but never panic-stricken.

Betty's mind wandered back in time when sex was exciting and enjoyable to her. It all started in high school. She attended St. Anthony's High School in Bay Ridge, Brooklyn. Always in the top ten percent of her class scholastically, Betty was active in several clubs and wrote for the school newspaper. It was when she made the cheerleading squad, that Betty's social life began. She attended parties with the athletes of the school and felt flattered when she was asked on a date by the handsome and popular quarterback of the football team, Michael Marino. The relationship began slowly, but soon they were seeing each other on a regular basis. In the beginning it was movies at the RKO Albee on Fulton Street and a bite to eat in Bickfords or the Automat. When Michael got his driver's license and the use of his father's car, they went to Long Island and nightclubs. By the Spring of their senior year, Betty and Michael spent a lot of time in the parking lot of Prospect Park, where their petting sessions were approaching flamatory proportions. When sex was finally consummated, Betty was relieved, and happy to find it so enjoyable.

Michael was a kind and patient lover, and Betty believed she loved him. The Santini family grudgingly had to approve of the Marino family, because Michael's father was a fireman. The only one who completely disapproved of Michael was Peter. He hated the way Michael bragged in the locker room, always hinting of his conquest. When Peter confronted Betty and she readily admitted having an affair with Michael, he blew his top. He agreed not to give her away only when she reminded him of all the scrapes she got him out of that the family never knew.

Remembering her teenage years, Betty cried herself to sleep. The vision of Frank's bloody appearance, the result of her latest bout with her neurosis about sex, tore at her heart. She felt he was the man to end the twenty-six year drought without sex, but would she kill him first?

Peter lay on his side, facing the window that was faintly illuminated by the street lamp across the street. He watched the curtains doing an acrobatic dance spurred on by the cool summer's breeze. A smile curled the corner of his mouth as he remembered his sister's face and how shocked she had looked at seeing him. He wanted to crush her in his arms. Instead he chained her to a pipe.

Betty, his alter ego until the age of twenty-one, when they both joined the Force and went their separate ways, was now a bounty hunter. He was the prey. He couldn't hate her for that. After all, she was here at their father's bidding. He couldn't fault his father. He had a right to want to clear the family's name. It was a smart decision to send Betty. His younger brothers hardly knew him. They just grew up in the same house.

But Betty knew him better than he knew himself, and she was certainly smarter. "Dammit," Robert yelled out loud, as his right fist punched the palm of his left hand, I have to put myself in Betty's head. It didn't take her long to trace me to Buffalo, he thought. I have to fool her and that's going to be tough. She's one of the best damn detectives in the City of New York and that means in the whole damn world. She would expect me to run, so maybe I should stay here. No, that big Mick detective got a good look at Mary and me, and it would be just a matter of time before we we'd be caught. So, where? Miami? LA? Mexico? She'd expect me to go south or west, so I'm going to go north and east. Yeah, upper New York state, or New England. Yeah, sister Betty, I'll give you a run for your money this time. A quarter of a million in cash, and Mary's clean, legitimate papers can give us an undisputed clean start anywhere, he reasoned.

At breakfast, Robert told Mary the plans he had formulated during the night. Their flight together from the Buffalo area to parts unknown seemed adventurous to her. They would co-habit as man and wife and the sneaking around would cease.

Mary's chest swelled with the feeling of sweet anticipation and she was impatient to get started. She telephoned her brother Vincent, whom she nagged, pleaded and coerced until he agreed to come right over. When he arrived, Mary sat him at the kitchen table, shoved a cup of coffee in his face, and with energetic gestures of both hands, excitedly told him of her plans to sell him her house and car.

Vincent was overwhelmed. He wanted to jump up and leave, but when he heard his sister say she didn't expect any money up front, he began to concentrate on what she was proposing. It was a sweet deal and a no-lose situation for him.

They shook on it, kissed on it, and the deal was complete. Vincent would handle all the paper work and Mary was free to leave. Informing her tenants of the change in ownership of the house was the only slight regret Mary felt before leaving. Her life in Eggertsville was over. Now she understood the lines in English movies. The King is dead, long live the King. Goodbye Eggertsville, hello anywhere.

Chapter Fifteen

After an agonizing night on the couch, Betty woke to the aroma of brewing coffee. She started to stretch but stopped when she felt pain from every joint in her body.

"Christ, I feel like a crippled old lady," Betty complained out loud.

"That's because you're a stupid, old broad," Frank answered from the kitchen amid the sounds of rattling pots.

Frank came into the living room, dressed in jeans, a muscle T- shirt and sneakers.

He was freshly shaven, hair combed, and his cheeks seemed to shine.

Betty was impressed. He certainly looked years younger, dressed so casually. Then she realized this was the first time she saw him dressed in anything but a suit.

"Be careful not to look in the mirror when you go into the bathroom," Frank said softly, "You look like a three day old D.O.A. with that dried blood all over your face. You could suffer a severe shock."

"Fuck you, Frank."

"I see you're your usually sweet self this morning. Move your ass, breakfast is almost ready."

Frank's expression was soft, almost loving, a far cry from the tough, Irish cop look he projected while working. Slowly, Betty got off the couch, wrapping the blanket tightly around her. Looking at Frank, her face colored. "About last night," she stammered.

"Stop," Frank ordered, holding up his hand like a traffic cop. "Forget last night. I'm going to try to put it out of my mind. I hope you're mature enough to also."

"Frank, I don't think --"

"That's the trouble with you. Sometimes you don't think. Last night I told you I loved you. That wasn't an easy thing for me to do. I'm forty-eight years old. Never told that to a living soul. I've been horny lots of times, but I never said those three little words. I couldn't, because I never felt them before. This morning, I came in here and knelt by the couch, just staring at your face. I prayed for the first time since I was a kid. I had to thank God for bringing you into my life. And I prayed even harder for help to keep you in my life. Maybe for a little miracle, too. That you could care for me."

Tears filled Frank's eyes. Embarrassed, he turned and walked into the kitchen. Betty was shocked at Frank's outburst of emotion, at the depth of his feeling for her. She was sorry now for her reaction to his sexual advance on her. Betty realized now it wasn't just a casual attempt at a one night stand, but a natural extension of his feelings.

But even now, knowing of Frank's deep feeling for her, Betty knew she couldn't have gone through with a sexual experience with him. She wasn't ready, and didn't know if she would ever be. However, Frank was certainly entitled to an explanation-- one that Betty feared she didn't have the strength to make.

With a troubled heart, Betty made her way to the bathroom. She noticed that Frank left out a big, fluffy bath towel for her, and that her clothes were neatly folded on the hamper. She made the shower as hot as her body could take, changed the shower head to the massage setting, and relaxed as the water beat the pain from her joints.

She luxuriated under the steamy water until it ran cold. Betty toweled and powdered her body, dressed, and took much longer than usual to put on her make-up.

I'm stalling," she thought. I'm afraid to face him. Afraid of what I have to tell him and I'm terrified of how he would react to my disclosures. Damn him. Why do I have to tell him anything? Because men want sex so badly. Why can't people live together without sex? After all, I've lived without it for the last twenty six years. Why has it suddenly become so big an issue in my life? Because I found Frank and I don't want to lose him. Shit. I came to Buffalo to find my brother and I fucked up my whole life.

"Hey, move your fanny. My breakfast is getting cold," Frank yelled from the kitchen.

"I'm coming, I'm coming," Betty yelled back.

"You should be so lucky," Frank grumbled.

"Why does everything have to have a sexual connotation?" Betty asked as she sat down at the table.

Frank came to the table carrying a pot of coffee. He stopped short and stared at her.

"Shit," he whispered as he exhaled.

"What?" Betty asked, avoiding eye contact.

"You're beautiful, like an angel. How can I stay mad at you?"

"Frank, I have so much to say to you," Betty stammered. "So much explaining to do, I don't know where to begin."

"You don't owe me an explanation. Anything you feel you want to tell me can wait. Right now, we have to go downtown and face the music. Heroes one day, bums the next. If one son of a bitch even smiles at me, I'll break his face."

Betty raised her head, her eyes meeting Frank's. "Thanks, pal, for changing the subject. I never realized how sensitive you really are. So different from the image you project. You're right, we have to get back to the real world. I never gave Peter a thought since we got here."

"Well, you better get on it, because I have a feeling he's going to move fast after last night. Jesus, can you believe that little shit. We spend weeks scouring the city for that guy, and suddenly he falls in our laps in the restaurant. But he's a lot smarter than you described him. He got rid of his woman and got the jump on us. Either he's sharp, or we're pretty lousy cops."

Betty beamed. She almost felt proud of her brother. "Yeah, he's pretty sharp," she said, thoughtfully. Then she slammed the table with the palm of her hand, and as if waking from a dream and said fiercely, "But I'm a lot sharper. I'll catch that little shit, if it's the last thing I do."

"You mean *we'll* catch the little shit, don't you?"

Betty colored. "Yes, Frank," she said softly, "I mean we."

Robert cursed under his breath as he tried to squeeze one more carton into the Explorer. "These goddamn cars have a lot of uses, but moving isn't one of them," he grumbled.

"I don't know why you insist we take so many of my things," Mary complained. "We can afford to buy new things when we get settled somewhere."

"Waste not, want not, my mother used to say. I can't see throwing out perfectly good things and then buying the exact same things a few days later," Robert said as he forced the last carton into the car. Then with a sigh of satisfaction, slammed the door.

"My clothes will look like shit when we take them out of there," Mary whined.

"You're the one that insisted on laying them down on the rear seat. I told you to put them into valises," Robert said coldly.

"Well, I didn't think you'd take my big TV, toaster and can opener. I'm surprised you left the refrigerator."

Robert's lip turned up into a wisp of a smile before he answered. "For a moment I thought of renting a trailer and taking it, but then I realized we might have to go off-road in an emergency."

Mary threw her arms into the air and cursed in Italian. as she expostulated:

"Men!"

They drove in silence for more than forty five minutes until they reached the Canadian check-point in Niagara Falls.

"Can you tell me why we're going into Canada?" Mary asked, almost shyly.

"I think the drive East will be a lot safer in Canada, than using the Thruway. And remember, Mary, I'm your husband Robert Russo now. Don't forget it. We're an old married couple. Capische?"

"Capische," Mary whispered, wishing with all her heart it could be true.

Robert answered the few questions the border guard asked, with a confident air. The guard didn't bother to ask for any papers.

"Amazing," Robert said with a laugh. "Going from one country to another with just a wave of the hand. Amazing," Robert repeated.

"What now?" Mary asked, worriedly.

"What do you mean 'What now?' We're goddam tourists, so we'll act like tourists. We'll stop at the Thousand Islands, Three Rivers,

Montreal, Quebec, the whole nine yards. My sister Betty will be looking for us West or South. I know how she thinks. I mean I know how she thinks I think."

"What the hell are you talking about?" Mary asked, with a scared look on her face.

"Forget it, Mary, leave the worrying to me. Just act like a tourist and enjoy yourself. I'm sure as hell going to try."

"I can't help worrying, Bob. My whole world is changing. As long as I'm with you, I don't mind the changes. Now, at least I feel alive, instead of feeling like a dried-up old Guinea widow."

Robert laughed, as he pounded the steering wheel with his fist.

"Yeah," he shouted, "Like the man said, `Free at last, free at last,'"

Chapter Sixteen

Frank turned crimson as he listened to the tirade given by his cigar-chomping C.O. Betty smiled as she watched in fascination the way Frank's neck swelled when he got angry. She was waiting for the button to pop off his collar.

Not able to take it anymore Frank exploded: "Why don't you save that speech for the goddam rookies, Captain. Betty and I have over fifty years experience between us. Nobody, and I really mean nobody, could have acted differently in a crowded restaurant without endangering innocent people."

"Stop the shit Frank. Why don't you admit you're over the hill? The other night this lady-cop had to bail you out at Charley-O's, and last night the uniforms found the both of you trussed up like two pigs in a meat locker. It's embarrassing. Captain Riley downstairs has been riding my ass for the last two hours."

"Over the hill? Bullshit. I'm the best you've got and you know it. Now I want you to get on that phone and call Betty's C.O in New York and request she be temporarily assigned to our squad. Her vacation runs out tomorrow, and we're very close to catching her brother. You owe me, Captain. I'm calling in one of your markers.

Captain Dellasandro was so enraged that he nearly swallowed his cigar. He rose from his chair and started pacing behind his desk. Pointing his cigar at Frank, he bellowed: "You fucking Micks have some balls. I call you in here to chew your ass out and you ask for a favor. What if I said no?"

Frank slowly stood up and walked directly in front of his superior, nose to nose. "You know the answer to that question," Frank hissed. "My retirement papers would be on your desk this afternoon. But I promise you this, you'll never make deputy and you'll be hard pressed to keep your ass out of jail."

The captain's eyes retracted to mere slits as he stared at Frank. The sound that came from his throat was barely a whisper. "Are you threatening me, Detective Mullin?"

"Not a threat, Captain. Like I said, a promise."

"Get the fuck out of my office, you Irish bastard, and take this bimbo with you.

"Look at my rod bend, I must have hooked a whale!" Mary screamed.

"For chrisssakes, sit down before you capsize the boat," Robert yelled.

"Help me. He's pulling the rod out of my hands. I don't know what to do."

"Give it to me," Robert said, laughing. He took Mary's rod and slowly began to reel in some line. He kept the line as taut as possible to keep the fish from jumping and spitting out the hook. After several minutes of playing with the fish, Robert swung his prize into the boat.

What a fish it was. Big and fat, at least five pounds, the small-mouth bass would make a delicious meal for two.

Mary clapped her hands in glee like a child, and kept repeating: "My first fish, my first fish."

"After you clean that monster, he'll make a helluva meal for both of us," Robert added, smiling.

"Me? You want me to clean that slimy thing?" Mary screeched.

"Then back it goes, I'm sure as hell not cleaning it," Robert said as he lifted the fish over his head.

"No, no, don't throw back my first fish."

"Okay, okay," Robert laughed, "I'll show you how to clean it."

It was their second day in Canada. The first day they spent like other honeymooners, gawking at the magnificent Niagara Falls and strolling leisurely among the young lovers. The second day they rented a cabin in a town called Geninocque on the St. Lawrence River. They rented the cabin for three days. An aluminum row boat came with it, complete with fishing gear. Mary drove the Explorer into town to purchase the fixings to go along with her fish. Later, she fussed over the meal and it truly fulfilled its promise.

"That was great," Robert said as he finished his second cup of coffee. "I'm glad we rented a cabin with a kitchen. I never realized it before, but you're a great cook. In fact, you cook the same style as my mother. Sicilian style."

Mary blushed slightly as she got up to clean the dishes.

"Outside of bed, you never say anything nice to me. Thanks, Bobby."

"Don't call me Bobby. It sounds like you're talking to a kid."

"Well, you look younger since you let your hair grow in and that Vandyke beard makes you look like royalty. A duke, maybe."

Robert laughed. "Some duke. I'm a hood, running to save his ass. You call me royalty? What a joke."

"You look like someone special. Don't you think I notice how all the women turn to look at you? They must wonder what you're doing with a fat old bag."

"Don't talk like that, Mary. I love you very much. You make me feel safe, even peaceful. Except for not having my kids with me, I've never been happier. When we make love, it's always special, like hitting a home run in the bottom of the ninth to win the game. That's it," Robert shouted. "You make me feel like a winner, when all my life I felt like a loser."

Robert got up from the table and brought some dirty dishes to the sink. He started to go back to the table, then changed his mind.

He stood behind Mary and hugged her, placing both hands on her large breasts.

Mary screamed and hit him in the groin with her butt. "Don't start with me while I'm working," she scolded, but obviously pleased with the attention.

She turned around and Robert kissed her deeply, while she put her wet, rubber-gloved hands around his neck. The kissing excited them both and soon they were frantically undressing one another, their lips never parting. Like horny teenagers, they made love against the kitchen sink.

It was past 2:30 in the afternoon, and Frank and Betty were sitting at a quiet table in Frank's favorite bar. A long time had passed since either one spoke. Both mulled over the fast moving events of the last few days and the uncertainty of the future. Frank toyed with his unlit cigar, spinning it as it hung limply from his lips.

Betty fingered an errant curl above her ear. Frank's beeper made them both jump as if they came out of a trance. Without a word, Frank got up and went to the phone booth. A minute later he returned wearing a concerned look.

"What? What?" Betty asked, anxiously.

"That was Dellasandro. He said he spoke to your C.O. and requested your temporary assignment to our squad, but it was denied."

"Why?" Betty asked with a catch in her voice.

"He said your work was piling up and the City needed you more than some hick town."

"Shit," Betty exclaimed, as she pounded the table with her fists.

Frank sat down heavily in his chair, picked up his un-lit cigar, leaned back and stared at Betty. "What're you going to do now, kid?"

"I'm going to ask for a leave of absence, and if that's denied I'll throw my papers in."

"Please don't jump to a decision. You might regret it the rest of your life."

"I don't know," Betty said solemnly. "Since I came out here, the Job doesn't seem as important as it used to. Maybe you have something to do with that." A glimmer of a smile crossed her face.

Frank scowled as he pushed aside the three empty beer steins in front of him, and waved at a passing waiter. "I'm getting another brew. You want anything?"

"Yeah, vodka on the rocks."

"Wow, you must be pissed off."

"You can bet your big Irish ass I'm pissed off. I never asked for a single favor since I got on the Job. And the first time I do, it's turned down." Betty grabbed her purse and headed for the telephone booth.

Fifteen minutes later she returned to the table just as Frank added the fourth empty stein to his collection.

"Any luck?" Frank asked.

"That son of a bitch boss of mine was going to turn me down on my leave of absence request. But when I threatened to resign, he gave in. After I thanked him, he added a sixty day stipulation. What a bastard."

Betty sat down heavily and reached for the glass of vodka. She finished the drink in two gulps and signalled the waiter for another.

"You're supposed to sip hard liquor, lady," Frank said, smiling. "Not gulp it like beer."

Betty's answer was between a grunt and a belch. After a long period of silence, she sighed audibly. In a voice just above a whisper, she spoke as if to herself. "I've never been without a job since I was a teenager. Never had to think about money. My pay stops tomorrow. I got to learn to be economical."

"Why don't you give up that fancy hotel room and stay in my apartment? There's plenty of room."

"Jesus, don't you ever give up? We were both covered with blood last night. Think tonight would be better? I can tell you, it won't."

Frank blushed. "I didn't mean it that way, honey. I could sleep on the couch. Shit, I sleep there most nights anyway. You can have my bed. You can have my car, too. I have use of a department car anytime I want. How about it?"

"I don't feel right, putting you out of your bed."

"I'd love to have you. Anyway, sooner or later, I know you'll jump on my bones. My charm is irresistible."

Betty laughed, and thought, I could love this big buffoon. Then she said, "Okay, Frank, but there's one condition. Let me share the rent and the cost of food. I don't want to feel like a charity case."

Frank put on his best hurt look. He over-did it, like he was in a silent movie back in the Twenties.

"What? What?" Betty asked.

"You heard me tell you I loved you," Frank stammered. "Your condition's like an insult to me. There's nothing more I'd love in life than to take care of you. I mean forever."

"The condition stands, Frank. Take it or leave it."

"I'll take it," Frank answered, huskily. "But I ought to take you over my knee and spank the shit out of you."

"You wish," Betty said slyly.

Chapter Seventeen

After leaving Genonocque, Robert and Mary toured the cities of Three Rivers, Montreal and Quebec. They engaged travel agents to get them on every side trip available. Since money was no object, they stayed in the best hotels. Touring at leisure, it was four weeks before they crossed the New York border back into the United States and their former lifestyle of hiding and lying. They traveled south into the Adirondack mountains, taking all the back roads, constantly searching for an available business to buy. Along the way they read the business ads in all the local papers without success.

Fall was swiftly coming to the Adirondacks and the city-bred couple were overwhelmed by the brilliant colors that filled the landscape. Robert drove slowly, not wanting to miss a single sight. On a beautiful sunny day, neither spoke very much, both feeling as much in awe of Mother Nature as they did for the magnificent cathedrals in Montreal and Quebec. Mary finally broke the spell. "Bob, you're running out of gas!"

"Baloney," Robert answered. "I have enough to go another hundred miles."

"To me, it looks like you're riding on vapor now."

"Okay, okay," Robert conceded, "We'll have lunch and I'll gas up."

They found themselves riding alongside a beautiful body of water that bore the name of Stewart's Lake. Houses that bordered the lake varied from shacks to mansions, and all, even the poorest, seemed to be well kept. Everybody they saw waved at them, and they found themselves waving back. Mary spied a sign advertising a deli up ahead. Robert stopped the car in front of a store with a small sign that read Northside Deli. On entering, Robert and Mary were greeted by a very pretty blonde woman in her late twenties.

"Non-smoking, please," Mary said, evoking a laugh from everyone seated at the tables.

The blonde led them to the only empty table. The other five tables were filled with locals who might have stepped out of a Norman Rockwell painting. A discussion was underway that seemed to include everyone in the store.

"Welcome to our place," the blonde said with a warm smile as she handed them menus. "My name's Peg and the guy in the kitchen is my husband, Stanley. The little nature girl running around the store is our daughter, Joanie," she said proudly, pointing to a cute little girl pulling a large purple bear behind her. She was a miniature clone of her mother.

"Can I get you a couple of beers or some coffee?" Peg asked.

"Coffee would be fine for me," Robert said as he opened the small soiled, menu.

"Me too," Mary echoed.

"Today's specials are on that blackboard. Everything's made from scratch in this place, even the bread. I'll be back in a few minutes to take your order."

Peg went back to the kitchen and Mary leaned over the table and whispered, "Whatta dump. Think it's safe to eat here?"

"It's no worse than a lot of places I ate in when I was a cop. Sometimes a little place like this can fool you," Robert said hopefully as he scanned the meager menu.

Peg returned with two large mugs of coffee, and Robert ordered a Western omelet, home fries and toast.

"Me too," Mary echoed.

"What kind?" Peg asked, smiling sweetly.

"What kind of what?" Robert asked.

"Toast. We have white, rye, whole wheat or black bread."

"Rye for me," Robert answered.

"Make mine pumpernickel, un-toasted, please," Mary added.

"We don't have no pumper... or whatever you called it."

"You did say black bread, didn't you?" Mary asked curtly.

"Yeah, we have black bread but none of that pump bread."

"Okay, black bread, un-toasted would be fine," Mary said, smiling.

When Peg left, Mary leaned over the table and whispered, "Whatta hick."

Peg returned, carrying two huge platters filled with the omelets and potatoes.

"Wow," Mary exclaimed, "Do you expect me to eat all that?"

"This is egg country, Honey. When you order eggs here, you get four, unless you order jumbo. Then you get six," Peg said proudly."

"Didn't you people ever hear of cholesterol?" Mary asked, laughing.

"Sure, but that shit's for city-folk. Around here, we eat anything, smoke anything and drink anything. And everybody lives a long time. What's more, we don't worry 'bout nothing."

Peg smiled a beautiful smile as she turned and strode back to the kitchen, her high heel clicking on the worn wooden floor, her full buttocks doing a mesmerizing dance. Robert stared, then slowly wiped his mouth with his napkin. Then he drained his third cup of coffee.

"That was the best omelet I ever ate," Robert commented, "And you never have to ask for a coffee refill, it's always there."

"She fills your cup so often because it gives her more opportunities to shake her ass in your face," Mary said with a scowl.

"You're nuts. Her husband's right there in the kitchen, watching everything."

"So what? I read somewhere that in these small towns, everybody's related. That's why they're all crazy and have so many idiots."

"I think you're just jealous of her beautiful legs and ass."

"Fuck you, Bob," Mary said, haughtily, as she grabbed her purse and headed for the door.

Robert drove slowly along the lake road, admiring the breath-taking scenery of the lush green mountains forming the backdrop for the placid water. Speed boats roared by, dragging skiers behind. Serious-faced men sat on captain's chairs on their bass-boats, lazily casting their lines into the shadows. There was a buzz of activity all along the lake, but no one seemed to be working at it. As Robert approached an intersection at the south end of the lake, he saw a Mobil gas station called Jake's Place on his right and pulled in. The place looked deserted. Robert got out of the Explorer and waited patiently at the pumps for at least five minutes. No one came out to serve him. He walked into the office and found no one there. He heard a rapping noise coming from one of the two bays.

On entering the bay, Robert saw a Chevy pickup on the lift and a person dressed in overalls pounding away on a wheel with a large ball-peen hammer.

"Hello," Robert called, "Can I get some gas?"

"Help yourself," a deep voice answered, and Robert was surprised that it came from a woman.

Robert filled the tank with premium, then checked under the hood, discovering a need for a quart of oil. He left the hood open and walked back to the bay where the woman was still hacking away with the ball-peen hammer.

"I need a quart of oil," Robert called out.

"Help yourself, sonny," the woman answered.

"Oil's in the office. All grades."

Robert walked into the office and looked around for the grade of oil that he needed. He saw about twenty cases of oil stacked on the counter, a Pepsi machine, a coin telephone on the wall and a cash register with the drawer open and stuffed with green bills. He helped himself to a can of oil from an open carton, when he spied a "For Sale" sign on a small crowded bulletin board. A closer look showed that a gas station and its property were for sale.

Robert poured the oil, checked the other fluids, then slammed the hood shut. As he walked back to the office, the woman entered, wiping her greasy hands on a red rag. She checked the machine that indicated the gas sale then asked for twenty dollars for the gas and two for the oil. Robert handed the woman a twenty and a five. She rang up the sale and handed Robert his change, without closing the cash drawer.

"I saw a "For Sale" sign on that board," Robert said, pointing. "Does that mean this gas station?"

The woman, about sixty years old, white haired and heavily wrinkled with ugly features, stared at him for a moment then slowly drawled, "Yup. The station, the house, the land down to the lake. About five acres, the dock and the boat. The whole kit and caboodle."

Robert raised an eyebrow, thought a moment, then asked, "How much you asking?"

"As much as I can get," was the quick answer from the un-smiling woman. "How much you offerin'?"

"I don't know if I'm offering anything," Robert answered, coyly. "Can my wife and I see the house?"

"Sure," the woman drawled, "But you don't look like country folk to me."

Robert walked back to the Explorer and opened the door on Mary's side. He told Mary what he had found and waited for her to explode. She said nothing, just stared at his face.

"Would you like to look at the house?" Robert asked, pointing to a large three story house about a hundred feet behind the gas station.

"If that's what you want," Mary answered with a bored expression on her face.

"Jesus H. Christ, if you don't want to look at it, say so. We have to settle somewhere."

"Yeah, but a gas station? Somehow I can't see you pumping gas and fixing flats. What do you know about repairing cars, anyway?"

"Nothing. We'll hire a mechanic for the repairs. We can pump the gas. In fact, this woman made me pump my own gas. At least we'd be together, day and night. It's a great place to hide out. Betty would never find us here. Never."

"Okay, okay," Mary sighed, "Let's look at the house." She got out of the Explorer and the two of them walked in the station to meet the old woman.

The woman shook hands with Mary, and said, "Call me Henrietta."

She led them down a path made with colored patio stones that circled the gas station, and through a small orchard of apple trees. They walked up three stone steps onto a stone porch and stood before huge double entry doors, half glass, half polished mahogany.

"I was born in this house," the woman drawled as she fished in the pocket of her jeans for keys.

She unlocked the heavy door and pushed it open, revealing a large foyer with a marble floor and four large, polished columns. The two on the left side led into a dining room that contained a heavy looking table surrounded by eight chairs. The shine on the table made it resemble a mirror. The hutch displayed many fine pieces of china and cut glass. The other two columns led into a living room that had a huge fireplace as its focal point. Two high backed chairs with lace doilies on the arms, stood on both sides of the fireplace. On one wall there was a huge couch made with a dark brown velvet fabric, and two polished end tables with tall lamps. Large portraits adorned the walls.

Mary was impressed. Her eyes, opened wide, as they darted from article to article. "How old is this house?" she asked in almost a whisper.

"My granddaddy built it in 1890," Henrietta answered, in a voice that virtually boomed with vigor. "The furniture's original from that era. My Grandma, my Ma and I worked hard to keep it lookin' good."

By contrast, the large kitchen was a picture of contemporary grandeur. It was brightly lit by ten recessed fixtures, accenting white European cabinets and gleaming white appliances. A light colored dining set was in front of a huge picture window facing the lake. The downstairs bathroom was large and contained the latest fixtures done up in remarkably good taste.

"Wow," Mary whispered, as she punched Robert's arm. "Who would have believed it, looking at this big old barn from the outside."

Robert's answer was a muted grunt.

"We only used one bedroom upstairs since the kids left," Henrietta said as she led them up a carpeted, curving staircase with gleaming mahogany banisters. On the way upstairs, the walls were filled with family portraits.

"Of course the pictures don't go with the house," she added with a wisp of a smile. "Our whole family history's in those pictures."

The master bedroom featured a huge canopied bed and heavy pieces of furniture that had such a high shine that they dazzled Mary.

"It must take a helluva lot of elbow grease to keep them so shiny," Mary said.

Henrietta spoke in a subdued tone, "A little Guardsmen polish every Sunday morning keeps the furniture looking this way. It's really very easy. This bedroom set is a hundred and two years old. My grandfather bought it for my grandmother for a wedding present."

Mary exhaled weakly, then timidly asked, "Is this house for sale furnished?"

"Yup," Henrietta replied. "Everything goes 'cept the pictures and some small antiques I can't part with."

The woman led them through two more tastefully furnished bedrooms, and a very large bathroom on the second floor and three more bedrooms and a bathroom on the third floor. She opened the door to a large attic that was crammed full of trunks, boxes and furniture.

"Of course, I'll clean out the attic," Henrietta said, apologetically, "And the basement, too. Well, whaddaya think?"

"It's a lot more house than we figured on," Robert answered.

Mary pushed Robert out of the way, as if he had no say in the matter. "What're you asking for this house?" Mary asked, her firm expression belying the uncertainty in her voice and the butterflies she felt in her stomach.

"Make me an offer, lady," Henrietta said impatiently.

"I wouldn't even know where to begin," Mary said timidly.

"You either want it or you don't. Don't waste my time," the woman said gruffly.

"I'd be honored to own this house," Mary said with deep respect.

Henrietta eyed Mary, thoughtfully. "I have a feeling you'd fall for this old house. I intend to leave everything including the linens. My sister has room for me in Florida and she said I don't need a thing but my clothes. I can't stand the winters here anymore, especially since Jake died. And my kids are spread around the country. The place is yours if you can come up with fifty thousand cash money.

Mary inhaled deeply, but it was Robert's turn to push Mary aside.

"What does the fifty g's include?" he asked.

"The gas station with the tow truck, tools and everything, the boat, and the house as is. Oh, yes, five acres of land too," she added as an after-thought.

"How much do you owe on it?" Robert asked.

The woman was taken back, severely insulted. "Listen, sonny," she hissed.

"This place has been free and clear for over a hundred years."

"I didn't mean anything by it," Robert said apologetically, "I only wanted to know if we had to deal with a bank and you or just you."

"A cash deal is a fast deal. My lawyer in town can handle the paperwork in a matter of hours. It's up to you."

Mary turned and faced Robert, putting her hands on her hips in a belligerent pose. "Well?" she challenged.

"Well what?" he answered, his voice rising in anger. "Don't you think we ought to talk it over?"

"No," Mary said emphatically, "I want this house."

Robert stared at Mary's resolute expression. What he saw caused him to throw his hands in the air.

"Give her the fucking money, I'll empty the car," he shouted as he stormed out of the house. "I don't even know the name of this fucking town."

Almost a month had passed since Betty moved into Frank's apartment. They settled into a routine. One week Betty slept in the bed and Frank on the couch, and the next week they would switch. Betty seemed satisfied with this arrangement but Frank felt that it was unnatural, especially since it was unnecessary. Everytime he brought it up, Betty would cut him short and he dropped it.

Their days at work were becoming strained as well, their frustration mounting each day. Betty's brother seemed to have disappeared. The session with the police artist produced two versions of what the mysterious woman looked like. But the pictures produced no results in identifying her after days of leg work. Frank and Betty showed them to restaurant cashiers, super-market checkout clerks, cleaning stores, beauty parlors or anyone who would look at them. Checking the motor vehicle picture files produced negative results as well. The differences in the two versions of the drawings evoked hours of arguments between Frank and Betty.

"She was just a floozy he picked up," Betty argued, "A fat slob in a cheap dress."

"Bullshit," Frank replied, "I saw the way she looked at him. Like he was a god. Besides, she obeyed him without a word when he told her to leave. That means something to me."

"She was a pig," Betty added under her breath, as a mean expression took over her pretty face.

"I don't understand you," an exasperated Frank replied, "You sound like you hate her and you only saw her for a few minutes. Besides, I don't think she looked like a slob at all. A little plump, maybe, but she was curvy and had two wonderful --"

"That's enough," Betty said, "You're all alike. You see two big boobs and nothing else matters. You all think with the wrong head."

Frank laughed, "You sound like a jealous wife."

Betty jumped up and started fiddling with the coffee pot.

"Fuck you, Frank, You're an idiot. Want a cup of coffee?" Betty said, desperately trying to change the subject.

"Yeah, sure," Frank answered, looking at Betty through squinted eyes, trying to read her mind, her heart , maybe even her soul. "A few weeks ago you told me you had something important to tell me. Maybe this is the right time."

Betty stiffened and dropped the glass coffee pot she had just filled with water. Glass and water splattered all over the kitchen floor.

"Shit, shit, shit," Betty sobbed as she knelt down on her hands and knees and started to pick up the glass remnants with her bare hands. Tears streamed down her cheeks as she fought the urge to cry out loud. Twenty-six years of guilt welled up inside her and she felt like she would explode.

Frank joined her on the floor and helped to pick up the glass fragments. "What the hell are you crying about?" he said. "It's just a cheap glass pot."

"It's not the pot, you dumb fuck. It's the sad, sad story I have to tell you."

"Then don't tell me. I'm sure it's not that important."

Betty stood up and dumped the glass she was holding into the trash can. Then she took the glass from Frank's hands, and dumped that too. Avoiding Frank's eyes, Betty began to speak.

"I've never told my secret to anyone. But I have to tell you. I owe you that much."

"Why me?" Frank asked, fearfully.

Betty knelt down beside Frank and took his hands in hers.

"I think I love you, Frank," she stammered. "After you hear my story, I know you'll hate me. You'll spit on me."

A terrible sound escaped from Betty's chest, like a cross between a sob and a hiccup. Frank put his arms around her and drew her to him, burying her face in his chest. From this position, not having to look at Frank's face, Betty began her tale, her voice just above a whisper.

"It happened on my prom night. I was a cheerleader in high school and I dated the quarterback of the football team for about six months. He was very handsome and I thought I was very much in love with him. Our relationship progressed to the point where we had sex every weekend, and I expected an engagement ring on prom night. The prom was held at the Hotel St. George in Brooklyn Heights and it was a lovely affair. We travelled to and from the prom in a limosine, getting home about two-thirty in the morning. According to the custom of the school, everybody changed into jeans and went to Coney Island to watch the sunrise on the beach. Michael picked me up in his father's car and I was surprised to see two other couples in the car. Both men were team mates of Michael's and they were huge. I recognized their girlfriends as school whores.

When we got to Coney Island, we set up a large blanket under the boardwalk, out of sight from police patrols on the boardwalk. Soon everyone but me, was smoking pot and drinking whiskey. They teased me, then ridiculed me. They wouldn't accept my feeble excuse that I came from a police family. They said even cops smoked, drank and fucked. Michael was the most abusive, and the girls were a close second. He started to slap me around and I begged him to drive me home but he laughed at me. Before I knew it, I was held down in a spread eagle position and my clothes were ripped off. My screams were baffled when they held my mouth. Michael fucked me in front of everybody as they cheered him. When he was done, he invited his two buddies to have me too. All the while the girls took turns sitting on my face. When they were through, they left me naked on the beach. I contemplated going into the ocean and drowning myself. Instead I got dressed and called Peter. He came for me.

He was very silent as he drove home. To account for my bruised face, Peter made up a story for my parents that I was in a car accident. They never learned the truth. Within a week, Peter stalked and assaulted each one of the boys with a baseball bat. He crippled Michael so badly, he lost his football scholarship. None of the boys' families made a complaint against Peter.

When she was finished, an exhausted Betty collapsed against Frank, like a punctured, life-sized doll. The tension left her but now she could feel it in Frank's arms. Betty looked into his face and saw that his usual ruddy complexion had turned ashen. There were tears in his eyes. Then he hugged her so tightly, she could barely breathe.

"Please stop," Betty gasped, "You're hurting me."

Frank released Betty with a sudden thrust. "I'm sorry," he said, I didn't mean to."

"I knew I would disgust you," she said fearfully, as she turned her back to him.

Frank leaned towards Betty, and encircled her with his arms.

"Oh no, honey. I'm just heartbroken that you carried this terrible hurt for so many years. But it explains why you never married and why you have an aversion to sex. You certainly don't disgust me. I want to help you desperately."

"But Frank, raped--gangbanged. Is there anything more disgusting? I felt so dirty that hours of bathing couldn't make me feel clean."

"You were just a kid, a terrible incident in your life. You were not at fault. Why'd you carry all that guilt for so long?"

"It changed all my feelings. When a man touched me, I--. Well, you know. You saw what happened. I couldn't help it.

"Listen, honey, and listen good," Frank hissed, as he hugged her even tighter than before. "I love you and I want to help you. I'm no shrink, but if you trust me, we can work this out. What I am sure about is that I don't want to lose you."

Gently, Frank turned Betty around and tilted her face up to his. He caressed her lips with his, then silenced her sobs with a deep soul-searching kiss.

Chapter Eighteen

Robert and Mary jumped into their new country lifestyle with both feet. Mary turned the office into a mini-convenience store. She cleaned out the place, moving the cases of oil into the shop. Robert built shelves in the shop to hold the hundreds of catalogues, auto manuals and parts books that previously littered the office. Mary painted the office white and lined the walls with new shelves she purchased from K Mart. From Sears, she bought a huge side by side refrigerator,and filled the freezer with cold cuts, cheese and ice cream. She stocked the refrigerator with soda and beer. From a restaurant supply house she bought a grill to make hot dogs and hamburgers. She applied for and received all necessary licenses and permits and to make it all work, composed her own ad for the local newspaper and the Lake Association's monthly bulletin.

Mary pumped the gas, and ran the office and promoted the sale of all the merchandise she sold when she made change or took credit cards. She was thrilled when the grocery sales equaled the gas sales. Fishermen pulled into their dock to fill gas cans. While they waited, they purchased cigarettes, a hot dog and a coke and sometimes a newspaper or a girlie magazine. Mary used every available inch of space to cram full of things to sell. She chatted easily with the locals and soon found herself listening to their troubles and dispensing advice. As the weather turned colder, she started to sell hot coffee and hot soup and took in a line of danish and doughnuts.

Robert ran the shop and was having equal success. He advertised in the local paper for a mechanic and was flooded with applicants. It felt strange to him to interview people, all desperate for a job, and he felt badly that he couldn't help more than one.

He hired Raymond Curtis, a young man in his late twenties, married and the father of two small children. Raymond came to work equipped with a full set of tools, a ready smile and an embarrassing stutter. So it became Robert's job to talk to the customers after Raymond estimated the cost of the repair and wrote the estimate.

Raymond proved to be an excellent mechanic and got his work completed on schedule, which pleased the customers as much as Robert's fair prices. Soon word got around that it was a good shop to get a car fixed, and the shop prospered. As an added bonus, it turned out that Raymond was involved in stock car racing and before long the shop was crowded with race cars to be fixed or modified. The locals had to make appointments in advance to get service. "Jake's Place" was never busier.

Robert was happy. He felt secure in his new life and the fear of being a fugitive was diminishing. He chatted easily with the customers and took payments in installments when the they couldn't pay all at once. The locals grew to like him and invited him on hunting trips. It wasn't long before Robert and Mary were invited to the Lake Association meetings, and they both became active members.

Robert drove the tow truck on emergency calls, and soon became proficient in jumping dead batteries, changing flats, and diagnosing minor troubles. If he encountered anything serious, he would tow the vehicle back to the shop. He frequently assisted Raymond, and slowly gained the skills to do minor repairs on his own.

Time flew for Robert and Mary Russo. Winter came early in the mountains and a seven inch snow fall covered the Village of Stewart in mid-October. Driving was dangerous on the steep, curvy roads, especially at night when they became slick with ice. It wasn't unusual for cars to skid off the road into the drainage ditches, and several times a week, Robert would be awakened by emergency calls. He would have to leave his warm bed to respond with his tow truck to aid his unfortunate customers. Since most of the vehicles in the area were equipped with CB radios, Robert installed transceivers at his bedside, in the office and in his tow truck to better serve his clientele.

Robert was surprised that so many of the emergency calls at night were made by women traveling alone. Many were so grateful for his quick response in the wee hours of the morning that they offered payment with sex. This embarrassed Robert, who was by nature a monogamous person. He felt no guilt living with Mary as husband and wife, for in his own mind he felt divorced from his legal wife, Alice.

So, Robert politely refused the friendly offers of sexual favors. It took him quite a while to realize that the locals considered sex between friends perfectly natural, and that many of them changed spouses more often than they changed cars. A quick roll in the hay between two friends was not usually a subject for gossip.

A brilliant sun was just setting when Robert received a panic call from Susan Robeson, who lived at the north end of the lake. It was the Friday following Thanksgiving, and her children were off from school. Susan explained that she promised to take her two children to an early movie in Lake George, but skidded off her driveway and needed a tow truck. This was the third time since Robert bought Jake's Place that Susan called for help.

The last time she called, Susan, a widow of about thirty-five years of age, blonde, curvaceous, and horny, came to the door wearing an old bathrobe and nothing else. The bathrobe hung open revealing nearly all. She insisted that Robert come inside to have a hot cup of tea to warm himself.

The emergency turned out to be that it was over a month since she had sex, and her need had reached emergency proportions. Since Jake's Place was listed under her emergency numbers, she decided it was Robert's turn for service.

When he declined, Susan had directed a stream of profanities at him as he ran to the safety of his tow truck.

This time, Robert was reluctant to believe her sad tale, but the screaming children in the background convinced him that there was some validity to her story. Fifteen minutes later, Robert pulled up to the Robeson Farm and saw Susan's pickup sitting dangerously in a ditch at a sixty degree angle. Robert feared the pickup might capsize when he tried to pull it out. Susan was pacing back and forth.

"This is a tricky one," Robert called out.

"Can you hurry it up, Mr. Russo. We gonna be late for the picture show. The damn kids have been irritatin' me all day. I just hate when they're home from school. And don't call me Mrs. Robeson. Call me Susan."

"Okay, okay, Susan, I'll do my best," Robert answered, as he tried to figure out the best angle to place the tow truck.

As Robert maneuvered the truck, Mark Robeson, a tow-headed boy of about eleven was playing with his big black Labrador Retriever directly in Robert's path. When his mother yelled at him to get out of the way, Mark crossed the road and wandered out onto the newly frozen lake. He sprinted about ten paces then set his feet so that he would slide. Each time he did this, he ran a little further and slid a little further. The dog was barking up a storm. The barking attracted Robert's attention and he turned in time to see Mark's legs go out from under him, propelling his chubby body high into the air, then come crashing to the ice and through it. The dog ran toward Mark, but the ice broke beneath the dog and it, too, was in the icy water.

Susan screamed, "Oh, my God," and started to run toward the lake.

Robert jumped from his truck and caught Susan by the arm, pulling her up short. "Go inside and dial 911," he ordered, "Ill get the kid."

Robert jumped into the truck and backed it to the edge of the lake. He got out and released the brake on his tow line, hooking the line to the back of his belt. Very carefully, he made his way out on the thin ice, pulling the tow line behind him. The reel ran out of line at fifty yards, five yards short of the hole in the ice.

Mark was splashing the water with his arms, as he desperately tried to stay afloat. His water-logged winter clothes tried to pull him under. The hysterical boy was tiring rapidly, and his threshing arms slowed. Then, suddenly, he was under the ice. Robert disconnected the tow line from his belt, then lay prone on the ice to distribute his weight as much as possible. Slowly, he inched toward the hole in the ice.

When he saw the boy's head disappear, Robert increased the speed of his creeping, trying to make up his mind what to do next. The ice made up his mind for him, by cracking, propelling him into the icy water.

The sudden shock of the bitterly cold water against his body sent Robert into a frenzy of motion. He swam the three yards to the barking dog in three strokes, where he saw the blurred form of Mark sinking into the darkness. Never a good swimmer, Robert forced himself to dive down after the boy.

Swimming downward with all his strength, Robert strained to keep his eyes open as the icy water shot them with arrows of pain. The tips of his freezing fingers touched the boy's jacket, and Robert managed to get a grip under the boy's armpit. Robert felt like his lungs would burst as he pumped his legs and thrashed with his right arm, trying to rise to the surface, pulling the heavy weight of the boy behind him. Looking up, Robert saw the light in the hole of the ice, but he had no idea how close he was to the surface. He battled to keep his mouth shut and the water out of his nose. He felt that he was losing ground and that he would have to drop his heavy load. His mind screamed at him: "You fucked up your own life, you have to save this boy."

With the last of his strength, Robert pulled frantically at the water when his fist broke into the clear. Then his head broke the surface and he drew the welcomed icy air into his lungs. Pumping his legs, he reached down with his free arm and pulled the boy to the surface. With his remaining strength, Robert heaved the boy onto the ice, pushing him as far away from the hole as he could.

Taking a breather for a few seconds, Robert noticed the black dog was now beneath the surface of the ice, but still moving its legs. Robert pulled as much air into his lungs as he could, then ducked beneath the ice and grabbed the dog's collar and pulled him toward the hole in the ice. "This goddam dog must have swallowed half the lake, he weighs a ton," Robert thought.

Robert's head broke the surface again and he gulped at the air, pulling the dog with him. He grabbed the dog around its belly and heaved it onto the ice. He could hear sirens in the distance. His strength now almost completely depleted, Robert tried desperately to climb onto the ice, but every attempt resulted in more and more ice breaking off. All he could do now was to lay his chest on the ice and hold on. The sharp pains in his legs, which were submerged in the water, started to fade and Robert realized they were becoming numb. Now the cold feeling on his cheeks was warming and he fought to stay conscious. He concentrated on the distant sirens, and smiled when he realized they were getting louder.

The next sensation Robert felt was his cheek sliding over the bumpy ice, and he imagined that his jacket was pulled over his head. Suddenly, he heard a loud cheer from a chorus of voices, as strong arms lifted him off the ice and onto a hard object he figured was a stretcher. A feeling of relief passed through him as he slipped into unconsciousness.

Mary was horrified when she learned over the CB radio in her office that Robert was one of the subjects of the immense rescue operation going on at the lake. She picked up her microphone and called for information. A sheriff deputy came on the air and instructed her to go directly to the emergency room of the Richard Bain Pavilion at the Glens Falls Memorial Hospital.

Mary called to Raymond Curtis, working in the bay, to take charge of the office and informed him of Robert's accident. She left immediately in her Explorer, asking for directions on her CB. A deputy came on the air and instructed her to go back to the gas station, and that he would pick her up and bring her to the hospital in his cruiser.

A half hour later, Mary pushed her way through the noisy crowd as she fought to get to Robert's side. The crowd was mostly the residents of Stewart Lake, who had followed the ambulance to the hospital like an Arab caravan. Mary saw camera flashes everywhere, as she saw people pointing their cameras toward the emergency room. She was almost in a panic as she finally broke through the crowd and entered the emergency room, closing the door behind her.

"Please, no pictures," Mary pleaded to the locals in the room, "Robert hates pictures."

How could she explain to these kindly people that any leak to the outside media would be a death sentence for Robert? Mary felt relieved when she saw a team of green-clad technicians working over Robert, completely shielding his face from view. Nobody could recognize Robert from a picture taken of this scene. She hoped nobody had taken any pictures of the rescue at the lake.

Mary took over as security officer. She thanked everyone for their help and concern as she eased them from the room.

Alone at last, it seemed like hours that Mary watched the green-clad people working over Robert. When they finally straightened up and removed their masks and gloves, Mary held her breath. The doctor in charge led her to a chair and sat her down. He pulled up another chair and sat next to her.

"My name is Dr. Scarpati," he said, as he shook Mary's hand, "I'm a neurosurgeon. Your husband is definitely out of danger from the exposure. He'ill recover nicely. However, he seems to be paralyzed from the waist down. I'm not sure why. It may be temporary as a result of shock, or it may be from an injury we can't detect. All the x-rays were negative, the spinal chord is intact. What he needs most is complete rest. What he did out there was a most remarkable feat, almost superhuman. Considering the temperature of the water and the weight of his water-logged clothes, I consider it a miracle that he saved himself, and the fact that he saved that heavy boy. Then to go back in to save a dog, well, I consider your husband truly the rarest of human beings, a bonafide hero. You should be very proud."

Tears streamed down Mary's face as she grabbed the doctor's hands. "Doctor, does that doctor-patient secrecy stuff extend to his wife?"

Doctor Scarpati, looking surprised, stammered, "I'm not sure, but I suppose it could. If you're acting as his agent. What's the matter?"

"Doctor, Robert's a wanted man. Any publicity could ruin him. He knew that when he went to save that boy, and he went anyway. He can't have pictures taken or any interviews. Will you help us? Please?"

"What's he wanted for?" Dr. Scarpati said.

"Murder," Mary whispered. "But it was an accident."

The doctor inhaled deeply.

"In my eyes, he's even a greater hero. He had much more to lose than a normal man in those circumstances. I'll help all I can. I'll really put a lid on him."

Detectives Frank Mullin and Betty Santini, riding in their un-marked police car, were busy canvassing yet another neighborhood in Buffalo, showing their pictures and police drawings to whomever would look at them. Suddenly, the radio dispatcher broke the silence with an excited call.

"In the fourth precinct, a ten-thirty in a liquor store, Piedmont and Tenth Street. One officer down."

Frank immediately reached for the mike and announced, "Car nine seven one on the way."

He hung up the mike and placed the portable red strobe on the dashboard, turning on the light and the siren.

"We're only four blocks away," he said to Betty as he gripped the steering wheel tightly and floored the accelerator. "I want you to stay in the car when we get there, do you hear? You're not on official duty anymore, and not covered by insurance. Get me?"

"Fuck you, Frank. If you go, I go."

"Please, you're not wearing a vest."

"Tough shit, I never seemed to have a vest when the situation came up. I survived."

"Betty, you're not just a partner now. I love you."

"That's very sweet of you, Detective. Now drive."

Frank took the last corner on two wheels and pulled up behind the radio motor patrol car with flashing red lights. The police car was parked about fifty feet from the liquor store and one officer was lying face down in a pool of blood on the street, about twenty feet from the entrance to the store. Shattered glass from the liquor store was all over the street. The other police officer was lying on the street behind the open door of his radio car, firing his weapon at the liquor store. Two men were crouched behind the counter in the store firing long bursts from AK-47 assault rifles.

"Get on the floor and stay there," Frank ordered as he opened his door and crawled to the street on all fours.

Betty crouched down in the car watching the action, her handgun, cocked and ready. She saw Frank, on his hands and knees, join the other officer and commence firing. Betty saw both robbers reload their assault rifles. Then with guns blazing, both made a dash for the front door, emerging on the street, but were met with a hale of fire from the two officers.

Frank hit one of the gunmen in the chest and he went down. The other gunman fired a long burst at Frank, who dove for the safety of a parked car. The last burst caught Frank and the officer next to him and both writhed in pain on the street.

Seeing what happened, Betty radioed for more ambulances, then left her car, and crawled behind a parked car, hoping that the last gunman didn't see her. Feeling sure he hit the two officers and was safe now, the gunman rose to his feet and started to run, right in Betty's direction.

Betty fired the entire magazine, fifteen shots, hitting the gunman in the face and chest, killing him instantly. Slowly, Betty got to her feet. She examined the man whom she had shot and nearly vomited. He had no face left. She ran to the other gunman who was writhing on the ground and crying. Betty kicked away his AK-47 then ran to Frank's side.

Frank had two slugs in his left arm and was bleeding profusely. The other officer took a slug in his right thigh and already used his belt for a tourniquet. Betty removed Frank's belt, then his jacket, and fixed a tourniquet on his injured arm.

Within minutes, siren-screaming cars converged on the scene from all directions. A uniformed captain took charge, issued orders, and everything that needed to be done was being done. Betty was in a daze as she watched the wounded and the dead being loaded in the ambulances. A detective tried to question her, but she refused to answer any questions at the scene, insisting that she had to accompany Frank to the hospital. She told them she would co-operate there.

Hours later, Betty sat at Frank's bedside, holding his hands as she watched him sleep off the anaesthetic from his surgery. She had completed her report, answered all the supervisor's questions and even participated in the tiresome session with the news media. She was exhausted now, but tried to stay awake watching the TV tapes of the shooting scene on the news.

Later, she listened to the anchorman describe a heroic rescue of a boy and his dog from beneath the ice in an up-state lake. He explained they had no tape of the hero because he was too badly injured to be interviewed, but they did show a tape of his wife pushing people out of the hero's room. Betty watched through half closed eyes, but then jumped to her feet as her tired brain recognized the woman's features. "That's her," Betty yelled at Frank, but got no response. "I told you I'd never forget that whore's face."

Betty picked up the phone and had the switchboard operator connect her with the TV station. After being switched from person to person, an official told her that the story came over the wire, and that all the details were sketchy. Further details on the story were unavailable, as all the townspeople were reluctant to talk. All further attempts to get information were dropped because the shooting at the liquor store pre-empted the story of the ice rescue.

Betty went back to Frank's side and held his hands again. Her fatigue, momentarily put on hold by the picture on the TV screen, was swiftly returning. She put her head on Frank's pillow and closed her eyes. Was it really her brother's woman she saw on the TV screen, or had she imagined it? Before dozing off, she made a mental note to go to the TV station tomorrow and review the tape.

Chapter Nineteen

When the sun lit up the brightly painted room in Mercy Hospital, Frank opened his eyes and panic gripped him for the moment. He always felt panic when he was temporarily disoriented. Seeing the intravenous stand holding an array of plastic bottles, all connected to a single plastic tube ending in his right hand, brought Frank back to reality. The last thing he remembered was being wheeled into surgery with Betty clinging to the side of the gurney.

His right hand felt something silky, and he looked down and saw his hand was entangled in a clump of dark auburn hair. Under the hair was Betty, sound asleep, with her face buried in his lap. A warm flush permeated his body as the feeling of love filled his heart and mind, pushing away the dull ache in his left arm.

"I love you, my darling. I love you so much," Frank whispered, as his fingers made waves in her hair.

Betty stirred then sat up with a start. "Oh, I'm sorry. I must have dozed off. I was awfully tired. How do you feel, honey?"

"Not as good as I felt a minute ago when you had your face on my ding dong."

"You are a son of a bitch. I was worried sick about you all night, and you wake up with something dirty on your mind. Men!" Betty scolded, a faint smile on her face.

"Give me a kiss to drive the pain away, and I don't mean a peck on the cheek," Frank pleaded theatrically.

"There's the buzzer. Call your nurse, I'm no angel of mercy."

"You're some pal," Frank whined.

"Huh, I saved your ass last night."

"That's right, you did. You're making a habit of it lately. This is the second shooting you came out a hero. You're ruining my reputation."

"Well, the mayor and police commissioner were here last night. Worried about you. And they gave me a pat on the back, too."

"Was that bastard C.O. of mine here?"

"You mean Captain Dellasandro, who said you were over the hill?" Betty asked teasingly.

"Yeah, that's the asshole."

"No," Betty answered, "But the emergency room was full of brass. I didn't know this little hick police force had so much brass. By the way, I'm grateful that you were so lucky last night."

"How'd the other guys make out?"

"Not so good. The guy next to you caught a burst in his leg. A lot of bone shattered. He's facing a lot of surgery before he walks again. The poor guy lying in the street when we got there was D.O.A.. They put him in the ambulance in pieces."

Frank moaned. "And the bad guys?"

"The one you shot is making it, the one I shot didn't," Betty answered as tears filled her eyes. "This has happened to me so many times in the last twenty two years, but it still breaks me up."

"That means you're still a human being. Thank God for that," Frank said, sighing.

"Something else happened last night, Frank. I think we finally got a break."

"I'm afraid to ask. You big city cops scare me. What break?"

"While I was sitting here watching our exploits on the TV, they put on a story about a rescue at some up-state lake. They didn't show a picture of the hero, but they did show a picture of his wife pushing people out of the room. I think it's the broad we're looking for. I called the station but they didn't have any details. I was too tired to pursue it, and I wanted to discuss it with you."

"You and I have two different pictures of what that woman looked like. Before we do or say anything, let's get that tape and study it. Call the station house for me, honey."

It was ten o'clock when a uniformed police officer entered the hospital room, carrying a VCR and a tape. He stood on a chair to connect the VCR to the TV then went on his way.

Betty, now washed, combed and refreshed, put the tape in the machine. It took only thirty seconds to review the entire story, but Betty replayed the tape about twenty times.

"Well, what do you think?" Betty asked anxiously.

"No question about it. That's just how I pictured her in my mind."

"You're so full of it. Your version of the police drawing doesn't look anything like her."

"Neither does yours," Frank said, pouting.

"The only information the TV station had was that the tape was filmed in the Glens Falls Memorial Hospital. Can I use your car to drive up there? It's about a five hour drive. I'd like to mosey around and see what I can find."

Frank looked hurt. "You mean you want to go up there without me? After all the work we both put into this case? I can't believe you."

"Don't give me guilt. It may be nothing."

"I'll be out of here in a day, two at the most. Wait for me."

"Five days, Frank, I asked. Do you expect me to wait five days?"

"Yes, I really do. I think you owe me that."

Betty blushed, half in anger, half in guilt. It was so hard to consider someone else's feelings after living alone for so many years and thinking only of one's self.

She loved that big mug. Even had sexual fantasies about him lately. But how could she wait five days to check out a hot lead on a case that was stymied for so long?

"Frank, er...," Betty stammered.

"Damn it," Frank said, "This guy's going to be my brother-in-law. Don't you think I belong there?"

Frank's question shocked Betty. She couldn't read him. Was he being funny or serious?

"Well?" Frank asked seriously.

Betty walked over to the bed and threw her arms around Frank's neck and watched him scowl in pain. "I'm sorry if I hurt you, my darling. But I just realized something. A family that shoots together must stick together. Of course I'll wait for you."

"I'm hurting bad, and you make jokes?"

"Stop bellyaching, you dumb Mick. I don't think I could be separated from you, anyway.

It was nearly midnight when Mary, completely exhausted, pulled up on the gas station and parked in her usual spot. She nearly overlooked a strange car parked near the path to her house, and when she spotted somebody sitting behind the wheel, she became terrified. She turned on her CB and reached for the mike. She wished she had a gun instead of the mike.

The door of the car opened and the courtesy light illuminated a stocky figure, wearing a hunting jacket, getting out. Mary was scared, but the urge to urinate took precedence over her feeling of fear.

"Mrs. Russo," the man called out. "It's me, Jim. Jim Frazier. You know, the president of the Lake Stewart Improvement Association. I hope I didn't scare you sitting here like this. But I've been waiting for hours. I'm representing the LSIA and Mrs. Frazier and myself."

"Jesus, you scared the piss out of me. Come inside, it's freezing out here."

Jim Frazier followed Mary into the house, but she left him standing in the foyer.

"You'll have to excuse me for a minute, Jim, but I have to go to the john. It's your fault anyway."

Moments later, Mary rejoined Jim Frazier and took his coat.

"Come in the kitchen. I'll put up a pot of coffee."

"Can you make it decaf, Mrs. Russo? At my age, I'd be up all night on regular coffee."

"No problem, but call me Mary. What's this all about?"

"Well, we, I mean the LSIA, had an emergency meeting tonight. We came up with the following motions, which I hope you let us execute, you know, carry out."

This guy drives me nuts, Mary thought. He ends every sentence with a question mark.

"What motions?" Mary asked.

"Well, with Robert laid up, we'll have a man here every day to help you run the station. And, we'll have a man standing by at night to take the tow truck out on any emergency call that might arise."

"Jesus," Mary exclaimed. "I just can't believe it."

"And that's not all," Jim said, as he puffed out his chest. "We'll have a woman at the station to run your little luncheonette whenever you go to the hospital to visit Robert. My wife, Ethel, will take the first shift."

"I'm not only amazed, I'm overwhelmed," Mary said, putting her two palms to her cheeks.

"And that's not all," Jim said, beaming. "We plan to have a parade in Robert's honor, and invite the media to let the world know that Lake Stewart has a real live hero."

"Oh, my God. No, no, you can't do that," Mary shouted as panic spread over her face. "It has to be our secret. Nobody outside this village can know about it. Please, it's absolutely essential, unless we lie and say somebody else was the hero."

"But it's Robert we want to honor, not somebody else. What's the matter with you?"

Mary began to sob, much to the bewilderment of Jim Frazier. She clutched his hands and raised them to her lips. "Promise me you and your friends will keep our secret. Promise me," she pleaded.

"I don't know what I said or did to upset you so. We're only trying to help," Jim said in frustration.

"Listen," Mary whispered, as if there were enemies all around. "Recently, Robert got into trouble, and we don't want anyone to know where he is. We love this little village, and we don't want to run again. Do you understand, Jim?"

"You mean that Robert's on the run?" Jim asked incredulously.

Mary shook her head as tears streamed down her cheeks.

Jim frowned, then in a determined Yankee manner spoke:

"Try not to worry. I'll see to it that every pair of lips in this village is sealed. I mean every man, woman and child."

"Thank you. That would be the greatest honor you could bestow on Robert.

Jim silently finished his coffee, stood and hugged Mary, kissing her on both cheeks.

"Trust us, and God bless you both," Jim said as he donned his jacket and left.

Mary sat down on a kitchen chair and wept bitterly. She realized that Robert's paralysis was the least of his troubles. Had the beans been spilled already?

Chapter Twenty

"The Glens Falls exit is coming up in two miles," Frank instructed as he folded his map one-handed and put it in the glove box. "You made terrific time. Four hours and forty five minutes. Not bad for a woman. I couldn't have done better myself."

"I can read the fucking signs, Frank, even if I am a woman. You chauvinist pigs piss me off, thinking that a man just naturally does everything better than a woman."

"I can't understand you. If I pass on some information you jump all over me. With my bad arm, I can't help with the driving, so I try to help with the navigation. Are you doing me a favor by taking me along?"

Betty's face reddened. She inhaled deeply then let the air out slowly. "I'm sorry Frank. I feel so apprehensive and I'm taking it out on you. I have this funny feeling that we're very close to finding Peter. I feel it in my bones. If we find him, how're we going to take him? We don't have a warrant and he won't come without a fight. I know that little shit better than anyone. He's not a brain surgeon, but he does the right things instinctively and he's strong as a bull."

"You're jumping the gun. We don't know for sure he's the guy in that lake rescue. The woman in the video looked familiar, and we're assuming your brother was the hero they were talking about. Just like you assumed it was your brother who came to that policewoman's aid a few months ago."

"But I was right that time, Frank. It was that story that brought me to Buffalo in the first place. And we met him face to face.

We can't forget how he embarrassed us. This time we have to act decisively and fast."

"We have to find him first. If we do, we can always get a local warrant to hold him. Either on the homicide charge in New York City or the felonious assault charge in Buffalo. These local cops would be glad to help us. It would give them something to talk about for years.

"I don't want him hurt, Frank," Betty pleaded, "He's my twin. There's nothing closer than that."

Betty exited the Northway and headed toward Glens Falls, following the signs with the big "H" on them. Ten minutes later she pulled into the parking lot of a huge hospital.

"Some big hospital for such a small city," Frank commented.

"Over five hundred beds. I looked it up before we came," Betty added.

Minutes later, Frank and Betty sat in the administrator's office and explained their mission.

"Dr. Scarpati handled that case. I believe he's in his office on the third floor," the administrator said in a curt manner. "I'll call ahead and let him know you're coming up. That's Room 330B. I hope you find what you're looking for," he said as he stood and extended his hand.

Dr. Scarpati, a dark and handsome man in his late thirties welcomed them with a broad smile and a vigorous handshake. "Sit down, please," he said, as he wheeled two large chairs in front of his desk. Can I get both of you some coffee?"

"That would be fine," Frank answered, "We had a long drive coming here, and we're a little tired."

Dr. Scarpati picked up the phone and placed the order. Then leaning back in his chair, he took a pack of cigars from his inside jacket pocket. He offered one to Frank, who accepted. The two men lit up, filling the small office with a thick, aromatic haze.

"Oh, I'm sorry, Detective," Scarpati said, looking at Betty. "I forgot to ask if the smoke will bother you. Will it?"

"No," Betty answered, smiling, "As a matter of fact, both my father and grandfather smoked cigars. I'm rather fond of the smell."

"Now down to business," Scarpati said, as he once again leaned back in his chair. "The Administrator told me that you're two police officers on the trail of some criminal. How can I help you?"

"We understand that you treated a man who went into a frozen lake to rescue a boy and his dog. We need whatever information you can give us on this man," Frank said, speaking in his most official manner.

"There's very little I can tell you that wouldn't violate the patient-doctor privileged communication."

"Come on, Doc. If this guy is who we think he is, he's wanted for homicide. Can't you at least give us his pedigree?"

"The man put down his name as John Smith, no address. He checked out yesterday and paid his bill with cash. That's all I can tell you."

"Doctor, this man may be my twin brother. Can't you tell me how he is? As family, I must have some rights?"

"Sorry. He checked out of here against my wishes. I felt a deep respect for that man. He's truly a hero. I know of no one who would go under the ice, fully clothed in heavy winter garb, and dive to the bottom of a lake to pull up a hefty boy, and then the boy's dog. He did this, knowing it would put him in grave danger, health wise and otherwise. So, you see, I wouldn't help you, even if I could."

The tension in the room was intense. A nurse entered the office carrying a tray with three mugs of coffee and a plate of danish. They ate and drank in silence. The phone rang and Dr. Scarpati answered it. He listened for a while and then mumbled something. He stood up, headed for the door.

"I'm wanted immediately in the emergency room. Stay as long as you like, but I'm saying my goodbyes now."

Frank and Betty sat dejectedly in their car in the parking lot.

"Well, that bastard was no help," Frank muttered. "Now the real leg work will begin. There must be fifty lakes within a fifty mile radius of this hospital."

Betty cursed softly under her breath, a worried look on her face. Suddenly her face changed. "I don't know why I didn't think of it before," she said, "But that kid must have been brought to this hospital. We should be able to get his name and address."

"See. That's why I love you so much. You're not only beautiful, you're smart, too," Frank said, smiling in admiration.

The two officers were out of the car in a flash and ran all the way to the accounting office of the hospital. A show of credentials and a few crisp orders brought instant response from the clerk. Within minutes, she handed Frank a slip of paper on which was written, "Mark Robeson, 11, mother Susan, 316B East Lake Road, Lake Stewart,N.Y. Phone 518 969-3742."

"Bingo," Frank shouted, "We're in business now."

Forty-five minutes later, Betty and Frank were driving south on the west shore of Lake Stewart. Betty drove slowly trying to avoid patches of ice that littered the road, but mainly to admire better the spectacular scenery all around them. "Just look at that panorama. Have you ever seen anything so beautiful?"

Frank grumbled. "If you've seen one mountain, you've seen them all. I'm starved."

"Sometimes you act like a dumb Mick. That's one of God's masterpieces out there, and all you can say is `I'm hungry'"

"Hey, that sign says the Northside Deli is one mile ahead. Let's stop there for lunch. We can ask where this Mrs. Robeson lives.

In a town this small, everybody must know everybody," Frank said enthusiastically.

Frank and Betty entered the small store, both squinting, trying to adjust to the dim light inside. All the tables were empty.

"Sit anywhere you like," a voice called from the kitchen, "At this time in the afternoon, we're pretty slow."

They chose a table closest to a pot-bellied stove. "What a joint," Betty whispered, "I hope we don't get poisoned."

"Sometimes, a place like this can fool you. You might be pleasantly surprised," Frank answered in a whisper.

A pretty blonde woman emerged from the kitchen carrying two menus. "Welcome," she said, showing a dazzling smile, "My name is Peg. The guy who does the cookin' is my husband Stanley, and that little naked girl in the corner over there is our daughter Joanie. She's the floor show in this cabaret. Two coffees?"

"Yeah, please," Frank answered, "You can hold the menus. Just bring us two burgers with everything and two large fries."

"I just love a man who knows what he wants," Peg said with a flirting look.

She went back to the kitchen, wiggling her buns all the way.

"Jesus H. Christ," Frank uttered, "Is that broad put together or what?"

Betty answered with a swift kick to Frank's shins.

"Hey, what was that for?" Frank complained.

"You're not supposed to admire anyone's ass but mine.

"You're acting like a wife, but you're not," Frank said, pouting.

"We're living together, that gives me the right," Betty said coyly.

"We're residing at the same abode. We're certainly not lovers."

"You haven't even tried lately," Betty whispered, her face reddening slightly.

"Are you kidding? My wounds haven't healed from the last time I tried," Frank said, looking into Betty's eyes for a possible hidden message.

Betty stammered, trying to put together an intelligent answer, but then Peg's arrival with two steaming mugs of coffee was like the arrival of the cavalry.

"Your food will ready in a few minutes," Peg said, smiling at Frank in a provocative manner. She shimmied back to the kitchen.

"Jesus, her jeans must be painted on," Frank whispered.

"I heard you, you pig, slobbering over this slut."

"Slut? How can you call her a slut? You don't even know her."

"Only a slut would wear five inch heels when she's working."

"That must be your professional NYPD opinion," Frank said, picking up his coffee mug as a signal that the discussion was over.

Later as Frank stood at the register paying his check, he asked Peg for directions to the Robeson residence.

"Why?" Peg asked suspiciously.

"We're journalists and we'd like to interview the family for a magazine article. The rescue story sure stirred up a lot of interest in that boy. It might be worth a lot of money for that family if we get that story," Frank said, winking at Peg.

"No kiddin'," Peg answered, wide-eyed. "She's a widow tryin' to raise a family. She sure could use it. Continue south on this road about a mile. At the end of the lake is an intersection. A Mobil station is on the right. Turn left and go about a mile and a half. You'll see the name painted on the mailbox."

Peg smiled broadly when she saw Frank's huge tip. "Come again, sometime, she called after them, as they left the store.

"It's fucking freezing in this car," Betty said, shivering as she started the car.

"Yeah, the temperature drops quick here in the mountains," Frank commented as he adjusted the sling on his arm to cover his cold fingers.

"I hope that gas station the waitress mentioned is still open," Betty said, "I'd hate to run out of gas on one of these roads. It looks like the North Pole up here in the dark."

A few minutes later, Frank spied the lighted Mobil sign on a high pole. A red neon sign spelled out Jake's Place in the office window.

"Stop at the high test pump. Betty. In this cold, I feel safer with the higher octane."

Betty stopped at the pump, but didn't shut the engine. "This damn car is taking a long time to heat up. You ought to get it checked," Betty said, rubbing her hands together.

"Yeah, yeah," Frank muttered, "When we get back to Buffalo.

A short person came out of the office, dressed in a dark parka that was trimmed with dark fur. The hood was up framing the person's face, making it difficult to discern the person's gender. Betty rolled the window down about two inches and yelled, "Fill it up, please." She rolled up the window.

"Regular or Super?" the attendant asked in a loud, feminine voice.

Betty rolled down the window and answered, "Super," as she stared at the woman's face.

Betty rolled up the window again, and nudged Frank. "Look at the woman's face. Could it be?"

"I really can't tell from here. I need cigars. I'll go into the office and pay for the gas and buy some. I'll get a better look at her in the good light."

"If you think it's her, give me a wave and I'll come in."

Frank got out of the car and walked quickly toward the office. Inside, Frank made notations on a pad, getting the owner's pedigree from the licenses that hung on the wall. The proprietor was named Mary Russo. He put the pad away just as the gas attendant came into the office. He paid the gas bill with his Mobil credit card adding a five pack of cigars to the bill. The woman pulled back the hood of her parka, smoothing her hair with her hand. Frank studied her features as she rang up the sale. Excitement rose in his chest. He was sure this person was the same woman he saw in Buffalo with Betty's brother Peter. He waved to Betty, who immediately got out of the car and hurried to the office.

"Can I use your john?" Betty asked, as she studied the woman's face.

"Sure," the woman answered, as she handed Betty a key ring, "It's around the back."

As Betty left the office, she nodded to Frank.

He waited anxiously for Betty to return, going over their next move in his mind. When Betty returned, Frank noticed that she held her shield in the palm of her hand. After she returned the key to the woman, Betty showed the woman her credentials, and introduced

Frank as her partner. The woman instantly paled, but struggled to keep her composure.

"Don't you remember us," Frank asked, "We met you and Peter Santini in a Buffalo restaurant a few months ago."

"I don't know what you're talking about," the woman stammered.

"Stop the bullshit, lady. I want to see my brother. We've got an important subject to discuss."

"My husband is Robert Russo, and I don't know any Peter Santini. Now will you please leave? I have to take an inventory of the food so I can call in an order."

"We can do this the easy way if you take us to Peter," Betty said harshly. "Or the hard way is calling in the State Police and getting a search warrant. Believe me, the easy way is a lot kinder to your furniture."

Mary Russo turned her back to the policemen, to hide the sudden rush of tears that filled her eyes. In a choked up voice, she answered, "Why don't you leave us alone. My husband is in no condition to see anyone.

He's very sick and I don't want to upset him."

Now it was Betty's turn to pale. She grabbed Mary's arm and swung her around. "What do you mean he's very sick? Tell me, quickly. You see, I'm his twin, I have to know." She squeezed Mary's arm even tighter.

Mary looked into Betty's eyes and saw deep concern. With tears streaming down her cheeks, she spoke very softly. "Let me lock up the office, and I'll take you to my husband."

They all brushed the snow from their shoes on a large hemp mat in the foyer. Betty looked around the dimly lit area, and could see enough to admire the grand old house. "Your house is magnificent, Mrs. Russo," she said politely, as Frank grunted in agreement.

"Thank you. Please call me Mary. We're pretty informal in this part of the state," she said as she led the two officers to the end of the hallway and opened the door.

Mary opened the door to the study that was turned into a bedroom. "Please come in," she said softly Betty entered first, followed by Frank. She wasn't ready for the sight that greeted her. She saw her brother lying on his stomach, strapped onto a contraption with his head lower than his feet. A stand loaded with intravenous solutions was at his side, all feeding into one tube that was attached to his wrist. A woman dressed as a nurse sat at Peter's side, reading a People Magazine. Betty ran to Peter and dropped to her knees, so that she could look up at her brother's face. His eyes were closed.

"Wake up, Petey. It's me, Betty," she said, her voice cracking.

She took his unencumbered hand and put it in hers. She raised his hand to her lips and covered it with kisses.

"Please open your eyes, Petey. Talk to me," Betty pleaded.

His eyes fluttered, then opened. His dazed expression changed to a joyous one as he recognized his sister. She put both her hands on her brother's cheeks as she covered his face with kisses. Frank and Mary watched from across the room. Frank seemed puzzled by Betty's show of emotion, but Mary was obviously touched by the tenderness that Betty displayed. She turned to Frank and whispered.

"You and Betty stay here tonight. We have plenty of room. Besides, you're family."

Frank started to object, but the touching scene of Betty's reunion with her brother, stopped him.

"Yeah, we're family," he muttered.

Chapter Twenty-one

Later that night Frank, Betty and Mary sat around the kitchen table. Betty and Mary sipped black coffee in accordance with Italian tradition. Frank drank a Bud.

"I think you people are nuts, drinking regular coffee before you go to bed," Frank said as he wiped a trace of foam from his mouth.

"Ah, you're the smart one," Betty answered with a smile. "You drink a six-pack and spend half the night getting up to pee."

Mary found it hard to join this frivolous conversation. Robert's welfare occupied her every waking moment. His pursuers were sitting in her kitchen. Her lover was in the study trussed up in a machine called a Prone Stander.

"What's going to happen now?" Mary whispered, her thoughts accidentally articulated.

"What?" Betty and Frank asked in unison.

"What's going to happen to Robert, er, I mean Peter?" Mary repeated.

"Obviously, we can't take him in now, considering his condition and all," Betty answered, a tremor in her voice.

Frank interrupted. "We'll probably get a warrant, arrest him and have the State Troopers place a guard here twenty-four hours a day until he's well enough to go to court."

"Oh, my God," Mary blurted, placing a fist in her mouth.

"You really love him," Betty said, making it a statement more than a question.

"With all my heart and soul," Mary answered, as her tear- filled eyes stared into Betty's. "And I'll fight for his health and safety with all my might against you, your cop family, and the whole state of New York if necessary."

Betty was stunned at the passion in Mary's response, and felt a pang of guilt that she couldn't join her in her brother's defense.

Mary broke down and sobbed openly. Betty got up and went to Mary's side and embraced her. Then she, too, began to cry.

Frank, troubled by this display of emotion, went to the kitchen door and opened it, letting in a blast of icy air. "I'm going out for a smoke," he grumbled, showing his displeasure for the crying session. Embarrassed, he went out into the freezing night coatless.

As his body shivered, Frank thought, This is the God damndest arrest I've ever been involved with in twenty-five years on the Job. I honestly don't know what to do next. I'm a guest in the home of a fugitive wanted for homicide, who happens to be the twin of the woman I want to marry. How can fate deal me such a hand?

Frank inhaled deeply, then slowly exhaled, the cigarette smoke merging with the vapor from his breath. He looked through the kitchen window and saw Betty pouring coffee into Mary's cup. He watched as Betty sat next to Mary and placed her hands on Mary's knees. He felt uncomfortable as the two women carried on a tear-filled conversation. He dreaded going back inside, but he had to before he turned into an icicle. His injured arm in the cast was aching from the cold. Frank tried to visualize how Peter must have felt, submerged so long in the frigid water of the lake, as he made that Herculean effort to raise that water-logged boy to the surface. He shook his head as he shivered uncontrollably.

"This is the most fucked-up case I ever heard of," Frank muttered, as he flipped his cigarette butt into a snow pile.

When he returned to the warm kitchen, Frank brushed off the light snow that had fallen on his shoulders. Betty turned and faced him with a look of determination.

"This is how it's going to be, Frank. We're going home. I mean we're going to New York City for Christmas. I'm bringing you home to my family and we're going to announce our engagement. We're all going to sit around the table telling exaggerated police stories as we fill up on canoli and coffee. My mother will prepare enough food for an entire platoon and Christmas dinner will last at least four hours. Mamma will cry when I tell her I'm finally going to marry, and my brothers will pound my back till I scream. Papa will look me in the eye and ask `Where's Peter? I gave you a job to do and you fucked up. It took you forty-four years to find a man who'd marry you, how long will it take you to find your brother?' What am I going to tell him, Frank?" Betty shouted hysterically. "I'm being torn apart. Happy that I'm marrying you, and so sad about my brother. Did my father realize what he was asking when he sent me to bring Peter in?"

Frank stared at Betty, so upset by Betty's hysterics that a cold sweat appeared on his brow. He felt like he was about to explode. "What the fuck am I doing here? I'm on sick report, confined to my house according to regulations, but I'm four hundred miles away from my house. You're making all the decisions, and I'm sitting here like a nebbish."

"What decisions?"

"You said this is the way it's going to be, Frank, like my opinion was unnecessary. First, we're going to New York City. Then, I'm going to announce our engagement. Jesus H. Christ, I'm going to be forty-nine years old next week. Too old to be told things. Besides, a fella likes to be asked. If I'm going to get a complaint for being AWOL, it ought to be partly my idea."

Betty's face took on an expression of utter confusion, her eyes widened wildly. She spoke and her tone was pleading. "Oh, I'm so sorry, Frank. I took it for granted that you felt the same as me." Betty broke down. Her sobs seemed to come from deep within. Frank hurried to her side and embraced her with his powerful arms, crushing her head to his chest.

"We'll work it out, honey, we'll work it out. I'm on your side. Calm down before I start crying too."

After several minutes, when Betty's breathing returned to normal, Mary spoke.

"I have to prepare your room, or rooms. Which'll it be, one or two?"

"One," both answered simultaneously.

"Second floor or third?" Mary asked slyly.

"Third," Betty answered with a slight blush. "We have a lot of things to work out, and we don't want to disturb anyone."

Mary nodded and left the room. She went to the linen closet to get the sheets and towels that were needed.

"Holy shit," she whispered out loud, "These are the first guests Robert and I ever entertained. And it has to be the two cops that we've been running away from. Unbelievable!"

Later, after Frank had brought their valise up from the car, Betty unpacked their pajamas and toiletries. Then she helped Frank, who was awkward using one arm, to undress.

"Why did you choose one room when you could have had the privacy of your own room?" Frank asked.

"I'm not sure," Betty stammered, "But it's about time I started working on my problem. What kind of a wife would I be, the way I am?"

Frank grinned.

"Oh shut up," she said, punching him in the shoulder.

"I'd like to shower. Could you help me put that plastic bag over my cast?"

"Sure," she answered, then tied a large brown trash bag over his arm.

"Later, I'll use it for a condom. I'll need something that big after waiting so long," Frank kidded as he escaped to the bathroom.

Betty threw the toiletry case after him, yelling, "You're a son of a bitch!"

"Don't insult my mother till you meet her," Frank called from the bathroom.

Frank came out of the shower wearing a big bath towel tied around his waist.

Betty was standing in front of a full length mirror wearing a shortie nightgown. She was examining herself from every angle. "Not bad for a forty-four year-old lady," she mumbled.

Frank came up behind her and hugged her waist. "You look terrific," he whispered into her ear. "A helluva lot prettier than any cop I ever worked with."

"Jesus, sometimes you talk too much," Betty said angrily, as she spun around and faced Frank. "If you stopped at `terrific' it would have been romantic. But adding the `any cop' jazz makes me feel cheap."

Frank chuckled as he drew Betty close. "Where's your sense of humor, kid?"

"Honestly, sometimes you're an insensitive shmuck. I"m so scared I'm fighting off diarrhea, and you're making jokes."

"Betty, I watched you in two shootings, and I never saw anyone so cool under fire. Now you're telling me you're scared to make love? It's the most natural thing in the world for two people in love. Just let it happen."

"I love you deeply, but I'm still terrified."

Frank's expression changed from smiling to one of concern. He drew Betty close, pressing her head against his chest, kissing her hair. "Listen, honey, for a moment I forgot the war that's waging in you. We don't have to jump into this with both feet. A little at a time's okay. You know, `the testing the water' bit."

"You're sweet. But let's just go to bed. It's chilly out here."

Frank turned the three-way lamp on his night table to its lowest setting, and threw his bath towel on a chair. He pulled back the comforter to climb into bed and saw, to his surprise, that Betty had removed her night gown. He stared at her naked form and murmured: "God, Betty, you are beautiful. You have the body of a young girl."

"You don't have to bullshit me. Just get into bed. I'm freezing."

Frank got into bed, his good arm closest to Betty. He drew her close and felt every muscle in her body tense. He could bet her fists were clenched. If he moved too fast, he was sure she'd punch him out, like she did before.

Slowly, he caressed her shoulder and then her back. He wondered if it was his imagination, but he felt the rigidity slowly leaving her body, like a blow-up doll with a slow leak.

Was that a low moan he heard or his imagination again? Frank shifted his body so that he could place light, tender kisses on her forehead and cheeks. Betty turned her head and kissed Frank on the lips, a hard, urgent kind of kiss.

"How come you rarely kiss me, Frank?" Betty asked, hoarsely.

"Are you kidding? I'm scared shitless of you. Besides, I make it a policy never to be aggressive with girls that pack a nine millimeter."

"Well, I'm not packing now. So really kiss me, you big Mick. No excuses."

To Frank's surprise, Betty took the initiative. She pushed Frank flat on the bed, climbed on top of him and kissed him deeply and passionately. When they came up for air, Frank was flushed and seemed confused.

"Jesus H. Christ, Betty, what --"

"Shut up, Frank," Betty interrupted, "And do as you're told."

"But, but, I'm supposed to --"

"Yeah, yeah, I know you're supposed to. But you're a cripple and I have to bail your butt out again," Betty said as she silenced Frank with another deep kiss.

Like a lazy summer day that is suddenly attacked by thunder and lightening, with pouring rain that sends picnickers scurrying for shelter, so was the complete personality change for Betty Santini. Forty-four years old, celibate since the age of eighteen, she unleashed suddenly all that stored up passion with a frenzied need, coupled with a tireless energy. All accompanied with animalistic sounds.

The emergence of all this frenetic activity scared the hell out of Frank. He felt like a prisoner of war, robbed of the masculine dominance that was supposed to be his, forced to accept the passive role that drained him of his normal turgidity.

"Don't leave me now, Frank," Betty shouted, as she came down the home stretch, like a sweaty, foaming race horse. Her hands gripped his shoulders with unnatural strength, when suddenly her entire body tensed and for several long seconds she emitted an un-recognizable sound from her chest. Then she seemed to wilt and uncontrollable sobs replaced the animalistic sounds.

After a while, Betty calmed down. She turned away from Frank, seeking the edge of the bed and as if ashamed, covering her head with a pillow.

Frank was speechless. He didn't know what to say or how to act. He was in a state of complete bewilderment. He got out of bed and walked around the room naked, oblivious to the cold. He found his jacket and searched for the five-pack of cigars he purchased earlier.

Then Frank pulled a chair in front of a window, sat with his feet on the window sill, and lit up his cigar. He puffed away for an hour or so until the cigar was a mere stub, almost burning his fingers. The ash tray on the window sill was filled to capacity.

Frank felt a shiver run through him and he realized that he had been sitting naked in this cold room for a long time after raising quite a sweat a short time before. He returned to the bed and switched off the light. The bed felt wonderfully warm and Betty turned over and nestled in his arms. Frank heard a muffled whisper.

"Are you awake?"

"Yes, honey, I am," Frank answered.

"I'm terribly sorry. I don't know what happened to me. I was out of control, like riding a wave at Coney Island."

"There's nothing to be sorry about. Now go to sleep."

"Yes there is. I'm sorry we wasted all this time. It was wonderful. You were wonderful. Frank, will you marry me?"

"I don't know, honey," Frank answered sleepily, "Ask me in the morning."

Frank rose early. He dressed quietly, spent some time in the bathroom and went downstairs to the kitchen. He was surprised to find Mary already there and the aroma of coffee filled the room.

"What're you doing up so early?" Frank asked.

"Dr. Scarpati will be here at seven-thirty to examine Robert...I mean Peter. I'm hoping for some good news."

"What exactly is wrong with Peter?"

"He has no feeling from the waist down. Dr. Scarpati says that he sees no damage to the spine. The nervous system may be in some sort of shock from the exposure and the tremendous exertion he suffered. He hopes for a complete recovery."

"Does this Scarpati know what he's talking about? He's only a hick town doctor."

"He's a specialist, Chief of Neurology at the Glens Falls hospital. But he did say that if he sees no improvement today, he would send Peter to Mt. Sinai in New York City. To that doctor that successfully treated that football player on the New York Jets. Sit down Frank, I'll make you a nice breakfast.

"I feel awkward. I'm here to arrest Peter and you're treating me like honored guest."

"I'm an Italian mother. You're a policeman. We both have to do what we're trained to do."

"No hard feelings?"

"Not against you personally. But if the occasion arises that I have to fight you for Peter, I will. I'd kill for him. Can you understand that?"

"Yes," Frank answered sadly. "I can understand that. Even admire you for that. Peter's lucky that he found you. I feel lucky I found Betty."

"Are you two really going to get married?"

"We plan to in the near future."

"Now I envy you," Mary said, her voice cracking as she turned toward the stove. "Help yourself to juice from the refrigerator. What can I make you? Eggs, an omelet, French toast? Name it. I'm a good cook."

"Ham and eggs would be a treat."

"No problem. Home fries okay?"

"Don't put yourself out."

Betty walked into the kitchen looking refreshed, younger. "What's everybody doing up so early?" she asked, "It's only six o'clock"

"Dr. Scarpati will be here soon to examine Peter. I'm very nervous," Mary answered.

"Can I sit in on it?"

"Of course, there's no one closer to Peter than you. I could use the support. The neighbors have been just great, but it's not the same as family."

Betty walked over to Mary and kissed her on the cheek. "You really are a very sweet person, Mary."

"We were really very happy here, Peter and I," Mary said sadly as she worked on Frank's breakfast. "But it was only for a short time. Then our whole world collapsed with Peter's stupid act. But it's those things that make me love him so. I can't believe he's wanted for murder. He's one of the kindest men I ever met."

"I don't believe he meant to hurt his partner. Maybe it was an accident. I just don't know," Betty said wistfully. "Most Sicilian families band together when someone's in trouble. My father's values are all New World. The Job's more important than family. When I go home, I'm going to bring that up. It may break up our family."

"When're you going home?" Mary asked.

"Today. After we hear what Dr. Scarpati has to say. Do we have time to go to church before the doctor comes?"

Mary glanced at the clock and said, "Yes, if we hurry." She took off her apron and handed it to Frank. "You'll have to finish your own breakfast, Frank. First things first."

Frank was amused at how fast the two women got out of the house. He burned his eggs and threw them in the trash can, then settled for a buttered roll and coffee.

Chapter Twenty-two

There was absolute silence in the room as Dr. Scarpati examined Peter. Mary's palms were pressed together as she was obviously praying. Betty's face showed the tremendous pressure she was under and Frank's face showed concern, the nurse's merely curiosity. Though the room was very cool, Peter's face was covered with sweat as he waited for the doctor's verdict.

Dr. Scarpati pulled the sheets up to Peter's chin, signalling the end of the examination. A slight smile cracked the serious expression on his face. Everyone in the room crowded around him, all tensed with anticipation.

"I'm hopeful, mind you, just hopeful that Peter will in time have a complete recovery," Dr. Scarpati said with a quiver in his voice. "I'm almost positive now that his paraparesis is temporary.

That his body went into shock due to hypothermia," Dr. Scarpati lectured, his voice gaining strength as he assumed the role of teacher. "It's a condition that results when the body loses enough heat to drop its core temperature in the brain, lungs, heart and spinal cord dangerously low. The result is that the heart and lungs can't work properly, and the arms and legs become numb and a swimmer can lose consciousness. Drowning can and usually results. That Peter saved that boy and his dog as well as himself in that frozen lake was not only a remarkable heroic feat, it was a miracle. God was certainly with him. Peter's body temperature was seventy-eight degrees when they put him in the ambulance."

"Why do you say you're hopeful of a complete recovery, Doctor?" Mary interrupted.

"Because Peter shows a slight response in both feet, and his entire body has lost some rigidity."

"What happens now?" Mary asked, excitedly.

"I'm going to put him under the care of Dr. Levy, a physiatrist. He'll treat him twice a day. First, he'll get passive range of motion exercises, then, I hope, advance to active range exercises. I hope that God will not abandon Peter now, but will help him make a complete recovery."

"Thank you, God, thank you," Betty cried. I'm so glad I went to church this morning. The first time in about twenty years. Do you think He listened, Frank?"

"I'm sure He did, honey," Frank whispered, as a tear appeared in the corner of his eye.

"I won't feel so guilty now, when we go home to my family to announce our happy news. My father will ream my ass for not bringing Peter back. That's all he'll hear when we tell our story."

As Betty and her brother said their tearful goodbys, Peter asked, "Betty, could you do me a favor when you get home?

"If I can, Petey, what is it?"

"Saturday is my daughter Marci's 7th birthday. Could you get her a gift for me and put in a nice card? Be sure to tell her I love her and I miss her terribly."

"Sure, Petey, no problem."

"Would it be asking too much if you could get a little something for Tess, also? I miss those kids something awful."

"I'll talk to both of them, don't worry. I'll take care of it. By the way, how about Alice? Is there something you want me to say to her?"

Peter thought for a while then shook his head no. He didn't trust himself to speak. He cleared his throat and in almost a whisper, said,

"Give Mom a hug and kiss for me and send my love to my kid-brothers, Jimmy, and Mike and his family." After a slight hesitation added, "Pop too. Mary will give you money for the presents."

"I think I can handle the money. You'll need all you've got to pay for your treatments. I don't think you'll be sending the bills to the NYPD."

Peter laughed. "Jesus, Betty, I forgot what a good sense of humor you have. Come to think of it, I haven't given much thought, lately, about how much I love you. You know, running from you, hiding out. What a joke, you always knew what I was thinking before I did, How did you find me?"

"You were great, Petey. I didn't have a clue where to look for you after Buffalo. It was just a fluke that I spotted Mary on TV. Your story was on a national TV network. I wasn't even positive that it was Mary. I only saw her that one time in the restaurant when you tied Frank and me to that steam pipe."

Peter chuckled. "I bet Frank had some explaining to do after that one."

"Yeah. They're still ribbing the pants off him."

Hardly a word was spoken on the four and a half hour trip from Lake Stewart to New York City. Both Frank and Betty were immersed in deep thought about the forthcoming meeting with the Santini clan. Betty was in dread of her father's irascible temper. She knew he was sure to erupt when she told him that she found Peter and didn't bring him home. Frank, on the other hand, wondered if this volatile family would accept him as Betty's fiancee.

"I'm forty-nine fucking years old," Frank exploded out loud. "Why should I give a shit what they think of me. I'm not going to ask your father for permission to marry you. And why, goddammit, didn't you stop at the last rest stop? You knew I was out of cigars!"

"Calm down," Betty responded with a smile. "My mother's cooking will cure whatever ails you. Besides, you'll feel like you're in the back room of a station house. Everyone's a cop in that house except my mother."

Frank's answer was a grunt. Then he asked, "What're you smiling about?"

"I was just remembering how Peter teased me about cuffing us to the steam pipe."

"Huh, that's no laughing matter. We'll never live that one down," Frank said, pouting. "By the way, how much longer before we get there? My ass is getting numb."

"You sound like a kid," Betty answered, laughing.

Traffic slowed as they approached the George Washington Bridge. It was five o'clock, the height of the rush hour.

"Normally it should take about an hour from here to my parent's home. But in this traffic, it could take us a lot longer. Why do you ask?"

"My bowels are in an uproar," Frank growled. "I don't know if it's from something I ate or just plain nerves."

Betty glanced in Frank's direction and smiled. "My money's on the nerves."

Two hours and ten minutes later, Betty turned into a tree-lined street in the Bay Ridge section of Brooklyn. She parked the car in front of a neatly trimmed lawn that surrounded a white-painted three story house. Four cars were parked in the driveway.

"We're here," Betty said wearily. "I'm surprised they left me a parking spot. Two of those cars belong to my kid-brothers, and the Legend on the end is Alice's, my sister-in-law. The house'll be a bedlam, with five grandchildren running around. Plus my parents, my brothers Jimmy and Mike, and Mike's wife, and now us."

"Jesus, let's split. I'll never remember all those names. I can't write them down on a clipboard. Let's come back tomorrow."

Betty laughed. "For one big, tough Dick, you sure are chicken-shit."

The front door of the house opened and five children burst through, led by the two oldest girls.

"Here they come," Betty said excitedly. "Those two beauties in front are Tess and Marci, Peter's girls. The two older boys are Mike Jr. and Ralph, and the toddler bringing up the rear is Jason.

Betty quickly exited the car and was besieged by the mob of kids, all jabbering at once. They climbed all over her.

"Oh, how I missed you guys," Betty giggled as she knelt down to hug each one. "I love you, I love you, I love you all."

"What did you bring us?" the chorus screamed in unison.

"I didn't get a chance to shop yet, but I promise to get everybody a present. Just whisper in my ear and maybe, if you're good, you'll get it. Okay?"

Hugs and kisses followed, and each child took a turn to whisper into Betty's ear. Suddenly, the massive form of the unsmiling Frank Santini Jr. appeared in the doorway.

Though sixty-eight years old, he still was an imposing, almost menacing figure. Tall, at six-foot-two, and a whopping 260 pounds, ex-Sgt. Santini had a full head of white hair, and the face of a Georgia red-neck.

"Hello Betty," he said in a low, deep voice that was almost a growl. "Welcome home."

Betty stood up slowly, scanning his face, trying to decipher his expression. "Hello Pop," she answered in almost a whisper, "And Merry Christmas."

"There will be no Christmas in my house this year. This house is in mourning until your twin is booked and tried. Who's that guy sitting in the car?"

"I'll get him and introduce him to you," Betty said with a tremor in her voice. She walked back to the car slowly, her eyes searching out Frank's, begging him to stand by her. "Come, Frank," she whispered as she opened the car door, "Come and meet my father."

Frank was surprised by the fearful look in Betty's eyes.

"Sure, kid, sure," Frank answered as he got out of the car, unwinding to his full height.

Betty took her fiance's hand and led him up the steps of the porch to introduce him to her father.

"Frank, meet Frank," Betty said, forcing a smile. "Pop, this is Detective First Grade Frank Mullin of the Buffalo Police Department."

Both Franks shook hands, both unsmiling, like two behemoths sizing each other up before a battle. They were almost nose to nose and by the redness that appeared in the older man's face, she surmised that her fiance was exerting maximum pressure in that handshake to establish his presence, to impress this stern-looking man twenty years his senior.

"Welcome, Mullin, come in and meet the family," Santini said.

Betty took Frank's hand and led him into the house, followed by her father. The family was in the kitchen, seated around a huge table with steaming cups of coffee in front of each person. At the sight of Betty, her mother jumped up from the table and her face mirrored her happiness. She ran to Betty and embraced her, showering her with kisses.

"Mamma, meet Frank Mullin. He's a detective from Buffalo," Betty said softly, her eyes tearing as she looked into her mother's eyes.

"So, my daughter went out and got her own Frank," she softly spoke in Italian, "And a big one like her father. What's the matter, you couldn't find an Italian one. You've been looking for twenty-five years?"

"Mamma, please speak English. Frank doesn't understand Italian."

"It wasn't meant for his Irish ears," her mother muttered in Italian." Turning to Frank Mullin, Anna Santini took his hand and with a smile lighting up her once pretty face, said in a warm, firm voice, "Welcome to our house, Frank Mullin."

She led him to the table and introduced him to everyone, and they all greeted him with warm smiles and firm handshakes. Everyone but Alice, who refused his hand but mumbled a greeting. The look of disgust on her face belied the words she spoke.

"Take a seat, Frank," Santini said, offering Mullin a chair. "And have a cup of coffee, unless you want something stronger. You being Irish and all."

"No, coffee's just fine," Mullin answered, "My mother taught me, `when in Rome, do as the Romans do.'"

That remark amused Santini, for his hard face softened and a trace of a smile appeared in the corner of his mouth.

"Betty, go help your mother," Santini ordered, forgetting for the moment that his daughter had been living on her own for the past twenty-three years.

Betty smiled sarcastically, but dutifully obeyed her father.

Anna appeared with a steaming cup of coffee and a platter of canolis and placed them in front of Mullin.

"Eat, you must be starved after your long trip. Dinner won't be ready for another hour," Anna Santini said without a trace of an accent.

As soon as Frank picked up his coffee, it was if a signal was given for the interrogation to begin. Questions about the Job in Buffalo flew from every corner of the table. Mullin tried to answer everyone, until Frank Santini hit the table with his fist. Then a respectful silence prevailed.

"Give the poor guy a chance to relax before you bring him in front of the civilian review board."

"C'mon Pop, give us a break," Michael, the thirty-nine year old son with sixteen years on the Job, remarked. "We're all interested in how a small town police force operates."

Betty came to the table, her eyes smoking in anger. "You're all a bunch of creeps, especially you, Mike. Goofing off in that rest home you call the 62nd Precinct. Buffalo, block for block, is just as active as any in New York City. In the short time I worked with Frank, I was involved in two shootings. How many times have you had your gun out of its holster? Why do you think Frank's left arm is in a cast? He didn't break it picking his nose."

"Calm down, Betty," Mike answered, smiling, "We were only teasing, just a little friendly rivalry."

"Jesus H. Christ," Frank Mullin muttered under his breath, "You don't have to stick up for me. I'm a big boy now."

"Okay, Frank, you're on your own. I know what it feels like to have my father and brothers ganging up on me, even though I'm a detective first grade. None of my brothers even made sergeant."

"You forgot I made sergeant," her father interrupted.

"Yeah, Pop, it took you thirty years to make it. I made sergeant in seven."

"But I had a family to raise. Who could study in this madhouse? You had peace and quiet in your own apartment. How can you compare?" the father answered hotly.

"Shut up all of you," Anna shouted, hands on her hips. "Mr. Mullin must think we're all barbarians."

"If he did, he'd be right," Alice added sarcastically.

Everyone turned and looked at the sad-looking woman with the beautiful face.

"Then, why do you come here, Alice?" Anna challenged.

"I'm sorry I said that, but you know why I come. My children love it here. They play with their cousins. At my parent's home, my children and I are constantly berated because of Peter. You know how the Irish are," Alice said in almost a whisper.

"We all apologize to you, Mullin. The Italian side and the Irish side. It seems we're all lacking in manners," Frank Santini said sullenly. It was obvious that this was not a man who apologized easily. He stood up, straightened his torso to its fullest height, then looked directly at Frank Mullin, and asked, "Just why did you come to Bay Ridge, Frank?"

Mullin was silent for an embarrassing length of time, mulling over in his mind the answer he would deliver. He, too, stood up to his fullest height, looked directly at Frank Santini and took a deep breath. "I came here with Betty to meet her family. You see, we're getting married very soon. I believed it was the civilized thing to do."

Silence followed Mullin's brief statement. All that could be heard was the chatter of the children from the living room and the TV program they were watching. Frank Mullin looked into everyone's face in consecutive order, as if challenging them. No one picked up the gauntlet, so he slowly sat down.

Betty came to his side and reached for his hand. In a voice that was barely audible, she said, "We're a little too old to ask for your permission, Pop, so this is more like an announcement. We hoped for your blessing."

Betty looked around the table, studying everyone's face. She saw tears in her mother's eyes and shock in her father's.

Alice stared into her coffee cup with an icy expression. Mike and Jimmy and Mike's wife were all smiling. Suddenly, there was an eruption of noise and everyone, with the exception of Alice, stood up and encircled the engaged couple.

Kisses and backslapping followed. The children peeked into the kitchen to see what the commotion was all about. Alice ran to the bathroom, sobbing. Frank Santini came to the table carrying a bottle of Scotch and a bottle of Rye. Like magic, a jug of ice cubes appeared along with bottles of ginger ale and soda.

Anna kissed and hugged her daughter and whispered in her ear,

"I guess my going to mass every morning for the past twenty-five years finally paid off." Then Anna approached her husband and hugged him. Then looking him square in the eye, said, "God blessed us by letting us live long enough to see our daughter get married. No more mourning in this house. I want the Christmas decorations up today and

I want a tree in the house by tonight. We have a wedding to get ready for. So let the moths out of your wallet, open your vault and dust off your checkbook. Our only daughter's getting married."

Frank, and everyone else in the room, were shocked by the outburst in such a loud, firm voice from the usually soft spoken woman. Betty burst into tears as she watched her mother hug her fiance, kissing him on both cheeks.

The Sunday afternoon dinner at the Santini home was prepared by Anna with Betty's help. It was a five course meal served to the thirteen people present. The two sister-in-laws sat like ladies, waiting to be served. Each course was enough to be a meal, but everything was so delicious that everyone somehow managed to consume every morsel set before him. Joviality reigned at the table in honor or the engaged couple. For a while, the tragedy concerning Peter, was set aside and not discussed.

Instead, the inevitable Job talk began, and even Frank Mullin joined the conversation by relating the two shooting incidents that he and Betty were involved in. Frank didn't have to enhance the stories, they were exciting even when told truthfully. Betty's brothers sat in awe of their much decorated sister.

Even Frank Santini wore an expression of pride, and when Mullin was finished, Santini commented, "I'm not surprised. She was always the spunkiest of all my kids. The smartest, too. She's been one of the best cops I ever saw since her rookie days. I'm proud to say she takes after me and her sainted grandfather, who got the Medal Of Honor. I can't say the same for my sons."

"C'mon, Pop, be fair," Jimmy retorted. "I've gotten three awards, Michael has five, and Peter must have at least ten. We're certainly holding up our end."

"Enough," Frank Santini shouted, as his huge fist slammed down on the table, making the dishes jump 3 into the air. "I don't want his name mentioned at this table. Jimmy talks of the honors my sons brought to this family, but doesn't mention the shame and disgrace that his brother brought. That's why I insist that a Santini bring in that son of a bitch. To show that the rest of the family still has some pride. Betty do you have a report to make to this family? What've you been doing the past six months?"

"Sit down, Frank, and shut your filthy mouth," Anna hissed. "You have no class. This is supposed to be a happy day, one I've been waiting twenty-five years for. I'm not going to let you spoil it. Take your sons and our guest into the living room and smoke your smelly cigars. The women will clean up here. Yes, all of you," Anna ordered, as she glared at her daughters-in-law. "Then we'll have coffee and desert, and maybe say a little prayer of gratitude. We haven't had anything to celebrate since Jason was born."

Silence followed this tirade. After a while, the men sauntered into the living room and the children went out to play. The women sullenly began the task of cleaning up after the feast. Later, after everyone left, Frank and Anna sat on the couch, and Frank Mullin relaxed in the deep easy chair. Betty sat on the carpeted floor, leaning back against her fiance's legs. Both Franks puffed on newly-lit cigars.

"I love when they all come," Anna sighed, "But I must admit it feels good when they finally go home."

"Are your parents alive, Frank?" Santini asked.

"My mother's alive and well, but my father drank himself to death fifteen years ago," Mullin answered.

"Ah, yes," Santini remarked, "It happens all too often like that in Irish families."

"Shame on you, you hypocrite," Anna retorted, "Your own father was reported to have had a snootfull just before he bought it on Forty-second Street. Lying in the gutter with his face in the mud, and in his own blood, isn't exactly the ideal way to meet your maker."

"Jesus, Anna, show a little respect. He died a hero's death."

"May it be God's will that my children not be such heroes, and live long lives instead," Anna said, holding her hands together in a prayerful fashion. "It would be better if we talked about the wedding. When do you children plan to marry?"

"After Christmas but before New Years, before we go home to Buffalo," Betty answered.

"So soon?" Mullin asked, obviously shocked.

"Yes," Betty answered, turning around to look at Frank's face. "Any objections?"

"No, no," Frank stammered, "You took me by surprise."

"We can't prepare anything decent in so short a time," Anna said in her usual sad fashion.

"Mom, Frank and I are no spring chickens. We're practically middle-aged. A ceremony in church, a meal in a good restaurant for our families and some people from the precinct -- it's more than enough. Maybe I'll buy a new dress and Frank a new suit."

"You mentioned going home to Buffalo," Frank Santini said quietly. "Does that mean you're quitting the Job? Jesus, Betty, you could make captain. You're young enough. There's no telling how high you could go."

"No, Pop, my place is with my husband. Maybe I could get a job teaching in their police academy. If not, I'll concentrate on raising a family, if I'm lucky."

Anna tried to stifle a sob but couldn't and gave in.

Betty went to her mother's side and embraced her. "Why the tears, Mom? You were happy for me a little while ago."

Anna raised her tear-stained face and looked at Betty. "It's going to be very hard for me to lose both of my twins. Twins are special, like a double blessing. Sometimes, when you were children, I felt like you shut me out. You had each other. My other children needed me more. Peter came to you with his troubles and sometimes, I was jealous. Oh, I don't know why I'm telling you this now. I'm so mixed up. I'm happy and sad at the same time. I can't help crying. Please forgive me. I'm not like your father, I'm glad you're quitting the Job. I worried plenty about you, patrolling those dangerous streets at night. Believe me, taking care of babies is much more rewarding than catching crooks."

Later that night, Betty lay in the bed that she used throughout her childhood. It was a narrow twin bed with a lumpy mattress. She shivered under two blankets and wished with all her heart that she could be snuggling in Frank's bear-like arms. It was so warm and safe there. The events of the day flashed across her mind like a kaleidoscope. She tossed and turned and found it almost impossible to fall asleep.

At the end of the hall, in Peter's old room, Frank also was very restless. He felt uncomfortable, lying in the bed of the felon he was tracking for the past six months. He, too, reviewed the day's events in his mind. He focused on the face of Frank Santini and could understand his passionate fixation that a member of the Santini clan be the one to capture and return his son for trial, to face the masked lady holding the scales of justice. His family's accomplishments on the Job, past and present, superseded anything else in his life. This could only be understood and appreciated by other families, long ensconced in family traditions. Traditions built by generation after generation in the military, or by the attendance in the same university. A renegade member of the family brought shame and disgrace, and it could only be eradicated by the family itself, cleaning up its own mess.

Frank Mullin lay in Peter's bed, trying to feel any vibes that might give him a clue to the make-up of this hero-villain -- loved by so many in the village of Lake Stewart and reviled by police officers of New York City, and possibly by his own family. Did anyone bother to listen to Peter's side of the tragedy? Not one word was mentioned around the dinner table in Peter's defense.

Frank thought of Betty and how his love for this woman had grown to mean more than life itself. How could he track and possibly hurt a man with almost the exact genes and chromosomes as his future bride? He honestly couldn't, and in the morning he would inform Betty of his decision. In his heart he knew he could not exert any force that might be necessary to effect the arrest of Betty's twin brother. To expect Betty to do so would be a heartless, cruel expectation.

Chapter Twenty-three

After a fitful night, Frank Mullin felt a hand shaking him. He opened his eyes and saw a smiling Frank Santini, cigar in the corner of his mouth, standing at his bedside.

"C'mon Frank, I need your help picking out a Christmas tree. Anna and Betty have been decorating the house for over an hour. Move your ass."

"Sure, Frank," Mullin laughed. "Just give me a few minutes to shower and shave. Do you have a plastic garbage bag I can tape over my cast?"

"Of course," the older Frank replied. "I'll bring it right up."

A half hour later the two huge Franks left the house together, chatting as if they knew each other for years, both enjoying the comradeship they shared as police officers.

Betty and Anna were left alone in the house hanging the holiday decorations. Betty wore a calm and peaceful expression, feeling more relaxed than she had for a very long time. In contrast, Anna's expression portrayed a troubled mind that was full of anxiety. Unable to remain silent any longer, Anna spoke. "Betty, I know I shut your father up yesterday when he tried to question you about Peter, but my reasons are different. I've had this terrible feeling that Peter isn't all right. That something terrible has happened to him. Please, if you know something, please tell me," Anna said, her voice cracking with emotion as she looked into Betty's eyes.

"Yes, Mamma," Betty answered, her own voice cracking. "Let's sit down and have another cup of coffee. I have a long story to tell you."

Half an hour later, Betty felt exhausted, but relieved that she could share her feelings with her mother. She dreaded the moment when she would have to tell the story again to her father. She studied her mother's face and believed she could actually see it aging. Wrinkles appeared between Anna's eyes and dark circles beneath them. Her mouth, usually upturned with a ready smile, turned down at the corners, changing the once pretty face into the sorrowful face of a Sicilian widow. All that was missing was the black dress and stockings.

"I just knew it," Anna said, holding a clenched fist to her breast. "I felt a constant pain here. But somehow I knew it wasn't a pain coming from me, but to me. Can you understand that?"

Betty, not trusting her voice to answer, just nodded. Without another word, Anna got up from the table, walked to the hall closet and took out her faded, drab winter coat.

"Where are you going?" Betty forced herself to ask.

"To church. I have to light a candle."

When the two Franks returned, struggling with a huge Christmas tree, Anna had already returned from church and was seated with Betty at the kitchen table, drinking yet another cup of coffee. The two Franks trimmed the tree to make it fit into the living room and the one good-armed Frank helped the older one decorate the tree.

There was much laughing and loud talking emanating from the living room, a sharp contrast from the silence in the kitchen. Frank Santini noticed the unnatural silence and bellowed in his usual manner. "Hey, what's going on in there? Before we left, you two were talking a blue streak, making all kinds of plans. Now there's silence. What happened?"

"Nothing. Nothing happened, Pop," Betty called back, trying to make her voice sound happy, but failing miserably.

Frank Santini put down the Christmas lights he was holding and walked into the kitchen. His eyes studied his wife's tear-stained face and he felt a sudden pressure in his chest.

"What? What's going on? Goddammit, is somebody going to tell me?"

Anna stood up and approached her husband like a zombie. She pounded his chest with both fists and shrieked, "Your son Peter is paralyzed. Are you happy now?"

Santini's face reflected confusion. A redness replaced his usually swarthy coloring. He grabbed his wife's two fists in his large hands and with a barely audible voice, asked, "How do you know? Who told you?

"Betty just came from his bedside," Anna said tearfully.

Frank Santini, in a sudden rage, dropped his wife's hands and in one motion, pulled Betty from her chair.

"You found him?" he yelled in a hoarse voice, "You found him and you didn't call me immediately? You bitch, how could you?" The father, in his frustration and rage, shook his daughter by the shoulders like a rag doll, her head rolling uncontrollably.

"Stop, you animal," Anna cried out, "You'll kill her, stop it, stop it!"

Frank Mullin rushed into the kitchen and viewed the shocking scene. With his one good, powerful arm, he swung the older man around, forcing him to drop his grip on Betty's shoulders, then pushed him down into a kitchen chair.

The old man's pumped-up chest deflated like a punctured balloon and his florid face turned pale as his head sagged into a cradle formed by his two hands. "Why didn't you bring him in?" Santini moaned. "You know the whole department is looking for him. That was the job I gave you. `Bring him back' I ordered you. `The honor of the family is at stake.' "

Anna flew at her husband, her face twisted with hatred. "What kind of a father are you?" she spat at him. "You're worried about honor? Didn't you hear me? Your son is paralyzed.

Don't you care? Go to him, put a bullet in his head and you'll end his suffering and put honor back into this family."

Santini was obviously shocked by the intensity of his wife's attack on him and by the venom she directed at him. He was confused by the hate in her face. He turned and looked at Betty and could have only seen anguish there. "I'm, I'm sorry, Betty," he stammered. "I hope I didn't hurt you. It's just that I waited for so long for some news, but you never called. I didn't know what was happening. The only news I got was from your C.O.. You called him regularly. Didn't I deserve a single telephone call in six months?"

"Till a couple of days ago, I didn't have much to tell you. When I finally found Peter, I was heartbroken by what I saw. I stopped acting and thinking like a cop and became his sister again. Can you understand that? I found my brother trussed up in a machine like a barbecued pig. Pop, all my love for him came rushing out. Can you understand that?

At that moment I didn't give a shit about family honor. Can you understand that, Pop? Answer me. Can you understand that?"

The huge man with the white mane looked up at his daughter, his eyes filled with tears. With a voice so husky that it was barely intelligible, he spoke.

"Yes, I can understand that. Since you were babies you took care of him. Fought for him, lied for him. You know Peter better than any of us. That's why I chose you to find him and bring him home. You always knew how Peter thought, and the fact that you are an outstanding detective made me sure you could find him. I never gave one thought to the cruelty of it. For that I apologize. But if I had to do it over again, I still would choose you. Can you tell me the whole story now?"

Betty looked into her father's tortured face and nodded.

"I'm ready to tell you everything. Let's go into the other room and sit down. It's a long story and I want Frank next to me. It's his story too. He was with me every step of the way, almost from the beginning. He was the one who listened to his head instead of his heart."

So, Betty began the tale. She told of the long, exhausting hours she spent on the computer until she discovered Peter's new name, his escape plan, and a possible new face to go along with his new identity. She described the lucky break when a state trooper called in response to the APB, giving Peter's direction of travel. She told the policewoman's story of an anonymous person who came to her rescue in Buffalo and saved her life, and the encounter in a Buffalo restaurant when Peter embarrassed them by capturing them instead of the other way around. The big break came when she spotted a face on TV that she thought might be Peter's new companion. The hunch panned out and they were able to track Peter to Lake Stewart. Betty described in great detail of Peter's heroic actions to save the life of a little boy and his dog, which had paralyzed Frank Santini's son.

When Betty finished her story, she examined her father's face. He seemed to be in deep thought. His eyes had a faraway look that was non-committal. Betty didn't have a clue to what her father was thinking.

Without a word, he slowly stood up from the sofa, stretching to his full height, and left the room.

Frank Mullin looked at Betty's puzzled face and asked. "Well?"

Chapter Twenty-four

For the next three days Frank Santini was more of a ghost in the house than a presence. He could be seen from time to time going from one room to another or hanging up his coat after a long walk outdoors. He never participated in his daughter's wedding plans. The family's consensus was that a New Years Day wedding would be most convenient for all.

With so little time left, Anna And Betty were busy from morning to night, putting together and executing the plans for the wedding in a precise and efficient manner. The Pentagon couldn't have done a better job. Arrangements were completed with the parish priest, organist and a singer for the church. Dresses for Betty, Anna, Alice and her daughters were ordered, fitted and delivered.

Both Franks were always absent from the policy making sessions. Mullin by choice. Santini just ignored them.

Anna wanted to make the wedding reception at home, but Betty vetoed that proposal since Anna hadn't fully recovered from the monumental strain of the Christmas dinner. The leading caterer in the neighborhood was engaged, but with Anna and Betty supplying non-stop suggestions from dawn to dusk, the caterer was driven to the brink of retirement.

Christmas day at the Santini's went reasonably well. There was a minimum of arguing between the adult siblings. Betty carried out Peter's request by giving Marci a birthday gift and card from her father, plus a generous gift for Christmas. Betty also supplied gifts for Tess in Peter's name and, as an afterthought, one to Alice as well. This brought on a huge crying jag from Alice.

Because of Frank Santini, the subject of Peter was rarely brought up, but the gaiety usually supplied by Frank's boisterous personality was missing this year. There was no singing of carols around the piano, and even the children seemed more subdued. They spent most of the evening watching a tape of A Christmas Carol in another room instead of nagging and being punished by their parents.

Three days before the wedding, Frank Santini sought out his daughter and invited her to his little office in the basement where he had his photography room. This was the place her father spent most of his spare time, never inviting his children to participate in his hobby.

"Sit down, Betty, we have to discuss a few things," Frank said, as he paced back and forth in his tiny office. An un-lit cigar dangled from the corner of his mouth.

Betty's heart ached for her father as she saw the pain that was etched into his face. She noticed there were stains on his shirt and his white shock of hair, usually neat and trim, was uncombed. This was far from normal for the usually impeccable ex-sergeant.

"I'll come right to the point. After your wedding, are you going to bring Peter in?"

Betty looked into her father's eyes and saw a desperate, tortured soul. She knew her answer would add additional pain, but her mind was made up. "No, Papa. I will not bring Peter back. When he goes on trial, I'll be sitting right next to him, supporting him. Not on the side of the prosecution."

Betty's answer evoked a gasp from her father and she watched the color drain from his face. Unable to face his daughter with the next question, Frank Santini turned his back on her and asked,

"Is your decision irrevocable, or is there a slight chance you might change your mind?"

"Why me, Papa?" Betty cried as she jumped to her feet, and tried to turn his large bulk around to face her. She couldn't.

"Why me and not Michael or Jimmy?" she sobbed. "In fact, why not you? You have so much time on your hands. Besides, this means more to you than anybody." Betty waited for an answer but none came. She pounded her fists on her father's back and asked again as tears streamed down her cheeks. "Why not you, Papa, why not you?"

"Please, don't ask me that," Frank answered in an un-recognizable voice. "For the past few days I've been asking myself that same agonizing question, and I can't come up with an answer. So don't ask me, please, Betty." Frank turned and faced his daughter.

She was shocked by how much he seemed to have aged, but she was relentless. "Why not you, Papa. You have to answer me."

Frank stared at Betty, his mouth moving as if trying to formulate an answer. He grabbed Betty by the shoulders with his huge hands, hurting her. Finally he emitted an intelligible sound.

"Because I'm scared. I've gone over a possible encounter between me and my son and it always ends with a `what if.' What if he refuses to come with me? Do I physically pick up my crippled son and carry him away? Do I pull a gun on my own son and order him to come with me? Do I shoot him if all else fails? He's my son and I love him. So you see, I can't do it. It has to be one of you."

"No, Papa, we all love Peter. Let the state police handle the job. Then we can all sit in Peter's corner like a real family, with pride and unity."

"My father would turn over in his grave if he knew someone else was putting the collar on his grandson. No, no, it has to be a Santini or we'll wallow in shame forever."

"That's bullshit, Papa. You have more love for your dead father than you have for your living children. You --"

A ringing slap to the cheek interrupted Betty's criticism of her father, a slap with so much force that her knees buckled. Frank had to catch his slumping daughter and he crushed her to his chest.

"Oh, God, I'm so sorry, Honey. I didn't mean that. Please forgive me."

"Goddammit, Papa," Betty responded, as her dizziness ebbed. "I'm okay. I'm just mad as hell you never considered the possibility that Peter's shooting his partner might have been an accident. You completely forgot that for twenty-three years he was a great cop. Decorated at least ten times. And dammit, Papa," Betty said, sobbing uncontrollably, "Even on the run, he disregarded everything and risked his life to save a kid and his dog. That village will defend him to the last man, woman, and child. Can his family do less?" Betty felt the steel-like grip that held her, gradually loosen.

Her father gently pushed her aside, and as he left the room, he stared into her eyes and muttered under his breath, "My son is a pimp, that much we're sure of."

The next few days flew by. Anna and Betty were constantly busy rushing to the dressmaker or to the caterer, solving problems and minor emergencies. Frank Mullin found it hard to stay out of the way, but he succeeded. Frank Santini appeared now and then, looking like a man in a trance.

New Year's Eve came and the Santini household was quiet, somber, and sober. For better or worse, all the wedding chores were completed and exhaustion had set in. Frank Mullin and Betty sat on the couch, embracing and speaking quietly.

From time to time Frank would kiss Betty's hair, and she would scold him for messing her hairdo that cost so much at the beauty parlor. Anna was busy on the phone, issuing last minute instructions to family and friends. She wanted everyone there on time and sober, at noon on New Year's Day.

Late in the evening, Frank Santini brought out a tray with a bottle of champagne and four glasses. He invited Anna, Betty and Frank Mullin to join him in a toast for the new year. Anna started to protest but was cut short by a severe look from her husband. As the world watched the ball in Times Square start its slow descent, Santini popped the cork and filled the four glasses. He handed everyone a glass and held his high. His voice cracked with emotion as he made a toast.

"I'm asking God to bless this marriage between my beloved daughter Betty and Frank Mullin, as I bless them. Betty, my only daughter, has been the apple of my eye since she was a small, beautiful child. No father could be more proud of his daughter than I have been. She was always respectful of me and her mother, a good sister to her brothers. Maybe too good to her twin. When she became a police officer, I can't tell you how proud that made me. Even though I worried so for her safety. Every year brought her new honors, which meant new honors to this family. At this time, Betty, I beg your forgiveness for asking too much of you. As you pointed out, the task of finding your brother should have been my job. Now I toast you both, Betty and Frank, and have a lifetime of love and happiness. Happy New Year."

Everyone emptied their glass, and Anna looked suspiciously at her husband. His toast was a complete reversal of his actions the past week. Why? Betty finished her champagne and went to her father and hugged him.

"Don't feel bad that you sent me to find Peter. How else would I have met my Frank?"

"Does that mean you're going back to bring Peter home?"

"No, Papa. After our honeymoon, I'm going back to Buffalo to set up a home."

"I expected that. I'll only ask you to tell me where to find him. I'm going to bring him home myself."

"You mean *we* are going to Peter," Anna said in a loud, firm voice. "Whether we bring him back is another story."

"That's ridiculous," argued Santini. "You can't go on this trip. It may turn out nasty."

The discussion escalated into a real Italian argument with all four people talking loudly, at the same time. Mercifully, the telephone rang. Everyone stared at it as it continued to ring. At the sixth ring, Anna uttered an obscenity in Italian and rushed to the phone. All watched as she picked it up and spoke. The answer to her greeting caused her to clutch her heart and she began to softly sob.

"Happy New Year to you, too, my son."

Everyone in the room knew instantly that it was Peter.

"Tell me, my darling, how do you feel? How are you getting along?"

The answer on the other end was long and mostly encouraging, for Anna kept muttering "I see, I see," then a long delay. Then,

"Thank God for that." Another long delay, then, "I'll light a candle for you tomorrow, and may God watch over you. I'll see you soon."

Anna kept nodding her head as Peter ended the conversation. Then turned to Betty, offering her the phone. "Your brother wants to wish you luck on your wedding tomorrow."

Betty eagerly took the phone and excitedly spoke to her twin, as Anna took her husband's arm and led him into the kitchen. "Your son sent his love to you. But he said he wasn't strong enough to handle talking to you directly. He wished you a Happy New Year and congratulations on your daughter's wedding."

"I understand his not wanting to talk to me," Frank said sadly. "In his place, I wouldn't have the guts to speak to my father, either. By the way, how did he know when Betty was getting married?"

"He said Betty speaks to him every day. He laughed when he said you'd have a stroke when you got your next phone bill."

Chapter Twenty-five

Like a well planned military campaign, the Santini-Mullin wedding went off without a serious glitch. The bride was beautiful, her mother radiant, her brothers suitably drunk and the kids were predictably boisterous. The bridegroom was beaming with happiness. To fall in love at the advanced age of forty-nine, and have his beautiful bride love him was the fulfillment of his dreams and fantasies.

Alice came dressed in a stylish outfit that Anna bought her. She looked ravishing but sad as she sat with her celebrating sister-in-law. Frank Santini looked handsome in his new suit as he shook hands with all the guests, a smile never leaving his face. He was, however, uncharacteristically subdued and did very little drinking. Even his trademark cigar was missing. A close look would have revealed the sadness in his eyes.

"How is it possible to feel so happy and so sad at the same time?" Anna asked her husband as they danced together.

"I feel the same way. But I'm not smart enough to answer that," Santini whispered in his wife's ear.

Later, as Frank danced with his daughter, he held her close and felt pressure build up in his chest. His voice was barely audible above the loud music as he spoke to her. "Your mother and I are leaving tomorrow morning for Lake Stewart. How do I find Peter's place?"

"Oh, Pop, that's not a good idea," Betty answered, her face clouding with worry. "Peter is just starting to improve. To take him away from his treatments now would be devastating."

"I have no immediate plans to bring him back now. It's your mother. She feels he needs her now, and she has a great guilt that she's not there to take care of him."

"He has a woman living with him who loves him very much. She's extremely capable and might resent Mom butting in."

"Don't worry, your mother's a great negotiator. She'll work it out."

"Her name's Mary, and she's a Sicilian. Can you imagine two Sicilian women negotiating for power over one man? C'mon, Pop. I can't."

"Ha," Frank smiled, "It may turn out more interesting than I figured. You didn't tell me how to find Peter's house."

"Just look for a Mobil gas station at the North end of the lake. It's the only gas station on Lake Stewart."

"That makes it easy," Frank murmured, his voice trailing off with his thoughts.

"Somehow, I can't see Peter running a gas station, fixing flats and all."

"From what Mary told me, it's a successful venture. The shop is doing well. Mary started a small luncheonette that's doing well too. The village people helped them run the place when Peter was in the hospital. Now that he's home, a volunteer comes everyday to help out. Can you imagine your neighbors in New York City helping you if you were in trouble? You'd be damn lucky if even one family member came to help."

Frank's face flushed with guilt. Before he could comment on Betty's last remark, the music stopped and the dance was over. Betty was immediately surrounded by her friends and the touchy conversation with her father was over. Activities at the reception continued at a frenzied pace and, when it was over, Mr. and Mrs. Frank Mullin left for their honeymoon.

Frank Santini was alone now with his wife Anna to sort out their plan of action. Anna was solely concerned with Peter's health problems and refused to discuss his legal problems. Frank's plans were no longer clear and precise. His feelings as a father were starting to dilute his firm resolutions as caretaker of the family honor.

The Santini household, a day after the wedding, was extraordinarily quiet compared to all the excitement of the past week. Frank sat in his favorite chair, watching the late news on TV as he puffed on a cigar. Anna was upstairs packing. Not familiar with the winter weather in the Adirondacks, she decided to pack for every contingency. Even their length of stay was unknown. When Frank walked into the bedroom and saw four large suitcases sitting there, he nearly bit through his cigar.

"Jumpin' Jesus, Anna," he shouted. "Where the hell do you think we're going, the North Pole?"

"I heard it's very cold in the mountains in the winter. Besides I couldn't think of borrowing anything from that woman,"

Anna answered. "C'mon, help me close these suitcases. Make yourself useful for a change."

"Huh, you pack them. That's the easy part. I'm the one that has to lug them."

By eight o'clock the following morning, Frank and Anna were on the New York Thruway heading North. Frank was sipping coffee from a Thermos cup and driving with one hand, his mind deep in thought.

"How come you're only driving at fifty-five? Usually, I'm fighting with you to keep it under eighty."

Frank didn't answer her. He didn't understand it either. Could it be that he was reluctant to meet with his son, afraid of the outcome of such a meeting? The sight of his once powerful son reduced to a paralytic cripple wouldn't be easy to take. How would he explain to his eldest son that he was there to take him back to face a murder rap? What section of the Police Department's *Rules and Regulations or Manual of Procedure* covered this set of circumstances? He needed more time and belligerently gave the finger to every motorist that passed him with a blaring horn.

"I need more time," Frank muttered under his breath, as Anna gave him a puzzled look. "What do we do, just knock on his door and say, `We're here. Let us in or we'll blow your house down.' Suppose he slams the door in our faces and sends us away? What do we do then? Get in our car and go home? Don't you think it would be wiser if we stopped and called him to see if we'd be welcome?"

"*Estupida,*" Anna answered vehemently. "He's our son, our flesh and blood. We don't need an invitation. Is that floozy he's living with going to throw us out? I'd like to see her try! I'll scratch her eyes out."

Anna's fury built. A series of old, almost forgotten Italian curses flowed from her mouth, as tears streamed down her cheeks.

"I'm his Mama, dammit. No one has the right to stop me from seeing my son," Anna shouted.

"Take it easy," Frank said, as a rare grin appeared on his face. "You're getting yourself pissed off at this woman and you don't know her, or even have an idea of what she's like. Betty liked her."

Anna crossed her arms on her chest and vented her anger. "Peter never needed me as a child. He was weak, hung out with trash and was always in trouble. Betty fought his battles and saved his ass many times. I don't know how she kept him out of jail. He never came to me, did you help him much?"

Frank was slow to answer. "No, but the truth of the matter is I never encouraged his confidence. I was always mad at him. I let Betty handle him. Maybe the trouble he's in today is partly my fault. The only help I've ever given him, was using my influence to get him on the Job." "Well, he was a chip off the old block once he got on the Job. Maybe it was in his genes, but he made some dandy arrests. He was accepted in the Honor Legion his first year on the Job. I was so proud of him."

"When did he go wrong?" Frank asked.

"It all started when he married that Irisher. After Tess and Marci were born, she closed her legs to him. She took that stuff the priests were handing out too literally. Italian women were too smart or too hot-blooded to fall for that. Alice drove him into the streets at night to find what she denied him. Can you blame him for that?"

"I can't blame him for wanting to get laid once in a while. But starting a whorehouse and selling drugs was a sin and an insult to our family and to the Job . Maybe that's why God punished him by paralyzing him," Frank said, almost in a whisper.

"Shame on you for saying that, you bastard."

Silence prevailed for a long time in the car, as both parents were deep in thought. Anna glanced at the speedometer and saw that Frank was now driving at fifty.

"Why are you driving so slowly?" Anna asked softly, startling Frank.

"I'm admiring the beautiful scenery," Frank stammered, "We should really get out of the city more often."

"Well, speed it up a little," Anna urged, "I'm really anxious to get there. I know my son needs me."

Frank's foot felt like lead when he tried to depress the accelerator. It felt as if the pedal was pushing back at him. The sound of the engine was mocking him. He could hear it or feel it confronting him.

"You're a hypocrite," it seemed to be saying. "Are you going to your son as a grieving father or a pursuing policeman? You're a phoney, you're a phoney," the tires sang in Frank's head as they rhythmically hit the expansion joints in the road.

No matter how reluctantly Frank drove, time ate up the miles and at a little after one o'clock, they arrived at the southern end of Lake Stewart. The Santinis had to make a choice, for the road split into two roads, West Shore and East Shore. They didn't know on which side of the lake their son's gas station was.

Frank pulled over to the side of the road and parked. He fished in his pockets, looking for a slip of paper and, after much effort, finally found it. He read it to Anna. "He goes by the name of Robert Russo. His woman's name is Mary. Don't forget it, Anna."

About fifty yards away, Frank noticed a young man romping in the snow with two small children. Frank left the car and approached the man.

"Could you kindly direct me to a gas station?" Frank asked. Frank remembered Betty telling him that Peter's gas station was the only one on the lake. He figured a resident would more likely give him information of the whereabouts of a gas station than a person. He was unaware of how thoroughly the residents of Lake Stewart were instructed not to give information to strangers about Robert Russo or his location.

"Well," the man drawled, "There are gas stations in Fort Edward, Hudson Falls or Lake George. Just keep headin' North."

"I was given to understand there was a gas station somewhere on the lake," Frank added, hopefully.

"Then you don't need my help," the man responded with a sneer as he turned his back on Frank and resumed romping with his children.

"Can you at least tell me if it's on the east side of the lake or the west side?" Frank called after the man.

The man's answer was complete silence.

"Rude son of a bitch," Frank said, as he got back into the car, shivering. "In the city, people will always give you information, even if it's wrong."

Anna studied the map, carefully tracing the road around the lake. "East Lake Road continues around the north side of the lake and circles around, becoming West Lake Road. So it doesn't matter which side you choose."

Frank chose the West Lake Road and drove slowly, admiring the breathtaking scenery of the lake cradled among snow covered mountains. Most of the houses along the shoreline could have served as models for a Currier and Ives print. Frank also noticed how cleanly West Lake Road was plowed. There wasn't a trace of snow, slush or ice on the roadway or shoulders, yet the snow on the banks remained pure white.

"Move it," Anna urged, "We're so close and I'm anxious to see Peter.

Anna's voice brought Frank out of his daydreams and her words seemed to register on his mind in slow motion.

"Take it easy," Frank answered. "The sight of your son may shock you. Remember, he's a paraplegic."

"My son? He's our son, Frank. Even though you've disowned him in your mind. A man can't abandon his own flesh and blood," Anna said as her eyes scanned her husband's face.

A certain look appeared on Frank's face. The look lingered a while, then disappeared as Frank changed the subject. "We just passed a sign advertising the Northside Deli. Do you want to stop for lunch?"

"No," Anna answered, visibly agitated. "Let's get to Peter as soon as possible."

A few minutes later, a tall pole with the familiar Mobil sign on top came into view. Frank drove onto the station and stopped at the gas pumps.

A cheery voice came over a speaker at the pumps. "Gas is self-service, but come on inside. We have hot food to warm you."

"Go on inside. I'll fill the tank," Frank said wistfully, trying to delay the meeting with his son as long as possible.

"You don't need gas, you coward," Anna hissed. "You've got more than half a tank. Come in with me."

Frank put his arm around Anna in a rare show of affection as they walked across the snow packed surface of the gas station toward the luncheonette.

"Boy, it's cold as a witch's tit," Frank mumbled under his breath.

"What? What did you say?" Anna questioned.

"Nothing. Just complaining about the cold."

Frank opened the door and they were greeted by a feeling of warmth and a nice smell of cooking food.

"Welcome to Mary's Place," a robust, smiling woman said. Her swarthy complexion, very similar to Anna's, easily identified her as being of Sicilian extraction.

"Won't you please take a seat?"

"No, I'm afraid not," Anna answered curtly, "We've come to see Peter. We're his parents."

The smile was wiped clean from Mary's face and a look of fear replaced it. She started to extend her hand in greeting, but seeing no encouragement in the faces looking at her, quickly withdrew it. "I'll make a call and get somebody over here to take care of the place, then I'll take you over to the house to see your son," Mary said respectfully.

"Oh, we don't want to bother you. Just point out the way and we'll go ourselves," Anna said coldly.

"It's no bother at all," Mary answered, as her Sicilian temper started to show itself.

Frank, recognizing the signs of two hot-blooded women sizing each other up, stepped in between them. Forcing a smile, he said,

"Oh, we'd be happy to wait, Mary."

Mary calmed a bit and smoothed her hair with her hand. Forcing a smile, she said, "Please sit down and have a cup of coffee."

"Only if you join us," Frank said in his best negotiating manner.

Frank and Anna sat at one of the small tables as Mary made her phone call. Then she filled a platter with her homemade pastries and put them on a tray with three cups of coffee. She carried the tray to the table. Mary sat down and unconsciously brushed her hair back with her hand, a nervous habit whenever she was uptight.

"I'm Mary Russo. Peter and I've been living together for the past six months. I want you to know from the start that I love him more than life itself, and I'll fight anyone -- and I mean anyone who tries to harm him in any way."

Anna was taken back by the passion in Mary's voice and in her face. She looked this woman over very carefully. Mary had a pleasant face but was certainly not a beauty like Peter's wife, Alice. And she was obviously several years older than Peter, and saying that she was buxom and full-figured, was being kind. But the love Mary had for Peter was clearly written in her eyes.

"This is a very nice luncheonette you have here," Frank said, making conversation.

"Thank you," Mary answered, with a note of pride in her voice. "I've put a lot of effort in here just as Peter has put a lot of effort into the shop over there. We're both doing well, and we're making a comfortable living."

"I can't picture Peter as a mechanic. As a boy, he couldn't fix his own rollerskates," Frank commented with a smile.

"Well, he was learning very fast. Before his accident, he did all the minor repairs. Our mechanic did all the big stuff. Peter did all the tow car runs," Mary answered, proudly.

To emphasize Mary's remarks, a loud hammering was heard from the shop area.

"Since Peter's accident, the village people have volunteered to help us run this place. I don't know what we'd have done without them," Mary said, her voice cracking.

"Yeah, Betty told us," Frank said as he nibbled on one of the pastries. "Hey, this is delicious."

"Thank you," Mary said, "It's homemade."

"How do you find the time?" Anna asked.

"Oh, I keep to a tight schedule. I take Peter to Glens Falls twice a day for his treatments and run this place. In between, I clean, cook and bake. I'm busy from early morning to late at night."

"You make it sound so simple, and I'm sure it isn't. I remember taking care of the house while I was raising twins. It wasn't easy doing the shopping, cooking and cleaning while diapering and feeding two babies. Sometimes, I forgot which one I fed. It was exhausting. I admire you," Anna said reluctantly.

"I've never been happier," Mary said as she made eye contact with Anna.

Anna nodded, getting the message.

Frank, trying to change the subject, asked as he bit off the end of a cigar, "Mind if I smoke?"

"Yes, I do," Mary answered firmly, pointing to a sign that thanked everyone for not smoking.

Frank, embarrassed at being rebuffed, tried stuffing the cigar back into its box, but broke it. He cursed under his breath.

"I'm sorry," Mary said, as a trace of a smile brightened her face.

Anna smiled, too, as she whispered to herself, "This is a woman to be reckoned with."

The door of the luncheonette opened and a blast of cold air bathed everyone. A middle-aged woman, dressed in jeans and a parka, burst into the shop. "I dropped everything and came right over," she said breathlessly.

"Thanks, Martha, I appreciate this," Mary answered. Without introducing anyone, Mary rose and invited the Santinis to follow her.

She donned a parka similar to Martha's and led the Santinis out the back door. She followed a shoveled path from the gas station to the house. Anna was surprised to see such a large, stately house hidden from the road. Once on the porch, Mary brushed the bottom of her shoes vigorously on a mat, wordlessly setting the example for Frank and Anna to follow. She opened the door and led the Santinis into a world of sparkling, high polished floors, gleaming, massive furniture, and a dazzling, huge kitchen. The Santinis stood speechless, but with their mouths open as they gazed at their surroundings.

"Be it ever so humble, it's our home," Mary said as she scanned their faces for approval.

"For just the two of you?" Anna asked in wonderment.

"Yes," Mary answered, "We saw it, liked it, and the woman made us an offer we couldn't resist."

"This house is magnificent. I've never seen anything like it," Anna said with honest admiration.

"That's some staircase," Frank commented. "I'm sure Peter can't get up there."

"You're right. We made Peter's study into a temporary bedroom."

"A study? That's impressive. I was never in a house that had a study. What the hell is a study?" Frank's voice boomed.

"It's sort of an office and library combined," Mary explained as she led them toward the rear of the house. "Robert -- I mean Peter -- is probably sleeping now. He gets knocked out from his morning therapy. I'll check." Mary opened the door to the study and found Peter sitting up in the rented hospital bed, rubbing his eyes.

"Hi," Peter greeted her. "I could have sworn I heard my father's voice echoing through the house. It must've been a dream."

"You weren't dreaming, Honey. Here's your mother and father," Mary said in a voice tinged with fear as she pointed toward the door.

The color drained from Peter's face. He held up his hand like he was directing traffic and yelled, "wait," with such vehemence that everyone stopped dead in their tracks.

"What?" Mary asked, her eyes pleading with Peter.

"I don't want them to see me like this. Tell them to wait a few minutes while I get dressed. Take them inside," he ordered.

"Do you want me to help you?"

"No, Goddammit, I'll do it myself."

"OKay, oKay," Mary answered, fighting back tears. When she left the room she slammed the door as hard as she could.

Peter reached down and grabbed his legs, and with a Herculean effort lifted them over the side of the bed. He reached for his walker, one of the newest types that had wheels and hand brakes. Peter struggled to a standing position with most of his weight on his arms. He manipulated his walker to the commode where he relieved himself, thankful that he was no longer in diapers and felt more like a man. Then he maneuvered his walker to the chair on which his pants and shirt were neatly folded.

With great difficulty he managed to seat himself on the chair and began the battle to dress himself. After an exhausting effort, Peter was dressed in a casual tan shirt and tan Dockers. He managed to get his feet into a pair of slippers.

Almost worn out from his effort, Peter smiled in triumph, proud of his accomplishment. For the first time since his accident, he peed by himself and dressed himself. He struggled to his feet, grabbed his walker and propelled himself across the room to a wheelchair. He transfered his weight from the walker to the wheelchair with relative ease, using his upper body strength. He wheeled himself out of the study, through the foyer and stopped at the entrance to the living room. Peter observed his mother and father seated on the massive antique couch, and Mary, on the other side of the room, seated in a deep armchair. His parents were the first guests ever invited into this room and he felt suddenly choked up.

"Welcome to our home," Peter said, straining to keep his voice under control. "Mom and Pop, thank you for coming."

Anna jumped to her feet and literally ran across the large room, knelt in front of Peter and hugged him.

"Oh, my darling Peter," she cried. "It's been so, so long since I saw you. My God, you're so thin. Doesn't she feed you? How do you feel? How can I help you?"

"Jesus, Mom, one question at a time."

Frank followed Anna across the room and awkwardly extended his hand to Peter. "How are you, son?" he asked in a hesitant voice.

Peter took his hand and squeezed with all his might, forever in competition with his powerful father. Secretly, he always felt his father was toying with him, and exerted only enough pressure to make the encounter interesting.

"Hiya Pop," Peter said, almost in a whisper. "I'm coming along real well. In no time, I'll be up and running."

"Your running days are over, Peter," his father said sadly.

"Don't be too sure, Pop. You always underestimated me."

"Maybe so, but one thing's for sure, I never understood you."

Mary, feeling the tension mounting between father and son, stepped between them and pushed Peter's wheelchair close to the couch. "Mr. and Mrs. Santini, please sit down and talk to Peter while I prepare lunch. You both must be starved after your long trip."

"Oh, don't bother," Anna was quick to answer.

"It's no bother at all," Mary said sternly, "According to my Italian up-bringing, it's a necessity."

Mary laid out the ground rules and Anna was quick to acknowledge them. Tradition would govern their behavior and Anna knew she was on foreign turf.

"In that case, allow me to help you," Anna replied.

"Of course," Mary answered, nodding at Anna, but with cold eyes, realizing that Peter's mother would be a strong adversary and that she would have to be careful to maintain a strong position and not lose ground to this wise old woman. The two women left for the kitchen.

Peter was very uncomfortable to be alone in his father's presence. They never had a warm relationship. When Peter was growing up, his father spent his spare time with his photography. Peter was never invited to observe or participate.

Small talk always involved talk of the Job, mostly glorifying his father's or grandfather's experiences. It was always taken for granted that Peter would follow in their footsteps and join the police force as soon as he was old enough. Sometimes, Peter had resented the fact that it seemed he had no choice in the matter, but he went with the flow as if it was his only destiny.

When he joined the force, he did extremely well. He was never really a rookie, for in his mind and heart, he was always a cop. But his father was always there, forever the sergeant, forever criticizing, forever advising. Never a good word for jobs well done. That was expected. But plenty of criticism at other times. They were on the force thirteen years together, until Frank retired. During that time, Peter was always in his father's shadow, or in his twin sister's. Although he was more prominent than his younger brothers, he never assumed the role of top gun in the family. And once in a while he had a little twinge of jealousy toward his sister, who had become a shining star in the detective division.

Peter squirmed in his wheelchair, sure of the inevitable lecture, the condemnation for his misdeeds. He couldn't look his father in the eye, for his guilt gnawed at his very soul. His father's voice shocked him back to reality.

"Is there something I can do for you, Peter?" his father asked softly, with a heavy heart.

"No, Pop, I'm oKay," Peter stammered. "Physically, it's all in God's hands."

"Maybe I can help with the gas station. Pump gas, run for parts, anything. I've got plenty of time since I retired."

"Thanks, anyway, but everything's under control. I have a really dependable guy running the shop, and the neighbors volunteer to help run the gas station and Mary's luncheonette."

"How about money?" Frank asked hesitantly. "I can spare a few bucks."

"No, Pop, I don't need it. Our business here is doing well, but thanks, anyway."

Frank was disappointed. His son wouldn't let him in, even a little bit. He knew that he would be hated when the time came for him to take his own son back to face the entire world for his crimes. An embarrassing silence followed as father and son stared at one another. Frank knew that there was so much that had to be said, though he hadn't the guts to start. The rattle of dishes from the kitchen was the only sound heard. A deep sigh escaped from Peter.

"There is something, Pop. It's laying heavy on my heart. It's about Alice and my kids. I worry about them, whether they have enough money to live on. I couldn't send them any without giving myself away."

"If that's all that's bothering you, you can stop worrying. They're all right," Frank answered with contempt in his voice.

"How? I mean who?" Peter stammered.

"Me. Your family, and even the guys from your precinct took up a collection. A lot of people care. We wouldn't let them down. It wasn't their fault you turned out to be a... a... Jesus, I don't know what to call you."

Peter's head dropped, his chin on his chest. When he finally raised his head to speak, there were tears in his eyes. He started to speak but was interrupted by an angry, authoritative voice.

"Enough," Mary bellowed, her hands on her hips. "Did you come here to destroy him just when he showed signs of getting better? He doesn't need to be torn down after we worked so hard to build him up."

"It's all right," Peter said softly. I asked him a question, a favor and he answered it. He didn't do anything."

"Okay, Okay," Mary said, as she walked behind Peter's chair. "Let's go into the kitchen. Lunch is ready."

They ate in silence. Anna looked around the kitchen in awe. There was every gadget the high-tech world could produce. The white European cabinets glistened, and so did the white tiled floor. "Your home is really beautiful," she said with a little bit of envy.

"It's our home, Peter's and mine," Mary answered, searching Anna's face for some hidden meaning. Then she trembled. The pressure in her chest expanded, and she felt she was going to explode. Mary couldn't breathe and her eyes widened in panic. She fought a nausea, looking as if she would bring up the lunch she had been eating.

"Excuse me, I'm going to be sick," Mary said, clutching her mouth with both hands as she ran from the kitchen.

Peter followed her in his wheelchair to the bathroom, just off the laundry room. He tried to enter but Mary had locked the door. He could hear her retching so severely that he became frightened. Peter never heard a more pathetic sound and he needed to help her. He pounded on the door and shouted, "Mary, open this door, let me help you."

She answered with the sound of more retching and gagging. Gradually, the retching subsided, and was replaced by the sound of pitiful, heart-rendering sobs.

"Mary, Goddammit, open this door," Peter yelled, pounding on the door.

"Go away," she answered weakly, "Leave me a little dignity."

Peter slowly wheeled his chair back to the kitchen and looked at his bewildered parents. "I don't know what happened to her," he mumbled apologetically. "If I live to be a hundred, I'll never understand women."

"Huh, you're finally wising up," Frank said with a trace of a smile on his lips.

"I can't believe men are so stupid," Anna hissed. "Stupid and heartless."

Peter looked shocked at his mother's outburst, but his father threw his hands skyward.

Anna walked into the hall, deliberating whether to go after Mary. Turning to Peter she said, "The poor woman. What she must have gone through with you the past few months. All alone, not knowing what God had in store for the two of you. Does she have any family?"

"Two married daughters she rarely speaks to. But they live far away and don't know what's going on. She has a couple of brothers in Buffalo, but the Mafia won't let them associate with her. But that's another story," Peter said as his voice faded away and his thoughts wandered.

After a while, an embarrassed Mary came back into the kitchen. Peter and his father were sipping a third cup of coffee. Anna got up from the table and approached the distraught woman. She reached out with her hands and took Mary back to the table.

Anna had a warm, sympathetic look on her face that somehow transmitted a feeling of fellowship to Mary, who returned a look of gratitude. Anna was acting on instinct, her heart overruling her mind. She obviously had a need to become this sad woman's friend, to show her appreciation for what this woman did for her son.

"I want to thank you," Anna stammered, but Mary instantly cut her short.

"Please don't thank me, Mrs. Santini. What I did for Peter, I did for myself. You see, I love him more than life itself. My first husband was murdered in front of my eyes and my house trashed. For five years, I didn't care if I lived or died. My children were married and had moved away. I had no one. I turned my house into a rooming house just to have people around me. When Peter came into my life, I felt re-born. I grew to love him dearly, and I was grateful for a second chance at happiness. I don't care what he's charged with. My heart tells me this man couldn't kill anyone. His paralysis is the badge he wears for his goodness."

Tears filled Anna's eyes as she stretched her arms out to Mary and the two women embraced. Anna had never felt a closeness to Alice in all the years she was married to her son. But in a short time, Mary had won Anna's respect and a feeling she couldn't yet define.

"Show me the rest of the house. I'm dying to see it," Anna said, embarrassed by her show of emotion to this stranger.

Mary led Anna away, leaving father and son alone in the kitchen, both sipping coffee, both on opposite sides of the table, deep in thought about ways to make some sense out of their relationship.

Later that night, Anna and Frank lay awake talking in bed. They were warm and cozy in the antique bed on the third floor of the stately house. Words came hard between them, a new and unpleasant feeling, after forty-six years of a good marriage. Their attitudes toward the strange predicament they found themselves in were worlds apart.

Anna's feelings were a mother's concern for her injured son and had definite priorities. First, her prayers were for a complete physical recovery, and second for a complete vindication of the charges against him.

Frank, in contrast, chafed under the stigma that this son brought on his family's reputation. It was in his power to bring him to justice and prove to the world his family's strength. He felt so strongly that if a Santini brought in this rogue cop, the family's honor would be restored. This feeling was stronger than a father's concern for his son's health and welfare. When Frank outlined his intentions to Anna, they were met with instantaneous rejections.

"You'll do nothing," Anna hissed. "We've come here to help and that's what we're going to do. Your honor will have to wait until our son gets more treatment and a whole lot stronger.

"It's something I just have to do," Frank said sadly.

"What kind of a monster are you?' Anna sobbed, as she pounded her fists on her husband's chest. "Don't you have even an animal's concern for its young? You're a freak. It's unnatural."

"Stop it, Anna," Frank exclaimed, as he caught her fists, "Don't get hysterical. Okay, okay, I'll wait a few weeks. But I'm not going to let him get strong enough to run again, or we'll be back to square one."

"You're all heart, Frank," Anna said as she turned away from him and covered her head with a pillow.

Chapter Twenty-six

A month passed, and during that time it was Frank Santini who drove his son to the Glens Falls Hospital twice each day. He watched as Dr. Levy and his therapists worked diligently on Peter with the passive range of motion exercises. It was with some degree of pride when he saw Peter advance to the active range of motion exercises. He smiled the day he heard Peter plead with the therapist to extend the session because he was making so much progress. It was into Frank's arms that Peter first walked without the aid of a walker.

But in a way, it saddened Frank because he knew the time was swiftly approaching when he would have to take Peter back to New York City. During the past month, he spent more quality time with his son than anytime in his life. He never realized the fine qualities Peter possessed, and secretly felt proud of him.

Another month passed, and on a sunny morning in the beginning of March, there was a hint of spring in the air. A warm breeze blew, and the ground was wet with melting snow. There was mud everywhere, especially on all the cars pulling up at the station for gas. When Frank drove Peter to the hospital for his treatment, he saw farmers working on their tractors. Some were bare-chested, for God's sake. The temperature was still in the high thirties and Frank was thankful for his heavy jacket. But these farmers, who were accustomed to much colder temperatures, were anxious to get on with their spring chores.

Peter had graduated from the hospital to a rehabilitation center. He soon became a star. Never had a patient responded so positively to their treatments. Peter's walker was now history. He walked everywhere, sometimes with a cane, mostly without. He swam like a fish for an hour daily and doubled the required time on all his exercises. Frank watched with pride but felt a deep sadness. He couldn't put it off any longer.

After lunch, father and son sat in Peter's study, watching CNN on the TV. Frank took a deep breath, then told his son of his intentions. Peter struggled to his feet and looked at his father with disbelief.

"Are you fucking crazy?" he screamed. "You're not taking me anywhere. You never even asked me if I was guilty, or even for my side of the story. Why should I go with you?"

"Because a Santini has to be the one to bring you in," Frank shouted back.

"Why?" Peter asked, a bewildered look on his face.

"For the honor of the Santini family. For years, the Italians have fought for equality with the Irish on the Job, and the Santini Family was a force to be reckoned with. We built a legend to equal any Irish family for the past hundred years. Until you ruined our reputation. With four children on the Job, it has to be me to take you in. Can't you understand that?" Frank pleaded.

"That's bullshit, Pop. Your place is by my side, and I'll decide when I'm going in -- if I'm going in," Peter shouted.

Anna and Mary, frightened by the shouting, hurried to the study. They opened the door and witnessed father and son in adversarial positions, nose to nose. Anna ran between them and pushed her husband away. Mary helped Peter to a chair and made him sit on it. Peter's face was scarlet with rage.

"I think it's time for you and Mom to go home," Peter shouted at his father. "I want you out of here today!"

"Please, Peter. Don't talk like that," Mary pleaded.

"Shut the fuck up, Mary. I want them gone, do you hear me?"

"I'm not leaving without you. Even if I have to take you by force," Frank shouted at his son.

"What are you going to do if I won't go? Shoot me?"

"Goddamn right," the angry father shouted as he pulled his Police Special revolver from its holster. "You're coming with me, one way or another."

Mary knelt in front of Peter, clutching his legs. With a voice cracking with emotion, she cried out, "I had one husband shot and killed in front of my eyes. I can't go through this again. Why don't you leave us alone?"

Hearing this, Anna flew at her husband and attacked him with such a fury that he stumbled backward, accidentally discharging a round from his revolver. The errant bullet struck Mary in the back of her head and she slumped in Peter's lap.

Peter screamed her name as he raised her head and saw the lifeless eyes, frozen forever with a look of fear. He cradled her head in his arms as he rocked her back and forth, her blood turning his arms crimson. A pitiful gurgle escaped from his throat as he wept.

The odor of burnt gunpowder permeated the room, as Anna and Frank, embracing, stared at the pitiful sight of their son hugging the lifeless head of his beloved. They were both ashen white, shocked beyond comprehension.

Frank dropped the gun in a reflex motion, as if it was hot and burned his hand. He tried to say something to his son but only a sob escaped from his throat.

Peter watched his father's agonized face and with tears running down his face said, "See how easy it is, Pop. With almost no effort at all, the honorable Santini family now has two killers. What're you going to do now, Pop, run? Maybe the Santinis will have two cops on the run. Maybe, we can run together. What do you say, Pop?"

Anna sank to her knees. Her agonized shrieks filled the room as she beat her chest with her fists.

Frank Santini felt he was going to be sick. He ran from the house, across the porch, and down the steps and heaved his guts out in the bushes. Coatless, he shivered as he stumbled toward his parked car. The sound of the shot was still echoing in his ears and he felt that his brain would explode. He had to think, to sort things out, but he knew he couldn't think here. He reached in his pocket for his car keys and like a zombie in a trance, got in his car and drove away.

Frank drove aimlessly, and had no idea where he was. He maneuvered his car down treacherous mountain roads, his reflexes so slow, he barely managed to make the hairpin turns. He found himself in Glens Falls and followed the signs to Interstate 87. Maybe he could think on that highway and straighten out the mess in his head. Still shivering, he turned the heater on high and found the north entrance to I-87. After two hours of driving, his mind was still a blank, but he was shocked back to reality when he read signs depicting the mileage to Montreal.

"That's it," his mind screamed, "A few days in Canada will straighten me out. I'll have the time to think and decide what to do."

Thus, with his destination decided upon, his foot lay heavy on the gas pedal. He cursed out loud when he heard the whine of a siren, and saw blue lights flashing in his rear view mirror. He felt his heart pound as the state trooper directed him off the road and onto the shoulder. Frank started trembling with fear. Could Peter have sent the state police to apprehend him? He reached for his gun but his holster was empty. Maybe he was only being stopped for speeding. He had his shield with him. It always worked before. He could certainly talk his way out of a summons.

Frank Santini drove up onto the shoulder of the road and shut off his engine. An amplified voice ordered him out of the car and told him to face the car with his feet spread. That was embarrassing for a man who spent thirty-five years on the Job, but he complied. For the first time in his life he was the searchee, not the searcher, and felt the indignity of it. Then he was ordered to turn around.

"Where's the gun that belongs in your holster," the trooper questioned.

The voice sounded very familiar, shockingly so. When Frank Santini looked at the face of the state trooper, he felt a severe pain in his chest and felt himself blacking out.

He heard voices, so Frank Santini opened his eyes. The fog started to clear out of his brain. He glanced around and recognized that he was in a hospital. There was this thing blowing oxygen into his nose, and an IV was hooked up to his left wrist. He choked, and the sound from his throat alerted a tall nurse who came over and grabbed his right wrist and took his pulse.

"Welcome to the land of the living," she said sweetly. "Can you understand me, Frank?"

They know my name, thought Frank. I better play it dumb till I find out what they really know.

Frank stared blankly at the nurse, not answering.

"C'mon Frank, we know your pedigree from the papers in your wallet, and we know you're a retired cop. But we don't have anybody to notify. You know the routine."

Frank answered with a blank look. Suddenly the face of the trooper jumped into his mind and curiosity overcame his decision to keep still.

"Who brought me here?" he whispered.

"A state trooper," the nurse answered. "He also left you a present, a summons for driving seventy-five miles an hour."

"Where is he?" Frank whispered with trepidation.

"Back on patrol, I guess. He brought you in three hours ago. By the way, my name is Nancy. You can call me by pressing the button pinned to your pillow. I'm going to call your cardiologist now, so get some more rest."

In Lake Stewart, the weather changed abruptly, like the mood in the Russo household. From the beautiful spring-like day, it darkened considerably and a cold brisk wind blew from the north. It looked and felt like snow was inevitable. Inside the Russo home, Anna and Peter struggled to put Mary's heavy body on Peter's hospital bed. Peter knelt beside the bed and embraced Mary's lifeless form and cried bitterly.

"Why'd this happen, Mama? For the first time in my life I was truly happy. Now I'm responsible for her death. I have nothing to live for."

"Don't talk like that, Peter. You have two wonderful daughters who love you very much and who need you. Live for them, Peter, and for me too. Your Papa's going to need you now."

"Me? The son of a bitch wanted to take me in and wound up killing the only woman I truly loved. He needs me? I hope he rots in hell."

"Don't say that. You know it was an accident. He held the gun but I was the one that made him shoot it. Please don't blame him."

"Bullshit. If he didn't pull that gun, Mary would still be alive. A cop is always responsible every time he pulls his weapon. My partner would still be alive today if he didn't pull his gun. His shot was an accident too, but it killed him, not me."

What're you going to do now, Peter?"

"What do you mean, Mama?"

"Mary's dead, your father ran, we have to call somebody. Do you want to get away first? Tell me how much time you need."

"I'm through running, Mama. I'll call the sheriff. He's a good friend of mine."

Charlie Templeton, Sheriff of Lincoln County, acknowledged Peter's request and came to the house without siren or flashing lights. It seemed like a social call. He had come to check on Peter's recovery several times before. Charlie listened patiently as Robert Russo revealed his true identity as Peter Santini, a police officer on the run, an alleged felon. Peter described all the facts leading up to the current tragedy.

"Jesus, you've been one gigantic pimple on my ass since you settled here. My life was much simpler before. Now Lake Stewart and Lincoln County will never be the same."

Peter said sadly, "By arresting me, you'll become a national celebrity. You'll probably run for governor or congress, but it comes with a price tag. Before any part of my story becomes public, I want you to promise me that my father will be found first, and the reason for his search will be kept out of the media."

"C'mon, you're asking for a miracle. What can I use as a reason for the search?"

"Use the missing person routine. You know, retired police sergeant, possible Alzheimer victim. It warrants an APB. Please, Charlie, don't book me till we find my father. I promise I won't run. I'm begging you."

"You don't have to beg me. In my book you deserve any favor you ask. Give me the information on your father and his car."

"My mother can help you. She has a picture of my father. I've got calls to make to my brothers and sister."

"Okay," the sheriff said, as he sympathetically patted Peter on the back,

"You have my condolences. Mary was loved by everybody in Lake Stewart."

"Thanks, Charlie, "Peter whispered, as his eyes filled with tears.

"Don't worry about the arrangements. I'll stop in to see the mortician. His family's been serving the people of Lake Stewart for generations."

"Thanks again, Sheriff. You're a real pal," Peter said, as he shook the man's hand.

By 10:30 that night, Michael and Jimmy had arrived at Peter's home and Betty and Frank Mullin were on their way. Anna, heavily sedated, was sitting in the living room with a faraway expression on her face. Peter was holding up with the aid of Jack Daniels, a long forgotten friend. He wobbled when he walked and found it safer sitting down. The reunion with his kid-brothers was emotional, but the wishes of sympathy from them wore a bit thin, since neither had ever met Mary. Peter longed for Betty to arrive, for it was in times of severe stress that he depended on her the most. He had to stop drinking, the JD was lousing up his walking, and even more, his thinking. The grief he felt for Mary was overwhelming. She took the bullet that was meant for him. How would he ever live with that? He couldn't decide whether to wait for morning to notify Mary's daughters or to do it now, so late at night. Betty would know the right thing to do. He'd wait for her before deciding.

"Mary, Mary, Mary," Peter mumbled out loud, "How am I going to live without you? I didn't tell you enough how much I loved you. Please listen to me now. I hope they send me to prison for life. I don't deserve to live."

Peter wallowed in his grief for hours, and everyone left him alone. Jimmy Campbell, the mortician, had arrived about midnight with Dr. Curtis, the county coroner, and removed Mary's body. By one o'clock, Anna, Michael and Jimmy were all asleep in the living room, while Peter sat alone in the kitchen.

His mind bounced like a tennis ball-- from the wonderful, private times Mary and he had together to the times she had nursed him so lovingly after his tragic accident. He thought of the happiness they had with their new life, their wonderful house, Mary's success with the luncheonette. All gone now, completely destroyed by a single shot from a pistol.

A gentle knocking on the back door brought him back to reality. He looked at the clock on the wall and it read 2:15. Peter struggled to his feet and shuffled to the back door. To his relief, he recognized Betty and Frank. He opened the door and fell into his sister's arms. The dam of his grief opened and the sobs came pouring out.

Betty's strength prevailed and she took over as head of the family, the decision maker. Early in the morning, Peter notified Mary's daughters of their mother's death.

He was shocked to hear they wanted their mother's body shipped back to Buffalo, and that he had no say in the matter since he was not her legal spouse. Anna refused another tranquilizer, and took over Mary's kitchen. She regained some of her strength by preparing breakfast for all of her children. While everyone was seated at the kitchen table, the front doorbell rang. Peter admitted Sheriff Templeton and invited him to join the family for breakfast and he accepted.

Seated at the table, the sheriff made his shocking announcement: "I've got good news and bad news. The good news is that we found Frank Santini."

At first all the faces brightened, but then quickly turned apprehensive, waiting for the second shoe to fall.

"I sent out an APB for a missing person late last night. Early this morning I received a phone call from a state trooper named Scott Andrews, from the Plattsburg Barracks. He told me Frank Santini was pulled over for speeding on the Northway, and during his interrogation and search, Mr. Santini suffered a heart attack. Trooper Andrews put him in his patrol car and drove him to the hospital in Plattsburg. He called for a tow car to remove Mr. Santini's car to the Plattsburg Barracks. Your father is now in the Cardiac Care Unit at the hospital and his condition is now listed as serious but not life threatening. After I get a warrant, I will be going to Plattsburg to place him under arrest. Anybody here's welcome to come with me."

Utter silence followed Sheriff Templeton's announcement for several minutes. Finally Peter cleared his throat and asked,

"Does that mean my father's well enough to travel?"

"No. But he will be put under guard around the clock, until he is well enough to be brought back to Lincoln County to be booked."

Anna began to weep and Betty got up to comfort her.

"Is there a Catholic Church nearby?" Anna asked, tearfully.

Betty answered, "Yes Mama, I went to one a few months ago. I'll take you."

No one felt like finishing breakfast. The sheriff left to get his warrant, assuring Peter he would do his best to keep the media uninformed. Peter asked his brother-in-law, Frank, to join him outside for a small conference, both men neglecting to don their coats.

"What is it?" Frank asked.

"Frank, I know you and Betty have been tracking me for a long time. By rights, you should be the ones to arrest me. But I cut a deal with Sheriff Templeton to give him the collar in exchange for some time until Pop was found. I feel like a rat about it but --"

"That's okay," Frank said, smiling as he put his arm around Peter. "Betty and I decided the last time we were here, that neither one of us would make the collar. We both would rather sit in your corner than sit with the prosecution. Betty retired and I asked off the case. We turned over all the paper work to another team. We never wrote anything up about tracking you to Lake Stewart, so Templeton will have the collar all to himself."

Peter hugged Frank and thanked him.

"It feels good to be surrounded by family, but I don't think I'll ever be able to forgive Pop for Mary's death. It was all so unnecessary. A few days ago, Mary and I both agreed it was best that I should give myself up and stand trial. But Pop got me so mad with his demands and that honor bullshit. I never got to tell him our decision. Now Mary's dead, and Pop's wanted for homicide. I can't take much more, Frank, I feel like I'm losing my mind."

The two coatless men were beginning to shiver as a light snow began to fall.

"Let's get inside, kid," Frank said affectionately. "We can't afford to get sick now. We're going to need all our strength."

Frank avoided answering Peter's last remark. He was at a loss for words and couldn't think of any to comfort his new brother-in-law.

Later that morning, four Santinis and two Mullins were packed tightly in Frank's Buick as they drove on the Northway toward Plattsburg. The cast had come off Frank's left arm weeks ago, but he was still on sick report. He drove slightly above the speed limit, trying to avoid attention from the state troopers, even though the car was full of cops. The two hour trip was made in almost complete silence, and the fact that the weather turned so bad increased the tension in the car. The snow was sticking on the roadway and getting deep in spots. Driving was becoming treacherous and Frank's heavy Buick was weaving and sliding from time to time. The usual two hour trip lasted more than three hours, and sighs of relief could be heard when Frank finally turned into the hospital's parking lot.

Anna was frantic when she saw her husband asleep in the hospital bed. He was in a tiny cubicle. There were machines on a shelf that were beeping and showing green electronic signals, and an IV stand with several bottles of medicine, all leading into one tube connected to his left wrist. An oxygen line was connected to his nose and he wheezed when he breathed. Somehow, her big, burly husband looked small and vulnerable, even older, lying in that bed. She knelt by his side and whispered Italian endearments in his ear. Up close, his color was chalky. Frank Santini's four children stood silently in the tiny room and sadly watched their parents.

An hour dragged by and the tension in the room was interrupted by the phone ringing on a table next to Santini's bed. Betty answered it. She listened, nodded her head a few times and whispered a few words before she hung up.

"The state trooper, A Scott Andrews, that brought Pop into the hospital wants to see how he's making out. He's coming up now," Betty said in an undertone.

A few minutes later, Peter Santini felt himself being moved aside as the uniformed officer pushed into the room. Peter looked up into the man's face and was shocked. The face he saw was his, a mirrored image of his own. Shock registered on the face of the state trooper as he looked at Peter, his mouth opened as if to speak, but no sounds came out. The trooper's features were visible to everyone in the room. Peter Santini and Scott Andrews were the same height, same approximate weight, and exactly the same coloring. They were identical in every way as they stood nose to nose. What kind of trick was Mother Nature playing in this tiny hospital room? Betty was the first to utter a sound, an exhaled exclamation.

"I'll be a son-of-a-bitch. I can't believe my eyes!"

Anna pushed her way through the astounded bodies to get a closer look at her son and this stranger. She felt her heart racing and she was getting light-headed. She grabbed the trooper's coat with both hands and stared into his face. Anna gently touched his face, then fainted. The stranger caught her before she fell and carried her to the lounge across the hall and laid her on a couch. A nurse was summoned and immediately tended to Anna. Trooper Andrews stared into this woman's face. He mumbled, only loud enough to be heard but not understood, that he felt his life would never be the same.

Peter, who could stand for only short periods of time, sat down on another couch. He studied the face of the trooper which was exactly like his own face, and his curiosity inflated to the bursting point. He signalled the trooper to come over and sit beside him. They shook hands as they greeted each other, and soon were engaged in a serious conversation. Betty watched from across the room and soon became consumed with curiosity. She noticed that even their mannerism's were identical. Betty knew that she and Peter were fraternal twins, and resembled each other greatly, but she was looking at two people that had to be identical twins. Was it possible that she was a triplet? Unable to resist any longer, Betty approached the two men and joined in their conversation. The rest of the family watched the animated trio with awe. Anna was sitting now, very alert but visibly pale. After a half hour, Betty approached the family and spoke, her voice filled with emotion,

"There is no doubt that we have all witnessed a miracle. An open pandora's box may be a more accurate description. Scott Andrews has the same birthday as Peter and I, and was born in the same hospital in Westchester. There is no doubt he's family. What happened is a mystery. Scott was adopted by a rich family from Westchester. He graduated from Yale and earned an MBA degree from Wharton, the best schools in the country. With all those advantages, you'd expect that he would have entered his family's business, the banking business. But he described the overwhelming obsession he had to go into Law Enforcement and has been a state trooper for over twenty years. Can you believe this shit? But it's absolutely true. Family, meet your long lost brother, Scott. I think Frank and Anna Santini have a lot of explaining to do."

Everyone in the room turned to Anna, who burst into tears.

"I swear by everything that's holy that I never laid eyes on this man and never had an inkling that he even existed. How I could have borne this child without ever suspecting it, only proves my stupidity. To me it's a mystery, but that man lying in that room may have the answers. A few weeks ago, I asked him how he could abandon his own flesh and blood, referring to Peter. That question brought on the strangest, and now as I look back on it, the guiltiest expression I had ever seen on your father's face. Please leave us alone for a while."

Anna pulled a chair up to the bed and gazed at her sleeping husband. The lines in his face seemed deeper somehow, and there was no doubt that he definitely aged in the past twenty-four hours. How could he have done that despicable deed without her knowledge? Was she really such a stupid person? Unable to find the answers to her questions, Anna, in her frustration, shook her husband until he opened his eyes. Recognition came slowly and with it an expression of fear, so alien to this powerful man. The expression of fear slowly metamorphosed to one of guilt, so pitiful to behold.

"Look at me, you bastard, and tell me how you could live with me for forty-six years with that terrible sin in your heart and never tell me? Tell me now, you fucking Judas, or I'll turn these machines off and kill you now."

"Go ahead, Anna, you'd be doing me a favor. I'd just as soon die," Frank whispered. "I never meant to hurt that woman, but I'll never go to jail. I'll kill myself first."

"I don't care about that now, you asshole. Tell me what you did forty-five years ago when you gave away our flesh and blood!"

Frank turned his head away from Anna and his breathing became labored. Instead of becoming scared, Anna became angrier.

"Talk to me, you despicable creature before I rip your face off. What did you do with my baby?" she screamed.

Frank turned back towards Anna and cleared his throat. His eyes seemed to be sinking into his head.

"Anna," he whispered, "I'm begging you, please get me a priest. I know I'm dying and want to make confession. Please."

"Up yours, you animal. You have to confess to me first. I won't let you die. I'll make you live a few more years so I'll have time to make your life unbearable. Now tell me what you did with my baby," she screamed again.

"You saw him?"

"Yes, I saw him. Now talk."

Frank inhaled deeply and a gurgling rattle sounded deep in his chest. He looked at Anna like she was a stranger and he began to speak.

"When Doctor Miliotti told me that you were going to have triplets, I was frantic. We were living in a three room cold water flat and I was making $2900 a year. Out of that I had to pay taxes and pension, and don't forget my loan for the uniforms and my gun. Then there was Station House Tax and PBA dues. How could we live on $89 twice a month? I would have had to turn crooked like some of the other guys. You know I couldn't live like that. One baby would have been tough, but three? You were so little and so frail. Taking care of three babies would have overwhelmed you. Working around the clock, I couldn't have given you much help.

Do you remember how you struggled with just Peter and Betty?" Frank asked, as he started coughing violently.

Anna gave him some water and the coughing subsided. Frank gave her a glance of gratitude.

"Keep talking, you shit," Anna hissed.

"I told Doctor Miliotti my troubles, and he said there was a chance he could help me. He told me about a wealthy couple from Westchester, who wanted to adopt a baby desperately. But only from a good family. I said no, absolutely not. He told me to think about it and he would talk to the people in Westchester. A few days later, he called and said they investigated our background and were willing to take the baby. He said they were willing to pay $10,000. Do you remember what $10,000 meant in 1949? It meant we could buy a brand new house and furnish it. It wasn't like we were condemning this baby to a terrible life, he was going to live better than all of us. I wanted to go through with it but I was scared. He assured me it would be okay. He said that if you gave birth in a small maternity hospital he ran with a few other doctors in Mt. Vernon, he could take care of all the paperwork and keep the legal fees to a minimum. There would be no risk, no chance of disclosure. I thought about it for over a week, then I consented. I never told you or asked you because I knew you'd never agree. We would have struggled the rest of our lives. Instead, we lived a comfortable life and brought up the rest of our kids in a good house in a nice neighborhood. So, we told you that you were delivering twins and you never suspected a thing."

"You told me your grandfather left you the money, to be given to you when you had a family," Anna said, sobbing softly.

"You never questioned it. I carried the guilt for forty-five years, never daring to tell a soul. Do you think that was easy for me? I was positive that Peter's crimes were God's way of punishing me. Betty was an old maid. I felt all along that my sins were put on my children. From time to time I would call Doctor Miliotti to find out how the child was doing. His glowing reports made the hurt a little easier. I was proud of him. Miliotti told me how much the adopted parents loved the child, so I made no attempt to see him. He was loved, Anna. Not that we wouldn't have loved him too. Inside, I suffered, Anna. I suffered a lot."

"How could you constantly preach to your children about honor, when you sold your own flesh and blood?"

"Because I had no honor and I desperately wanted them to have it. Can you understand that?"

"No I can't. Oh, how I hate you."

"Please Anna, enough. I beg your forgiveness before I die. I was never unfaithful to you and I tried with all my might to be a good husband. After that terrible tragedy with Mary, I panicked. I had to go someplace to be alone, to think. Canada seemed like a good idea. Yesterday, when I turned around and looked into the face of that state trooper, I knew that God was playing the ultimate trick on me. I was going to be arrested for murder by my own son. Who said that God had no sense of humor?"

As the confrontation was taking place in the tiny Cardiac Care Unit, another kind of confrontation was taking place in the lounge. The four Santini siblings were trying to get acquainted with their long lost sibling, the existence of whom they learned about only minutes ago. After all the introductions were made, the Santini clan seemed a little happier about the unexpected event than the aloof, almost rude Scott Andrews. Peter, while explaining their presence in the hospital, described the tragedy that had taken place the day before in his house, and how the death of Mary occurred.

"You mean your father was a fugitive for homicide when I pulled him over? Hah, then I'm entitled to the arrest," the animated trooper exclaimed.

"But he's your birth father," Peter answered.

"I don't give a shit. He's just another Dago to me," Scott retorted.

Peter bristled at the bigoted remark, but strained to keep his cool. "That makes you a Dago too, you asshole."

A look of disbelief crossed the trooper's face. He leaned back in his chair and raised his eyes to the ceiling, as if he were looking for a divine explanation. "I can't believe I'm a Dago," Scott shouted in disgust, as he stood and paced about the lounge. "I've always disliked Dagoes. Our gardener was a Dago, for Christ's sake. Even the grocery store owners where we shopped, and all the gangsters in the movies. How can I be a Dago?"

Everyone in the room was shocked at the outburst, and disgusted with their new relative. He was obviously very ashamed to learn that he was of Italian descent.

"Listen, you jerk," Michael said belligerently, "We did fine without you. We're not too happy with you either."

"You can say that again," Jimmy added, as he looked over his new brother with disgust.

A wet-eyed Anna entered the lounge and looked around the room. She was surprised at all the tense faces and clenched fists that she saw. "What's going on here?" she asked, tentatively.

"Nothing, Mama," Betty answered, as she came over to Anna and hugged her. "Did Papa tell you anything?"

"Yes. He told me the whole story. He's sleeping again, the bastard. Telling me the story nearly killed him," Anna said, her face gray with anger.

"Come sit down, Mama, you don't look so good. Remember, you fainted a little while ago.

Anna looked around and saw Scott sit down on a small couch, away from everyone in the room. She walked over to him and asked,

"Do you mind if I sit next to you?"

"I guess not," Scott stammered, his face reddening with embarrassment.

Anna sat stiffly on the couch next to her son. She tried to think of words that would be relevant at a time like this. She decided to be honest, and speaking softly said,

"It's hard to find the right words. I don't know if there was ever a situation like this before. I want you to believe me, Scott," Anna said, touching his arm. Scott drew back as if the touch scalded him. "I had no inkling you existed before today. My husband gave you away for adoption without my knowledge. Only the doctor, my husband, and your parents knew the truth."

"Look, Lady," Scott interrupted, "I had two perfectly good parents that I loved, and I'm not in the market for two more. You don't owe me an explanation, and I'm not looking for one."

The trooper got up, leaving a hurt Anna seated on the couch, and walked out to the hallway. He placed a cigarette in his mouth, but didn't light it. He paced back and forth in an agitated manner. Peter joined him, and with a scowl on his face, said,

"It's obvious that you want no part of us. What the fuck are you hanging around for?"

"I'm waiting for the sheriff. If this guy was a fugitive, then I'm entitled to the collar and I damn well intend to get it."

"Yeah, you'll certainly get plenty of media attention," Peter said sarcastically. "I can see the headlines now, `Trooper Busts Birth Dad For Murder.' That should make you world famous, the darling of every talk show and every super-market tabloid. To me, you're a real shit and I'm tickled pink I didn't have to grow up with you."

Peter's outburst startled the state trooper. He took the unlit cigarette out of his mouth and pointed it at Peter.

"Now you listen to me," the agitated trooper said.

Before he could continue, Scott was pushed aside as Sheriff Templeton, dressed in his ostentatious uniform, entered the lounge with two deputies. He looked around, spotted Anna and came over to her.

"How's he doing?" the sheriff asked.

"Not so good,"

"I could tell by everyone's expression."

"You don't know the half of it," Anna continued. Take a close look at the state trooper that brought my husband in here."

Charlie Templeton turned and looked at the state trooper pacing nervously back and forth in the hallway. "Holy shit," he shouted, "He's the spitting image of Peter. What's the story?"

"It's a long story, Sheriff. My husband just told it to me.

The son-of-a-bitch, I hope he rots in hell for eternity. That man is my son and I never knew of his existence for forty-five years."

An agitated Scott Andrews burst into the room. He swung Sheriff Templeton around and addressed him officiously. "I summonsed this guy on the Northway, yesterday, and if he was a fugitive, I deserve the collar. It's only fair."

"Get out of my face, you asshole, and never put a hand on me again or I'll take you apart," a fuming Templeton shouted. "You know, a guy that's so anxious to bag his own father, is a shit in my book. Get the fuck out of here."

"OK, but I'll be back with my supervisor. The State takes precedent over the County."

"Go ahead, Asshole," the red-faced sheriff shouted. "You don't even know what's going on. Get out before I throw you out."

Scott Andrews stormed out of the lounge, too much in a hurry to wait for the elevator. He took the stairs and went down two at a time. He left without a glance at his newly found family and disappeared as suddenly as he had appeared. But the impact of his presence, changed the lives of everyone in that waiting room and especially the sick man asleep in the CCU.

"I wonder if he's married," Anna said sadly. Do you think I might have grandchildren that I never saw?" Anna burst into tears.

Peter came over to console her, and hugged his mother. "Don't cry for him, Mama, he appears to be a bigger loser than me, and that takes a lot of doing."

Anna raised her tear-stained face and looked into Peter's eyes. "Peter, my son, don't run yourself down. There's a lot of people in this world that love you, and there's a little boy and his dog running around and playing, that owe their lives to you."

"Yeah, Mama, remember there's a police officer and a wonderful woman dead because of me. Do I deserve to live?"

"Stop it Peter, stop it right now. I want you to remember what you have to live for, not what you should die for. Live, my son, for your two lovely daughters that adore you. For them, no one could ever replace you. I don't deny you a time for grieving. But after the grieving, life must go on."

The sheriff came over and tapped Peter on the shoulder. "C'mon, Peter, we have to talk."

Peter got up and followed the sheriff into the hallway.

"Peter, I was up all night thinking of you and your father. If the facts are presented fairly to the Grand Jury, I don't think your father will be indicted. By your own admission, the gun went off accidentally when your father tried to take you into custody for a felony that was allegedly committed in New York City. I don't think there's a grand jury in this country that would indict him for that. That's my opinion, for what it's worth, but I have a warrant for his arrest, and I have to put him under twenty-four hour guard until he's well enough to be booked. It's all for show."

"How about me?" Peter asked.

"I've got a warrant for you, too. I know you for about six months now, and I never met a finer man. I don't know the facts in your case, but I don't want anyone taking you back to New York City but your father. It's what he wants so badly. How do you feel about it?"

"I don't know," Peter pondered. "If I went back with him, then Mary died for nothing. She took the bullet meant for me."

"That's bullshit," the sheriff exploded, "The gunshot was an accident. It was not meant for anybody."

"He pulled his gun on me," Peter argued hotly, "That's intent enough for me."

"How about what happened in your case? Did you intend to kill your partner?"

"That was different, Charlie. I didn't pull my gun, my partner did. I can't testify what his intent was. We were mixing it up and the gun went off. It could have just as easily killed me, but it killed him. What does it all mean?"

"Beats the shit out of me, Peter, beats the shit out of me," the sheriff said sadly. "Follow me outside, I think we need a drink. That's an order."

Chapter Twenty-seven

The wake for Mary Russo at the Campbell Funeral Home brought out most of the population of Lake Stewart. Peter, sitting with Betty, received the condolences from all of his friends and many people that he barely knew. As the long day continued into late evening, he became more and more confused and agitated. Finally, as an act of mercy, Sheriff Templeton called an end to the proceedings and took Peter home.

Betty and Frank Mullin followed, and in Peter's study, decisions were made. Betty and Frank would accompany Mary's body back to Buffalo where Mary's daughters made arrangements for her internment. All the costs were to be paid by Peter. Sheriff Templeton turned down Peter's request that he be allowed to go to Mary's funeral, since he was now a prisoner, released from jail in the sheriff's custody.

Anna and her two sons, Michael and Jimmy, attended the wake only briefly, since Frank Santini was now on the critical list. They had taken residence in a motel close to the Plattsburg Hospital, but spent most of their time at Frank's bedside trying to convince him that life was worth while.

It was a Wednesday morning in early March and a warm breeze was melting the snow as Peter and Sheriff Templeton stood outside of the Campbell Funeral Home, watching Mary's hearse disappear from sight. Betty and Frank followed the hearse in their green Buick. Then Charlie drove Peter to his gas station, still called Jake's Place, for a meeting with

Raymond Curtis, Peter's mechanic. Seated in Mary's luncheonette, Peter was close to tears as he looked around, remembering what it looked like when he and Mary bought the place, and seeing all the changes that Mary had so proudly made.

"I'm promoting you to a junior partner, because all the responsibility is going to be yours. I have no idea how long I'll be gone, and I want you to be fully rewarded for your efforts. How about twenty-five percent of the profits, and double your regular salary, Ray? How's that sound to you?"

Ray stuttered, "I never dreamed that someday I'd be an owner of such a fine station. Bein' that I don't have a penny to my name. Jenny's gonna be thrilled when I tell her. Kids, too. Thank ya, boss. And God bless ya, too."

"I want you to hire a good woman to run the luncheonette and the office, and maybe a young kid to operate the tow truck and be your assistant in the shop. The shop's busy enough to support two mechanics, but I'll leave that up to you. Be sure the woman runs the luncheonette like Mary did. I want it clean. Serve good food. And let people run a reasonable tab if they're short of money.

I want you to send me the receipts every week, no matter where I am. Any important judgement calls are to be made by me. I'll be a telephone call away. Okay, Ray?" Peter asked.

"Anything you say, boss," Ray said, stuttering badly, "But can I ask you a favor?"

"Sure, Ray, just ask."

"Can I hire my wife to run the luncheonette? She's a hard worker and we could use the extra money. I know she'd take care of the place like it was her own. And another reason, she could help me talk to the customers. You know..."

"Damn good idea. And since you're part owner now, the luncheonette really is your own. Good luck, partner," Peter said, forcing himself to smile as he shook hands with Raymond Curtis.

Charlie Templeton put his arm around Peter's shoulders, as he led him to the patrol car. "Let's see if we can keep the wolves away from the door, until your father gets well enough to take you back," he said, solemnly.

Scott Andrews was an angry and totally confused man when he left the Plattsburg Hospital. He was angry at the lack of respect he received from that Lincoln County sheriff, and confused by the lack of support from his superior officers. Confused, also, by the sudden appearance of a new family. Being adopted, he always knew there were relatives out there somewhere, but he never had the desire to search for his roots. Now they were suddenly dumped into his lap and he was very unhappy to find out his true genealogy. Italians, for Christ's sake, idol worshipping Catholics. His dark complexion always stood out from his blue-eyed, blonde-haired parents, of Scottish descent. But when your parents were the powerful Harry and Helen Andrews, Wasps of the first degree, nobody asked questions. Not outwardly, anyway.

Scott Andrews grew up as the only son of a wealthy banking family, whose history and business dated back over a century. They were real "Yankees" these Andrews. Scott was a pampered child, doted on by his parents, his nanny, and the many servants that made up the Andrews household. As a pre-schooler, he had no playmates and never learned to share his many toys and pets. He lived solely with adults, all of whom found it easier to give him his way than put up with his tumultuous tantrums.

As he grew older, Scott attended only fashionable private schools, but made no close friendships. He was always a loner, an excellent student, but not one to join fraternities or clubs. He had no desire to play or watch sports. His leisure time was spent reading every Police publication he could get his hands on. His love expanded to firearms, and he subscribed to every magazine and catalog on guns. At a very young age he pestered his father for a BB gun and finally won his campaign on his eleventh birthday. At thirteen, he owned several .22 caliber rifles and target pistols. He taught himself to become an excellent shot.

Scott had nagged his father to take him hunting, but his father refused. He compromised by taking his son to the country club for Skeet Shooting, a gentlemen's game. Scott convinced his mother to allow him to go deer hunting with the family's Italian gardener, where he learned the thrill of killing a living creature. It gave him a feeling of power.

At his father's insistence, Scott attended Yale University, his father's *Alma Mater,* and graduated *Cum Laude.* While at Yale, Scott continued his loner way of life, rooming alone, joining no fraternities, clubs or athletic activities. Harry Andrews, convinced that his son would follow him into his banking empire, pressured Scott to continue his studies at Wharton School for Business.

To avoid ugly scenes with his father, Scott attended Wharton and graduated with honors. Like a pre-programmed robot, Scott joined his father's banking firm. At the country club, he was introduced to Nancy Phillips, the beautiful daughter of one of his father's wealthy associates and before long a marriage was arranged.

All the while, Scott felt like all the events in his life were happening to someone else, like some mini-series on TV. He felt like an observer to his own life instead of a participant. His real interest, the love for law enforcement and firearms, burned deeply in his soul.

After their wedding, Scott and Nancy lived at the Andrews mansion. Several months passed and Nancy announced she was pregnant.

Scott panicked and felt completely overwhelmed. He was drowning, but fought back instinctively. He resigned from his position at the bank, and he and Nancy moved out of his father's mansion into an apartment in Albany, N.Y. There, he sought and obtained an appointment to the State Police. Scott and Nancy moved to Plattsburg when Scott was assigned to the Plattsburg Barracks. For the first time in his life, Scott Andrews had been happy, finally settling into his element.

Nancy, however, was unhappy. She found it difficult to live on a policeman's meager salary, refused to do all the menial jobs of a housewife. Most of all, Nancy detested the nights she spent alone. She couldn't get used to the loneliness and after a while, managed a few short affairs. After her son was born, Nancy had rebelled at having to care for the child without help and moved back to the palatial mode of life she had grown up with, taking her son, Robert Philip Andrews with her.

Scott dismissed this episode of his life from his mind. Feeling no remorse, he went on with his life, alone. He built a magnificent loghouse in the Adirondack Mountains that cost over a million dollars and he lived there alone.

Scott's mother, Helen, died four years ago when Scott was forty years old. A year later, his father Harry entered a posh nursing home where he remained, suffering from advanced Alzheimer's disease.

Scott became the head of his father's banking empire, but gave it as little time as possible, preferring his lifestyle as a state trooper. Scott remained a loner, but had taken vacations at fashionable "Waspish" resorts and did have occasional relationships with wild women from this social structure. Somehow, he got on the mailing lists of several white supremist organizations, and the deluge of propaganda that he received piqued his interest. He toyed with the idea of attending one of their military style training camps, but never sent in an application. Then he encountered Frank Santini, who turned out to be a killer of a woman and was trying to escape to Canada. When Scott tried to summons him for speeding, he suffered a heart attack. Certainly, he thought, he deserved the collar for apprehending a killer and all the glory that went along with it.

Scott had a day off, after the chance meeting with all the Santinis at the Plattsburg Hospital. He sat alone in his den, drinking scotch and sodas one after the other, thinking of the man he arrested and his family. He was distressed to find them Italians, but the fact that almost the whole family were police officers was a redeeming feature. He felt a little jealousy when he realized that all of them had active careers in municipalities, their experiences far more exciting then his twenty-three years in sleepy Plattsburg.

He wondered if that old man, what's his name, Frank Santini, would survive. He also felt a little guilty the way he treated the old woman. Maybe she really didn't know of his existence. Maybe he ought to take a ride to the hospital to see how they were doing. Maybe they could use a hand, even if they were Dagoes and killers.

Scott drove his Corvette into the hospital's parking lot, and found a spot away from other cars. He didn't mind a longer walk as long as he felt his car was safe from accidental scratches. He strode through the melting slush, without a thought. His mind was uneasy, knowing he was going to encounter these strange people. At the reception desk, he announced he was going to visit Frank Santini, but the clerk informed him that no visitors except immediate family were allowed, since the patient was under police guard. Scott flashed his badge, turned his back on the clerk and headed for the elevator. The clerk caught up with him and repeated only immediate family was allowed to visit.

"That old man's is my father," Scott mumbled, feeling an immediate shot of guilt. Why did I say that? he thought.

Scott got off the elevator and slowly walked through the corridor, wondering what he was doing there. When he reached the lounge opposite the CCU, he looked inside and found the room was empty. He went across the hall and entered the CCU and approached Frank Santini's cubicle. Frank was alone, except for an attending nurse.

"No visitors?" Scott asked.

"His wife and two sons went to dinner about a half hour ago. They should be back soon. Who are you?" the nurse said pleasantly.

"I'm the trooper that brought him in here the other day. How's he doing?"

"Still touch and go, but his pulse is stronger and his pressure's down. It looks better."

"Can he talk?" Scott asked.

"Sure, when he wants to," the nurse said, smiling. She picked up a tray and left.

Scott pulled up a chair near the old man's bed and sat down, secretly pleased the rest of the family was absent.

Frank opened his eyes and looked at the trooper's familiar face. He cleared his throat for a time, then he spoke softly,

"How could you write me up for seventy five? I showed you my `Tin.' "

"I never give anybody a break, even cops," Scott boasted.

"Asshole," Frank muttered. "Whoever taught you how to be a cop? Didn't you ever hear of professional courtesy? It's practiced the world over. Don't you have any pride in your job?" Frank whispered as he lapsed into a coughing jag.

"Take it easy. Don't talk so much, you're too weak," Scott admonished, smarting under the old man's criticism.

Frank nodded, his eyes never leaving the younger man's face. After a while the coughing subsided, and Frank reached and grabbed Scott's wrist, his eyes pleading with the man to listen.

"There's so much I have to say to you. To explain. To apologize for," Frank whispered weakly.

"You don't owe me any apology, Mr. Santini. You did me a favor. I grew up better than all of you. I had the best of everything."

"Did you have a brother or a sister?" Frank asked.

"No," was the quick answer.

"Then I cheated you. You see, there's no substitute for family. In the long run, it's more valuable than money," Frank said as he resumed his hacking cough.

The nurse came in and offered Frank a drink. Turning to Scott, she ordered, "I'm afraid I have to ask you to leave. You're exciting him and he's too weak for that right now."

"Okay," Scott answered, "So long for now, Mr. Santini. I'll see you later."

"Thanks for coming," Frank whispered between the coughing. "And don't call me Mr. Santini. Call me Frank." He squeezed the man's wrist then let go as he watched his long lost son leave the room.

Scott, upset with this verbal exchange with his birth father, went into the lounge and sat down. He put his head into his hands and tried to evaluate the feelings he was having. He felt choked up, a feeling he experienced only once, at his mother's funeral. Suddenly he thought of his own son and a feeling of guilt flushed through him. When was the last time he visited with him? He couldn't remember but he knew it was months.

I can remedy that, he thought. Then his mind flew to the statement the old man had made, about being cheated for not having a brother or sister. What would my life have been if I had a brother or sister, he thought. So much for that bullshit about twins. I had an identical twin and a fraternal twin and I never felt a thing in forty-four years, not even an inkling.

Scott's thoughts were interrupted by a tap on the shoulder. He lifted his face from his hands and looked around. There was this guy standing there smiling. What's his name?

"Jimmy, Jimmy Santini. We met here the other day."

"Yeah, yeah. I remember," Scott said, standing up and shaking Jimmy's hand.

He looked around and saw two more Santinis standing in the doorway, Mrs. Santini and another son. Anna's smile was the only greeting she gave, as she chose a chair and sat down. Her son, Michael, stood behind her chair like a bodyguard.

"Did you people have dinner?" Scott asked, trying to make conversation.

"Yeah, we grabbed a bite in that greasy vest on the next block," Jimmy said cordially.

"Too bad," Scott responded, "We could have had dinner together. Maybe we'd get to know each other."

"Well, you could have called. That ESP shit doesn't work with me," Michael answered, sarcastically.

"Pardon me," Scott said angrily. "I made the mistake thinking you Dagoes were civilized."

"Jesus Christ, Mama, he's just like Peter. If I closed my eyes, I'd swear it was him," Jimmy said, astounded.

"Yes," she said sadly. "He has the same talent to turn a conversation into a fight in the blink of an eye."

"Bullshit," Scott yelled, "That goofball behind your chair started it."

"It's amazing," Anna said, "You've been brothers for one day and you're fighting like you knew each other a lifetime. It must be the genes."

Anna's reprimand put a stop to the angry confrontation, and the pugilistic expressions were replaced by sheepish ones.

Scott chuckled, got up and approached Michael, extending his hand. "Maybe it would have been fun, growing up with brothers. I never had anyone to fight with, so I ordered servants around like a brat."

The brothers shook hands and smiled at one another, measuring each other.

"Are you married, Scott, do you have children?" Anna interjected.

Scott turned and looked at Anna, as if he was annoyed that she invaded his privacy. He could tell her off, but decided to be civil.

"Yes," he said in a monotone. "Yes to both questions. I'm married and I have a ten year-old son. I rarely see them. We've been separated for nine years. My wife couldn't live on a cop's salary and moved back to her family's mansion."

"But I understand you're wealthy. Why did she have to live on a cop's salary?" Anna questioned.

"I felt that if I wanted to feel like the average cop, I had to know the struggle to make a living. Well, that feeling didn't last too long. I found that being poor is no great shakes. I like being a police officer, but I like my comfort too. I built a great house in the Adirondacks and live there alone."

"Why didn't you have your family move back when you built your house?" Anna asked.

"I didn't love her in the first place. It was a marriage arranged by two wealthy families. I'm happy I don't have to listen to her whining. She was really a tramp. So, maybe things happen for the best."

"What about the boy? Don't you miss him? Don't you want to be a father to him?" Anna asked and admonished at the same time.

"I'm as much a father to him as mine was to me. The boy has everything he wants and goes to a fine private school."

"Oh, that's so sad," Anna said.

"Goddammit," Scott exploded. "What right do you have to lecture me? Don't you ever do that again, or--."

"Or what, asshole?" An angry voice from the doorway. There stood a fierce looking Peter, with the sheriff standing behind him. Peter took three large steps and confronted the trooper nose to nose. "If I ever hear you speak to her like that again, I'll rip your fucking heart out. Get me?"

"She had no right to interrogate me. I owe her nothing," Scott answered with as much venom in his voice as Peter.

"Please stop it, both of you. I apologize. I had no right to ask you anything. I was just curious to know if I had a grandchild I never met. Please forgive me," Anna begged with much emotion in her voice.

The twins backed up and walked away from each other, taking seats on opposite sides of the room. The tension in the room eased only slightly.

Sheriff Templeton pulled up a chair and looked around. "How's the old man?" he asked.

"We just came back from supper. We checked on him but he seemed to be sleeping," Jimmy answered.

"I spoke to him while you were gone," Scott interjected, "But he did most of the talking and it tired him. He also coughed a lot."

"That's what worries me," Anna said. "The doctor said if he developed pneumonia, he's finished. I hate him tonight, but I loved him all my life. I don't want him to die. Prayers from all of us could only help."

"Don't worry, Mama," Peter said softly, "Papa's too ornery to die. You'll see. In a few days, he'll be ordering all of us around."

A few muted chuckles seconded Peter's statement and then an eery silence settled in the room. Everyone seemed content to adjourn to his own thoughts. After a long silence, Scott got up and approached Peter.

"How about if I bought you a drink?"

"Sounds good to me," Peter answered, as he turned to Charlie Templeton for permission.

Charlie nodded, and the two identical men left the room together, as if the tension between them moments ago never existed.

They left the hospital and walked three blocks to Main Street. In the middle of the block they spotted Murphy's Tavern with a large, green clover lit up in neon lights. From the time they left the lounge outside of the CCU until they entered the tavern, neither man uttered a word.

"This joint's okay," Scott muttered. "I've been in here a lot of times."

Scott didn't hold the door for Peter and it slammed shut in Peter's face. Peter uttered an obscenity under his breath, opened the door and followed his brother into the tavern. Scott had already picked out a booth in the rear of the darkly lit room and seated himself. Peter followed and without a word seated himself in the opposite seat.

Both men slipped out of their heavy jackets. Being early in the day, there were only a few patrons at the bar, most staring at a soap opera on the television. All the booths were empty except one, where two young women were eating sandwiches and sipping beer. It took five minutes before a waitress, clad in a very short skirt, came over to take their order. She recognized Scott and greeted him.

"Hiya handsome. Long time no see."

"Hello Fran. Nice seeing you again," Scott responded.

"Who's your friend?" Fran asked casually. "Holy shit, I've got double vision," she screamed.

"Meet my brother, Pete," Scott said nonchalantly, but cut off further discussion by ordering a bottle of beer.

"The same for me," Peter echoed.

Nether man spoke until the waitress returned with the beer. Batting her eyes at Peter in a flirtatious manner, she said,

"I hope you're friendlier than your brother. I never could get him to take me out. Are you available?"

"Lay off, Fran. He's in mourning," Scott growled.

The smile disappeared from the waitress's face and she quickly mumbled an apology and a word of sympathy, then left.

"Thanks," Peter mumbled.

Scott just nodded and sipped his beer. Minutes passed in silence until Scott broke it with a question: "How'd you get so fucked up?"

"It's a long story," Peter answered in a low voice.

"I've got plenty of time. I don't go back to work till tomorrow at midnight."

"Okay, you asked for it. It all started about seven years ago when my younger daughter Marci was born." Peter went on to tell Scott his entire story, right up until his escape to Buffalo and settlement in Lake Stewart. Scott appeared to know the rest of the story.

Scott drained the rest of his beer and signalled the waitress to bring another round. He was very quiet after Peter finished his story. He reviewed everything that was said in his mind. Would he have reacted the same? No. He realized he was different in a lot of ways. Maybe it was a result of their different environments. Maybe they had very different personalities.

Scott, in his analysis, realized that sex was much less important in his life than in Peter's. The fact that he was independently wealthy would have made it much easier for him to resist going into an illegal enterprise, and he felt his lifelong love affair with law enforcement would have prevented him from doing anything illegal.

The letter of the law was his bible, and even this was criticized by the sick old man in the hospital. His analysis of Peter's story was interrupted by the return of the waitress with the beer.

"Thanks Fran," Scott said, as he dropped a ten dollar bill on the table. "Just keep them coming."

"My pleasure, handsome. You've got the bucks, I've got the beer," the waitress said, laughing.

"Yeah, you got that right," Scott growled.

"How about you?" Peter asked, after the waitress left. "How'd you get to be such a sweet personality?"

"Shit, you don't have to be a brain surgeon to figure me out. I was really brought up by a bunch of strangers, hired help who didn't give a shit about me. They gave me anything I wanted just to make their job easier. My parents were always someplace else. When they were home, their only interest in me was to make sure that I fit into their world.

They couldn't care less about my desires, my needs, or my ambitions. As soon as I was old enough, I created my own world where I made all the rules. To make their lives easier, my parents and the hired help stayed out of my life, and I made very few waves, just to keep my privacy. Even my marriage to a beautiful, rich girl was arranged. To keep the family goodies from falling into the wrong hands. I went along with that shit for as long as I could, then I rebelled. I left the family empire, quit the bank and became a state trooper. Moved with my wife Nancy from paradise to a small house in Plattsburg. I wanted to live like the average cop, so I tried to make it on a cop's salary. I did okay, but Nancy hated it. She grew up in luxury and refused to understand my motives. She hated her life, my hours, my job, and grew to hate me. She played around and I found out. She argued that it was common and acceptable in our former lives. Why change the rules? When she became pregnant, I wasn't sure I was the one responsible.

After the baby came, she refused to do all the dirty work by herself. She took the baby and moved back to her family and her former life. The funny part of it all, I didn't miss them. Never really loved them. I don't know what love is, or whether I'm capable of it. After they left, I had a great house built to my specifications. I now live in luxury. Have all my little toys that make my life tolerable. And work at a job I love. I live the life I want to live. If that's happiness, then I'm happy. The arrival of you and your family into my life is just one big pain in the ass."

Peter had listened very attentively to his brother's narration. He mulled it over in his mind and took his time before he commented on it.

"When our parents produced triplets, they sure screwed up. Not one of us knew happiness over the past forty-four years, or had what people would call a normal life. Hey, do you mind if I switch To Jack Daniels? This beer is doing nothing for me except making me pee a lot."

"I don't give a shit," Scott answered as he waved for the waitress.

Fran came over to their table and gave the twins a broad smile. "Another round?" she asked.

"This time bring us two Jack Daniels on the rocks, and make them doubles," Scott ordered.

"Is this conversation getting serious?" she asked.

"Just serve the drinks, Fran, and save the comments for another time," Scott growled.

"It's your nickel," Fran called over her shoulder.

There was silence between the brothers until Fran brought the drinks and left with a twenty dollar bill in her hand.

"What's the female part of the triplets like? What's her name?" Scott asked.

"Betty," Peter answered. "It's hard for me to tell you just how important Betty was in my life when we were growing up. I was constantly in jams. Betty was my savior. She fought for me, lied for me, guided me, and tried to teach me. We were closer than I was with my brothers. When I recently got into trouble and went on the lamb, it was Betty that hunted me down and found me."

"Why did she do that?"

"My father gave her that job. He said it must be a Santini to bring me in, and since Betty was a great detective, it had to be her. It was the only way to restore the family honor. What bullshit. All it accomplished was to get my Mary killed. Just take my word for it. I have the most terrific gal in the world for a sister. When she became a cop, her career took off like a rocket. I can't tell you how many big collars she made or how many shootouts she's been in, but it's an awful lot. She was the most decorated female on the NYPD. She retired a few months ago as a Detective First Grade and was high on the captain's list."

"Why'd she retire, being so close to a promotion?"

"She fell in love with a detective she worked with, when she went out to Buffalo, hunting me. You met him a couple of days ago. He was the huge guy with the Irish face, Frank Mullin. They got married on New Year's Day and Betty threw in her papers to live with him in Buffalo."

"But to give up a promotion to Captain doesn't make any sense," Scott said, with vehemence. "I couldn't pass a single test. Not that I studied very hard."

"Betty never met a guy she fell in love with until she was forty-four years old. When she fell, she fell hard. Frank was more important to her than making captain," Peter said as he leaned back in the booth, slowly sipping his Jack Daniels. "Betty's one terrific person and I'm very proud of her. Someday, you will be too, if you ever get to know her."

Scott, unaccustomed to long conversations with anyone, started to doze, to the amusement of Peter. Feeling himself collapsing on the table, Scott jerked to attention and apologized, then said, "You make her sound great, I'd like to meet her. Maybe get to know her. By the way, what's going to happen to you now?"

"I'll be picked up any day now, and brought back to Brooklyn to stand trial. I had hoped the sheriff could stall it long enough for my father to bring me in. But that isn't likely. We don't even know if he's going to make it. The shock of meeting you -- on top of his accidental shooting of Mary -- was too much for his old heart. I hope he does, he's really a pretty good guy. He was smart enough not to waste too much time with me."

"Sounds like sour grapes to me," muttered Scott, his words slurring. "Sorry for yourself?"

"Ha, wouldn't you be?" Peter exploded. "You have no idea how many guys I'm going to meet on the inside. Guys that I put there. I bet they're licking their chops now, planning a great reception for me. If Sheriff Templeton wasn't such a good guy, I'd take off again. I gave him my word I wouldn't, and I never went back on my word yet."

"Let's have one more for the road," Scott said as he signaled the waitress. "If I were in your shoes, I'd be sipping drinks on a small island in the Caribbean, one that had no extradition agreement with Uncle Sam."

Fifteen minutes later, the two brothers were slowly walking, or rather, staggering back to the hospital and a very worried sheriff. Everyone in the lounge breathed a little easier when they appeared. Anna stared at the twins and wondered what might have been. She smiled.

Chapter Twenty-eight

Three days later, Peter was awakened at six in the morning by Sheriff Templeton's phone call and was told to pack his bag and report immediately to headquarters. On his arrival, Peter was introduced to Detectives Shapiro and Ryan of the 78th Squad, New York City Police Department, who held extradition papers for his return to their jurisdiction. Peter held out his hand in greeting but was snubbed by both detectives.

"Fuck you, cop killer," Shapiro sneered.

"Hey, where's the `presumed innocent till proven guilty' routine?" Peter said as his face reddened with shame. "You ever hear of an accident?"

"Steve Moran was busting you for being a pimp and pushing drugs. In my book that makes you a fucking low-life. Can you deny that, asshole?" Ryan said, his voice dripping with hate.

"What does that make all the brass and cops that took my money to let me operate? I'm sure the two of you have some skeletons hidden in your closets, you just haven't been caught yet. So don't throw stones at my glass house," Peter said with a cracking voice.

Shapiro pulled Peter's arms behind his back and cuffed them tightly, causing Peter a great deal of pain. Then Ryan belted the defenseless prisoner in the gut with all his might, causing Peter to drop to his knees in agony. Charlie Templeton picked up a chair and hit Detective Ryan in back of the neck with it, splintering the chair while rendering Ryan unconscious.

"If either of you bastards lays a finger on this man again, you'll answer to me," Templeton roared. "In these parts, Peter Santini's quite a hero. I hear he's been decorated many times in your neck of the woods. I'm sending my best man with you to see that he's treated with respect on the trip back to New York City. He'll have my orders to cripple anyone who even comes close to Peter. You understand that, Shapiro?"

Detective Shapiro glared at Templeton, but reluctantly nodded his head.

Peter's trip downstate was uneventful, but very uncomfortable, as he remained cuffed all the way. He was tired when he was finally brought to Central Booking and booked for homicide, pimping, selling drugs, and fleeing the jurisdiction to avoid prosecution. After he was fingerprinted and photographed, Peter was sent to Rikers Island where he was incarcerated. Peter refused to answer any questions until he had legal representation.

He was allowed to call the law firm that represented the PBA: Parsons, Parsons, Kelly and Leibowitz. Mr. Kelly showed up to interview Peter and informed him that none of the partners wanted to handle the case. An associate, Kathleen Fitzgerald, volunteered to represent him and Kelly assured Peter that she was a very able litigator, the most promising young attorney in the firm.

It was a little past noon on the following day when Peter was brought to the interrogation room to meet his new attorney. She was sitting at the table, her hands clenched tightly on top of a legal pad.

Kathleen Fitzgerald didn't rise when Peter came in, but she asked him to be seated. Her voice sounded soft and strangely resonant.

Peter sat down and extended his hand in greeting but the attorney ignored it. Peter felt a coldness emanating from the person across the table. They made eye contact, but no words were spoken as they sized each other up for an embarrassingly long time. Peter studied her face and saw a fine featured, almost delicate face, that could have been described as beautiful except the coldness in the light blue eyes spoiled the illusion. Somehow, Peter sensed an illness, but he couldn't tell if it was mental or physical. He felt her scrutiny but shrugged his shoulders as if to say "I don't give a damn what she thinks about me."

Finally Kathleen Fitzgerald spoke. "I've read all the affidavits, and I think I can help you. Some of the charges against you are serious, but there's room to maneuver. I don't think this will ever go to trial, because you have so much to deal. However, plan on doing some time. You had so much exposure in the media that it isn't realistic to hope for anything less. But you never know."

She went on and on, discussing each and every charge and her plans to counter them. Never once did her tone of voice change nor did feeling of any kind enter into her conversation.

Peter listened very carefully to every word his attorney said, and a chill ran up and down his spine. He felt like she was discussing the sale of his car -- not his very life -- so cold and lifeless was her delivery.

"Everything isn't so cut and dried," Peter said. "I'm a human being. And as such, there were reasons for everything I did. I'm not a stranger to the law. I've been a police officer for most of my adult life, enforcing the written law. I have enough experience to know that the Penal Code of the State of New York is a living, breathing document. Written by human beings."

"I'm fully aware of all that, Mr. Santini," the attorney said. "We'll spend a great deal of time going over your background until I know every single thing about you. Before I'm done, I'll know every thought you had in your head and why it was there. I'm extremely efficient and very thorough. I'll know you better than you know yourself. I'm confident I'll get you the best possible deal."

Peter stared at the young woman after she stopped speaking. He shivered as he realized that never once had she smiled or even changed expression during her entire presentation. Was Kathleen Fitzgerald a robot? Was a robot what he needed at this stage of his life?

"I'll be back tomorrow with a tape recorder and we'll start working. If you have any objections to my methods, or dislike me personally, speak up now, and we'll get you another attorney," Fitzgerald said, as she rose and faced Santini.

Peter stood up and hesitated before answering. He really would have preferred more time before making a decision, but then remembered what Mr. Kelly said, that no partner in the PBA legal firm wanted to handle his case. Kathleen Fitzgerald was the only volunteer. With an eerie feeling that he was making a mistake, Peter extended his hand and said, "You've got a deal."

Kathleen Fitzgerald just tapped Peter's hand with her legal pad and without another word, turned and left the room.

Six weeks had passed since Frank Santini was first admitted in the Plattsburg Hospital. Michael and James had returned to work a month ago, leaving their mother, Anna, alone to see Frank Santini through his slow convalescence. She wasn't alone for long, for she had a frequent companion. Scott Andrews started to come around more often to keep her company.

He had long conversations with Anna and even some with Frank. Scott never showed any warmth towards his birth parents, but here was a magnetism that kept drawing him back. A force that he couldn't explain to himself. He found himself to be a daily visitor to the hospital and became impatient with the care that Frank was receiving from the burdened nurses. At his expense, he hired private nurses to care for Frank around the clock. After driving Anna back to her motel one rainy night and observing her dingy quarters, he insisted that she move to his house in the Adirondacks. Anna, tired and weak from the recent tragic events that had befallen her family, agreed. Scott rented a car for her so that she could come and go as she pleased while he was at work.

Anna spent many hours alone in Scott's large home, roaming through the rooms. In this way gained a better understanding of her newly found son. She supervised the cleaning lady that came in three days a week, and started to cook elaborate meals for her son, introducing him to her Italian background. When the cardiologist suggested that Frank's recovery would be improved in a home environment, Scott insisted that Frank be brought to his home where he could rest and regain his strength before returning to Brooklyn. He hired a full-time registered nurse to help Anna.

Both Frank and Anna were overwhelmed by their son's strength and indulgence. Puzzled by his desire to help them, yet he remained cold and remote. His personality emphasized his upbringing as a Wasp, a sharp contrast to the hot-blooded devotion of their own children.

Scott, Anna and Frank began to spend long evenings in front of a tantalizing fire in Scott's den. Anna and Frank fondly recounted episodes of their children's childhood, but the stories of Betty rescuing Peter from the brink of disaster time and time again particularly intrigued Scott.

He couldn't get enough of these stories, sometimes imagining himself as a participant in their escapades. He realized how barren and sterile his childhood had been. Scott couldn't remember a single time that he and his parents spent a close and intimate evening in front of a fire. He couldn't remember his parents doing much parenting at all. Scott felt cheated and angry. Being rich, never gave him the warm feeling that he felt now, sitting in front of a fire with Frank and Anna Santini.

Scott spent a restless night, reviewing in his mind the many stories he heard about Betty and Peter. He felt a need to know them better. After all, he was one third of the triplets born in that Westchester hospital, forty-four years ago. Scott remembered with warmth that one evening he spent drinking with Peter. It felt so natural. He wanted more. Peter, now in jail, was out of the question. But Betty? Why not? The next morning Scott obtained Betty's phone number from Anna and called her.

"Hello Betty, this is Scott. Scott Andrew. Your brother."

"What's wrong?" Betty shouted, anxiously.

"Calm down, nothing's wrong. This is just a social call."

"Oh?" Betty answered, her voice two octaves lower.

"As you know your folks are staying with me for a little while. Until your father's strong enough to make the trip back to Brooklyn. But he's still pretty weak," Scott answered sheepishly.

"You mean our parents, don't you Scott?"

"Yeah, that's what I mean. Jesus, Betty, I can't say it, yet. Can you understand that?"

"Sure, I can understand. I have a helluva time calling my husband's mother Mom," Betty said, laughing.

"Betty, small talk is fine, but I want to get right to the point," Scott said, his voice turning deadly serious. "A few weeks ago I didn't even know you existed. But the last few nights, I've been listening to your mother and father tell stories about you and Peter during your childhood. I have to admit I'm jealous. I missed an awful lot. Growing up as a rich kid isn't all it's cracked up to be. Your memories are worth much more than money. Betty, I hope it's not too late for us. I'd like for us to really get to know each other. Could you come for a small visit? I'll send you the air fare. You could give your mother a hand taking care of your father. He's a tough and ornery old man. I'd take part of my vacation so I could spend a lot of time with you. Please, say you'll come."

"Jesus, I don't know. Frank's clearing up all his pending cases, then he expects to put his papers in and retire. I just found out I'm pregnant and I'm not feeling too great. But I can't tell you how shocked I am to hear that Mom and Pop are staying with you. It's certainly a surprise. Dammit, I'd love to come. It will give me the chance to tell them about my pregnancy. Give me a few days to straighten things out here, then I'll drive up. Do me a favor and don't tell the folks I'm pregnant. I want to tell them myself. They've been bugging me for the past twenty-five years and now I can fulfill their wishes."

"That's swell. But why drive? If you're not feeling well, flying's easier. I can pick you up at the airport. It's no trouble."

"No, I'd rather drive. If I get sick, I can always pull over and rest. I feel more in control when I'm driving. I'll see you in a few days, just give me the directions."

"Having a family is a new feeling for me and, I have to tell you, it feels good."

"Even if we're Dagoes?"

"Gimme a break."

Chapter Twenty-nine

Peter lay fully clothed on his bunk, his thoughts drifted to Mary, and his heart ached. Oh, how he loved her. The ten months they spent together were the happiest of his life. Surely, God's taking of Mary was punishment for becoming a dirty cop. He never blamed himself for the death of Stephen Moran, for in his mind, it was self defense. The struggle over Moran's gun could have gone either way. In Peter's mind, it was God's choice , and the errant bullet found

Stephen's head, not his. Now his fate was in the hands of a woman, Kathleen Fitzgerald.

Peter tried to conjure up the face of the new woman in his life, but it was hazy. As he thought about her, Peter realized that this Fitzgerald woman was as opposite from Mary as she could be. Where Mary was full figured, Kathleen was slight, almost anoretic. Mary had dark Sicilian features, black shiny hair. Kathleen had light, delicate, Celtic features, with strikingly large, light blue eyes. Mary's smile lit up a room and her warmth made the room feel cozy and safe. Kathleen never smiled and her presence gave off an aura that was cold, almost ghost-like. Peter hugged himself, but his arms ached for Mary.

"Why did you leave me now, when I need you the most," Peter whispered out loud.

Hearing his own voice shocked him and he felt ashamed. Suppose the prisoner in the next cell had heard him. He would be a marked man. It was bad enough everyone knew he was an ex-cop, and he was hated by every prisoner in the place.

Peter's mind drifted again, reviewing his own life. Decorated nine times for bravery -- what a farce. He never considered himself a brave man, one fully in control. For the first twenty-one years of his life, there was always Betty to make things right for him, to bail him out of his jams, to ease his fears and make him strong. The next phase of his life, he was influenced by his wife Alice. But the rigid rules in her house, her quest for hospital-like cleanliness, the coldness of her bed after she decided against more children, drove him to the streets at night and eventually into the arms of prostitutes. What followed wasn't entirely his fault, he reasoned. It was Alice's fault. If she was more loving and understanding like Betty or Mary, he wouldn't now be lying in a prison cell.

"Damn you, Alice. You're to blame," he shouted out loud. "I hate you."

Peter was instantly filled with guilt. He knew he could only blame himself. He always knew he was a weak-willed man, and he knew he honestly could never hate Alice. He loved her deeply once, and even now revered her beauty. After all, she was the mother of his two beautiful, darling daughters. He would owe her forever for that. Why, he asked himself? Why was his life always tied to a woman like an umbilical cord that he couldn't cut?

The night was interminably long, and Peter tossed and turned. He got up at first light, shaved and made himself ready the best way he could. He had to face this new woman with a show of dignity and strength. He recalled with pleasure the recent months he spent in Lake Stewart, where he basked in the sunshine of being considered a hero for saving the lives of a boy and his dog. He relished the respect of the people in that small community and how everyone, every man woman and child, tried so desperately to protect him by guarding his identity. How the people contributed their time and effort to help him and Mary to come through those difficult days of his recuperation. "God, how I could use their help, now," he thought.

After breakfast, Peter was brought to the interrogation room where he found Kathleen Fitzgerald seated at the table. She greeted him with the icy statement, "I hate this place. Everytime I come here I feel like I'm being rowed across the River Styx to hell. The first thing I've got to do is get you out of here. We have to get a bail hearing. Can you get me any character witnesses? Your family doesn't count or any friends you might have left on the Police Department."

"I think so," Peter stammered. The Sheriff of Lincoln County, and most of the people in Lake Stewart were behind me a hundred percent."

"Good," Kathleen answered, "I'll get in touch with the sheriff this afternoon. Maybe he'll get me in touch with other prominent people from your community. Your medals on the job will help, too. We'll delay these interviews until we get you out on bail. I'm going to work on a bail hearing right away."

Without another word to Peter, Attorney Fitzgerald stood and walked to the door. She signaled the guard who opened the door. She left without turning to wave or acknowledge Peter at all. Her coldness depressed him. Somehow, he felt she hated him. Why did she take his case?

Ten days passed before Peter heard from his attorney. He tried calling her three separate times, but was told she wasn't available.

It was late Friday afternoon when Kathleen Fitzgerald finally called Peter. He was so anxious, his hands shook as he picked up the phone. He scowled at the guard, but the guard wouldn't leave to give Peter a little privacy. As soon as Peter said hello, the attorney started to speak, without uttering one word in greeting or asking he if he needed anything.

"Your hearing's set for Monday morning. I subpoenaed Sheriff Templeton and he promised to bring a large number of people from Lake Stewart. Your family will be there to show support. Over the weekend, your wife Alice will bring you your Wedding-Funeral suit. Make sure your shoes are polished and remember to shave. You have to look like a human being."

Peter was shocked that his attorney didn't even wait to hear if he had a question. She just hung up abruptly as soon as she dispatched her message. Peter was getting pissed off.

On Sunday afternoon, Peter was notified that he had a visitor. He was brought to the visitor's room and saw Alice sitting there, as beautiful as ever. Visitors and prisoners weren't separated, and when Alice greeted him, she didn't offer a kiss, only an extended hand. Her smile even seemed forced. Peter held onto her hand as they found two seats in a secluded corner.

"How's Tess and Marci?" were Peter's first words.

"They're fine. Getting big. Both getting very pretty. We're being bothered with boys coming around to see Tess and she's only nine," Alice said proudly.

"Why didn't you bring them? Children are allowed."

"How can you ask me that? Did you really think I'd bring them to a place like this? Would you really like for them to see you here? I don't know why, but they worship you. Marci blows up if I say anything unfavorable about you. And Tess sulks for hours. You don't know what those kids went through because of you. You were on television so often, and you know how cruel kids can be at school. Tess is always black and blue fighting for you."

Peter stood up and turned his back on Alice. He couldn't let her see the tears that suddenly came to his eyes, and he was afraid to speak because the lump in his throat felt like it would choke him.

Finally, Alice stood and walked to Peter's side, putting a hand on his shoulder.

"When you go to prison, how am I going to pay the mortgage on our house or support the girls? I'm tired of accepting charity from your parents and your friends from the 78th Precinct. I never worked and I don't have a trade. All I could be is a waitress and I couldn't afford the house and pay for a babysitter, too. What am I going to do, Peter?"

"Listen to me, Alice, and listen carefully. I've given this a great deal of thought. First, put the house in Bellmore up for sale. After ten years we should have some equity in it. Plus the property values are way up since we bought that house. Sell the Acura, too. Then take the kids and move up-state to Lake Stewart. My house there is very beautiful and it's free and clear. Your only expense would be taxes and they're pretty low compared to Long Island. I have a gas station there that'll give you a pretty good income. The kids will have a fresh start and no one will hassle them there. The schools aren't as good, but we can't have everything. I have a Ford Explorer for you to use. It's four- wheel drive and you'll love it in the snow. What do you think?"

"I, I don't know," Alice stammered. "It means leaving my friends, my parish priest, and your family. You know how they help me."

"Well, I have a newly found brother who lives up north. I'm sure he'll give you a hand. He's a state trooper, looks exactly like me and is probably just as obnoxious," Peter said with a slight smirk on his face.

"Lucky me," Alice retorted. "Instead of one son of a bitch to contend with, I'll have two. What did I do to deserve such great luck?"

"Listen, Alice. Don't break my balls. I have enough to put up with without you pouring salt in my wounds. At least my plan will put a good roof over your head, give you plenty of spending money, and provide a fresh start for the girls. Is that bad?" Peter said, his face flushed with anger.

"Do you really expect me to sleep in the same bed where you fucked that whore?" Alice responded, equally angered.

"Get the fuck out of here. I almost forgot what a bitch you really are."

Betty felt strange as she drove into the driveway that was marked by a sign with the name ANDREWS burned into the wood. It was a long, twisting road that ended in a circular path in front of a huge, loghouse. It was set back in the woods and landscaped in a natural style. No manicured trees and shrubs here.

The front door was thrown open and a man walked out waving his arms in greeting. If Betty didn't know better, she could have sworn it was Peter. She couldn't detect a single distinguishing mark or feature that would single out one brother from the other. Even the voice was exactly the same as Scott shouted his hello. "Jesus, Betty, you look great. Actually radiant. Some women look better when they're pregnant," Scott said warmly.

What a change, Betty thought. The last time I saw him he was a sullen, angry man who seemed ashamed of his newly found family. Now her family are his house guests. He hugged her and kissed her cheek.

"How about a kiss for me?" Scott said.

"Cut it out. I don't even know you.

"What's that supposed to mean?" A puzzled Scott asked.

"I don't hand out kisses, not even friendly ones."

She popped the trunk lid and Scott lifted out her heavy suitcase. "How's Mom and Pop?" Betty asked, changing the subject.

"Pretty good," Scott answered. "Your father's gaining his strength back pretty fast, and your mother seems to enjoy ordering the help around. My house was never so clean"

"I see you're still having trouble acknowledging them as your parents."

"In my mind I can, but I can't say the words. I feel mixed up and disloyal to my own parents. Even though I was never really close to them. The last couple of weeks have been strange. In the evenings we sit in front of the fire and talk for hours. I never did that with my Mom and Dad. I'm developing feelings for Anna and Frank. Anna's very warm toward me, and I love listening to Frank's police experiences and about his father's too. He brags about Michael and Jimmy, but mostly about you. He makes you sound like Dick Tracy and James Bond rolled into one. What a guy."

As soon as Betty and Scott entered the house, they were surrounded by Anna and Frank. The maid came and took Betty's heavy suitcase and literally dragged it up the stairs. After the hugs and kisses, Anna held Betty at arm's length, eyeing her suspiciously.

"You've put on a little weight, dear. Have you got something to tell me?" Anna asked slyly.

"For God's sake, Anna, leave the girl alone. She's a married lady now. Every married woman puts on a little weight," Frank said, his booming voice echoing in the cavernous foyer of the house.

"I see Pop's feeling better," Betty laughed, "His voice is back to normal. His arms, too. He only broke three ribs when he hugged me."

"Let's all go into the living room," Scott said, breaking into the conversation. "I'll make some cocktails."

"None for me," Betty said, a slight blush appearing on her face. "I don't drink."

"Since when?" Frank bellowed. "You could always drink your brothers under the table."

"Since I got married," Betty stammered.

"Bullshit. You married an Irisher. He certainly ain't gonna discourage drinking."

"Leave the girl alone, Frank," Anna said as she pulled Betty away from her father. "She doesn't have to make excuses for not wanting a drink."

"A little orange juice will be fine," Betty said.

Later, after dinner, Scott, Betty, Anna and Frank relaxed in the den in front of a roaring fire. Betty thought about dinner. They all sat at the table and were served by the maid and the cook. It was like the movies. Betty never believed it actually happened in real life.

The best part was after dinner. No Cleanup. They just got up and walked into the den. Scott put on some soft music, then he and Frank lit up two smelly cigars. Betty was brought up with cigars. Her father and grandfather always smoked them after dinner. Her own husband smoked cigars. But tonight, they made her nauseous.

"What's the matter?" Anna asked, studying her daughter's face.

"I don't know why, Mama, but the cigars are bothering me tonight."

"Of course, I understand," Anna said. "Put those lousy cigars out," Anna ordered loudly, "Can't you see Betty's pregnant and they're making her sick?"

"How'd you know, Mama? Scott tell you?"

"No. A mother knows her own daughter. You're a little heavier than when I saw you last, and you have that look."

"What look?"

"I don't know. A sort of radiant look. Anyway, you have the look. I knew right away. Thank God. I never believed it would ever happen to you. I've waited a lifetime for this. Tomorrow, I light a candle. What's the matter with you, Frank? All of a sudden you can't talk? Say something to your daughter."

"I can't," Frank whispered. I'm afraid I'll bust out crying."

"This calls for champagne," Scott said cheerily. "I'll go get some."

Later that evening, after the eleven o'clock news, Frank cleared his throat and announced he had something serious to say.

"So, say it," Anna said, impatiently.

"Peter called me today. He's having a hearing on Monday to decide whether he gets bail or not. He asked me to come if I was feeling up to it. I believe we should all go. You know, to show family solidarity."

"Why, Papa? A few months ago you didn't allow his name to be spoken. Now you want all of us to stand behind him. Why?" Betty said.

"After what I did to his Mary, I owe him," Frank answered with a tear in his voice. "I never would or could believe it was an accident when he shot his partner. All I knew is that he disgraced this family and I wanted him to pay for it. He had to be brought in by a Santini to save the honor of the family. When I was in the hospital, not knowing whether I'd live or die, I did some serious thinking. I realized I never heard Peter's side of the story. I condemned him by what I read in the papers. What kind of a father doesn't give his own son the benefit of the doubt? When my gun accidentally killed his Mary, I realized this could have happened to Peter, also. I, too, panicked and ran. But my family didn't condemn me. Everyone stood behind me. Can I do less for Peter? God forgive me, I was wrong. Dead wrong."

Chapter Thirty

Monday morning at ten o'clock, Peter was brought into the court wearing handcuffs. Gasps and murmuring could be heard from all over the crowded room. Family and friends were obviously disturbed at seeing the police officer treated like a common criminal. The correction officer removed the cuffs and Peter was seated at the table with his attorney, Kathleen Fitzgerald.

She was a sight to behold, her long blonde wavy hair cascading down the back of her dark blue tailored suit. She looked different to

Peter and he studied her intensely to find the difference. Ah, he found it. She was smiling. He never once saw her smile before. But on closer scrutiny, Peter observed that only her lips were smiling, her eyes were still that same old, icy blue, and her face retained the rigidity of a robot. It sent a shiver down his spine.

Peter looked around the courtroom and saw that it was filled to capacity. Directly behind him was the Santini contingent filling up two rows. His mother and father wore worried expressions. But his brothers, Michael and Jimmy, looked belligerent, ready to take on the court in their big brother's defense. Peter was surprised to see Betty and his brother Scott there. Both greeted him with their eyes. On the other side of the room, Peter was pleased to see a large number of people from Lake Stewart, led by Jim Frazier, the president of the Lake Stewart Improvement Association. Mark Robeson, the eleven year-old boy that Peter saved from drowning was there with his mother who, for once, was dressed fashionably. Ray Curtis, his partner in the gas station was there with his wife. Sheriff Charlie Templeton looked magnificent in his dress uniform as did his two deputies. Bill Dunn, the Fire Chief was there with more than half the fire department. A lot of the Lake Stewart people Peter only knew by sight, and couldn't remember their names. All in all, it was a tremendous turnout in his behalf, and Peter felt very humble and appreciative. Tears suddenly appeared in his eyes.

All the cross-conversations in the room came to an abrupt halt with the arrival of the judge. The black-robed figure blew into the room with her red hair flying. She rapped her gavel loudly and called for order. Judge Janet Graves was an imposing figure on the bench. The tall, husky, florid- faced woman with her hawk-like features, looked as if she could conduct this bail hearing with an iron fist. Without a civil greeting to anyone in the court, the Judge called on the District Attorney, Leon Blum, to proceed.

In a dull, monotone voice, the short, heavy set, balding DA outlined the State's position, which was to deny the defendant bail. In great detail, he described Officer Peter Santini's flight to avoid prosecution, and his preparation for that flight. He enumerated the many charges that were to be brought against the defendant, and the severity of those charges. Blum spoke for forty minutes. He brought the parents of Stephen Moran as witnesses before the bench, and led them through passionate testimony. He concluded with a heated plea to reject Peter Santini's request.

In contrast, Defense Attorney Fitzgerald was a pleasing figure to look at. Her voice was soft but resonant, which made everyone in the room strain to catch her every word and she had everyone's attention. Her plan of action was to first establish the merits of the defendant's character. She brought character witness after character witness, all of whom praised Peter Santini and vouched for him. No less than sixteen people brought the deeds for their homes to guarantee Peter's appearance in court when the trial commenced.

The most stirring appeal in Peter's behalf was from Susan Robeson, the mother of the boy whom Peter pulled from the depths below the ice of Lake Stewart. She recanted tearfully how she watched him go below the ice a second time to rescue the boy's dog at great danger to himself, and how he indeed became paralyzed from the neck down from hypothermia. She went on to describe how so many prayers from so many people influenced God himself, who cured Peter's paralysis. She asked the court to be lenient.

Under such a steady barrage of testimony extolling Peter's virtues, and after banging her gavel for order to silence the large number of people pleading to testify, Judge Janet Graves capitulated. She granted Peter Santini bail, set at 500,000 dollars and granted his custody to his attorney, Kathleen Fitzgerald.

Alice watched Peter's reunion with his daughters. It was almost painful to see as Tess and Marci flew into his arms with such force he was knocked to the ground. They smothered him with kisses as they crawled all over him. They tried to evoke from him a promise never to leave them again, and wouldn't accept from him the lame excuse that his destiny was in the hands of the court. From a corner of the foyer, a sullen Alice watched the wild display of love and affection. She wished she had it in her heart to participate in this warm welcome, but the small spark of affection she once had for Peter was extinguished long ago. She longed to put a stop to this vulgar scene, for she rarely showed any outward signs of affection for her beautiful girls and they never showed any for her. They were always Daddy's girls and she often felt the pangs of jealousy.

Alice agreed to allow Peter to live in the house, for after all, he did pay the bills and she had no legal separation. The girls couldn't understand why he couldn't resume his proper place in his old bedroom, but his sleeping on the convertible couch in the den was better than not having him home at all. They could still wake him in the mornings with their frantic pleas for a story, where their Daddy made them outrageous heroes in wild escapades.

As days passed even Alice, in her own way, was glad that Peter was back home. She certainly slept better. She left the worrying to him, and she ignored all the subtle noises, the creaks and groans that the house made all night long. Cooking for him and washing his clothes was a small price to pay for the feeling of security that his presence in the house gave her. As payment for her services, Peter made an offer of an amorous nature. She quickly cut him short on that.

Three times a week, Peter drove his almost brand new Acura from Bellmore to Queens to his attorney's office. There, Kathleen Fitzgerald taped the long interviews as she attempted to learn every facet of Peter Santini's life. Knowing her client completely gave Kathleen the direction her plans of defense would take. Sometimes the taping sessions were as long as fifteen hours a day, carrying them through lunch and dinner. They ate in the best restaurants Queens had to offer.

Kathleen learned everything there was to know about Peter, but he learned little about her. Once in a while she would throw in a little item about her own life that would correspond to his, but on the whole their relationship remained strictly business. She was a driven woman, and at the present, she seemed obsessed with freeing her client from all charges against him.

Peter, who had bathed in the warmth of his relationship with his beloved Mary for almost a year, was now involved with two beautiful blonde women, both icy cold. But his wife

Alice, the woman with the padlocked legs, appeared as a hot-blooded Carmen compared to the frozen-faced robot with the emaciated body, Kathleen. At dinner, Kathleen would refuse every offer of alcohol, with the excuse that she preferred to be in complete control of her senses. She claimed that even one glass of wine made her lose her sharp focus. Often, Peter wondered what this woman would be like if she ever relaxed and tried to enjoy herself.

As months passed, Kathleen informed Peter of the progress she was making in the plea-bargaining sessions she had with the district attorney. Kathleen learned of the difficulty the DA was having trying to get the businessmen from Peter's sector to cooperate and testify against him. The Puerto Rican prostitute twins employed by Peter had disappeared, and possibly had left the country. The homicide case against Peter was very weak and leaned strongly toward self-defense. The only fingerprints on the pistol found on the scene belonged to Stephen Moran. The Grand Jury refused to indict Peter on the homicide charge. The only charge against him that seemed irrefutable was his flight to escape prosecution. On this charge, Kathleen was fighting for a suspended sentence on a cop-out. She felt she was wearing the DA down, and kept requesting postponements to further this end. The DA requested postponements to continue his search for cooperative witnesses, but failed.

When the case came up for the thirteenth time, Judge Janet Graves exploded when neither side was ready to proceed. She refused to grant even one more postponement and ordered both sides to proceed, or she would throw the case out of her court. The Judge ordered both sides to reach a settlement by the second call of the calendar or the case would have to proceed.

District Attorney Leon Blum and Kathleen retired to the DA's office where they haggled over a settlement for two hours. Blum's shirt was soaking wet with perspiration as he fought with the cold-blooded female defense attorney. Kathleen remained very cool and determined. Finally, they shook hands and returned to the courtroom.

When the case was called, Judge Graves pushed her eyeglasses up on her forehead and stared down at the two lawyers. "Well, have you come up with a settlement or do we proceed with the case?" she asked.

"Yes, your Honor," the DA answered eagerly, "We have an agreement. The defendant agrees to plead guilty to fleeing to escape prosecution, a felony, and the people of the State of New York agrees to drop all other charges. But we strongly recommend to your Honor to give him the maximum punishment the law allows. The defendant, at the time the crimes were committed, was a police officer in the New York City Police Department, known world wide as `The Finest.' His actions brought disgrace to that fine body of men and women and three generations of his family's dedication. His punishment should reflect the peoples' wishes."

Judge Graves slowly removed her eyeglasses and deliberately cleaned them, using her black robe for a towel. Her hawk-like features portrayed deep thought as the creases in her face became more visible. Her delay in answering only heightened the suspense in the courtroom. The room was so quiet that individual breathing could be heard.

"Mr. Blum," the Judge said, slowly and deliberately in her deep, masculine voice. "You ask for the maximum penalty for the defendant in the name of the people. But this courtroom is full of people who want to see this defendant freed. They want it so much that they're willing to put up their entire life savings to keep him out of jail. Testimony in this courtroom showed that this defendant, while in flight, was willing to put his life on the line to save another human being. As a result, he suffered paralysis and months of tortuous rehabilitation. To me, that showed the very essence of three generations of service to the people. He knew his very actions would expose him to the media and certain capture. His duty came first.

I apologize to you, Miss Fitzgerald, for doing your closing statement for you. The issues in this case are complex, but I won't need anymore time to render my decision.

Please stand, Mr. Santini. Since you pleaded guilty to a felony, I sentence you to three years, but I'm suspending your sentence to five years probation and a fine of 25000 dollars.

As the judge pounded her gavel to indicate the session was over, the spectators erupted with an explosion of hand clapping, giving the judge a standing ovation. This brought a blush to her cheeks for the first time in her twenty-five years on the bench, and she scurried to her chambers before anyone could notice.

Not everybody was celebrating, for the family of the late Police Officer Stephen Moran wept as they slipped out of the courtroom unnoticed.

Peter turned to his attorney and extended his hand in gratitude, but she pushed it away.

"Don't you think I deserve more than a handshake for all my efforts?" Kathleen asked, with a trace of a smile on her face.

"Damn right, you do," Peter exclaimed, as he hugged her tightly, lifting her off her feet as he planted kisses on her cheeks.

Peter was immediately surrounded by family and friends. Everybody was kissing and hugging and some of the people didn't know each other. Anna hugged her son as tears streamed down her cheeks.

"You'll come for supper, Peter. I'm going to make the biggest feast this family ever saw," Anna cried happily. Turning to Kathleen Fitzgerald, Anna hugged her and kissed her on both cheeks. "Please come tonight, Miss Fitzgerald. You'll be our guest of honor," Anna begged.

"I'm afraid I can't," Kathleen stammered, "I'd be frightened to travel to Brooklyn at night by myself."

"Don't you worry about a thing, Anna said, "Peter will be glad to pick you up and take you home. Isn't that right, Peter?"

"Damn right, Mama," Peter answered, grinning from ear to ear.

"What time?" Kathleen asked in a voice barely above a whisper.

"About seven. I'll be there with bells on!"

Chapter Thirty-one

At seven sharp, Peter rang the bell at Kathleen Fitzgerald's high-rise apartment in Bayside. Kathleen opened the door, revealing an apparition that startled Peter. Her beautiful blonde hair was made up like she was Marie Antoinette. Her usually pallid cheeks now displayed a subtle blush of pink, make-up transforming the almost perfect features into a work of art. She wore a dark green dress that fitted her like a glove, low-cut, revealing a heretofore unseen cleavage. Peter's mouth sagged in astonishment.

"Kathleen?" Peter said, tentatively.

"Yeah, yeah, it's me," Kathleen answered with a hint of a smile on her face. "Help me on with my coat. I'm afraid the dress will split if I try to put it on by myself."

"Jesus H. Christ, you're stunning," Peter gasped.

"Stop the shit and let's get going," Kathleen shot back at Peter, the returning robot expression shattering the illusion. "The quicker we go, the sooner we get back."

Peter instantly bristled. "Why go at all?"

"I couldn't think of a way to say no to your mother without hurting her. She seemed so happy planning this `feast' as she put it."

"As I remember, she made you the guest of honor," Peter said sarcastically. "Look, you don't have to go just to satisfy my mother. I'll make excuses for you. I don't want your shitty attitude offending my family. I gave them enough heartache the past two years."

"Well, I spent a lot of time putting on this face and I don't want it to go to waste. Besides, I heard you Italians put on a pretty good party. I can use a few laughs."

The forty five minute trip from Bayside to Bayridge seemed like an eternity to Peter. Everytime he started to say something, he realized he would only exasperate the situation, so he remained silent. Kathleen said nothing and the silence increased the tension. Finally, Peter turned into his parents' street, and could park no closer than a half a block away.

As he escorted Kathleen up the front walk, the door opened and Tess and Marci came flying out. They jumped all over their father in an exuberant display of love and affection, initiating a feeling of sadness for Kathleen. She remembered as a young girl the happy greetings she gave her own father, and the hurt she felt knowing that such greetings would never be in her future.

The girls, noticing Kathleen standing there, suddenly became quiet and shy. As

Peter introduced them they stood in awe before Kathleen's beauty.

Anna appeared on the porch and warmly greeted Kathleen, kissing her on both cheeks. She held Kathleen at arm's length, looking her over from head to toe. "You were always so business-like in the courtroom, I never realized you were so gorgeous," Anna said. "Come inside. My sons will love you and their wives will hate you."

Anna led Kathleen into the living room where they were swallowed up by the rest of the family. Peter's arm was grabbed by his father.

"Let's go downstairs to my photography room. We can be alone there. I have to talk to you," Frank Santini said, a serious expression on his face.

"Okay, Pop, no problem," Peter said as he followed his father down into the basement.

Frank lit the light in the small office and reached for a bottle of Chianti that was on the shelf above his desk. He went into the darkroom, washed out two tumblers that had held chemicals, and brought them into the office. He filled both tumblers to the brim with the wine and handed one to Peter. They touched glasses and Frank whispered, "salute."

"Salute," Peter answered, then took a sip of the sour liquid.

Frank chug-a-lugged the wine and commented, "Ah, that's good," then sat down at his desk. "Sit, Peter. We gotta have a talk."

"Why so serious, Pop. I thought tonight's a celebration?"

"I can't celebrate until you forgive me."

"For what?" Peter said, feeling very uncomfortable.

"For being a lousy father to you. For always being a lousy father to you, since you were a little boy. You were the type of child that needed a lot of guidance. That should have been my job, but I gave that job to your sister, Betty. Maybe you would have turned out better if I did my job, but I failed you. Then when you got into trouble,

I should have stood by you. That was my job as your father. But instead, I condemned you. I cursed you for the shame you brought on the Santini name. I went to the cemetery and cried on my father's grave and I swore we would clear the Santini name by having a Santini bring you back. Oh, the shame I felt that you were a felon. Your grandfather got the Medal of Honor. I had fifteen citations. Betty, Jimmy and Mike, all had citations up the kazoo. Then you... a felon on the run. You broke my heart. But I realize I was wrong and I beg your forgiveness."

"You fucking well told, you were wrong. You talk of the Santini's honor. You worship your father. Look at the truth. Your sainted father was a crooked cop. He told me all the stories of how he put the arm on the bootleggers during Prohibition. The fact that everyone did it, from the mayor on down to the cop on the beat, didn't make it honest. He was a dirty cop. He got the Medal Of Honor because he was shot dead in a gunfight. He was so drunk that he couldn't shoot straight, but killed in action means an automatic Medal of Honor. The honor in this family goes to you and my brothers and sister. Grandpa Frank was as dirty as I was."

Frank Santini paled at his son's outburst. Anger started in his chest but quickly subsided, because he knew Peter spoke the truth. Frank idolized his father and his mind managed to throw out the facts and replace them with stories that now became legend. Why could his other children remember the legend and forget or forgive the facts. Only Peter was mean enough to taunt him with facts, maybe to justify his own sins and show that like his grandfather, he, too, was human.

"There's more, Peter. There's so much I have to apologize for. So much you have to forgive me for," Frank said in a strained voice.

"Then why the fuck don't you go to confession. I'm a cop, not a priest," Peter shot back.

"Because Jesus might forgive me, but it wouldn't mean anything to me unless I heard forgiveness from your lips."

"For what, Pop, for what?" Peter shouted.

"The three or four months that your mother and I lived in your house in Lake Stewart, we saw you happy for the first time in your life. Your Mary was a saint. She loved you dearly and treated you the way you should have been treated all your married life. And it was obvious how much you loved her. I'll never forgive myself for trying to bring you in and then pulling a gun on you, my own son. Then God punished us all by letting that bullet hit Mary. I can never forgive Him for that. That bullet should have been meant for me, the real evil person in our family. I'm afraid to die now, because I could never face my father. How could I explain to him that the life I led here on earth was a charade? Taking money from bootleggers was nothing compared to the sins I committed. I, I..."

Frank got up from his desk, took a few steps and sank to his knees, his hands clutching his ears. Sobs came from deep within his chest. Peter got up and went to his father's side, sinking to his knees and hugging his father.

"Please, don't do this, Pop. Don't do this to yourself. You'll give yourself a heart attack. Everything's working out. I'm going to be free. God's forgiving all of us for our sins."

Frank's tortuous sobbing finally subsided. He turned and faced his son. With tears running down his grizzled face he said,

"Can you forgive me, Peter? Can you forgive me for a lifetime of failing you? Can you forgive me for Mary?"

Tears came to Peter's eyes as he tried to answer his father. He tried to speak, but he was so choked up that no sound came from his throat. He swallowed several times, then managed a whisper, "I forgive you, Pop. I forgive you for everything."

Frank kissed Peter on both cheeks, then struggled to his feet.

"Now I go to beg forgiveness from your twin brother."

"Jesus Christ, Pop, you're a glutton for punishment. You don't owe Scott a fucking thing. You did him a favor. He lived a better life than all of us, thanks to you. You apologize to him and he'll think you're a fucking nut. Leave it alone. Beg forgiveness from Mama. She's the one you cheated."

As Peter rose to his feet, he looked around the photography room. He noticed it hadn't changed at all since he was a kid. Father and son, arm in arm, went up the stairs to join the festivities that were going on in all the rooms of the first floor. Everyone looked flushed and well on the way to being drunk, with the exception of Betty, who was abstaining from alcohol because of her pregnancy.

Scott was busy handing Kathleen a line. She looked amused. She was finishing her third drink and was feeling wonderful. Anna, Betty, and the two daughter-in-laws were busy setting the table in the dining room and bringing trays of food to the table. Everyone looked happy with the exception of Alice, who at every opportunity looked at Kathleen. Suddenly, Alice had a rival for being the prettiest woman in the house.

Dinner started and Anna, with the help of the other Santini women, brought endless courses of delicious food to the table. The wine flowed freely as did the words in the many speeches that were made. Kathleen was indeed the guest of honor, for every speech glorified the wonderful job she did for Peter, and each speech ended with another toast to her.

By midnight, all the children were asleep on the floor of the den as the TV blared. Jimmy, Michael and Scott were engaged in a noisy game of billiards in the basement, drunkenly shouting at one another. The women, with the exception of Alice and Kathleen, were busy cleaning up in the kitchen.

Kathleen waved to Peter and signaled him it was time for her to go home. She stood on wobbly legs and made her rounds saying goodbye to all of Peter's relatives. When she got into Peter's car, she asked him to unbutton the back of her dress. "I can't remember when I've eaten so much," she said as she leaned back, stretching out her legs and kicking off her shoes. "I feel like I'm going to explode. Everything was so delicious I had to have it all. And that Italian wine. It tasted sour in the beginning, but every drink kept getting better and better."

You're soused," Peter muttered.

"Yes I am and it feels wonderful!" Kathleen shouted in an unaccustomed gleeful manner.

Peter drove in silence. The episode with his father unnerved him and his mood never came up to the level of the other revelers in the house. Kathleen took off her seat belt and snuggled up to Peter, her left hand holding his arm, while her right hand dropped nonchalantly into his lap.

"Why're you so quiet?" Kathleen asked quietly. "Don't you like me?"

"What kind of a nut are you?" an exasperated Peter asked. "For the last four months you gave a pretty good impression of the Ice Maiden. Never once did you give me a civil greeting or engage in a personal conversation. Now you snuggle up to me and ask me if I like you. What gives?"

"When I'm working, I'm all business. I completely focus on my subject. I have no time for anything else. But the job's finished and you are a handsome man. Sexy, even. So cool out."

"Cool out? Jesus H. Christ, where did you come up with that one?"

"I grew up on the streets of New York just like you did. I wasn't born in law school, you know," Kathleen cooed as she stroked his thigh, causing Peter to jerk his hand, pulling the steering wheel sharply to the left.

The tires screeched and Peter fought to settle the car back in lane. "You better cool off, or we'll never get back to Bayside," Peter admonished, smiling.

"Who cares," Kathleen shouted, as she gave Peter's penis a squeeze.

"Holy Mother of God, are you crazy?"

"No, just horny. You must have noticed in all the times we ate together, I never took a drink. Not once. Alcohol makes me horny. So, can't you drive a little faster?"

"Wait a minute. Don't I have anything to say about this?" Peter said, as he stole a glance at Kathleen's beautiful face.

With the buttons of her dress open, the bodice hung loosely, revealing two large, full breasts. Larger than he imagined. The mood in the car was catching, and Peter, against his wishes, became excited.

"Oh my, this looks promising," Kathleen teased, as she stretched her head and put her tongue in Peter's ear.

"Cut it out, or I'll have to park the car right now. Damn it, I'm not a teenager. I outgrew fucking in cars twenty-five years ago."

Kathleen's answer was an attempt to open Peter's fly, but he pushed her hand away.

"We'll be at your apartment in fifteen minutes, please wait," Peter pleaded.

True to his word, fifteen minutes later Peter half carried, half led Kathleen into the lobby of her apartment house. She carried her shoes in her hand. Peter held her purse. Kathleen started to undress in the elevator, and at the door it was Peter that had to fumble in the purse to find her keys. When Peter finally opened the door, Kathleen was down to her panties and a half bra. She made a bee-line for a liquor cabinet and held up a bottle of Jack Daniels like a trophy.

"No more Italian wine, we're ready for some real drinking," she laughed as she filled two big brandy glasses. "I'm sorry I don't have ice here like they do in the movies, but booze is booze."

"I'll get the ice," Peter said, "Where's the kitchen?"

"Over there, over there," Kathleen said as she pointed to a door off the foyer, then collapsed into a chair. "I never noticed the floor was so wobbly."

Peter returned from the kitchen carrying a bowl of ice cubes. He put a handful in Kathleen's glass and then his own. He sat down on the couch and took his shoes off. Kathleen joined him on the couch and they touched glasses.

"Here's to us," she said thickly and downed the bourbon in one gulp. She put the glass on the coffee table and snuggled close to Peter, who was just sipping his drink. Kathleen unbuttoned Peter's shirt, and ran her fingers over his chest. She wrapped his long chest hairs around her fingers and toyed with his nipple.

Peter was so confused by the sudden change in Kathleen's behavior that he couldn't make up his mind whether to run or lean back and enjoy it. For over four months, this woman treated him coldly, almost with disdain, and he resented it. In her presence he felt inferior. Afraid to entertain a lustful thought in her direction. During times when she put him down, thoughts did enter his mind that what this woman needed was **a good piece of ass, to be fucked till she screamed.** But he never pictured himself as the one to inflict this punishment.

Kathleen kissed him passionately, and to his dismay, parts of him responded. "Oh, what the hell, I might as well," Peter muttered, in surrender.

The smell of coffee slowly brought Peter back to awareness. He sensed that he was alone in the bed and sitting up confirmed it. The blinds were open and sunlight streamed into the bedroom. Kathleen was nowhere to be seen.

Peter looked around and saw the room was beautifully furnished, although a little messy. Kathleen's bra and panties were draped over a lamp and his clothes were strewn around the floor. He got out of bed and searched in the pile until he found his jockey shorts, then opened and shut doors till he found the bathroom.

Half an hour later, he emerged refreshed and alert. He dressed then sought out Kathleen. He found her in the kitchen, sitting on the window sill sipping a cup of coffee and staring down on the street scene below. She was dressed in her bathrobe, her beautiful blonde hair pinned high on her head.

"Good morning," Peter said cheerfully, "How's your head? No hangover, I hope?"

Kathleen didn't answer. She turned and looked at him strangely. She wore an expression that seemed part smirk, part elation, like she was a conqueror. Whatever it was, it caused a shiver to run up and down his spine.

"What?" Peter asked. A sudden thought entered Peter's mind, that maybe he was less than adequate in bed and she was laughing at him. "What?" he repeated.

The smirk turned to a sneer, making that beautiful face look downright sinister.

"Yesterday, I got the court to dismiss that murder charge against you. But here in this apartment, I sentenced you to death. As sure as you're standing there, you're going to die, and it'll be a horrible death. Just like mine's going to be."

"What the fuck are you talking about? You're scaring the shit out of me. Are you still drunk, Kathleen?" Peter asked, terrified by what he had just heard.

"I was drunk, you asshole. So drunk, that I forgot how sick I was. So horny, that I went after you. You were easy. Like shooting fish in a barrel," Kathleen bragged. "You men think with your prick."

"Please, Kathleen," Peter pleaded, "Explain what's going on."

"Grab a cup of coffee and sit down, lover boy. Have I got a story for you."

Peter did as he was told. He filled a mug to the brim with the steaming coffee and found a seat at the kitchen table. He dreaded what he was going to hear.

"It all started ten years ago," Kathleen said, using her `opening statement' tone of voice. "I grew up in Brooklyn, in Flatbush to be exact. I graduated from Midwood High School and attended Brooklyn College. I lived so close to the school, I walked to class. When I graduated from BC, I matriculated at Brooklyn Law School in downtown Brooklyn. That's where I met Allan. He was in my class and we saw each other a lot. We studied together, shared lunches, and early in the second year, we started to go out socially. We fell in love. Couldn't stand to be apart. We decided to look for an apartment together and we found one on Gold Street, a few blocks from the school. It was a dump. We filled it with second hand furniture we bought on Myrtle Avenue, and to us, it was heaven. Both of us came from religious Catholic families. Both of us were disowned for living in sin. We were so happy, how could it be sinful? But both our mothers condemned us to hell.

But with graduation, our luck changed. All through school, Allan was the smart one.

Always knew his stuff and explained it to me. But on the exams, I always did better. Somehow, he froze on the tests. I wound up third in the class, Allan was three twenty-five. I passed the bar exam on my first try, Allan never did pass it. I was hired by Parsons, Parsons, Kelly, and Leibowitz. That's where you got me.

Allan couldn't get a job with a law firm. Only the lawyers that stood high in their class could get jobs. Allan became very depressed, because I was the breadwinner. Finally, he took a job with the NYPD. After the Academy he was assigned to the 16th Precinct in Manhattan. He reached top pay after three years and I kept getting good raises, so we moved to this apartment in Bayside. I was very happy and I wanted Allan to marry me, but he still felt inferior and wouldn't marry me until he passed the bar or the sergeant's exam, whichever came first.

Finally, our luck changed. In March, Allan took the sergeant's exam and passed. He stood tenth on the list, sure to be called before the end of the year. So, we planned to be married around Christmas time. Even my mother forgave us and agreed to make the reception if we were married in church. It was all planned.

Then Allan got a seat in a Radio Car, which made him happy. He was tired of foot patrol, and flying to every detail all over the city. He rode with a veteran cop who was as crooked as sin. Allan resisted the money his partner offered him for a while. But greed got the better of him and he gave in. He felt proud that he was bringing home as much as I did. Then disaster struck. Allan and his partner got caught in a `sting' run by Internal Affairs."

"What happened then?" Peter asked.

"Our world collapsed. Allan was devastated. Too ashamed to face me or his family, he ate his gun."

"Jesus," Peter said. "What a fool. There's more to life than the Job."

"He wasn't strong like you," Kathleen shouted. Then she sunk to the floor, sobbing.

Peter was bewildered. Kathleen's story was devastating. "How could it be?" he thought. "How could that PBA law firm let her defend me? What did she mean when she said she sentenced me to death?"

Kathleen was still sobbing on the floor, when Peter went over and placed a hand on her shoulder.

"Don't touch me, you fucking bastard. Don't you ever touch me again," she screamed.

"You were damn anxious to get into my pants last night. What are you a psycho?" Peter screamed back.

"No. Just a bad drunk. I lose control when I'm drunk. I'm HIV Positive. In fact I have Aids, and now you have it too."

Peter was stunned. He sunk to the floor alongside Kathleen. His mind raced as his heart crashed. Yesterday, he was at the top of the world. The murder charge was dismissed, he copped a plea and was given probation, what could be better. He planned to take the kids to Lake Stewart to live. With or without Alice. He had a good business there. Life would be just fine.

That was yesterday. Today, he better start looking for a cemetery plot. How could his cock do this to him? Was she telling the truth? Could he get infected just after one time?"

"Can I get infected just after one time?" Peter asked, not knowing if Kathleen heard him above her sobbing."

The sobbing wound down and Kathleen made an attempt to speak. "I did," she hiccupped. "I got infected after one time."

"How?" Peter asked.

"After Allan's funeral, I couldn't stand this apartment. I was heartbroken. It drove me crazy. One rainy night, it got so bad that I had to get out of here. I walked out in the pouring rain to an Irish Pub on Bell Boulevard. It was a miserable night and by nine o'clock I was the only customer in the place. The bartender started to give me free drinks and I got loaded. I don't even remember going home with him, and I was shocked when I woke up in his bed."

A new attack of sobbing overcame her. It was several minutes before Kathleen could continue. "A few months later I became ill. A consequent blood test revealed the HIV virus. I was so angry that I went back to that bar to confront that son of a bitch, but it was too late. I found out he died of Aids. That was six months ago. I've been hospitalized twice since then. Yes, I have Aids, and my days are numbered. I doubt if I'll see a new year."

"I can't feel sorry for you. You're a fucking murderer. You knowingly and deliberately infected me. I hope you rot in Hell for eternity, you bitch," Peter hissed.

"It's all your fault," Kathleen cried. "Your family got me drunk."

"Bullshit," Peter shouted. "You're just plain evil."

Kathleen flew at Peter, beating him with her fists and wailing hysterically. "You lousy pimp, you filthy dirty cop, you paid off all your bosses and they refused to do anything. You were responsible for Moran's death and you call me a murderer? It was your cock that got you into trouble then and last night you fucked me when I was drunk. You and your cock deserve to die."

Peter got into his car and couldn't believe how his life turned around since he left it the night before. He drove around the city as in a trance. He didn't know where he was and cared less. He drove until the car ran out of gas. Then he abandoned it and took to walking.

He walked with his hands thrust deep in his pockets, his body hunched over like an old man. He was approached by panhandlers, prostitutes and con men, but he didn't acknowledge them. He walked until his weakened legs couldn't go on. He found himself in a small park, and tried to make it to a bench about a quarter mile ahead, but he could go no further. Peter slumped down on the grass and fell asleep.

Chapter Thirty-two

HIV Positive? Are you sure?" a shocked Alice asked, clutching her heart.

"Yes, I'm sure, I got the lab report back this morning," Peter answered. "I haven't slept for days waiting for this."

"I can't believe it. How did you get it?"

"Jesus Christ, Alice, must you ask me that?"

"I think I have a right to know."

Peter sighed sadly. "I got it from Kathleen Fitzgerald, my lawyer."

"I just knew that woman was evil. I felt it in my bones. And the way the family was slobbering over her at your party last month. It was disgusting. How'd she do it? How'd she give you Aids?"

"I haven't got Aids yet. The doctor is going to start me on medication tomorrow. It could delay Aids for years. Maybe they'll come up with a cure before I get it," Peter said, wistfully.

"How'd she give it to you?" Alice repeated, impatiently.

"Well, when I drove her home, I had to carry her to her apartment. We started drinking, and I guess I wasn't thinking too clearly. One thing led to another and we did it."

"You son of a bitch. I knew that thing would be the end of you, sooner or later. Your whoring around got you in trouble in the first place and now it's going to kill you. God, in his unquestioning wisdom is punishing you for all your sins. My bed wasn't good enough for you. You had to be an adulterer. Pay the price, Peter, pay the price."

"Thank you, Alice. I appreciate all your sympathy and understanding," Peter said sadly. "A normal relationship with you could have avoided a lot of my problems. I can't understand how you consider yourself blameless. If you spent half as much time with me as you did with your parish priests, maybe we could have made it once in a while. Your legs were locked tighter than Fort Knox.

"Am I glad! God knows what you might have given me. But I'm going to make sure you don't give me or the children Aids. I want you out of the house immediately."

"Listen, if we just use common sense, I won't infect anybody. The doctor gave me a very long speech full of do's and don'ts. We can live a normal life here. Please listen."

"Haven't you brought enough shame on your two little girls? With your face in the newspapers and on the TV constantly, they've gotten into enough fights defending your honor. How're they going to defend you when everyone finds out that you have Aids? Do you know how cruel kids are? Leave now, before anyone finds out. Please. Do your kids a favor, go back to your house in the mountains and die there. Give us all a break," a dry-eyed Alice said.

Peter thought long and hard about what Alice had said. He could see the wisdom in her words. By leaving, he would eliminate any chance of infecting his beloved children. If and when he got really ill, he surely couldn't depend on that cold bitch to nurse him. He was glad he hadn't told anyone in his family about his latest problem. Recently, his mother and father helped nurse him through paralysis. That was a picnic compared to what is in store for him. He'd make Alice swear on her mother's grave not to reveal his secret. She was devout enough never to break that promise. As soon as he cleared up his business with Internal Affairs of The New York City Police Department, he would put his papers in, then leave. He would be on the run again. Only God knew for how long.

Peter said his goodbyes to the family in Brooklyn. He called his sister Betty and told her of his plans and finally he called Scott. He was getting very proficient in lying, which was good. He would live a lie for as long as he could. He would have to pay for care when the end came close.

The goodbyes to Tess and Marci were extremely tough to make, for he loved them with all his heart. Only God knew when he would see them again.

Peter settled in quickly, when he returned to Lake Stewart. He missed Mary terribly, but he felt her presence everywhere. The residents welcomed him back with open arms, and that eased some of the pain of his exile. He resumed his duties at his gas station, which pleased his partner, Raymond Curtis, greatly. The responsibilities of keeping the books, keeping up the inventory and trying to collect money from the customers were too much for Ray, and the pressure was destroying him. He was stuttering more than ever. Peter took back the responsibility of the tow truck and was available to serve his neighbors, day and night.

Peter's life was different than in the days with Mary. The beautiful house was never tidy, and the magnificent furniture lost it's glowing shine. Peter missed meals and when he did eat, it was sandwiches in the luncheonette, so he lost weight. He never knew if it was from the illness or just not eating right. The one redeeming feature of his present lifestyle was a very close relationship with his brother, Scott. They were so identical, it scared both of them. He was almost tempted to tell Scott of his illness, but was too ashamed.

One night during a snow storm, as Peter Santini sat at his desk in his office reviewing his accounts receivable, the phone rang. He picked up the phone and was surprised to hear the voice of his brother-in-law, Frank Mullin.

"Congratulations, Peter, you're an uncle again. Betty just gave birth to twins, a boy and a girl."

"Here we go again," Peter whispered, a large grin on his face, then raised his eyes to the heavens, and whispered, "Poor Betty."

About The Author

Arnold M. Pine is a veteran of twenty years on the New York Police Department, where he served as a very active "street cop". His experience with the criminal element on the street and in the department itself, enabled him to create memorable characters in thrilling situations. Enough to complete three novels on the subject. Mr. Pine attended Brooklyn College before and after his two year stint in the Navy during World War Two. He lettered in Wrestling, which prepared him for the battles he encountered on the streets of New York City. Upon retirement from the Department, Mr. Pine spent many years as the CEO of a water engineering business, before he engaged in writing as a full-time endeavor.

Printed in the United States
71191LV00001B/4